The

Syderstone Ghost

Victoria Hart

Red Raven Publications

1 – England 1549

What first strikes her about the boy is that he is tall, with dark eyes and a high forehead and a slightly concave line to his nose. His dark hair is carefully swept back beneath his hat, but not fussily. He is a man who likes his sport and keeps himself trim and neat for that reason alone. No wonder his careless, wild good looks have earned him the nickname 'the gypsy.'

She is slight and short, a little plump in the face, but with golden hair that hangs about her like a cloak. She is fairer than fair against his sultry darkness. Her mouth might be a little pert, her expression a little sharp, but she is lively and happy and he is in her home.

His name is Robert, hers is Amy. He is on his way to meet the Kett rebels with his father. Stanfield Hall, the family home of the Robsarts, is merely a stopping point in his travels. Sir John Robsart, his host, can hardly believe his eyes as he looks out on a sea of soldiers, perhaps as many as 10,000, no one is quite sure. But more than the old man has seen in his lifetime. The humble hall surrounded by fields suddenly seems to have become the centre of a military fair – tents litter the landscape and on the guest list for that evening's meal at Stanfield Hall is an earl, a marquis and three lords; not to mention the two young men who have ridden out with their father, the Earl of Warwick, John Dudley.

John Dudley's star is rising; after several successful military campaigns in Scotland and France, he has become one of Henry VIII's intimates and a leading proponent of religious reform. Two years ago he was made an earl, now he has been trusted with putting down Kett's rebellion in Norfolk. Can John Robsart help but be pleased at seeing the interest the earl's son, Robert, now pays his only child, Amy?

But Robsart is anxious too, as any man would be who finds his sister-in-law married to the leader of a rebellion against the king's administration. Robsart is married to Elizabeth Scott, the widow of Roger Appleyard, a once influential member of the Norfolk gentry. Stanfield Hall is, in fact, part of Elizabeth's inheritance from her dead husband; Robsart has chosen to live there because his own family home at Syderstone is lying in virtual ruins. Yet Roger Appleyard also had a sister, a woman named Alice Appleyard and she has married Robert Kett. To complicate the matter further, Robert Kett is in the midst of a long-running feud with local lawyer Sir John Flowerdew over the enclosure by Flowerdew of some common land. Flowerdew is the steward of Robsart's Norfolk estates and his son William is due to marry Frances Appleyard, John Robsart's stepdaughter and Roger Appleyard's child. Needless to say, Robsart is treading carefully around John Dudley and his entourage.

Poor Elizabeth Robsart, his wife, is beside herself with worry too, but for different reasons. News has just reached them that her sons John and Phillip have been captured by the rebels and taken to Mousehold Heath just outside the City of Norwich, where Kett has set up camp. Now there is an army outside her house and her husband is making it as plain as possible to the Earl of Warwick that he is loyal to the crown, despite his dangerous family ties.

And in the centre of it all is the pretty Amy Robsart. Seventeen-years-old and the only child from Elizabeth's second marriage. Amy is excited by the arrival to her quiet home of so many soldiers and gentry. She is dazzled by the horses and men in fine armour. Her eyes linger on the two young men who have joined their father in this testing mission. Ambrose Dudley is the older boy, as dark and handsome as his brother, but coarser in his manners. Robert Dudley, the gypsy, is too dashing in his fine armour to avoid Amy's eye, and he looks back at her keenly.

She vaguely feels she may have seen him before. In her short life she has travelled among noble families and picked up a good education for the daughter of a country gentleman. She writes in a neat calligraphic hand and is genteelly mannered from time spent with the grand Howard family, before their catastrophic downfall. Robert has the feel of a boy she has seen somewhere before, even if only fleetingly. But even if she is wrong, even if this is their first meeting, she is already in no doubt that Robert Dudley is the most handsome man she has ever seen and that he looks upon her, and even smiles upon her, more than she can bear.

When the men come indoors the talk will be about campaign tactics and politics alone, but she hopes secretly for a moment when she might steal a few words with the dashing Robert. Perhaps she might make a remark of some import that will lure his eyes to hers. Or is she being merely vain to think he looks upon her favourably? She is pretty, if not beautiful, and she is small and well-rounded. She takes great heed of her clothes, even if they may not be of the fashion in court. Should she not feel able to charm an earl's son?

In the morning he will ride to his first battle, would not a few comforting words from her help to ease his night? Perhaps she should wish him luck for the coming day? Whatever she says he must recall her in the morning, for she has no idea when they will next meet. He must remember her! She cannot let him forget this fleeting moment.

As he passes her in his armour – he will not take it off this night for fear of surprise attack – she steps a little closer, lets her skirts brush him. He glances up.

"My lord," a curtsey, slow and graceful as she was shown

by the Howards, "I wish God's grace to follow you tomorrow."

He smiles a little, his dark eyes take in this slip of a girl.

"My lady," he says with a bow, then he is away from her and with his brother, being ushered into the Grand Hall and towards the feast her father has speedily arranged.

But she is satisfied. He shall remember her, of that she is certain. She saw it just for a moment in his eyes.

2 – Syderstone, Norfolk 1955

"Reverend Fourdrinier!"

Norman Douglas Fourdrinier rose stiffly from his crouched position over a gravestone in the churchyard.

"Charlie Talbot?" the reverend pressed his hands into the base of his spine and tried to ease out a crink.

"What a surprise to see you here," beamed Charlie, moving over to the reverend and shaking his hand vigorously.

"What a surprise to see you in civvy clothes," Fourdrinier laughed. "It must be nearly ten years since I last saw you."

"1946. Before I was demobbed," Charlie stood back to take in the reverend. "You've aged, old boy."

"You've grown fat," Fourdrinier said pointedly, nodding to a round belly that threatened to pop out of Charlie's brown tweed suit. Charlie laughed.

"I'm a gentleman farmer now. I'm expected to grow fat!"

"Well, in my experience, reverends are expected to look old. It implies wisdom, which I always felt was a very unwise idea."

Charlie suddenly looked a touch abashed.

"I always meant to come and visit you in Norwich, you know. When I got the car I meant to plan a visit, discuss old times, the war and such. But you know how it is," Charlie gave a shrug. "Farming takes up a lot of time, not to mention all the committees you find yourself on. Farmer's Association, the Parish Council, Common Land Trust, you name it and I seem to be on it. Even the darts team has me signed up as a member."

"That doesn't surprise me Charlie, you were always the outgoing sort," Fourdrinier leaned back on a tomb and stared at his former curate. "How long have you been running a farm?"

"Oh, since '48. That's when father died. The war muddled me up slightly and I found it incompatible with my new views to return to the church. I still believe though."

Fourdrinier nodded.

"You don't have to apologise, Charlie, many men feel the same and as for the visit, well, I hardly went out of my way to find you either."

Charlie propped himself on a gravestone.

"Perhaps I was worried too. Worried you might want me to return to the church. I couldn't..."

Fourdrinier was moved by the younger man's sudden dismay. He had always had a fondness for the big, bluff Charlie Talbot who wore his heart on his sleeve.

"I wouldn't have done that," he assured him. "But it doesn't matter anyway."

The air had a damp taste to it in the graveyard and Fourdrinier found himself craving a warm fire and a pint of something wet and strong.

"Care to treat your old reverend to a drink?" he asked.

Charlie looked buoyant again.

"Certainly! What brings you to Syderstone, anyway?"

Charlie pointed to the churchyard gates and started to lead the way as he spoke.

"I am taking a service here on Sunday," Fourdrinier answered, noting the ornate A and R wrought into the iron of the gate. "I thought I would pay a visit to remind myself of the place. I'm working on a history of the Church in Norfolk."

"Really? Mind you, I always pegged you for a historian."

"You mean boring?"

"I mean curious," Charlie nudged him merrily. "And a nosey parker, all historians can't resist poking their noses into other people's affairs."

"Oh well, that I will grant you."

"So you will be writing a chapter on Syderstone?"

"I think so."

"There are certainly plenty of stories to tell about this place," Charlie and Fourdrinier paused as they came level with the former parsonage, now looking rather run down as its dark windows gazed across into the graveyard.

"I confess that is part of the reason I am here," Fourdrinier stared at the house that seemed deserted. "I was curious about the Stewarts. Reverend John Stewart was curate here in the 1830s and 40s. The grave I was looking at was for his daughter, Margaret."

"I don't know much about the Stewarts," Charlie shrugged. "I know there is a story that one of the curates here was a notorious drunk and had to have people cling to his surplice to prevent him falling into graves during funeral services."

"Ah, I think that will be William Mantle. I have only just begun to delve into his story. A curious character, actually."

Charlie gave a shrug and a smile.

"Aren't we all in Norfolk?"

"Speak for yourself," Fourdrinier answered with mock sternness.

Charlie's smile spread to a grin.

"And how is great aunt Ida?"

Fourdrinier groaned.

"You still remember her then?"

"She is rather hard to forget especially after the last occasion," Charlie smirked, "It was '36 and I do believe she turned up for divine service in Middle Eastern costume and insisted on calling herself Cleopatra?"

"She had just returned from that fateful Nile trip, convinced she was a reincarnation of an Egyptian queen. I felt half-inclined to have her committed there and then."

"Not dear Ida!" Charlie pretended to be horrified. "Where would we be without her informing us that the church cat was a sacred being from the time of

Tutankhamen and should be treated as a god?"

"At least we have ventured past that infatuation," Fourdrinier stifled a slight grimace.

"What preoccupies Ida now?"

"Spiritualism," Fourdrinier shook his head. "I offended her deeply last Christmas when I informed her that as an Anglican cleric I was fundamentally opposed to the premise. It hardly prevents her from pulling the drawing room curtains and summoning who knows what, of course."

They were at the door of the pub and Charlie opened it for the reverend.

"Aunt Ida is another reason I am here," Fourdrinier blushed mildly as he made his confession. "Ida read my first draft of the history of Syderstone parish and is now convinced she has made contact with the spirit of Margaret Stewart."

"The daughter of Reverend John Stewart?"

"Yes, look at this," Fourdrinier pulled a letter from his pocket.

Charlie took it as they nestled into opposite sides of the snug by the fire. Fourdrinier lifted up his aching feet and rested them on the hearthstone.

"Dearest nephew," Charlie read, "I hope you are well and enjoying the Norfolk air. I have heard pheasant are prosperous there and would be inclined for a pair if you might send them..."

"Skip to the third paragraph," Fourdrinier interrupted politely.

"We held a séance on Thursday last, I am certain you will be appalled, but after reading your latest draft about the Stewart household I had a strange notion that I just must contact one of them. I cannot explain these moods I have, not to a man such as you who is opposed to the matter so vehemently, but I felt something moving in spirit," Charlie cast his eyes up at the reverend, who was slumped back and rubbing his brow.

"It gets better," Fourdrinier prompted.

"So we held a séance. Nancy came, a pretty girl, very in touch with the other side. I shall not go into all the details. There was a great deal of noise that night from the old silver trumpet," Charlie paused. "Trumpet?"

"They use it to communicate with the spirits."

"Oh, right," Charlie quenched a laugh as he carried on. "Nancy slipped into a most delightfully deep trance, I was certain we would get a message soon and indeed we did. I record it here verbatim for I feel it is deeply important on a spiritual level and must not be ignored. Nancy spoke in a child-like voice and said, 'Do you know who I am?' I said no. 'You must know! She must know. I am Margaret.' Margaret who, I asked. 'Margaret Stewart. You know of me.' Yes, I do, I agreed at once. I was elated that my intuition was correct. I inquired of the spirit if she had a message for us, but at first it came all out as a whisper, then Nancy trembled and spoke louder, '...don't like it here. Want to be free. Soul....' What about your soul, I asked. 'Trapped.' She answered. That confused us for a moment, then Nancy seemed to whisper 'purgatory'. There was a silence when Nancy was breathing very deeply and I was growing inclined to wake her, when in a terribly bleak little voice she said, 'tell him to solve the riddle of the sealed room.' And suddenly Nancy came awake by herself.

"You see nephew, I am sure this is important. The little girl Margaret is clearly in some sort of spiritual torment, which we must resolve for her. I feel certain God has directed us to this lost soul to save her from her plight. I can only think the 'him' referred to you. There were no other men in the room and Nancy had no idea of your connection to Margaret Stewart. So I set you forth on a task to solve this mystery, you shall be my agent in this. Write soon with news, I shall continue to try and contact Margaret. Your eternally loving aunt, Ida."

Charlie laid the letter down on the table.

"She writes a good story, doesn't she?" Fourdrinier smiled miserably. "The truth of it is, I dread her disappointment enough that I came here with the purpose of looking up any details of Margaret Stewart. Aunt Ida has a weak heart and doesn't travel far, the doctors feel I should indulge her fancies as otherwise she becomes upset and that can damage her health."

"Has she ever been to Syderstone?" Charlie had a curious look on his face.

"Never. She only ever visited me in Norwich. She lives in London and hasn't left the city, oh, not since before '39. Her nerves were affected during the war, of course, she never quite recovered from that."

"And this riddle of the sealed room?"

"I know! I honestly don't know where they get this nonsense from! The papers perhaps? Or Nancy has a vivid imagination."

"Only," Charlie averted his eyes to the letter, "there is, or should I say was, a sealed room."

Fourdrinier sat up slightly.

"Do not jest, Charlie."

"I don't. Syderstone parsonage, the old one we just walked past, had a sealed room. No one knows why it was sealed, nor by who, but it was shut up for at least a century, certainly during Reverend Stewart's time here."

Fourdrinier hardly believed his ears.

"This is an old wives' tale!"

"No, the story was true enough. I dear say I haven't heard it spoken of in many years, not since the war at least. My grandfather told me about it, he heard it in the 1860s from his own father who recalled the room being unsealed. It was also said the parsonage was haunted."

"My aunt would have a field day listening to you," Fourdrinier shook his head. "Ghosts too?"

"The usual sort of tales, unearthly groans and footsteps. Some people claimed they saw the ghost of a man in a nightgown, they claimed it was Reverend Mantle back from the dead because of his wicked ways in life. There were also those who said the ghost was Amy Robsart."

"Who?"

"The Robsart family owned Syderstone in the sixteenth century. The town is linked with Amy after Walter Scott wrote a novel concerning her life and death. You saw her initials on the gate of the churchyard just now."

"Indeed I did. Why would she haunt the parsonage?"

"Syderstone Hall no longer exists. Fell into ruins centuries ago. Local legend has it, Amy's restless spirit moved to the next convenient location and that happened to be the parsonage, though no one seems inclined to explain why the ghost everyone claims to have heard and seen is distinctly male."

Fourdrinier let out a dark laugh.

"Would you care to go to one of my aunt's séances?"

"Don't you find it curious though, Fourdrinier? How could your aunt, let alone this Nancy, know of the sealed room? It is a local story that hasn't been spoken about in years. If your aunt has never been here, how could she know?"

"You are assuming a lot of creditability for the talents of Nancy. She may have been acting to please my aunt."

"But if aunt Ida had not mentioned Margaret Stewart, how would she know to drop in that information? How would she know to gather information about an old legend that no one hardly remembers?"

"Good fortune can provide some amazing coincidences," Fourdrinier answered.

Charlie frowned.

"Doesn't it interest you slightly? The possibility of a lost soul reaching out to us?"

"I believe in an afterlife Charlie, obviously," Fourdrinier carefully took back his letter. "But that we can communicate with the dead? No, that is not something I accept. It is against the church's teachings and it stinks a little sordidly of witchcraft and chicanery."

"But what if it were true?"

Fourdrinier hesitated. There was a look of absolute

desperation in Charlie's eyes. He had leaned across the table that divided them and was pleading with his whole being for Fourdrinier to give him some hope, some reassurance.

"We set ourselves the task of reaching out to lost souls in this life, but what about the next?" Charlie persisted. "If a person has never heard of God and dies, are they then condemned to forever drift in limbo? Or have we been given the power to help them?"

Fourdrinier was a touch shaken by his earnestness.

"Charlie, dear boy, I don't deal in ghosts."

"Why not?"

Fourdrinier didn't know how to answer him.

"Because I don't believe in them."

Charlie almost fell back in his seat. His expression was hard and determined.

"You are wrong Fourdrinier. I have seen... things. Things that made me challenge my old beliefs in the Church. Religion doesn't know everything."

"God does."

"Perhaps God is asking us to open our minds and to look at things differently. How confident are you in your beliefs to deny this child even just the chance of salvation?"

"You are confusing the issue."

"No, I am not."

Fourdrinier rubbed his old fingers. They were stiff from the cold and damp.

"Margaret Stewart died of tuberculosis."

"What does that matter?"

"I am dealing with facts, Charlie, be patient. Nancy's insights are not facts."

"The sealed room is. There was a sealed room and neither Nancy nor your aunt could have known about it."

Fourdrinier shook his head.

"I have barely examined the Stewarts yet, just mentioned them in passing at the start of a fresh chapter. My aunt has jumped upon them."

"Then perhaps it is time you investigated them. If there is something there it will either prove or disprove your aunt."

"Why are you so determined Charlie?"

The younger man was staring at him intently.

"I lied before, Fourdrinier. I did not keep my faith. I lost it somewhere between the streets of Paris and outside those hellish concentration camps the Germans built. It left a hole, an ache inside. I've been empty ever since, throwing myself into work and the community to try and ease it. I lost something important back there, but I can't bring myself to believe again. I'm a lost soul too."

"No one is a lost soul," Fourdrinier reached out to touch the arm of his old curate, upset to hear his honest confusion and keen to help.

"That is one of the things I wonder about being true. Fourdrinier, you talk of facts. I want a fact that will prove to me once and for all that God exists and is watching over us."

"I'm not sure that fact exists."

"No?" Charlie removed his arm bitterly from Fourdrinier's grasp. "What if this child, this lost soul from the other side is a fact? What if she is the proof that I need, that the world needs?"

Fourdrinier wanted to tell him he was clutching at straws, the séances and ghost stories were not equivalent to faith, but he snagged his tongue, knowing he would hurt his friend deeply.

"If I could, I would find you proof Charlie."

Charlie's expression, hard and angry, softened.

"You will be researching the Stewarts anyway?"

"Yes?"

"Meet me here again and tell me what you find, would you?"

Fourdrinier nodded.

"I can do that."

"I'm starting to feel it was fortuitous my meeting you

today," Charlie's smile had returned. "You will be here Sunday? Come for lunch at the farm, I'll pick you up in the car after the service."

Fourdrinier agreed, not pushing his luck to try and get Charlie to come to the service.

"What will you write to your aunt Ida?" the tension had lifted between the two men.

"The usual thing, that she is a nutcase, completely off her rocker and that I love her dearly and shall do exactly as she asks me."

"Then I hardly need have argued with you?" Charlie said incredulously.

"Oh I don't say that," Fourdrinier smiled. "You've given me something to think over and a challenge nonetheless."

"To help Margaret Stewart?"

"To help my old curate and friend." Fourdrinier said firmly.

3 - Norwich, Norfolk 1549

The Kett rebels are in the city of Norwich. John Dudley sits on his horse and ponders the situation. Nearby is his son Robert, his mind not entirely on the imminent attack. Every now and then his thoughts slip to the pretty girl at Stanfield Hall. He shakes himself, glances at his father. John mistakes the look for nerves.

"We will go in through the St Stephen's and Brazen gates. Northampton has failed, now the rebels are ransacking the city. Are you ready to fight, Robert?"

"Of course." Robert is surprised at the comment, he has been ready since they set out on this march, now thousands of soldiers stand behind them waiting for their commander's signal.

It is 24 August 1549. As day dawns they assault the city. The gates are ill-defended. Dudley's troops slam into them and force them open with little resistance. Suddenly the city is open before Warwick and his men. The rebels are running for their lives. What sort of chance do they stand against trained soldiers? They are angry farmers and irate labourers; Kett understands crops and sheep, not military tactics. The rebels flee through the cramped back streets of Norwich, setting light to houses, hoping the flames will slow down Warwick and his troops. Now Norwich is ablaze and her citizens are watching their world burn.

At 3pm Warwick's baggage train is lost in the part of Norwich known as Tombland. The horses stumble about on the cobbles, while their drivers try to make up for lost time and find their way. A rebel spots them as the lengthy line of carts rumbles down Bishopsgate Street; they are heading directly for the rebel army.

The rebels attack the baggage train and aim to capture it, including all of Warwick's artillery. The unfortunate drivers pay for getting lost with their lives and now Kett's men are better armed than their opponents. Except none know how to fire a gun.

Warwick sends one of his subordinates, Captain Drury, to recapture the guns. Bishopsgate explodes into a fierce battle as armed soldiers slaughter the under-prepared rebels. Blood makes cobbles slick. Men groan and scream. The narrow lanes are crammed with men trying to flee or fight, the baggage train now blocking them in, while panicked horses rear and crush the unwary. Despite the carnage, Captain Drury only rescues some of the guns.

As night creeps on the rebels set more and more fires, hoping to trap Warwick in a net of flame. Cries of alarm rise up everywhere. Robert is exhausted, but looks at the night sky now vivid with orange light. Like all his men he is in real danger of being burned to death. He summons the strength to create fire-fighting parties and slowly the fury of the fire is dimmed. The rebels have not slaughtered him this time.

A new day brings the sound of heavy artillery exploding against the north walls. Kett has had all night to learn how to use his stolen guns, now they are bombarding the north of the city near the Magdalen and Pockthorpe gates. The walls collapse, the rebels run in to retake Norwich. Warwick summons his men and his sons. They must take the attack forward, fight hand-to-hand in the streets if necessary.

Robert charges in with his men while overhead the crashing sound of cannon-fire echoes everywhere. Houses suddenly crumble to nothing. Falling masonry crushes a man before he knows what is happening. Young Robert sets his mind to his task. For the first time he is fighting for real; not the practice sparring matches he has been trained with. He is not afraid to kill a man. He has always known one day he would. His father is an old soldier and it was always expected Robert would follow suit. That is how the Dudley's gained favour with King Henry and it is also how they must retain it. All thoughts of a pretty blond girl in a country house are gone as Robert draws his sword and launches himself into the centre of the rebel forces.

Under his sword the rebels tumble. Men swing scythes and pitchforks at him, but they hardly know how to fight and he dodges their blows and pins them with his own. Men scream as he rams his blade into their soft flesh and feels it grate against bone. He has not known this sensation before; the bloodlust that fills him, the uncontrollable need to move and kill. He cuts to the right, sends a farmboy screaming to oblivion, swings left and takes a jagged chunk out of the arm of a carpenter. Their agonised cries fail to reach him. He ploughs on. Takes out each man who faces him without hesitation. Either side are soldiers in armour, lashing out with pikes and blades. Some are caught unwary, swamped by rebels who bludgeon them to death. Not Robert. He darts among them, draws them the rebels out. He is damp with sweat, his armour feels tight, his muscles stiff from exertion, but he keeps going. Every swing is one less man to fear, every lunge takes one more rebel out of the equation.

It is some time before he realises they are almost at the city limits. That no more rebels remain standing to fight him. He turns left and right, expecting the next attack. But the enemy are all dead or wounded. Despite the triumph the rebels still bombard the city, catching out the unwary who are killed just when they thought they had survived. Deep in the city the citizens cower and grimace, fuelled by a burning desire for revenge. Warwick knows this.

26 August. The soldiers rest. Warwick has news of German mercenaries arriving to aid him. 1500 foreigners armed with handguns and pikes. They look stern and fearsome. Hired help to rid the King of Kett's troublesome band.

Robert has hardly slept. He never takes off his armour.

He lies on a straw mattress and lets the day drift over him. Stanfield Hall feels a lifetime ago, but he keeps remembering her. He pictures her standing in the entrance to the hall, the fragile smile on her face, then the strange moment when they touched. She was so much shorter than him, yet so pretty too.

He washes blood off his armour, face and hands. He wants to strip off his clothes and bathe in a cold stream. He cleans his helmet, patiently picks specks of gore from its decorations. He thinks of Amy even as he works. Amy's face has become a symbol to him; a symbol of the world he is fighting for. He will cut down these traitorous rebels not just for the king, but for her, so she need not fear their banditry and villainy.

There is more news. The rebels have seen the reinforcements and they know Warwick has offered arms to the people of Norwich. Many citizens have joined him to take retribution on Kett for the wreckage of their city. Now the rebels are fearful and they leave their camp at Mousehold Heath, heading for lower land where they might better fight the coming battle. They are doomed.

It is 27 August and Warwick leads the charge onto a patch of open ground called Dussindale. The rebels are slaughtered. Thousands fall against the well-armed, well-trained troops. Young Robert has the chance to wet his blade again. As the rebellion is crushed, many flee the battlefield disappearing back into their mundane lives, hoping to never hear the name Robert Kett again.

3,000 rebels die. Warwick loses 250 men. Stragglers are rounded up and hung from an oak tree outside Magdalen gate as a reminder to the unwary what will happen to traitors. Kett has vanished. Warwick orders him found and men fly out across the country. The next day Kett is captured at Swannington and taken to the Tower of London. The rebellion is over. Warwick has triumphed and his son Robert has had his first taste of warfare and blood.

4 – Syderstone, Norfolk 1955

Fourdrinier carefully unwrapped a cheese sandwich prepared by his wife that morning and nibbled off the corner. Crumbs fell down onto his surplice, but he enjoyed every bite. Fourdrinier had a passion for cheese which had been severely curtailed by the war and rationing. The previous year cheese and meat had finally come off the government's rationing list and the last restrictions were lifted. Since then Fourdrinier had indulged his cheese obsession as much as possible and it had become a tradition to enjoy a cheese sandwich around nine o'clock on a Sunday morning. Fourdrinier found it helped to sustain him after waking at six to prepare his notes and travelling to whichever parish he was preaching in that day. There was a shortage of clergy post-war and smaller parishes had to borrow priests from other areas. Fourdrinier did not normally do Syderstone, but her usual preacher was ill with the flu.

He had ridden over on his bicycle. It was a long distance and not the most sensible journey for a man of his age but, without a car, what was he supposed to do? Now, tucked into the vestry of the church, he went through the various papers left for him by last Sunday's priest and took the time to search out the old parish registers. If his history was to progress at all he needed first-hand information on the people who had lived here, in particular the clergymen.

Fourdrinier ate the last mouthful of sandwich, savouring the sharpness of the mature cheddar. He had plans to seek out some French cheeses when next he could; he had a craving for Camembert, but for the time being he would make do with the comfort the small lump of Stilton in his larder at home brought him.

He wiped his fingers and carefully opened the register. Syderstone was a typical small parish, with typically small numbers of births, marriages and deaths recorded in the registers. He browsed through the earliest entries, glancing at familiar names. Edith Brown, born 1777, had a descendant living today who he happened to know. Her name was listed along with her twelve siblings, remarkably in an age of high infant mortality only one died young. Further on he found a Charles Talbot and smiled. Charlie had a long lineage in Syderstone and the farm had been in his family for generations. Unfortunately this Charles Talbot perished at nine months. Fourdrinier read on.

When he reached 1783 the historian in him became excited. This was the William Mantle period, as he liked to think of it. William Mantle had arrived in Syderstone from Hull, he had previously graduated at Cambridge and had married Octavia Huntingdon, (probably a childhood sweetheart) sometime between his ordination and instalment at Syderstone. Soon after they were blessed with a great number of children. In fact, much to Fourdrinier's amusement, the very first entry in the register by Mantle was the baptism of his own eldest child, named Octavia after her mother.

Fourdrinier had a strange liking for Mantle, even if his reputation was rather tarnished locally. Legend around Syderstone held that Mantle had fallen in with bad company, that he had been led astray into gambling and drink. Eventually Mantle was so thoroughly ruined in body and spirit that he died at the pathetically young age of 35. Despite his profligate lifestyle and dereliction of church duties, he was surprisingly well-liked by the population, and there was a certain degree of sympathy for his plight. Fourdrinier had to admit he had soft feelings towards the flawed Mantle. The musty register before him gave a rather brief glimpse into his short, but full, life.

At 20 he was married to a woman who was six years his senior, at 21 he had his first daughter. Another daughter, Ann Elizabeth, followed in 1784 and a son, William, was born in 1786. John Mantle was born in 1788, Joseph Mantle 1789 – only 13 months between the births – perhaps the reason why Joseph died and was buried only fourteen days later by his father.

The first sign of any oddness, if that was what it could be termed, came with the birth of a son in 1790 who was baptised Berry. It was a strange enough name, Fourdrinier considered, but it might have come from some family surname the Mantle's wished to honour. The more sensibly named Harriet appeared in 1792 and a final son, George, was born in 1794.

After George the entries in the register took on a significant change. It was quickly apparent to Fourdrinier's eyes that a completely different hand was writing the entries, despite the services allegedly being performed by Mantle. Where Mantle's handwriting did appear it varied from being exceptionally neat, as all his prior entries had been, to being messy, untidy, full of ink blotches and clearly written by someone struggling with some form of malady. The final entry from Mantle's era seemed rather under-stated, considering the story the previous entries had been telling. William Mantle was buried on 8 June 1797, leaving behind seven living children and the unfortunate Octavia.

Fourdrinier leant back in the hard wooden chair he had borrowed from the choir stall. What a strange and sad little life Mantle had had. There had been so much potential joy; it was a lucky soul in the eighteenth century who had seven of his eight children survive infancy. Yet something had tarnished it.

"I would like to give you the benefit of the doubt, old boy, and say you had some sickness," Fourdrinier mutter to the dry, stone walls as though Mantle's shade perched nearby. "The last four years of your life you were clearly a troubled man."

And all that misery, whether self-induced or by will of God, had led to the legend that Mantle's ghost haunted the parsonage. Fourdrinier smiled to himself. He was far from a believer in ghosts. He understood the concept, but as for actual proof? The Bible was rather amiss on ghost stories, but there was a certain sub-text that they were the sort of thing clergymen should refrain from believing in. Although he had to admit there were many among his number who were quite certain of their existence and would be no more shaken on that subject than on the reality of the crucifixion.

Fourdrinier checked his watch and then turned the next few pages of the register. A curate by the name of Skrimshire had served Syderstone at the turn of the nineteenth century, seeing in an age of great change; witnessing the emergence of Jane Austen and the end of the regency period. In 1831 he was retired and his place was taken by John Stewart, who arrived just before Christmas of that year. Fourdrinier knew little about Stewart, unlike Mantle his reign as a curate had been unremarked upon by local legend. To all intents and purposes he seemed a respectable man with a small family of three sons and one daughter.

Fourdrinier picked up his life story with his first entry into the register in April 1832. Very rapidly his face darkened. Stewart, it appeared, was a man of superior feelings and self-righteous pretensions. As Fourdrinier scoured the lines of script for baptisms and deaths he was appalled to see Stewart had taken it upon himself to mark out illegitimate children for special attention. Certain names were fiercely underlined in black ink and marked with large crosses that gave Fourdrinier a shiver as he remembered similar crosses he had once seen illustrated in a school-book, daubed on the doors of plague victims. To ensure Stewart's intentions were clear and that no one may mistake why he was picking out these particular infants' names for defacing he had added the words 'base born' beside them.

Fourdrinier sighed sadly as he tracked the defaced names. He was angered to see even an infant's burial entry had been tarnished in this way. He somehow doubted that Stewart would have been able to mask such vehemence in his personal dealings with the families, particularly the women involved. Stewart was on a quick route to making himself extremely unpopular. What a contrast between the flawed and beloved Mantle and the pompous, self-righteous Stewart. Fourdrinier flicked through the few years of entries for Stewart. By the 1844 page he was relieved to see Stewart's ministry at Syderstone had ended.

Where did that leave him? He now had a clearer insight into two of the men who would feature in his history. He would have to be careful over his wording of the Stewart section, there might just be some descendants of his alive who would take offence. But it was all grist to the mill and would spice up what otherwise was shaping into a slightly dull narrative. Just where that left the Syderstone ghost and Miss Margaret Stewart he did not know.

At precisely 11 o'clock, he took a short service for the small, regular congregation. He had toured parishes before and knew it was always tricky judging the sermon for the audience; each parish had its own thoughts and foibles, so he kept to a very neutral topic and discussed the story of the resurrection, since Easter was fast approaching.

As he shook hands with various people in the church porch he glanced over to the gate and saw Charlie leaning against a stone pillar and staring off into the distance. His heart sank a little; not because he wanted to avoid his old curate, but because he feared the next few hours – he feared he might do more to harm Charlie's hopes that he could somehow prove God existed, than help him. It was a cowardly thought, he realised. He spent much of his time discussing belief and finding a path to God with all manner of people. Charlie was just one more. Except he wasn't. Except he was a dear friend who Fourdrinier desperately wanted to help, who he wanted to bring back to God and give him the comfort he so longed for. Fourdrinier felt totally inadequate in the situation.

Saying goodbye to the last of his temporary flock, Fourdrinier travelled down the sloping path of the graveyard and emerged through the iron gates.

"A and R," Charlie said before they had even greeted one another.

Fourdrinier glanced at where he was pointing and saw the letters wrought into the gate.

"Amy Robsart?"

"I told you the village has a fondness for her. Do you like the car?"

Charlie proudly motioned to a black Humber, polished to a smart shine, but with clear traces of mud on the wheels, arches and doors.

"She is stunning," Fourdrinier nodded, his knowledge of cars being limited to complaining at the speed they went by him on his bicycle. "How long have you had her?"

"Got her just after the war. The old owner was ditching her, no petrol you see? Anyway, he said he hardly had the use of her and after six years of riding a bicycle he no longer had the inclination to drive a motor car. So she became mine," Charlie opened a door for Fourdrinier. "Hop in, I brushed down the seats this morning."

Fourdrinier did as he was told and stared about at the pale leather interior and walnut dashboard.

"Don't mind if she rattles a bit," Charlie grinned. "She needs a few new bits and bobs, but you know the way it is."

He pressed down on the accelerator and the Humber rumbled affectionately back.

"Just think of the rubbish those damn Germans are driving these days!" Charlie laughed as he dropped her into gear and sped off up the road.

Fourdrinier held firmly onto his hat with one hand and the car seat with the other. He experimented with shutting his eyes to try and calm his nerves, but the horror of not being able to see an upcoming bend proved worse than the horror of anticipation. Charlie took the roads with accustomed speed and grace, the Humber cornered as though she knew where she was going.

"I've been looking forward to this," Charlie shouted over a heavy rattling noise coming from the engine.

"Have you now? I hope I live up to your expectations, I fear the older I get the less I am good company."

"Nonsense Fourdrinier! You talk like a man who doesn't get out enough," Charlie took a tight corner and startled a pheasant. "Someone missed the guns!"

"I told Maud you were coming, Maud is the wife," Charlie continued. "She is preparing a roast bit of beef, she does smashing dumplings. She won't stint you on that front."

"I hope I am not inconveniencing her. With meat only just off the ration I do feel a trifle anxious when people cook for me that they will stint themselves for the rest of the week."

"You are an old coot!" Charlie laughed again. "Stint ourselves? Do I look like I stint myself?"

Charlie risked taking a hand off the steering wheel to pat his broad belly, then they were winding into a narrow bend and emerging into a sheet of sunshine.

"I've been thinking about our conversation all week," Charlie continued.

"Have you?"

"I was a bit, well, forthright when we spoke."

Fourdrinier glanced at his friend, looking at his worried expression in profile.

"I am always open to honesty, Charlie, you well know that."

"It's just... I came across rather blunt, and I know I was a blustering fool and a bully."

"You were eager and passionate."

"No, I was a bully. I shouldn't have pushed you so hard on the subject. I just want to know so badly, I want someone to point at me and go 'Charlie believe in God because I said so and here is my proof that I am right'. I suppose that is asking too much?"

Fourdrinier took a moment to consider his reply.

"Maybe not so much depending on the type of proof you require."

"That's just it Fourdrinier! I have no idea what proof I need!"

Charlie pulled the Humber into a muddy farmyard, sending a flock of chickens scattering into the air. He drove into the centre of a three-sided courtyard of barns and a farmhouse. A great plough horse gazed at them from its stable and a black and white farm dog bounced after the car and tried to jump on the running board. Charlie brought the Humber to a stop in front of an old, stone feeding trough and swung open the door to greet the dog.

Fourdrinier let himself out the other side, relieved to have firm earth beneath his feet, even if it did stink of various forms of manure. He exchanged looks with the plough horse, both feeling disinclined to this roaring, puffing machine man had invented and called a car.

"Go inside Fourdrinier. We'll have a drink before dinner. I dear say the skies are looking grey again and ready to rain on us. I'll drive you home if the weather deteriorates."

"I'm sure I will manage," Fourdrinier demurred, giving a gentle pat to the scruffy farm dog that jumped at his knee and smelt almost as foul as the farmyard.

Charlie pushed open the door of the old farmhouse and called out to his wife. Then he took Fourdrinier's coat and hat and hung them on a mahogany hat stand.

"Scotch?"

"With soda, please."

Charlie escorted them into the parlour and opened an elaborate drinks cabinet.

"By the way, don't mind Arthur if he wanders in. He's the wife's fancy."

Fourdrinier pricked up his ears. The wife's fancy what? He wondered.

"It was a good turn out today," Charlie brought over the drink. "No ice, sorry."

"I never have ice, old man, it is just added water."

"You don't change!" Charlie laughed and drained a finger of whisky. "Care for a cigar?"

Fourdrinier refused politely.

Mrs Maud Talbot appeared through another doorway.

"Take yourselves into the dining room, gentlemen. It will only be a few minutes more," she was a busy thing, who bobbed out into the corridor as soon as her message was stated.

"I was sorry to miss your wedding," Fourdrinier mentioned as Charlie showed him through into a long black-beamed room, a fire blazing in the hearth on one wall.

"It was a war-time thing," Charlie shrugged, "in Gibraltar. Maud was in the Red Cross."

"Still, congratulations," Fourdrinier patted his friend heartily on the back. "Only ten years late."

Charlie groaned at him and motioned for Fourdrinier to take the seat at the head of the table.

"Guest's privilege," he informed him as Fourdrinier went to protest. "Besides, I have plans to quiz you on all this haunted parsonage business, so I need to compensate."

"Really Charlie," Fourdrinier downed the last of his scotch and felt the heavy body of a dog rub against his knees. He reached down with his hand and scratched its side. He almost spluttered up his drink as his fingers touched prickly skin instead of fur. Reacting rather than thinking he disappeared under the table and came face to face with a rather large and peculiarly ugly pig.

"That would be Arthur," Charlie joined him peering under the table cloth. "He was a runt and the wife took a shine to him. Can't get him out of the house now."

"Is he..." the questions flew through Fourdrinier's mind,

"docile?"

"Oh yes, ever so good. And clean in the house too," Charlie nodded proudly. "Better than the dog, in fact."

Fourdrinier emerged from under the table with what little dignity he could muster and managed to mask his grimace as Arthur sat down heavily on his foot.

"You have really adapted to farm life, Charlie."

"It wasn't so hard, father loved it. I used to imagine I would be a town pastor all my life, but things change, do they not?"

Fourdrinier nodded.

"That they do."

Maud Talbot served up a fine joint of roast beef a few moments after Arthur's arrival. It was clear the pig had an unerring sense for when dinner was ready. Fourdrinier had his plate stacked with thick meat, roasted potatoes, carrots, dumplings and peas. There was lusciously thick gravy to coat everything and the meal caused the reverend's stomach to rumble appreciatively. Charlie was picking up his fork to spear a potato when Fourdrinier carefully placed together his hands, closed his eyes and said;

"Let us pray."

Fourdrinier gave his hosts a moment to recover from the surprise and respond in like before he carried on,

"For this meal make us truly grateful, O God, and for bringing old friends together we thank you. Amen."

Fourdrinier unclasped his hands and glanced over at his friend sheepishly. Charlie was smirking, but made no comment. Grace had not occurred at that table in so long that he had almost forgotten it.

"Charlie says you are writing a history on Syderstone?" Maud asked, her eyes averted to her plate.

"I am indeed, mostly focusing on the role of the parish priest in Norfolk, with a section on Syderstone. I fear it will be a very poorly circulated work. I have looked into printing costs already, just for my own amusement."

"I think it would be a grand thing," Maud contradicted.

"No one ever writes the history of little parishes. Perhaps if you could extend it to include a little bit of local history it might appeal to more readers?"

"That is a point. Did you have anything in mind?"

"Well, I'm not local. My folks are from Lincolnshire, but Charlie's family go back in Syderstone five generations."

"They do indeed," Charlie grimaced. "Regular stick-in-the-muds."

"I'm sure there must be other people you could talk to. Mrs Douglas at the paper shop, for instance. Her grandfather ran the post office."

"I think you make a fine point, Mrs Talbot," Fourdrinier told her warmly. "I must say Syderstone has caught my attention over all the other parishes I intended to focus on. There is something about it that fascinates me. So many stories seem to begin and end here, even the odd mystery or two."

"Aha!" Charlie looked pleased. "The parsonage ghost."

Maud Talbot offered her guest some pickled cabbage and the distraction was long enough for him to compose his thoughts.

"That wasn't precisely what I meant, yet, I confess our discussion earlier in the week has piqued my interest in certain curates of Syderstone."

"Such as?"

"Reverend William Mantle. I was looking at the records today and I find myself wondering whether the rumours of his alcoholism were true or whether he was really suffering from some form of disease?"

"That I can't help you with, what about the Stewarts?"

Fourdrinier felt that flicker of anger at John Stewart's defacing of the records burn bright again.

"I do not care for Reverend John Stewart's style," he said concisely.

Maud looked up sharply.

"What an odd thing to say about a person you never met. What has made you so certain about him?"

Fourdrinier glared at his plate.

"He took it upon himself to highlight and crudely annotate the entries of any child in this parish born out of wedlock. Whatever your views on illegitimacy, such behaviour in a curate is disgraceful."

"So he was bit of a prig?" Charlie inserted.

"I imagine he was brash in his manner and fervent in his belief in God, to the point where he would scorn and punish those who he deemed sinners, while all the time failing to see the sin within himself. Or at least that is my opinion."

"You sound angry."

Fourdrinier turned to his friend and saw a look of understanding.

"Men like Stewart do not spread God's word, they spread intolerance and hate," Fourdrinier sighed. "How can I have found this man so dislikeable when what little I know of him has come through the parish records?"

"Intuition?" Charlie suggested.

"If I pass my thoughts along to Aunt Ida, she will have Margaret Stewart popping up at her séances and spouting all manner of slander against the man."

"Seances?" Maud was curious.

"My great aunt dabbles in spiritualism," Fourdrinier shrugged. "On any given day of the week she may consider herself in touch with Sir Arthur Conan Doyle, Benjamin Franklin, Cleopatra, Nelson or any other famous person who fancies dropping in from the afterlife for a chat."

"I told you about dear Ida Fourdrinier," Charlie grinned at Maud. "Remember, the Egyptian encounter?"

"Oh that lady!" Maud's eyes glittered. "Does she really believe she can talk to the dead, Reverend Fourdrinier?"

"I dare say she does. She has now come to the conclusion she is in touch spiritually with the daughter of Reverend John Stewart who was once curate here."

"How I would love to have her come here!" Maud gazed wistfully at her husband. "If she would accept an invitation..."

"She never leaves London," Fourdrinier hastily added.

"But if she would, why I would make her perfectly comfortable. In the summer, perhaps, when the weather is fair. She might be able to tell us all manner of things."

"That might not be such a bad idea Fourdrinier," Charlie had a sudden mischievous look in his eyes. "Being in Syderstone she might find her connection with Margaret Stewart all the stronger."

Fourdrinier looked at him in disbelief.

"Oh do write to her and invite her!" Maud pressed. "I would so ever much like it."

"I think she would find it hard to resist," Charlie added.

"She would never come," Fourdrinier said staunchly.

"Then, it would hardly hurt for you to write and ask her," Charlie persisted.

"Oh please, Reverend Fourdrinier, please do!"

Fourdrinier felt hemmed in on all sides. At least he was consoled that there was no way his aunt would leave London, not with her various infirmities. Feeling frustrated by the eager, pleading faces looking at him and tied by his manners as a guest he finally conceded.

"All right, All right."

"That is so good," Maud smiled. "Thank you, Reverend. I shall fetch the apple crumble and cream now. Oh thank you."

Maud almost danced out of the room.

"In all seriousness," Charlie turned to the reverend as soon as his wife was out of the room, "I do think there is something in this story. Perhaps Margaret Stewart is calling out to us, or perhaps not, but there is a mystery here. Something went on at that parsonage, for all I know might still be going on. As a spiritual man you believe in demons?"

Fourdrinier felt flustered. He wanted to roll his eyes; it seemed such poppycock to discuss demons in the middle of the Twentieth century. Unfortunately, certain branches of the Church were of the opinion that there still existed such evil and Fourdrinier was a servant of that Church. Even so, he hated encouraging Charlie.

"If you mean the demons within us, then yes, I believe in such."

"No, I mean a demon that can attack someone. There was a recent case in Italy, a girl was exorcised."

"They are always doing that sort of thing in Italy," Fourdrinier puffed.

"But what if there is something at the parsonage? Why was that room sealed Fourdrinier? And why did your aunt suddenly know of it."

Fourdrinier studied his old friend quietly.

"What are you seeking, Charlie?"

"A light in the dark?" Charlie laughed, but it was forced. "I told you, I lost my faith in the war. Sometimes I think I lost my soul too. As a soldier you do things... Perhaps I am desperately looking for anything beyond this mortal coil, anything that will convince me this is not all there is. That is what you think, isn't it?"

Fourdrinier sighed as he leaned back in his chair.

"What is belief, Charlie? Is it knowing something is true, or just hoping it is? Aren't we all desperate for certainty?"

"Will you humour me then?"

"I'm concerned this ghost story will lead you down dangerous paths."

"I don't say your aunt can really speak to the dead, you know. Maybe it is all done by telepathy. There has been all manner of studies done on the subject, but... if there is something... can we afford to ignore it?"

"My aunt won't leave London," Fourdrinier avoided answering.

"But you will write?"

"Of course."

"Then, I suppose we must leave it in the hands of God or fate, whichever you prefer."

"I would much prefer if it wasn't left in the hands of my

aunt Ida," Fourdrinier puttered. "You will owe me a considerable number of Sunday dinners for this, my man."

Charlie grinned, satisfied that, for the time being, he had won.

⬚

5 – Greenwich, London 4 June 1550

She is more ecstatic then she thought possible. How could this have come to pass for a country girl who had only ever stood at the fringes of court-life? She has heard the Howard girls talk about the king's court and mention how it was in the time of Henry VIII, but never had she experienced, nor could she have ever foreseen, being married in a palace at Greenwich. More importantly, she had never expected to marry for love.

But there is her groom. Finely turned out in his best doublet and silver breeches. His tight white stockings emphasis his well-turned calves and his muscular bearing is evident as he walks towards her. Her stomach trembles with nerves. She feels a little sick. She has loved Robert since he came home victorious from Kett's defeat. John Dudley, his father, is more influential over the young king Edward the VI than any man alive. Some cast sly comments that, in reality, Dudley rules the country, but that means very little to Amy Robsart.

Robert could have married anyone. Many would have expected a prestigious match arranged by his father to strengthen his ties with various noble families. Amy's father, after all, is a mere gentleman-farmer. But she knows he could only ever have married her. He returned from war and declared his desire for her. Even now it seems impossible, but so it was, and so John Dudley, amused at his son's foibles and not unaware of the subtle connections to Norfolk gentry a Robsart match would bring, has allowed the wedding.

She does not mind that they have piggy-backed their

nuptials onto Robert's elder brother's own wedding. The younger John Dudley, who will become Earl of Warwick when his father dies, has taken the place of his unfortunate elder brother Henry, who was killed during the siege of Boulogne in 1544. Yesterday the future earl married Anne Seymour, daughter of the 1st Duke of Somerset and former Lord Protector of England.

The wedding festivities were extravagant and lively. Twelve-year-old King Edward attended and could not imagine a happier or more fun day. There were mock battles, dancing and a huge banquet. Amy had never seen the like and though many of her wedding guests have arrived this morning a tad worse for their indulgence of the night before, she would not change the excitement and thrill of that day for anything.

Her wedding is to be quieter. The marriage vows have been said and the same audience as the day before have mostly stayed awake through the service, though some are craving a quick retreat to the privy. A live goose has just been brought into the hall. King Edward peers around the crowd from his chair wondering what entertainment this could be. John Dudley treated him to a fine joust between two teams of six gentlemen yesterday, while Edward sat in his own special bower of woven branches. Few boys could have been disappointed by such a performance. But now there is a goose and they are hanging it by its trussed feet from a pole.

"What are they doing?" Edward leans and asks the nearby elder John Dudley.

"It is a game, your highness, a rural pastime. No doubt something the fair bride will be familiar with."

There are gentlemen gathered now, stripped of their doublets so only their loose shirts threaten to be ruined by the sport. The goose is flapping its wings and honking alarmingly as it tries to flutter free from the cross-bar where it has been tied. And the gentlemen have knives, which they laugh and point at one another, still a little drunk from the previous festivities.

"The winner is the first to take away the goose's head," the elder John Dudley informs his king.

"Oh," says Edward, considering it a far cry from the tournaments of the day before and rapidly losing interest.

At the far side of the room Amy averts her eyes to the spectacle, unaware of the comments of her new father-in-law. Robert sits at her side looking so handsome it is almost impossible for her to breathe without gasping aloud. That he is hers is worthy of a fairy tale.

"Do you care for goose?" Ambrose Dudley laughs at his brother.

Robert pulls a face.

"I would have preferred a joust."

"So you could show up these courtly popinjays, brother? You should be careful with that arrogance of yours. It will do you a disservice."

Robert laughs.

"Hark at him Amy, he calls me arrogant!"

Amy smiles at her husband and obediently replies.

"I do not think that of you, Robert."

"But you are love-sick, dear lady," Ambrose tuts at her. "You are blind to his failings, at least for now."

"I am not blind," Amy defends herself, insulted by Ambrose. She may be an adoring wife but she has not forsaken her own temper. "I truly do not think Robert is arrogant."

Ambrose masks his smile behind his goblet.

"Let me leave you in no doubt, my lady, your future husband is not perfect and does not deserve to be adored like a god. But as we are now family let us not argue over the matter."

Ambrose makes peace, but it is very much on his terms.

"Ah, there goes the head!"

With a splatter of blood over the warring gentlemen the goose is deprived of its head and its frantic flapping ceases. King Edward offers a mild applause and pretends not to yawn.

"At least any marriage I make cannot be over-shadowed by our darling brother John's extravagances," Ambrose mutters, rolling back his shoulders and stretching out his arms until they crack quietly. "But then I suppose it was a necessary evil, since father was trying to impress the Duke of Somerset."

Both brothers glance across the room where the younger John Dudley is feasting with his wife Anne Seymour and offering his new father-in-law wine. Somerset looks grim despite the joyful day.

"Somerset played a dangerous game," Robert lowers his voice. "His contradictory actions during the Kett rebellion could not be ignored. He sympathised with the rebels, it was plain to see."

"Seizing up his nephew and fleeing to Windsor castle hardly helped him."

"He feared arrest, doesn't any man who has tasted power here? He knew well enough the reign of Henry to have his doubts that he would survive a fall from grace."

"But father was gracious to him. Somerset's fall was our triumph," Ambrose grins. "Look how he hates us Robert. Our father took his place as Lord Protector, look how his piggy eyes glare. I would not be surprised to learn he still longs for revenge against us."

Amy pretends not to hear such disturbing news. Somerset was the elder brother of Jane Seymour, mother to the boy king currently trying to keep awake on his throne. He was Lord Protector until he was criticised during the Kett rebellion. He nearly plunged the country into civil war when he fled to Windsor with Edward. Everyone thought he would hang, that he didn't seems likely to be because Edward could not bear to have his uncle executed and John Dudley, the new Lord Protector, considered it in his best interests to not upset the young monarch.

Amy feels a frisson of fear within her. Her father has managed to avoid politics all his life, living a relatively peaceful existence, even if his finances could have benefited from the favour of the king. Now Amy is at the centre of it all. She feels a little scared. What dangers are lurking for her new husband in this lion's den? What souls smile and fawn at him, while all the time they plot revenge behind his back? She hardly knows anyone here, she hardly knows even her husband. Suddenly Amy feels like the helpless goose trussed by its feet in the air, awaiting the deadly cut that will end its life. The festivities feel hollow, the wine is sour on her lips. What, wonders Amy, has she risked uniting herself to the Dudley household?

6 – Syderstone, Norfolk 1955

Fourdrinier was dissatisfied with himself. He had written to great aunt Ida and, in loose terms, expressed the invitation Maud Talbot had extended.

"...the young lady has a slight interest in the art of séances and requested meeting you. As she is tied to her farm she wondered if you might pay her a visit and stay a few days. I politely explained your infirmities and said you would most likely decline, so do not feel at all obliged to make extensive communications on the matter, simply write back to me and I shall inform the young lady."

He had tried to avoid mentioning Syderstone, but inevitably it came up as he tried to explain away Maud's interest.

"...she is new to Norfolk, but her husband is Charlie Talbot who you may recall was once my curate. He has settled in his home parish and has taken an interest in my recent researches."

Aunt Ida, eccentric as she was, had a remarkable memory for details and easily made the connection with Syderstone. Her response filled Fourdrinier with despair.

"Dear nephew, the doctor has informed me I must take some country air or I shan't live through another winter. Quite absurd of him, but he has the idea London air is hazardous. So I am in the position of looking for a country retreat, of sorts, and what better place to spend it than in that remarkable town of Syderstone. Margaret, (you recall I mentioned the child?) was quite beside herself at the notion when she came through last night. I would of course bring Nancy, as my companion. Please pass my address on to

Maud Talbot, so I might make arrangements direct. I believe it will take around a month to get everything in order, so that shall make it April. I do hope you will visit frequently while I am in the area, I so rarely see you these days."

Fourdrinier duly passed on the news to the Talbots, feeling a heavy lump in his chest as he contemplated what was to come. Maud was ecstatic, Charlie seemed anxious. Fourdrinier refused an offer to stay for tea protesting he had a service to conduct in the next parish. In truth he was planning to curtail all this ghost nonsense before it grew out of hand. There was only one way to deal with this business and that was to go to the source and prove there was no such thing as a Syderstone ghost; that, in fact, the pretty parsonage was completely unhaunted and that the mysterious room had been sealed up for entirely logical reasons.

He therefore left the Talbots to pay a call on the current owner of Syderstone parsonage. The old cottage – and it was old, Fourdrinier was no architect but he recognised Tudor beams when he saw them – stood parallel to Syderstone church. In previous times the reverend had been most comfortably located next to his place of business, with a gate tucked into the hedge and leading directly from the parsonage garden to the graveyard. The cottage was long and narrow, with a thatched roof and small windows. There were two doors; one facing the church and the other on the back, leading out into the garden and towards the road. The whole quaint estate was guarded from observers by a sturdy, red brick wall, tastefully decorated with creeping ivy. If ever there was a place that was haunted, this was surely not it. With blackbirds singing in the garden and an early rose budding around the porch, the house looked distinctly untroubled by any noisy spirits.

Fourdrinier rang an old fashioned bell and hoped the owner would be amenable to his odd questions. It was several moments before he heard a shuffling of feet and an elderly man with long nicotine stained grey hair opened the door. He was a clear foot shorter than Fourdrinier and stared up suspiciously. After a moment he reached into the pocket of his waistcoat and removed a pair of round spectacles. Donning them he observed the vicar.

"Can I help you?"

"I am Reverend Fourdrinier," Fourdrinier offered a hand which the old man shook limply. "I do apologise for disturbing you but I am working on a history of the church in Norfolk and I do believe your house was once the parsonage for Syderstone?"

The old man cupped a hand around his ear as he listened and nodded along with the words. Then he smiled.

"An historian, huh? Well do come in. I'm a bit of a history buff myself. Used to be in antiques. I would like to chat about the place, the parsonage has quite the pedigree," the old man limped backwards and allowed Fourdrinier into a square hallway decked with rows and rows of old framed prints. "I'm a bit of a collector."

The man motioned to several Cruikshank cartoons from the eighteenth century mounted behind glass and caricaturing various celebrities of the age. Nearby were several old maps of Norfolk, half hidden in the dim gloom of the hall.

"Come through to my living room," the old man led the way out of the hall, down a corridor turning left to face the front door over-looking the churchyard, and then taking a door on the right.

Fourdrinier entered a dark, panelled room stuffed full of what he could only consider clutter. Fourdrinier was not the tidiest of men, certainly when it came to his papers he was a regular hoarder and stacked them wherever space allowed, his wife was forever complaining. But in comparison to this room his home looked positively Spartan. He was not certain how the old man had managed to negotiate three large, rearing stuffed bears into the room, one an Arctic polar bear that towered over Fourdrinier and was being used as a hat and umbrella stand. Completing the menagerie of stuffed wildlife was a disintegrating golden eagle, a grimacing fox in a glass case and a pair of squirrels boxing under a glass dome. Around the animals an assortment of ornaments jostled for space on a series of side tables and cabinets, that so dominated the room that only a narrow corridor remained for Fourdrinier to creep down and find a sofa. Even that was covered in cushions, rugs, old books and several glaring African tribal masks.

"Just move things off," the old man said, brushing aside some papers carelessly, but reverently removing the masks from the sofa. "Eighteenth century, North African," he motioned to the mask. "That there is a Meissen shepherdess."

Thrown for an instant Fourdrinier followed the old man's pointing finger and noted a white female figurine perched between some toby jugs, porcelain prancing horses and a match holder in the shape of a grinning pixie.

"I was in antiques," the old man repeated. "When I shut my shop I brought the stock I had left here. Sorry about the clutter."

"Not at all," Fourdrinier smiled.

"Would you like a cup of tea?"

Fourdrinier wondered where a tea tray could possibly fit.

"If it is not an inconvenience."

"Course not! My name's Donald, by the way, Donald Steward. I used to run Elegant Antiques in Dereham, ever visit it?"

Fourdrinier admitted he had not.

"Well, do look around won't you. If you want anything... look at me, I still think I have a shop. But do look around and if you like anything just say. It's got to all go somewhere eventually."

Donald limped out of the room and Fourdrinier stared around at the dingy clutter. The bears' various pairs of black eyes seemed to be fixed on him. He suddenly felt rather relieved he had never been inclined towards hunting.

42

There were sounds of water running through pipes and Fourdrinier was able to grasp an impression of the house while its owner was away. His aunt had a fondness for talking about 'atmospheres' within old buildings, but to Fourdrinier's senses the house seemed quiet and peaceful. Without the clutter he could imagine the room he was in being quite airy and bright. In fact, it struck him that this would make a pleasant family home. More than ever he was certain there was no haunting at the parsonage.

Donald returned, balancing a battered tea tray on one arm, while carrying a fancy biscuit barrel under the other.

"My daughter keeps me well supplied with biscuits," he directed the biscuit barrel at Fourdrinier who obediently took it, then he carefully placed the tea tray on a sofa opposite the reverend. "Now we can settle and have a chat. How far have you got along in your history, Mr Fourdrinier?"

The biscuit barrel was opened to display Garibaldis. Fourdrinier took two of the biscuits he always thought of as 'the squashed fly ones.'

"So far my research has been mainly involved with the formal side of the parish, the records and so forth. I certainly found my interest piqued by the contrast between the reverend William Mantle and reverend John Stewart."

"Two very different men," Donald nodded.

"Yes, well I don't seem able to get much further back than Mantle and beyond Stewart the history becomes, well, rather dull. I fear that is how my book will turn out unless I can fill out the bones of the story somehow. Records are all very well, but they don't tell you about the people. And, of course, there is this beautiful parsonage. Is the cottage Tudor?"

"Older," Donald poured tea. "The foundations are medieval, had an expert from Edinburgh come down and look at them once. He thought they could be fourteenth century. The deeds for the property seem to confirm that, though at one time I believe this was two cottages, hence the strange arrangement of doors. By the fifteenth century the house was one and being lived in by a local gentleman farmer. I've had work done on the fireplace in the past and they found small, medieval bricks and this."

Donald stood up and negotiated his way to a curio cabinet at the back of the room. When he returned he was holding a bundle of blackened leather. He placed it in Fourdrinier's hands and the bundled resolved itself, in Fourdrinier's mind, into a child's shoe.

"They used to place such things in chimneys to keep away witches," Donald explained. "The land around these parts is steeped in superstition. There is a pond just beyond the far hedge, once part of this property, where the ghost of a witch was said to have been laid."

That was the last thing Fourdrinier wanted to hear. He needed no encouragement for aunt Ida. Firmly putting the shoe aside he asked;

"When did it become a parsonage?"

"As best I can tell in the seventeenth century. Even then the parish tended to share its vicar and only a curate would live here. The right side of the house was rented out to a local family to subsidise living costs."

"It must have been quite cramped. Mantle had seven living children."

"I suppose so. This room and the one opposite were reserved for the curate's use. The room at the far right of the house was allotted to the renting family and the kitchen, pantry and larder were shared. Upstairs it was even more tightly packed. There are four bedrooms, excluding the room the stairs emerge in and a small, cupboard size room usually called a dressing room. Say the tenants were allotted two rooms, that only left the curate with two and a pair of attic bedrooms which sit in the eaves."

Fourdrinier was surprised at the minimal accommodation, no wonder the parsonage had eventually fallen out of favour.

"One of the bedrooms, I should add, has a tiny window.

I suspect it was once a storeroom, though the fireplace in it is pretty substantial which suggests it was in use a considerable time. Of course in Mantle's day people thought nothing of sleeping together in the same room."

On that front Fourdrinier agreed, though he wondered if lack of privacy within a busy and noisy family had driven Mantle to drink.

"Now, what about this business of a sealed room?" he asked slyly.

"Ah, you heard about that."

"A local in the village told me. I'm afraid I didn't believe him."

"It's true, all right. Here, I'll show you," Donald fetched a key off the mantelpiece and escorted Fourdrinier up a dog-leg set of stairs. "This is a right warren, my daughter thinks it would be best off knocked down and replaced with something more straightforward. I say this house has history and that is something you can't manufacture. This cottage grew around its occupants like a living thing. She doesn't understand that."

Fourdrinier smiled at the man's passion, he seemed deeply in love with his home and though it was cluttered it was clearly well tended to. Like an old rustic garden, there was a strange order among the disparate parts.

"This room I'm showing you, it was nailed up with boards across it for almost 100 years," Donald went down the corridor and came to an old latch style door, with a brand new lock in it. "It's called the haunted room. I keep it locked out of habit. My wife, bless her soul, felt it had a sinister air and insisted I fit a lock. What good is a lock against a ghost? I said to her, but she was adamant."

Donald unlocked the door and opened it to reveal a well-lit and completely empty bedroom. The room looked surprisingly clean and free from cobwebs and dust for somewhere shut up for years. On the far right there was another opening. Fourdrinier went to take a pace inside and hesitated without knowing why.

"It takes you like that," Donald said. "Some people just can't enter it. That on the far right is a maid's room backing onto the stairs."

Fourdrinier gazed into what must have been not only the biggest, but nicest room in the property and tried to rationalise why anyone would seal it up.

"Was the floor rotten?" he asked Donald. "Is that why they sealed it?"

"The floor is the same one today it was when Stewart opened the door."

Fourdrinier felt his thoughts jump.

"Reverend John Stewart had this room opened?"

"Oh yes, insisted, in fact. He turned it into a bedroom for his daughter Margaret."

There was a strange chill running down Fourdrinier's spine.

"If you look here you can see the holes where the boards were nailed in," Donald was pointing at the doorframe. "Beautiful room, isn't it?"

Fourdrinier deliberately took a step backwards away from the doorway. It was as though the air had been crushed from him. He was a little light-headed.

"No one has slept in there since Margaret Stewart," Donald continued, closing the door firmly on the room and locking it.

The world seemed to rush back in on Fourdrinier and he took a deep breath.

"Here, if you are writing a history on the parish perhaps I can help you a bit more," Donald seemed not to have noticed the reverend's discomfort, or maybe he had and was trying to distract him from it. "When I came to the house there were a load of old papers left in the attic with the deeds. Some are letters by Stewart, others by Skrimshire and a few are really early. There is also something I think you would really like. You were interested in William Mantle, weren't you?"

"Yes," Fourdrinier managed to say.

"Well, go back downstairs and I'll join you in a moment. I'll fetch those papers. They could do with being catalogued and stored somewhere," Donald bustled off towards the attic.

Fourdrinier climbed back down the stairs slowly. His legs felt oddly weak and he was still a little faint. He feared he had caught something riding his bicycle in the rain and was about to go down with the flu. He dabbed at his forehead with his fingers, it seemed cold rather than feverish. He made it back to the living room and dropped onto the sofa gratefully. He was determined not to acknowledge the fact that this strange sickness felt a good deal like acute terror, the sort of terror he had experienced during his first air-raid. Nor was he prepared to admit to himself that this terror had been induced by almost stepping into the upstairs bedroom. The haunted room.

What a foolish title. He scoffed at himself. Reverend Stewart had had the right idea; he had opened the door and restored the room to use. He would not suffer to be dictated to by the nonsense of a ghost story!

Fourdrinier's body was returning to normal. His legs had stopped quivering, his heart no longer raced, and his usual calm demeanour was restoring itself. He sank back into the sofa and began contemplating helping himself to another Garidbaldi biscuit when Donald reappeared.

"It's quite a collection," he handed over an old fruit box, heavy with papers, and sat down panting slightly. "Letters mostly, probably some bills too. But it's the top piece I think you will appreciate."

Fourdrinier picked up a bundle of paper, folded over on itself. It was discoloured at the edges, and a little ragged. He unfolded it gently and couldn't believe his eyes.

"The diary of William Mantle?"

"Remarkable, isn't it," Donald beamed merrily. "Imagine it surviving the persecuting eyes of reverend Stewart? He had no time for Mantle."

"Have you read it?" Fourdrinier felt his inner historian

welling up with excitement.

"Never had the time, do you think it will be useful to you?"

"My dear fellow, it could prove a breakthrough for my book!"

Fourdrinier stared at the neat handwriting he had become so familiar with in the parish register. Could this document prove the key to the mystery of Mantle's demise? What a treasure! His excitement over the find and what it would do for his manuscript completely overwhelmed the last dregs of fear that lurked within him. By the time he was saying his thank yous and goodbyes to Donald all thoughts of the strange sealed room had disappeared from his mind.

At least for the time being.

◌

7 - The Diary of Reverend William Mantle April 1783

Praise be to the Lord! My darling Octavia has been safely delivered of a daughter. The child is fair like her mother and surely I shall name her accordingly? I am beside myself with joy. Octavia beseeches me to calm myself, that I trouble her as she rests in her confinement. I prowl the house with my new dear in my arms, hardly paying heed to all the duties I must attend to.

Phoebe Steward is in the kitchen and is trying to pester me to eat something. How can a man eat when he is in such a celebratory mood? I beg her to bring me fine wine and we shall toast the child. She tilts her head in that scoffing manner she has and chides me.

"Mr Mantle, you would have the world think a woman never bore a child before."

Well, dear Mrs Steward, my woman never has!

Ah, but how can I explain to such a simple, practical person? She sees no beauty, no magic in this finest moment. I see the breadth and depth of God's work, of His will amongst us. I see such perfection, such tiny grace. I want to run to the church and ring the bells! I shall let all of Syderstone know that Octavia Mantle has just partaken of a miracle and William Mantle could not be more ecstatic if Jesus Himself stood before him!

Forgive my blasphemy, oh Lord! My agitation took over

the better part of my wits. If I say wrong it is only for being witness to your glorious wonder. I carry this child like a precious gift, I cannot contain my happiness.

Octavia still rests in my arms. Yes, I shall name the dear thing after her mother. At my side I have the registers I was carefully notating before my darling wife cried out her first pangs. Now I look back at them and my mind is blank as to what I should have been writing. All I can imagine is the space on the next line where I shall record the baptism of Octavia. That shall be tomorrow. Octavia, my wife, has given her assent, too tired to debate the arrangements with me. She merely gave a faint smile and requested I don't let the child grow too cold.

She is not cold. She curls up against me as blessedly content as a new-born lamb. One finger, the tiniest thing I have ever seen slips into the open button-hole of my jacket and latches hold as though I might slip away. I am a blessed man, oh God, and to think I dreaded coming to this place?

I could not shake my fears, though I told myself God had willed me to this part of the world. Norfolk has been favourable to me. After Cambridge I had little inclination to return to my hometown of Hull and then I was made curate of Terrington St Clement and St John. Octavia agreed to marry me that same week I had the news. We had known each other since childhood and we had always sworn one day we should pledge our hearts to each other. So I should feel no dread, no ill-fortune has come my way, nothing but good has followed me from my ordination.

Still, this parish chills me a little. Forgive me, no, not the parish. This place, this cottage. Something here sends a discomfort through me I cannot explain.

The tiny Octavia has begun to fret, she craves the comfort of her mother. I shall return her, though I can hardly bear to let her from my grasp. I have never felt worthy of much. My father reminded me daily that I was particularly contemptible. I never wrote well enough for him, or learned my Latin fast enough or could pronounce my sums like my brothers could. He was not a bad man, but I disappointed him. Is it too proud to say I finally feel I have become a part of something important? That this child is a sign I am not the worthless beast my father told me? Have I finally done something laudable?

My mind wallows in these thoughts. I have lost my joy and replaced it with confusion. Again I am taxed by doubt. Have I come here to do good or merely to pass time? I must move and do something. I must get out of the house. If I sit here any longer I shall stifle. Octavia wants her mother and I want my freedom.

~ ~ ~ * ~ ~ ~

I found Josiah Smith, Ernest Hemp and Edward Steward, (brother to Phoebe) at the White Stag. Josiah is a farmer and Ernest one of his labourers. Edward makes a reasonable living as a journeyman carpenter. I wonder at this most days since they are nearly always within the White Stag and also nearly always deep in their cups.

But I craved company, even ill company, of the male persuasion. Josiah Smith is also good for buying a man a mug of ale, which eases my conscience somewhat. Octavia disapproves of the money I spend on drink and, indeed, more than once my purse has run dry before my thirst has been satisfied and my eyes have wandered with a terrible temptation onto the small box we keep locked for church collections. It is a wickedness within me. I fear my father was right when he declared I was a bad soul, even if he was only angry over another failure in my Latin grammar.

I also had a desire to share the news of my joy. Josiah Smith has three daughters and two sons and understands such things as the novelty of a first child. He was most gracious when I told him my news and insisted I drink at his expense all night. I could hardly mask my delight, even if I had wickedly hoped he might be so generous. Father, forgive me!

Josiah is a man who talks much when he drinks and he talks loudly. I have drunk with him once or twice before, but rarely in such a friendly manner. He usually discusses his sheep or his cart horse, which he claims has won first place for 'finest horse' at the annual fair for the last five years. I always look at Ernest when this topic comes up to see his reaction, but presumably he is well used to his employer's foibles, he certainly never raises an eyebrow at the tale.

Tonight Josiah did me the courtesy of desiring to speak only of tiny Octavia, of the health of my darling wife and on fatherhood in general. We drank a toast to long life and many children and to each of our respective offspring. He drank a toast to his wife, with a smirk as he commended her firm thighs and broad hips, which make, as he tells me, for a fine brood cow. Ernest laughed heartily at the comment, Edward smirked. I was a little taken aback. Make no mistake, I am far from naïve about such discourses as wives' thighs and hips, but to compare a beloved to a cow seemed rather unpleasant. Josiah, seeing my confusion, assured me it was very natural in country areas to affectionately associate a wife with livestock.

I fear it was my obvious uncertainty that brought about a change of subject for the worse. For I have come home now with a loss of all my joy and instead a return of that old, creeping sense of dread.

"The poor curate ain't like us fools," Edward Steward told his drinking cohorts. "He thinks the world of his wife. The poor sod's madly in love."

"More fool him!" Ernest laughed loudly – Ernest, I hasten to add, is unmarried and I take his comments very lightly for he does not truly understand the delights of a wife.

"If he loves his wife so much," says Josiah, with a strange look in his eye, "why does he insist on staying in that thar parsonage?"

I must have looked at him goggle-eyed, for he roared with laughter and slapped me on the shoulder.

"Sorry lad, I didn't realise you han't a clue about the

stories."

"Stories?" I felt wrong-footed. I felt criticised and insulted. I felt my honour concerning my wife had been questioned.

"No one ever told you the story of Syderstone parsonage?" Josiah fixed his gaze on me. I suddenly doubted he was as drunk as he pretended to be.

"No one," I said. "Surely it is just a cottage?"

Josiah chuckled again.

"Thar house is haunted, young squire," he winked at me. "Ever since the dear Lady Dudley did perish in mysterious circumstances."

"Lady Dudley?" I flustered over the name, I could not think who he meant. "She lived in the cottage?"

Now all three men laughed loudly, and the other drinkers in the pub were looking over to see what was so amusing.

"Lady Dudley did live two hundred years ago at Syderstone manor house. She were the wife of Robert Dudley, Queen Elizabeth's favourite."

My history is rusty, but I recalled enough to know that Robert Dudley had played a dangerous game courting the queen while he was still married.

"Lady Dudley fell down a staircase and died," Josiah continued. "Some say she tipped herself down, some say she were pushed. Whichever way you look at it, Robert Dudley was immediately better off because he could openly court the queen."

"And what has this to do with the parsonage?" I was under the impression I was being goaded.

"Well, Lady Dudley's ghost walks because of her untimely death. Only Syderstone manor is no more than a few lumps in the grass, so she moved her spirit and set up home in the nearest place she found. Your cottage."

Now I snorted.

"You are implying my parsonage is haunted by the ghost of Lady Dudley?"

"You ask my sister," Edward piped up. "She has heard the ghost herself."

I had had enough of such talk. My ale tasted bitter and I had lost all my exuberance of the moment before.

"I don't believe you," I told them sternly. "You are saying this to frighten me."

"Ah curate! Why would we do a thing like that?" Josiah rested a hand on his heart and looked sincere. "I only tell you what is said in the village. I'm sure you don't need to be afraid."

"I would be," Edward said, his face suddenly very serious. "Spirits aren't something to be messed with. They can cause all manner of harm. Especially to women and young children."

"Leave the sod alone, Ned," Josiah snorted. "Can't you see how spooked the bugger is?"

But I was already on my way out and heading home as fast as I could. Those feelings of dread now took on a whole new meaning and I was cursing my failure to listen to my own senses.

The house was quiet when I arrived. Phoebe had gone home and not a lamp was burning. I took a candle from just inside the porch and used a flint to light it. I was trembling as I held up the flickering light and looked about my hall. Did I expect to see her in that dark place? Did I expect her to lurch at me from the shadows of the kitchen door? I cannot say now, I only know how I reacted at that moment.

I went upstairs swiftly, the boards hardly getting a chance to creak beneath me before I was on the landing and heading for Octavia's bedroom. There was a draught whipping down from the attic stairs that threatened to blow out my candle; someone had failed to close the door at the foot of the staircase. I confess I shook even more as I went to the gaping black hole in the wall that was the doorway and braced myself to face it.

There was not a soul there, yet still it disturbed me that the door had been so neglected. Octavia is always very precise about that doorway, she hates the cold. I pulled the door shut, listening as the black latch clunked into place. I felt safer just performing that action – that is how disturbed I was by this time.

I went back along the hall, casting my light at the shadows either side, trying to startle away the demons and monsters that now filled my mind. I wished I had not drunk so much. I am prone to attacks of my nerves when I have been drinking. Now my heart was dancing in my chest and I feared I would collapse before I reached dear, sweet Octavia and my dear sweet child.

Then there was the door! I grabbed for the handle, felt the latch lift and stumbled into the darkened room that had a slight smell of the sick-bed about it. I have never been good with disease or illness and for a moment the illusion the familiar scents of herbs, lotions and blood brought to my mind unsettled my fragile state of being. I edged towards the bed, convinced I would look upon some nightmarish scene, and there was my child! Her face turned into her mother, her tiny fists clenched and her chest rising and falling by the slightest of movements. I placed my hand lightly on her stomach and felt the rhythm of her breathing. My anxiety ebbed.

Next to her I looked at my Octavia, smiling in her sleep, as contented as the babe by her side. I reached to her too and held my hand just before her mouth, feeling the warmth of her breath upon my skin. I came within a fraction of falling to my knees and crying out "Hallelujah!"

Instead I held my nerve, what little I confess to having, and crept away. I came into my study where a bed has been kindly made for me by Phoebe Steward until my wife is fit to have me back in the bedchamber. I placed down the candle and cupped my head in my hands.

Can I express how foolish I felt? How I imagined the laughter of Josiah, Ernest and Edward as they joked to each other about teasing the stupid curate into thinking his house was haunted? How I had run, how the fear had taken the better of me! I am a man of God, yet I became a coward in the face of something I should not even believe in. A curate does not believe in ghosts, and certainly does not fear them.

Oh, I wish I was able to convince myself. I must say nothing to anyone about this. If I was so much as to ask Phoebe about what her brother said then I would be admitting to my actions – and what actions they were! Did I really believe some ghost could have acted upon my wife and child while I was absent, snatching their sleepy souls from me before I could act?

I am saddened by my failure. I am saddened by my lack of faith in God. I know the ale did not help, that it made me weak. I must never drink again, else I fear what future nightmares I shall conjure for myself. I should rest now. I am to baptise little Octavia in the morning. I shall think no more of ghostly ladies and fairy stories. I have been a dupe, but I shall not be one again. Oh God, save me from Josiah Smith and his mockery! Save me from making a fool of myself! Oh God, don't let me ruin what you have so graciously given me!

⬚

8 - Somerset House, London 1553

The world has changed yet again. Robert Dudley stands by the window of his new, luxurious home and gazes out at the passers-by. Somerset House was built under the orders of the man who gave it his name, Edward Seymour, Duke of Somerset. In 1549 he pulled down an old Inn of Chancery and put up the vast two storey house around a large quadrangle with a gate house rising to three stories. The building favoured European architecture and was designed to include sweeping curves, large, Grecian pillars and ornate details of cupids and flowers.

Dudley is mildly irritated with the fussiness of his new home. It seems far too fancy a place for a man who likes to ride out with the hunt, to joust and to dance, but he supposes it is the way things have to be. Somerset absorbed some of the chantries and cloisters of nearby St Paul's Cathedral into the property, making full use of the previous king's dissolutions of the monasteries to fuel his own grand designs.

What a fool, thinks Dudley. In the wake of his wedding Dudley has been promoted first into local county administration with his father-in-law Robsart and then into a gentleman of the Privy Chamber, where he has full access to the new young king. His father knows how to take firm control of the kingdom; with his son close to the king and himself the Lord Protector there was no hope for the temperamental Duke of Somerset. Since the wedding things have been uneasy. Seymour did not taken the unification of his household with John Dudley's well. He resented the man who took his place.

John Dudley did not like the sensation of Somerset's presence lingering around every corner. It made him uneasy. Two months after promoting his son to the Privy Chamber, he had Somerset arrested for plotting an assassination attempt against him, and he was executed with due speed. Robert Dudley is still not certain of the truth about the plot, but he will stand by his father forever and, besides, Somerset was a thorn in their side. Just a shame that it has cast a taint over his older brother's marriage. It is very difficult when your wife's father is executed by her father-in-law. No one discusses the matter, but Ambrose has hinted that the younger John Dudley is suffering in his marriage.

Robert has been too busy to worry about his brother. Life as a new husband has great dividends. Amy is a pleasant and amenable bride. That she has yet to fall with child has nothing to do with a lack of effort on either of their parts.

The promotion of Robert to Somerset House, to be its custodian for the king, has been an unexpected delight. Amy loves to look out on the Thames and Robert is so close to the court he never need fear missing any news or scandal.

In fact, he spends as much time at court as with his wife. Robert Dudley is growing into a fine man. His dark, curled hair is now complimented by a moustache and beard. He wears his finely cut clothes with pride, his athletic physique as pronounced as ever. If some of his compatriots still call him 'the gypsy' behind his back it is only because they are jealous. Indeed his skin has darkened with constant outside activity – he is always at the royal jousts, in December 1551 he ran six courses at the tilt for the Christmas entertainment. He ran again on Twelfth Night and eleven days later, the only men who could defeat him and his team were his brothers John and Ambrose. Ambrose still taunts him about that triumph.

Other men envy him. He is gaining more power daily;

just recently he was appointed Master of the Buckhounds and given the honorary role of Chief Carver. Dudley's star is rising rapidly, but there is one point that draws his constant attention.

Princess Elizabeth is occasionally in London. The half-sister to the king through the dishonoured Anne Boleyn, her appearances at court are infrequent. Some are coarse enough to whisper about her illegitimacy boldly. Dudley has known the princess since she was eight years old. He met her while he was a young lord attendant in Edward's household, prior to him becoming king. Elizabeth was a fleeting shadow in the household, a girl with thick, red hair that cast an eerie glow to her pale, white skin. She was always the outsider, uncertain of her position, yet strong enough to weather the storms that faced her. Dudley remembers her passion for learning that was limited to any free time Edward's tutors could offer her, until Catherine Parr married her father and ensured she had her own private tutor.

Dudley hadn't thought of Elizabeth in years. When Henry VIII died it was anticipated Edward VI would have a long reign like his father, the boy king was all that mattered for the moment. One forgotten princess was a trifle. Elizabeth went to live with Catherine Parr, her stepmother who had been the subject of court scandal since she took Sir Thomas Seymour, the younger brother of the Duke of Somerset, as a lover. Catherine fell with child, and there is talk Thomas turned his eye on the young princess.

Dudley has many reasons to detest Thomas, not least his treachery. In 1549 Thomas thought he could win over the king and gain influence, in the failures that followed he tried a desperate tactic of stealing away Edward in the night. A dog brought an end to his scheme, alerting the household as Thomas broke into the boy king's bedroom with a loaded pistol. He was executed, his warrant signed by his own brother who would later try a similar action with the boy king.

Thomas' advances towards the princess, still only thirteen, scandalised the court and troubled the Dudleys. The sooner the Somerset taint was cleared away the better. That Elizabeth wept over his death was a bitter pill to swallow.

Robert expects to see Elizabeth at any time. Since the destruction of the Seymours, Elizabeth has found more favour at court. She was treated on her last visit with full regal dignity and granted an allowance of £3,000. Robert has developed a renewal of interest in the long lost princess and with tonight being the Twelfth Night festivities at court, he duly anticipates seeing how the child he recalls has grown into a woman.

~ ~ ~ * ~ ~ ~

Amy is not comfortable at court; she finds it too demanding on her country manners and is intimidated by the other noble ladies. Robert was disheartened by this at first, but he has adjusted to the situation. If Amy is disinclined to dance there are many others who will gladly take the hand of the 'gypsy'. Robert is as accomplished at dancing as he is at riding and he earns the scowls of other noblemen at court. Not least the studious William Cecil, who acts as surveyor on the princess Elizabeth's new estate at Hatfield.

Amy places herself to one side of the hall in which they dance. A keen observer she prefers to watch than participate. Robert is handsome as he sweeps a young woman about the floor and she loves him all the more for his gallant display of dancing. She never fears if he loves her. His presence in her bed assures her he does and she has often heard it remarked at court than no other man was so enamoured of a woman. Does that make her proud? Indeed, but does she not have a right to be proud? Married to one of the inner circle of Edward's court, son of the Lord Protector and Amy a mere country girl from a remote Norfolk estate. She is indeed justly proud.

But Amy's eye drifts to the king. Sat on his throne at the

centre of the festivities, he seems oddly out-of-place in this gaiety. Amy thinks he looks pale and so very young, younger than her at her wedding. A youth really, who has already been on the throne longer than some kings of old. She wonders why he does not dance?

Edward, upon his pedestal, leans on a hand and feels a hot pressure behind his eyes. His skin burns and he feels too sick to partake in the feast that has been prepared for him. Peacocks are presented to him covered in gilt and spewing flame from their beaks, a boar's head garlanded with an apple in its mouth adorns the table and a swan, the king's own dish, is poised as if to fly away on a silver platter. But he has no appetite. Though he nods and smiles as he has been taught as the dishes are presented. He sups warm wine and tries to stifle the cough that keeps straining from his chest. The dancers look so happy, he hopes not to spoil it, but his head aches and his body is tormented by strange chills.

Finally he looks to John Dudley. Beckons him.

"Your majesty?"

"I am unwell Dudley, I wish to retire," no sooner has he said it the young Edward realises how ill he really feels. He coughs violently, no longer able to prevent it.

John Dudley gazes at him with a mounting sense of concern.

"I shall have you escorted to your chambers," he motions to servants and then turns into the natural politician as he wraps up the festivities as discreetly as possible.

But no one is fooled. The king has retired early, some, including Amy, have seen how frail and sick he looked before he was escorted away.

As Robert takes his wife's arm his eyes stray to look for his father. A sudden fear has snatched at him. If there were to be no Edward, then where would that leave him? The changing of kings is always a cause for concern and usually entails the downfall of someone. Somerset lost last time, this time is it destined to be the Dudleys?

9 - Syderstone, Norfolk 1955

Fourdrinier looked on despairingly as great aunt Ida descended from the black Ford draped in a flowing red and yellow kaftan. Her grey hair was swept back under a turban style headdress and she wore gold rimmed round glasses that hung on a chain about her neck. Fast approaching ninety and allegedly riddled with a number of health complaints, though none particularly life-threatening, Ida stood before the Talbot farmhouse looking like some mythical witch.

Just behind her, emerging from the other side of the car, came a woman Fourdrinier had only heard of – Nancy Hope Walker. She was younger than he had anticipated; only in her thirties and dressed rather plainly, (compared to his aunt) in a utility wear brown skirt suit that he suspected had first seen the light of day just after the war. Her only adornment, if such it could be called, was a dark orange hat with a pheasant feather sewn to the band.

After Nancy and Ida came Phillip, Fourdrinier's aunt's long-suffering chauffeur, there to drop off his charges and then run the car back to London. He was loaded with several suitcases and a hat box, but managed to juggle the load as he slammed the car door shut with his foot. He gave a smile to Foudrinier from beneath the peak of his hat, which had half fallen over his eyes.

"Morning, reverend."

"Good morning Phillip, might I help with the bags?"

Phillip was almost as old as his employer and unloaded the heaviest cases into Fourdrinier's arms gladly.

"And how is my aunt?" Fourdrinier asked, grunting as

the cases came into his grasp.

"Look at her! Right as rain. The doctor said to get some country air because of that pneumonia she had over Christmas, but I hardly think she needs it. That being said, it's grand to get out of London for a time. I can't remember the last time your aunt went visiting."

"Nor can I," Fourdrinier lied, visions of his aunt calling to Egyptian gods during Holy Communion sprang to mind.

That moment Maud and Charlie Talbot appeared out of their house.

"You must be Ida," Maud said ecstatically.

Ida smiled at her benevolently.

"Maud Talbot?"

"Yes, I am, and this is my husband Charles."

Charlie rolled his eyes at Fourdrinier as his name went under temporary refinement.

"Please come inside," Maud continued. "I have the guest room all arranged. It's next door to the bathroom. Charles' father had indoor plumbing installed just after the war."

"Well, well," Ida smiled. "I do appreciate my comforts. Now where is that nephew of mine?"

Fourdrinier obediently came into his aunt's line of sight.

"There you are! Are you well Norman?"

"Never better auntie."

"Call me Ida, you silly boy. Now, are we going indoors? These old legs of mine only do standing up for short periods."

Maud bustled her guests into her sitting room and, after assuring herself everyone would be delighted with tea and cake, took herself off to arrange it. Phillip made himself scarce to deposit the luggage in the guest room, leaving Fourdrinier and Charlie to deal with the two mystical ladies before them.

"I do believe this is Nancy?" Fourdrinier asked politely of the prim looking woman who had perched herself on an armchair and looked decidedly uncomfortable.

"Yes it is," Ida answered for her. "Nancy has been my spiritual inter-communicator for the last three years, as well as a companion. She has quite a gift for mediumship."

Fourdrinier studied the young woman who gave nothing away by her expression or demeanour.

"I know you don't approve Norman," Ida spoke up sharply. "My beliefs are my own, however. I have not been influenced or some other such nonsense. And this communication with Margaret Stewart is very real. The child is in some distress, Nancy has sensed it."

Nancy gave a small affirmative nod.

"That is why I am most glad for the invitation down here. I dare say it goes against every grain in your body Norman, but I am delighted."

Fourdrinier found himself hesitant to speak, he glanced at Charlie.

"My wife is interested in spiritualism," Charlie obligingly assisted. "My own stance is fairly neutral."

"It is a subject that has raised a good deal of debate. Norman fears I am communicating with demons," Ida scoffed. "I am not. I came to spiritualism after a journey to the East where I learned I was a reincarnation of an Egyptian priestess."

Fourdrinier shut his eyes and tried not to listen.

"I found myself confused but fascinated by the realm of spirit and started my own explorations. Unfortunately I was misguided in these wanderings until I came across a spiritualist society who put me onto the correct path. I encountered Nancy there and we were soon holding private sessions. While Nancy has the gift, spirits are drawn to me as a sympathetic soul. We have had some astounding results. A few have been published by the London Psychical Society."

Fourdrinier was terribly relieved to see Maud reappear with tea and fruit cake.

"I am so glad you could come, Miss Fourdrinier," Maud chirped. "This ghost business is quite a conundrum to us all and the mystery of Margaret Stewart has us all thinking. Do you really imagine it is the same little girl who comes to you?"

"I do Mrs Talbot, I do," Ida said firmly. "She has told me things only someone who has lived in Syderstone could."

"I was impressed by the information on the sealed room," Charlie added. "That is something only a local would know, and even then, not everyone does."

"Precisely!" Ida cast a satisfied smile at her nephew.

"Oh could we... oh but no, you must be tired," Maud blushed at her interruption.

"You want a séance?" Ida interpreted the unfinished sentence correctly.

"It was just a thought, but I am over-eager."

Ida smiled indulgently, clearly enjoying being the centre of attention, as any elderly lady who lived by herself would.

"I feel perfectly refreshed, so I have no objections. What of you Nancy?"

Nancy had spent the last few moments nibbling at a small chunk of fruit cake and taking minute sips of tea. Now she very carefully put them aside.

"I am perfectly ready," she said in a quiet voice.

"Then I shall direct Mrs Talbot on the preparations."

"Oh do call me Maud," Maud fluttered.

"Then call me Ida," Ida held out her arm to be helped off her chair. "Let's find ourselves a suitable location."

Fourdrinier watched the proceedings of the next half hour with the feelings of a man watching a stage being readied for a play. The dining room was purloined for the meeting. The heavy curtains were shut and pinned so not a chink of light fell through. The table was moved to the centre of the room and other heavy furniture moved against the walls. Five chairs were arranged in a circle and candles were strategically placed on the mantelpiece. Finally Ida saw to it that a wad of paper was brought to the table for note-taking. It was then, as the arrangements seemed to be drawing to a conclusion, that Fourdrinier decided to make himself scarce.

"I shall call again tomorrow then, aunt," he said, bending down to give his aunt a kiss on the cheek.

"You are not intending to leave?" Maud reproved him.

"This is hardly the setting for a Church of England vicar," Fourdrinier replied, already putting on his hat.

"Norman Douglas Fourdrinier, you will sit at this table and take notes for us," Ida told her nephew unequivocally.

"Aunt..."

"I did not give you permission to question my decision. I did not say you had to participate, you are merely an observer. An impartial note-taker, which is precisely what we need. Phillip sometimes does it, but his handwriting and spelling are appalling. Besides, I believe you know short-hand, Norman?"

Fourdrinier reluctantly admitted he did.

"Then take that seat and stop complaining."

Fourdrinier felt like a caned schoolboy before his friends. He glanced at Charlie who gave a sympathetic grimace. With as much dignity as he could muster Fourdrinier took a chair and made a show of arranging the papers neatly before him.

Aunt Ida settled herself in a chair, motioning that Maud and Charlie should sit opposite each other, either side of her. Nancy took a chair facing the old lady.

"Now dears, have you done this before?" Ida asked.

"No," Maud said, her excitement making her quiver.

"Well, it is best if we begin by holding hands and we sing a hymn to build the spiritual energy. Nancy will stay quite still and silent and channel whatever spirit deems to come through."

Fourdrinier shifted uncomfortably in his seat.

"Norman, I don't expect you to take part, so just settle yourself to one side and take notes," Ida glared at her nephew.

Fourdrinier reluctantly pulled over a side table and

moved away from the main group, wondering dismally what the bishop of Norwich would make of this.

"I quite feel like 'O Christ, the redeemer' tonight," Ida shuffled herself in her chair to get comfortable. "Relax and let your minds clear. Breathe deeply and try to avoid breaking the circle."

Ida took the left hand of Charlie and the right hand of Maud, across from her Nancy extended her own hands and allowed them to be clasped by their hosts.

"When Nancy drifts into her medium state it can be quite unexpected, so please do not panic or make abrupt movements. It is very unsettling for the spirits."

Fourdrinier stifled a small groan, though not well enough to avoid his aunt's attention. He made a fuss of his papers to avoid looking at her.

"Come now, let us sing," Ida closed her eyes and led the party in a hoarse rendition of the hymn. Maud stumbled on the words slightly, but Charlie got the tune admirably, calling into service his years as a curate. Fourdrinier stared at his paper. The afternoon was growing dark and he would soon be unable to see anything.

"Could I borrow a candle?" he interrupted.

It was Nancy who gave him a hard stare this time.

"If you must," Ida tutted. "Really, Norman, no more interruptions."

Fourdrinier retrieved a candle from the mantelpiece and the party picked up the thread of the broken hymn. They sang it twice over and then fell into silence.

Fourdrinier waited impatiently. It felt as though the party had fallen into a deep sleep. Nothing could be heard but the deep regular breathing of nearby Charlie and the faintest of rustles as a foot or hand moved. Fourdrinier checked his watch by the candle. It was drawing close to five o'clock. He had hoped to be heading home by now. His old bicycle had a battery powered lamp, but it was not much comfort on a dark country lane. He was just beginning to wonder if he could use his age and far-ranging duties as an excuse to the diocese to subsidise him with a car, when a movement from Nancy caught his eye.

It was little more than a stiffening of the body. She went rigid. But in the stillness of the room even such a slight action was noticeable. Fourdrinier studied the woman in the flicker of his candlelight. Her face had fallen into repose, the hardness of the features relaxed, but beneath her closed eyelids her eyes danced restlessly.

Her hair seemed to be coming loose from the pins holding it. That disturbed Fourdrinier for a moment. He blinked his eyes, certain it was the candlelight tricking him and when he looked again it seemed to have stopped, but now long stands of auburn hair were lying down Nancy's back.

She gasped quietly and gave a spasmodic jerk, though not enough to remove herself from the grip of Maud and Charlie. Her eyes fluttered a little.

"Who is there?" Ida asked, breaking the silence in a soft, solemn voice.

Fourdrinier obediently wrote down the question.

Nancy twitched a little, her head twisted to the side. She swallowed awkwardly, as though something was in her throat. Her mouth worked but no words came.

"Is that you Margaret?" Ida continued.

Nancy twisted her head the other way. She shrugged her shoulders as though donning a coat.

"...'es."

The voice was strained and high-pitched. Fourdrinier could not quite call it childlike, but it was certainly not Nancy's usual voice. He wrote down the quiet answer and wondered what new trick Nancy was about to perform.

"Do you know where we are?" Ida asked.

"Syderstone," the little voice said louder.

"Are you pleased we are here?"

"Yes."

"We hope to help you Margaret."

"Good," Nancy fidgeted in her seat. "Thank you."

Fourdrinier glanced at the rest of the party, he could only see the back of Charlie's head, but Maud was directly opposite him and he could see she had her eyes wide open and was staring with a mixture of fear and amazement at Nancy. She had unconsciously drawn herself away from the medium.

"Do you know the man who is taking notes?" Ida said. Fourdrinier scowled at her, sensing her mischief-making.

"Yes."

"What is his name?"

"Fourdrinier."

"He is supposed to be researching about you Margaret. The spirit world has eyes everywhere, has he been doing it?"

"Yes."

The answered seemed to surprise Ida for a moment.

"Really?"

"I don't lie. Only bad girls lie," Nancy's lips pouted petulantly.

"No dear, I didn't mean that," Ida responded hastily. "I hadn't realised he had had time, that is all."

"Ask him about the visit to Donald Steward," Nancy said in the childish voice that rose and fell in its squeakiness.

It was Fourdrinier's turn to be surprised. No one knew of his visit to Donald, so how could Nancy have discovered it? He was so stunned he stopped writing.

"I saw him with the diary," Nancy persisted.

"What diary?"

"I saw it."

"Margaret, what diary do you mean?"

"Solve the riddle of the sealed room," Nancy's voice was suddenly strained. "Goodbye."

She seemed to choke out the last words. Abruptly Nancy was coughing hard and shaking violently in her seat.

"Get her a drop of sherry, Maud," Ida instructed calmly.

Maud obeyed though she was as pale as a ghost herself and looked ready to flee the room. She handed the glass to

Nancy who was almost shaking too bad to hold it. Maud pressed it into her hands.

"Norman, turn on the lights," Ida commanded.

Fourdrinier did not hesitate to hop up and find the light switch. He was unsettled, perhaps even a little scared. Nancy had said things that she could not possibly have known. Perhaps someone had seen him go to the old parsonage and told Charlie... perhaps Charlie had somehow informed Nancy of that – but the diary? No one but himself and Donald Steward knew about the diary he had been given.

"Nancy will be all right in a moment. Margaret's wee spirit is a strong thing," Ida had folded her hands before her and was watching the younger woman closely.

"What did you make of it, Maud?"

"Fascinating!" Maud said with wide eyes.

"Charles?"

Charlie glanced at his elderly guest. He could not mask his disappointment.

"It was rather short."

"It depends on the spirit," Ida answered with practiced swiftness. "Some use most of their strength just coming through and cannot talk long. We rarely get Margaret for more than a few moments."

Ida cast her eyes about the room and spotted Fourdrinier snuffing the candles on the mantelpiece.

"And what about you, nephew? Was Margaret correct?"

Fourdrinier turned slowly to face his aunt.

"Have you been to see a man called Donald Steward?" Ida persisted.

Fourdrinier glanced at his curious friends.

"Yes, I have."

"And the diary?" Fourdrinier turned back to the mantel, for some strange reason which he could not define and which went against his usually honest character, he did not want to admit to the diary. He did not want them to know about it.

"I don't know anything about a diary," he said. "I visited Donald Steward who lives in the old parsonage as part of my research into my book."

"Perhaps you will come upon the diary later," Ida said, unfazed by the denial. "The spirits do not always get their timings right. The past, present and future is meaningless to them. Sometimes they say something has happened which has not occurred yet and they are often getting dates wrong."

Fourdrinier said nothing. His heart was still pounding in his chest and no matter how hard he told himself it was ridiculous, that there was a logical reason for Nancy knowing about the diary, he could think of none. Unless Charlie had, for some reason, visited Donald himself and learned about the diary he had given Fourdrinier? Yes, that could be it! That was the sane solution, even if Fourdrinier was not entirely clear how, or even why, the information was passed to Nancy.

"I expect you to keep investigating the sealed room mystery," Ida continued. "Something is afoot in the spirit world, I sense it."

"Would anyone like tea?" Maud was trying to return to normality, she was still uneasy when she looked at Nancy.

"Tea would be splendid, dear. Norman I want to see the notes."

Maud pattered off while Fourdrinier obeyed his aunt, then went to open the curtains and stare out into the darkening farmyard. After a moment Charlie joined him.

"That was... intriguing," Charlie mused. "I'm not convinced though."

"Charlie, did you know I had been to see Donald Steward?" Fourdrinier asked sharply.

His old curate looked at him curiously.

"No, I did not. Are you suggesting I fed the information to Nancy?"

Fourdrinier went to answer, then shook his head.

"No, you are not the sort. No, I'm sorry. I didn't mean

to imply anything."

"She has unsettled you."

Fourdrinier watched a star wink into life.

"I've unsettled myself. I'm making assumptions, confusing my mind. Thinking the impossible. Somehow Nancy learned I visited Donald Steward."

"How?" it was the simplest of questions, but the one Fourdrinier could not answer.

"This is all witchcraft, you know," he hissed instead. "Trickery and witchcraft."

"Calm down, Fourdrinier. I haven't seen you like this since you learned the choirmaster was getting too friendly with the choirboys."

"I will find a logical solution to this and then I shall feel a priceless fool," Fourdrinier assured himself.

"And if you don't?"

"You are hardly suggesting that was real?"

Charlie took his turn staring out the window before answering.

"I've believed in a lot of things in my time. A lot of what the Church says and holds true can seem odd to a sceptic."

"That is called faith."

"Still, I watched Nancy. I swear I saw her face change, it became wider, darker and... younger. Her voice... it seemed as though something was trying to take over her vocal chords, trying to get them to work for it. Did you notice the peculiar swallowing?"

"It was a good performance."

"Yes, and yet what if it was no performance at all? What if a spirit, the spirit of a child, was coming through?"

Fourdrinier felt a shudder of dread creep down his spine.

"That doesn't bear thinking about."

"From a Church perspective I agree it is very bad. Even from a secular perspective the idea of a ghost controlling a living body stinks of possession."

"I don't hold with that either," Fourdrinier said

staunchly. "Though I did know a Catholic priest who specialised in exorcisms. He was convinced on the matter."

"What about house blessings? Banishing evil spirits. You're bound to have been asked to do that once or twice."

"Well, yes."

"So, in the process of blessing a house, what were you doing? Because I don't believe you would go through a religious ritual if you thought it was pointless and a sop to the superstitious."

"I never said that," Fourdrinier rebutted. "If a person asks for a house to be blessed it is usually because they believe a negative force has invaded it. In that case, it is my duty as a Christian minister to dispose of that entity."

"You are very careful not to use the word demon."

Fourdrinier wondered how dark it would be before he got a chance to set out for home.

"A demon is a complicated thing. I have given the subject little thought, but thinking it over now, I would argue that we witnessed a demon coming through tonight and that is a very dangerous thing."

"I venture to disagree with you."

"As you may, but still I find this whole business unpleasant."

"Don't stop looking though, Fourdrinier," Charlie had that pleading look in his eyes again. "I think it is important for some reason that you keep looking. Promise me you will?"

Fourdrinier gave a sigh.

"I will, for the simple reason that doing such will prove this business is all nonsense. I shall find a very sane and very ordinary reason for the sealed room."

"Good," Charlie smiled. "Can I give you a lift home? It is too dark for a bicycle ride."

Fourdrinier contemplated the world shrouded in darkness and his bike with its abysmal lamp.

"Not tonight, Charlie. Tonight I need to clear my head

and do some thinking, and the most conducive method for doing that is riding a bicycle."

"Come back tomorrow then," Charlie persisted. "Your aunt would like it."

Fourdrinier allowed himself a groan.

"Yes, no doubt she would, to tax me with more questions about spirits and Syderstone. I'll pay a call if I can."

Fourdrinier said his goodbyes to the rest of the party and left the cosy farmhouse. In the darkness outside, as he wheeled his bicycle to the lane, it felt a lonely and empty world. For a moment it was just possible to imagine a ghost existing. Fourdrinier turned his mind back to Donald Steward and the parsonage, to the strange room no one used and the awful feeling that had come over him when he set foot inside. It was disturbing contemplating Donald being in that house right now, the night drawing in around him, the world vanishing, and overhead the locked room that no one had slept in since Margaret Stewart.

Fourdrinier shook his thoughts away like a wet dog shaking off rain. He would not allow his mind to stray like this. It was unbecoming in a churchman. He mounted his bicycle and set off down the lane. After five minutes the battery in his lamp died.

⌑

10 – London, July 1553

The king is dead. Even as his father tells him, Robert can hardly believe it. The boy king's last hours were wretched; too weak to leave his bed he laid there dying, coughing up a vile, black substance his doctor pronounced was full of carbon. Exhaustion finally overcame his body and all of John Dudley's plans.

"There was time to make a will," he stands before Robert in the fine palace at Greenwich. "Edward had a strong heart to the last. He would not allow a Catholic to take the throne."

Robert nods. Edward's half-sister, Mary, a pronounced Catholic like her mother, had been biding her time, expecting to be next to the throne.

"Then it is certain Jane will take the crown?" Robert asks with more than a touch of anxiety.

The king had originally planned that the crown would pass to the male heirs of his cousin Frances Grey – yet Frances only had a daughter. Sixteen-year-old Jane. In a hope to produce a male heir quickly, John Dudley concocted a brilliant plan. He married Jane to his son Guildford. For better or worse the Dudley fortunes were now inextricably linked with the monarchy.

"There was very little time, but God willed it that the king lived long enough to change his will. Jane is his sole heir."

John Dudley paces. The deadly game they are playing is far from over.

"I have taken the Tower, the guards have been doubled and the ports are being watched. I shall not allow any supporters of Mary to cause dissent among the people," he scratches at his beard. "Jane will be here in three or four days. We shall proclaim her queen in front of all of London."

"You are well prepared."

"Yet not prepared enough. Mary remains at large," John spins to face his son. "She has ignored my summons to come to court. I cannot risk her roaming freely about the country. She is residing at Sawston Hall in Norfolk."

Robert stands to match his father.

"You will send me?"

"Yes. Robert, you have influence in Norfolk, you have served the county well. You must ride there immediately and capture the errant princess. Need I tell you her support in the county is rising?"

"No," Robert assures him. "But I know the people of Norfolk. They shall not ride with Mary. I shall see to it."

"Then do so, my son. Go tonight. Remember mine and your brother's fate rest upon this matter. Take Mary and let no one resist you."

Robert does not need the warning. With gritted teeth he races for his horse. If this all goes wrong then the Dudleys will suffer the fate of Somerset. They have thrown their hand in with Lady Jane Grey; a terrified teenage girl now set the challenge of ruling a country. John Dudley has no doubts that he can control her. With Jane married to his son their position is cemented. Unless Mary raises the support so many fear. What would become of the country if Mary takes the crown and tries to turn the world back to Catholicism?

Robert sets off as fast as he can with several soldiers. Paying no heed to the strain on his horse he belts down the roads of the capital and out onto the highway that will lead him to Cambridge. He rides through the night, hardly seeing a soul and not caring. His time is precious, word of Edward's death will spread fast; he must reach Mary before she is warned.

And so he thinks of Guildford as his horse gallops. Only six weeks before his younger brother had been celebrating his wedding in grand style. At Durham Place, John Dudley's town mansion, Guildford had married Jane Grey. It was a double celebration as, also on that day, Robert's sister Katherine married Henry Hastings. The ceremony was accompanied by jousts, feasting, music, dancing and performing troupes. The lavish occasion, surpassing the marriage of the younger John Dudley to Somerset's daughter, had been attended by the Venetian and French ambassadors. Anyone would have sworn the dashing young Guildford was safely assured in his future.

Yet so much had gone wrong so soon. Guildford and many others were sick after the feasting, said to be caused by food poisoning due to an error by the cook. Robert can only feel the minor catastrophe has cast a pall of foreboding over the match.

Guildford is only 18 and Robert noticed a longing in his eyes at the wedding as he gazed on Jane. His brother was besotted with her already, and that troubled him. In the times ahead he fears there will be no place for soft feelings. His brother and sister-in-law now reside in the Tower of London under the protection of John Dudley's men and in great comfort – that, at least, is reassuring, though Robert can't help feeling a chill of apprehension.

He arrives at Sawston Hall as dawn breaks. His body aches all over and he is exhausted by his anxiety and the ride. He does not want to be delayed. Until Mary is safely in London his own life and that of his brother and father are in peril. He thinks of Amy momentarily, like the image he summoned when fighting the rebels at Norwich. What would become of her if he should perish? Amy has shown nothing but loyal devotion to him, would that devotion condemn her? Then there is the poor Jane. She looked so young at her wedding. Robert felt a pang of guilt looking at her. She reminded him so much of Amy who he is determined to protect. Jane is the sacrifice the Dudleys need to ensure their survival.

A man emerges from the door of the hall.

"I am calling for Princess Mary," Robert calls at the servant who cannot but help recognise him. The young Lord of the manor has been about enough for his face to be familiar. He also cannot help but know why Dudley is here. "Summon your mistress, she is due in London."

The servant comes a little closer, bowing slightly, grovelling, keeping a distance between himself and Robert Dudley's sword hanging from his belt.

"My mistress has gone, Master Dudley."

Robert's chest tightens. His temper flares.

"Gone?"

"To Framlingham castle, at the invitation of the Duke of Norfolk."

The Howards! Robert wants to yell furiously. Thomas Howard is a staunch Catholic and has been locked in the Tower since 1546, yet here he still manages to make his influence felt by aiding Mary!

"Does she know her brother is dead?" Robert snaps before he can help himself.

The servant's eyes widen.

"Does she?"

"No... no... my lord. She just received word that he was ill."

"So she has fled me, so be it," Robert's outburst has turned into a simmering fury. He knows what this disaster means. Mary will contest the crown. She will gather supporters and she will set an army against Lady Jane Grey and the Dudleys

He is too angry for further words, instead he looks at Sawston Hall where Mary has spent many happy hours and his ignominy boils over.

"Ransack the house and burn it down!" he cries to his men.

"My lord!" the servant begs him, but he is pushed aside.

The soldiers with Robert charge into the house, scare

out the remaining servants and strip it of anything valuable. Then they set it alight as though it were a pile of kindling.

"My lord! My lord!" weeps the servant. "What will my mistress Mary say?"

Robert hopes she is utterly furious. He wants her to wail like a banshee when she learns of what he has done. If she is so determined for war let her know the Dudleys will not limit the damage they will deal her.

He mounts his horse and with his soldiers rides away.

~ ~ ~ * ~ ~ ~

When Jane is crowned it is to a silent audience. A letter has arrived from Mary declaring she will not recognise the new queen. She is intent on taking the throne. John Dudley knows he must ride out and meet her, but that means leaving the new queen in the hands of his Council. He finds himself doubting their trustworthiness.

"If you mean deceit, though not forthwith yet hereafter, God will revenge the same," he tells them as he leaves his son and daughter-in-law in the Tower. Dudley's entire future now rests on the outcome of the next few days.

He has hardly spoken to Robert, he is furious with him. His rash act in burning down Sawston Hall has only infuriated the Catholics in Norfolk, not to mention severely worried other local landowners. Mary's army has grown since the bonfire.

John Dudley rides through London at the head of an uncertain army. He senses the unease about him.

"The people press to meet us," he whispers to a comrade, "but not one says God speed us."

It is quite different from the time a few years earlier he rode out to destroy the Kett rebellion. Then he was cheered by Londoners, now everyone seems afraid. Even his soldiers seem anxious and he fears their loyalty.

They ride to Cambridge. It is now the height of summer. Dudley's men have started to abandon him. They appear to have already decided he is a lost cause while Mary's forces are said to be growing. The earls of Sussex, Bath and

Oxford have now joined her.

John Dudley hides his concerns. At his base in Cambridge he continues his battle plans, but his worst fears are destined to come true. The Council has betrayed him. On 18 July they declare Mary queen at Cheapside. Dudley learns from the messenger that brings this sorry news that the crowds rejoiced and there was a great ringing of bells.

Appalled and aware his life is in grave danger Dudley tries to return to London, perhaps even change sides at this disastrous climax to his plans. But he is caught and arrested. He returns to London a prisoner to spend his last days in the Tower.

~ ~ ~ * ~ ~ ~

Robert has been trying his best to quell the Catholic tide against his family when he rides into King's Lynn and declares Jane the one true queen. He stands in the marketplace and with the support of the mayor and 300 townsmen he makes it plain there is to be no queen but Jane. Too little, too late. At the same moment he shouts his proclamation, in London the treacherous Council announce that Mary is queen.

Everything is going horribly wrong. Robert hardly knows what to make of this calamity. His father is arrested and Guildford has found his pleasant stay in the Tower now turned to imprisonment. Then men come for Robert and he is escorted to Framlingham.

Mary is waiting for him. Her chestnut red hair is pulled back and her pug-like face grimaces at him. She has decked herself in her best jewels and clothes, looking fit to be queen. Robert despises her, but he cannot let his feelings betray him. Now there is only time to save himself. His father's gamble has failed.

"Your Majesty!" he falls at her feet.

"You recognise me, Master Dudley? Last I was informed, you were declaring to a marketplace that only Lady Jane Grey might be queen."

"I was mistaken, your Majesty," Robert is trembling

slightly with fear, he tries to put on his best charms. "I have been foolish. I was misguided by my father's politics. But I now realise you are the true queen and I beg your pardon for my rashness before."

"Speaking of rashness, you burned down Sawston Hall."

Robert is breathing so hard he is sure everyone must hear it.

"I was not myself. I had ridden such a long way and in error. I acted without considering, afterwards I sorely regretted it."

"Many things we regret, Master Dudley."

"Your majesty, I beg your forgiveness and mercy."

Mary walks about the hall at Framlingham, looks out at the old medieval battlements and smiles to herself. Robert knows she is enjoying his predicament. He keeps his face lowered so she might not see him glowering.

"I have considered your plea, Master Dudley," Mary returns, a twisted smirk on her face. "I do not believe your excuses. I do not think you dull enough to be a slave to your father. You wanted me away from the throne too. Well, you have failed. You have failed with that wisp of a girl and your upstart schemes. You may have fooled my brother, but you do not fool me, Dudley."

Mary sneers.

"Take him to the Tower like the others."

Robert is yanked to his feet knowing his death sentence has just been read out. His heart pounds in a way it has never done in battle and how he wishes to cleave a sword in the breast of this obnoxious woman! But he knows his manners, knows how to play the game. He walks out with dignity and allows himself to be escorted all the way back to the Tower. To join his father, Guildford and Jane, and his unfortunate brothers Ambrose, Henry and John.

⸙

11 – The Diary of Reverend William Mantle
December 1784

I have looked upon my last entries in these pages and realised I have been neglectful. Little matter, the last news I imparted upon this paper was the birth of my darling Octavia, the fairest child a father could look upon. Now I write of another birth of another daughter. Ann Elizabeth, born this morning. She is healthy and well, as is her mother. Little Octavia is four months off her second birthday and is curious about the baby, but also a touch jealous. She complains of not seeing her mother, whimpers and cries. I am, apparently, a sorry substitute.

The parish blossoms with other bairns too. I baptised another Ann a few weeks ago, the daughter of a wretched creature I only know as Sarah. There was no father present, the girl is not married and looks entirely too simple to understand the concept of the sin she has committed. I felt a great deal of pity for her. When I asked her if she knew what baptism was, she said it was so the Devil would not steal her baby, then she wept a little and declared herself wicked. How can a man feel hard towards such sorrow? I've asked her to attend the small Bible class I have sent up in the evenings. I thought teaching her about Christ's Grace might comfort her.

Josiah Smith has been granted another son. His wife is a woman of wide girth and stout proportions. Now I understand why he cannot sometimes tell her apart from the heifers in his fields!

Ah, what a disgraceful thing to write. I am so taken by these spurious thoughts at times. There is no one to talk to in confidence about this parish. I must hide my true thoughts and not complain about those who I disapprove of. I am certain Josiah has taken up gambling again. His wife holds his purse strings very tight, but men such as he are resourceful. I have vowed I shall root out the cause of this problem and find the soul who is leading him into temptation.

I am not against gambling. I have played at dice and cards myself. But when it strips a man of his dignity and comes close to ruining him, then I am morally destined to intervene. Josiah Smith has a family to think of and cannot be allowed to run them into poverty. I have my suspicions as to who is behind the new craze. The local squire's son has returned home from a visit with a cousin in London, it was said he had to be sent there to avoid the magistrates, though that was before my time in the parish and no one talks about it. I believe this boy is wiling away his time with card games. His father seems unable to stop his wastrel habits. I shall put a stop to this before any other soul is dragged into his wickedness.

~ ~ ~ * ~ ~ ~

I have a toothache. Octavia tells me I am fussing over nothing. I saw her this morning and a contended being she looks nursing Ann. I took in little Octavia, but the chick cried fiercely and tried to climb into her mother's arms. I took her away before Octavia scolded her. She is inconsolable. I took her down to the pond at the bottom of the garden where she is not allowed to go by herself and showed her the ice forming at the ends in pretty patterns, and told her how the fish go to sleep over winter. She wanted to know if we could fish in the pond, and I said we might in the spring.

It is a truly awkward pond. I cannot fathom who chose

to construct it. It might be natural, I suppose, but it has the appearance of being manmade. It is too oval and neat at the edges, and by far it is too small. It is not sufficient as a stock pond for a fisherman or a cook, and I am not inclined to think former residents here were moved by ornamental ponds, as some of the bigger estate gardens are now being decorated with.

When little Octavia went inside with her nurse I walked the perimeter of the pond and concluded a man of my height could barely fit in it if he laid flat at its longest point. I drove in a stick to see how deep it was and was surprised, for the longest branch I could find was a good six foot, fallen in the wind from an old sycamore, and plunging it in it simply vanished from my hand before it reached the bottom. A strange little curiosity this is. I intend to take out a lead weight on a string next and try and judge the distance like a sailor would.

~ ~ ~ * ~ ~ ~

January 1785

I am almost convinced I am dying. This tooth has fretted at me through the night. I have been to the local surgeon who declares it needs to be pulled, but I looked at his forceps and pliers and found I had not the guts for the procedure. Instead he gave me a dose of opium for the pain and remarked merrily enough that he would see me soon.

I have taken the first grain of opium and some release found me. I was able to rest and then begin working on my parish chores.

Sarah has attended my Bible classes with surprising regularity. Far more so than my other students. She is not the quickest, but is easily the keenest. I see a great burning inside her to learn. What a shame such creatures are cast by misfortunes of birth into the poorest regions of society, where learning takes the form of knowing how to darn socks and make suet puddings!

My little Octavia and Ann shall not want for learning. I shall see to it they have many books and a good governess when they are old enough. I shall have them read and write and learn their sums, perhaps I shall be bold and teach them about Latin as though they were boys. I am thought of as mildly eccentric around these parts anyway, so teaching my girls shall not add much grist to the mill.

I have failed Josiah Smith so far. His wife was at church on Sunday in a ragged skirt, looking quite hard done by and with a fat bruise about her eye. I did not enquire, but it seems there was a dispute over money, she would not give Josiah anymore and he was not inclined to be denied. There is a rumour the newest babe is not so healthy as first thought and might die. I only hope Josiah sees sense soon. I intend to have words with that squire's boy. I promise it to God that I shall intervene.

Ah, this opium makes my eyes dull. I thought for a moment I caught a glimpse of someone from my window down by the pond. I looked again lest it was little Octavia, but there is no one. I hope this tooth eases soon so I might banish the drug.

~ ~ ~ * ~ ~ ~

March 1785

I try and keep a record here, but there is so much mundane work to do and such of little import to write. So I come to the one thing in this grey world that has been of excitement lately. I went to see the squire's son and have it out with him over this business of Josiah Smith. He was a vile thing, bloated and wretched, smelling of old beer and, I fear, his own vomit.

He admits to gambling but sees no harm in it. Says I am fussing like some old spinster. He inferred that God should not involve himself in his business and that I would be best to mind my manners in future. He implied he could have his father make trouble for me. I do not fear him, not as such, but I soon realised he was a lost cause. He sets up the tables, but has no inclination towards the men he ruins. He is idle and bored, life to him is tedious. I failed in my endeavour and must think again, but with Easter virtually upon me there is such little time. I shall try another approach; I shall seek out Josiah one evening and confront him with this problem. Perhaps then we shall have some solution.

The left side of my head pounds so. It is the tooth still, the surgeon confirms it. He very much wants to pull it, but I cannot face the operation. The opium dulls the pain until it is merely an ache and I can work through it. I ask God for the strength to continue. I find a little water and wine helps too, and seems to stop the burning the opium causes in my stomach. Octavia does not know about it, though she was concerned the other day when she saw the wine bill. Our housekeeper showed it to her. I managed to convince her I had used up the bottles celebrating the birth of Ann with our friends, but how long can I mask this from her? The tooth must finish its rot soon. Perhaps it shall fall out one night and then I can reduce my consumption of wine. Fortunately, I have been buying the opium outright, so Octavia has no knowledge of that.

Sarah still attends the Bible classes I hold in church. She has come out of herself a little since we first met. She has even confided in me, though not a great deal. Her mother is dead, so the girl lives with her father and several younger siblings who she cares for. Her father is a journeyman butcher and is away a great deal, I sense this is where problems have arisen. She likes the Bible and enjoys the learning I provide. She says she now thinks of God far more kindly, for before she was inclined to a fury towards him for snatching away her mother.

I have only once tried to broach the subject of her daughter's father. She told me bluntly she would not discuss it. I have thought of which boy in the village it might possibly be, but I cannot fathom why she would protect him. And there is something else in her manner. She hardens when I speak of the subject. She does not strike me as loving the young man who has so ruined her. If anything her tone suggests to me hatred. But I am digressing and yet again I have filled this paper with pointless gossip. My thoughts seem to wander from me as soon as I sit to write. Perhaps it is the medicine or the wine.

~ ~ ~ * ~ ~ ~

June 1785

Sarah told me a fairy story today which I thought it might be worthy to record. She says the pond in my garden was made by the Devil. Apparently he was in league with a witch in the village, but one day the villagers took the witch and drowned her. Outraged the Devil cast a stone at Syderstone church, but God deflected his evil and the stone sailed past the church and into the garden of the parsonage where it crashed into the earth.

It was a massive boulder and, half buried in the earth, it blocked the road running just outside the garden. The vicar of the time, Sarah is not clear when this was but states it was at least 200 hundred years ago, prayed on his knees near the boulder that God might do something about it. One night there was an awful storm, the rain rattled the windows and people thought the witch had returned to haunt them. The next morning the boulder had mysteriously vanished and in its place was a circular pool of water. The vicar was certain God had saved the village again from the wrath of the Devil and had removed the boulder so the hole it left might fill with the treacherous rain the witch had flung at them. To rid the village of evil once and for all, he determined to lay the witch's restless spirit in the pond and trap her there for a thousand years.

Men dug up the witch's body, a stake was thrust in her heart and her shoes and clothes weighted down with iron. Then she was buried in the middle of a crossroads and the vicar read the words of a service over her and commanded that her wild spirit be imprisoned beneath the water of the pond.

There was a terrible thundering around the village and the wind rushed down the roads and took the leaves off every tree. Then several people swore to seeing a white, cowled figure burst from the witch's grave and fly through the air. Some chased it and said it landed in the pond with a huge splash of water that drenched the parsonage and the church.

Sarah believes this story fully. I am a man of reason and follow the learned men in London who believe demons are metaphors. I do not think a witch's spirit was laid in my pond, but still, it is a fascinating local legend whose source would be most interesting to discover.

~ ~ ~ * ~ ~ ~

September 1785

I must write in haste. I must commit this to words on paper before events overtake me. I have been trying to confront Josiah on his gambling for months, but he has eluded me. The squire's son privately rents out the back room at the inn and I am prevented from entering, but tonight my fury is enough to take me through that door of wood and to that table of indiscretion and ruin.

I have just spoken with Sarah. She was in a pitiful state. Her babe Ann is sick with a fever that nothing seems to dim. She came to me in the church and we prayed together for the child to be saved. Afterwards she cried fitfully and told me she feared the babe would die because she was wicked and God would punish her.

I asked her, whatever could she mean? I thought I had shown her in our classes that God was gracious and forgiving. Sarah wept in my arms and confessed to coming close to drowning the infant last month. Apparently the family are in a poor way. They have not heard from their father in weeks and have very little in the way of money to sustain them. The infant is an added burden and last month Sarah reached a point I can barely imagine from my comfortable, safe position. The child was fractious and Sarah tired from working in the fields to sustain the family. She lost her patience, grabbed up the babe thinking they would all be better off if there was one less mouth to feed and she would be free to find other work, and went to cast it in the well. As she hung the babe over the edge, something stopped her from committing the awful act. So she tells me, at that exact moment a strange feeling came over her, a feeling of dreadful anguish and remorseful love. She clutched the babe to her and stumbled back from the well as if in a daze.

Sarah explained that up until that moment she thought she had hated the child; that had been another switch she had flayed herself with. It was only in that instant of terribleness that she realised, in actuality, she loved Ann. Now she fears God is punishing her for trying to kill the babe by sickening it with fever, so she might lose her just as soon as she realised she could not be without her.

Her thoughts were so confused and I did my best to calm her and explain that God does not punish us so. If the babe dies it is not because he wills it as a punishment but for some other, unknown reason that we cannot fathom. She must trust, I told her, and pour all her fears and feelings into prayers to God.

The talk seemed to calm her. Slowly she settled and was able to compose herself. When the worst was over I asked why she had been so convinced she hated the babe. Was it because the child was conceived out of sin?

Sarah shook her head. She put out her chin in a manner I have come to denote as meaning great determination in her. She looks the same when trying to understand a Bible passage that has confused her. I sensed she was about to confess something and I was not mistaken. She told me without delay that her child was not conceived out of her own sin, and though everyone thinks that, she and God, and now I, know it is not true. Sarah was taken against her will when she was tending to some sheep in the top fields. She has told no-one because of who the culprit was.

I held my tongue, but can I lie and say I was not already guessing names? When she declared the perpetrator I had no hesitation in believing her.

The squire's son took Sarah and is the father of Ann.

Tonight I shall confront him. Not over the matter of Ann, I have vowed that to Sarah for she saw how angry I was and was fearful I would do something foolish. But that boy has caused too much trouble in my parish. He is ruining the men and women of Syderstone with his wickedness and debauchery. Enough is enough! I shall march into that room tonight and demand he stops his antics else I shall go to his father and then even the magistrate, for I am sure we can find something illegal in his actions, and if nothing else works I shall ride him out of town myself. Like the pastor who laid the witch and routed the Devil from his garden. I shall rout out this devil!

12 – Tower of London, 1554

The Duke of Northumberland, once England's Lord Protector, is dead. His head was laid on a wooden block one hot August day and hacked off by the executioner. It could have been worse, it also could have been better.

John Dudley proved his loyalty to his family until his last breath. Begging that his sons might be spared as they had only obeyed him and not gone against Mary of their own free will, he even agreed to take part in a Roman Catholic Mass, publically declaring the country's error for following Protestantism these last 16 years. Robert Dudley and his brothers were forced to watch the charade, knowing their father was doing everything in his power to spare them. It was humiliating.

Robert's only consolation is that he now shares the Tower with his brothers. Ambrose is a constant source of comfort. He tries to keep merry despite the horrors that hang over them. Neither saw their father executed, but they witnessed his dismembered body being carted away for display around London. Robert has a hearty hatred for his new queen. It burns in his belly and makes him gag on his wine. He wishes her ill, he wishes her very ill.

It is winter. The Tower is cold. Icicles form on the windows, dripping down like long, frozen fingers. Robert wants to reach out and touch them, to taste for a moment the outside world. He thinks of his manor in the country and the palace he once graced. Will he ever look upon them again? He pushes outwards the small window of leaded glass and breaths softly into the cold world beyond. He is high up and can see the Tower complex stretching before him, see people going about their work; guards patrolling, servants vanishing from one stone building to another. Distantly the lions roar, housed deep in the menagerie, unaccustomed to a frozen English winter.

"Close the window," Ambrose glances up from warming his hands by the fire.

At least important prisoners such as themselves are not forced to suffer a cruel prison cell. They have furnishings and a fire. They drink and eat well, and can even walk about the Tower buildings for their exercise. Still, it is a tiresome life.

Ambrose has picked up a shard of stone and returns to the back wall where he has been working. Between the brothers they are drawing the family crest into the wall, etching away the surface of the stone. When it is done a bear will stand beside a ragged staff and below will be a verse;

"You that these beasts do well behold and see
May deem with ease wherefore here made they be
With borders eke wherin there may be found
Four brothers' names, who list to search the ground."

Robert intends to place his own motif in a border around the bear; an oak spray is his personal emblem. Then his name and that of his brothers will be engraved into the wall. Perhaps it shall be smashed after they are gone, or plastered over, but at least they have tried to immortalise themselves. Robert is still certain death awaits him.

Guildford and Lady Jane Grey, the girl his father had wanted to be queen, have already faced the Council and been found guilty of high treason. The punishment for such crimes is hideous; Jane would be burned at the stake, while Guildford would be hung, drawn and quartered. Fortunately, some mercy has been shown and the pair have had their lives spared and must instead endure a lifetime of captivity within the Tower.

Ambrose carves on. He can't keep still. His restless

energy has him awake at all times of the night. When he is able he walks miles about the Tower and climbs to the top to overlook the city he once thought of as his sanctuary. It seems a long time ago since his father was executed. It seems even longer ago that they sat at Twelfth Night with the boy king still alive and their father's position secure.

There is a knock at the door and a guard ushers in a woman. The instant he is gone she removes her dark veil and reveals herself to the brothers.

Robert rushes forward to embrace his wife.

"Amy! You are my salvation! Your face brightens my bleak day. I thought you would not come so soon."

Amy relishes his warm body against hers, her handsome gypsy is still so in love.

"I am better," she says softly in his ear. "It was only a minor sickness. Oh, but Robert..."

He pushes her back as her distress rings out, so he can see her face better. He searches for clues in her eyes. What must befall them now?

"I have terrible news."

Ambrose steps closer, his cheery face suddenly downcast. Even the fire cannot warm them now.

"Thomas Wyatt has led a rebellion against the queen," Amy says breathlessly.

Robert glances at his brother. He doesn't instantly understand. Thomas Wyatt opposed their father and Lady Jane Grey. He was an avid supporter of Mary. His betrayal does not make sense.

"Why, Amy?" Ambrose jumps in. "We hear so little in here, the guards keep news from us."

"The queen proposes to marry Phillip of Spain," Amy says.

"We have heard that announcement," Ambrose almost spits. "They were keen to tell us that. The engagement was officially announced last month."

"Thomas Wyatt is opposed to the Spanish," Amy continues. "He has been to Spain and seen the Inquisition in action. He fears a similar thing developing in England. He believes Mary will betray her people by marrying Phillip. He wanted to remove her from the throne and replace her with Princess Elizabeth."

"And he hoped to achieve this by rebellion," Robert turns away to the window angrily. "Surely Kett's example should have been warning enough?"

"Perhaps he felt there was no other option," Ambrose says lightly. "After all, in Mary's eyes we are rebels too."

Robert looks forlornly at his brother. He has never considered himself anything but a loyal subject to the Crown, but his mind turns guiltily to that moment when he went on his knees before Mary and begged for his life.

"There is worse," Amy lowers her head until all she can see is the floor. "The Duke of Suffolk joined Wyatt, along with his two brothers."

Robert reels as though he has been punched in the stomach. Ambrose lets out a moan and shakes his head. The room seems to swim about them. Robert clenches his fists on the windowsill and stares out onto snowy roofs.

His mind is churning over the news, his stomach follows. The Duke of Suffolk is Jane Grey's father. For her the outcome is inevitable, and perhaps for Guildford too. He wants to scream at the horror of it all. Guildford is still a boy with such hopes for his future, and he had fallen in love with Jane instantly. He had always been a dreamer and the shy would-be queen had stolen his heart. Now they will die together. He wants to curse his father for allowing his youngest son to stumble so blindly into this madness.

"What became of Thomas Wyatt?" Ambrose asks between his hands.

"He tried to march on London. You surely heard the commotion."

Robert merely nods. Yes, he heard the gunfire and the cannon shot. He heard the cries and shouts, the screams and death throes. He just had not known the cause.

"They say Mary was truly afraid at first. She took hostage

Princess Elizabeth, but this did not dissuade Wyatt. He wanted the Tower. It was the talk of London. He wanted the Tower turned over to him. Oh for a moment Robert I hoped..." Amy bites on her finger. "But the London people, they were with him until that moment, until they heard what he wanted, and then they turned against him. Mary was able to raise her army and occupy London Bridge. Wyatt was in Southwark but he was driven back."

Ambrose turns to his brother.

"Do you recall that trouble the other day? So much shouting in the corridors and someone yelling about Lord Chandos determined to turn the Tower guns on Southwark. I wondered why he would shoot cannons at the district," he looks back at Amy. "I tried to go to the top of the Tower and look at the scene but the guards refused to let me leave. So the commotion was Wyatt?"

"Tell me the rest, Amy," Robert says quietly.

Amy reaches out for his hand.

"They were driven out of Southwark, so marched to Kingston. There the bridge was destroyed, but they rebuilt it and crossed. They say no one tried to stop them and for a moment it seemed Wyatt would walk right up to the queen and demand she give up the throne, but then the people of Ludgate rose up and stopped him. His army had had enough. Many ran away. Wyatt surrendered."

"He was brought to the Tower?" Ambrose persists.

"Yes, they say he was tortured, but I do not know for sure. He was beheaded at Tower Hill, so was Lord Thomas Grey."

Robert collapses onto the bed. His face is so pale it matches the snow outside. Amy rushes to him.

"I am so sorry," she clutches at his hand. "I prayed so hard for a miracle to free you and in the madness of that day when Wyatt marched on London I thought my prayers answered. Instead, I fear I have condemned you with my hopes."

"Not I," Robert says hoarsely, his throat seems to have

swollen almost shut, he drags out the words. "Guildford and Jane. They will die."

"That bastard, Thomas Grey!" Ambrose slams his palm against the wall. "All he ever thought of was power! Now he has sealed his daughter's and our brother's fate. We must do something Robert!"

Robert tries to dredge some small grain of possibility from his despair.

"What can we do? We cannot even see the execution grounds?"

"We must protest to the queen!"

"She is a stone-cold bitch, brother! She has no interest in helping us. Her only interest is in finding a husband who might look past her withered garden and ugly features and try to plant a seed in barren soil!"

Robert abruptly stands and storms across the room. He feels helpless, useless and that makes him even angrier. His hatred for the queen rises into a bubbling, boiling fury.

"I shall request an audience," Ambrose insists.

"And even if she grants it she will never listen to what you say! If I was king I would not let Jane and Guildford live, not after this, not knowing how much hate I had engendered in my people. Mary is not forgiving, she is a spiteful witch and you will achieve nothing Ambrose!" Robert turns to the fireplace.

Ambrose goes to respond, furious at his brother's defeatism. Then he realises Robert is weeping. He hastily ushers Amy from the room. She must not see her husband like this. She protests, but he hurries her outside anyway. Then he goes to Robert and rests a hand on his shoulder.

"Will he have to endure a traitor's death?" Robert says, biting down fiercely on his emotions.

"I hope not," Ambrose answers.

"I will kill the queen if I am able!"

"Hush! Guards might hear!"

"I cannot hush! She has scorned and spat upon our family. Where will it end Ambrose?"

Ambrose shakes his head. Has no answer.

"Just think of your wife, Robert. Don't do anything that could have her at the executioner's block."

Robert shudders, but the thought reminds him that there is more to consider than just revenge. He slowly moves and looks at the crest they have been carving.

"We must etch in Guildford's name. At once."

Ambrose stares at the growling bear.

"Yes," he picks up a shard of stone and sets to work. Within a moment Robert joins him. They work until the day fades and then they light candles and carry on.

The next morning is 12 February 1554, the day Lady Jane Grey and her husband, Guildford Dudley, are beheaded.

⬚

13 – Syderstone, Norfolk 1955

Spiritualist volumes lay in a pile at Fourdrinier's feet as he executed the deft movements needed to install his bicycle clips about his ankles. It was a beautiful morning after the rain-swept night and, as he had promised, Fourdrinier was intending to call on his aunt and the Talbots.

He picked up one of the books and glanced again at its gold title. 'The Foundation of Spiritualism' it called itself. Fourdrinier had spent several hours last evening searching his over-stuffed library (an inheritance from the previous incumbent) and had turned up a number of volumes on the subject of spiritualism.

He had learned that it all began with the Fox sisters in America; the two young girls had learnt how to click their toes and produce rapping sounds. It was a parlour game; the bored sisters pretended there was a ghost in the house, using the disembodied raps as proof. Their parents were convinced and so were locals. Visitors flocked to the Fox residence to listen to the ghost rap and to ask it questions. Eventually the spirit revealed itself as a murdered man who had once lived in the Fox homestead. No one appeared inclined to check the truth of the ghost's story and very rapidly the case was deemed an extraordinary instance of paranormal activity.

The elder of the two sisters started to travel the country to perform her 'talent'. She was accompanied by the dubious Mrs Fish, in fact her considerably older sister, who seemed to realise the financial possibilities of a little girl who communicated with the dead.

By the time Fox mania reached England there was an

audience eager for it. The latest theories on evolution had thrown traditional religion into a tizz-wazz and people were reaching out for anything that proved there was life after death. God was optional, though many Fox followers believed the girls' gifts were from the Almighty.

Spiritualism was the result of all this fuss. Developed via the Fox sisters it quickly spread across Europe and Britain. Rapping mediums popped up everywhere and people flooded to them in droves looking for answers. Scientists were as enamoured as the ordinary man and the Church found itself being rivalled by a bunch of toe-clickers.

Of course, the enterprise quickly became infected by charlatans and the deluded. New mediums developed new tricks; objects moved about, hands appeared from nowhere and, most remarkable of all, some began producing full body manifestations. These 'ghosts' could prowl about a darkened room, talk and touch the sitters and behave very much like a living person. That they bore a striking resemblance to the medium was brushed aside by the believers.

Fourdrinier had wandered through time learning about people's desperation, about con-artists and hoaxers, about debunkers and the odd case that remained unproved and yet also far from disproved. He had scratched his head and contemplated ectoplasm, spirit photography and spirit writing. Slowly he had understood the appeal to people like his aunt, who found traditional religion cold or somehow unapproachable. What he also understood was that no medium emerged from the Victorian era untouched by exposure – none were safe from being called frauds.

That left Nancy. Fourdrinier put down the book slowly and took a deep breath. He had suspected from the start that she was manipulating his aunt. But while the possibility had existed that she might be telling the truth he had allowed his doubts to be overridden. Now he was certain. Nancy was playing a game with his aunt; maybe she believed she was talking with the spirits, or maybe she was deliberately playing his aunt for a fool. Either way it had to be stopped.

Fourdrinier checked his laces, collected his hat and set off once more on his bicycle. The day was bright, but the wind cold and he felt it beating against his face as he rode. His mind was working fast. He had to prove Nancy a fraud and he had to prove it as soon as he could, before Maud and Charlie were swept further into this nonsensical business of a haunted rectory. He could only think of one way to do that. He would go to the parish registers, locked firmly away, and he would pick out a few choice events with specific dates. Dates and events the real Margaret Stewart would know, and then he would ask Nancy to name them. She would be unable to, and then she would be held up before everyone as a fake.

He pedalled round a corner and veered out of the way of a car, the driver honking his horn furiously. There had to be plenty of dates he could choose from, he just had to verify them first. He eased off the brake and free-wheeled down a hill. Syderstone beckoned him. He cut around another corner and drove a pair of woodpigeons into the air. He was flying so fast now the cold wind was a distant thought and he was sweating in his jacket. He bounced over a pothole, snatched his hat from the air as it threatened to fly away and pulled to a furious, skidding halt just inside the gate of Syderstone church. Gravel flicked into the air about him and a woman tending a grave glanced up in surprise. Fourdrinier doffed his hat to her and hurried to the church.

He dragged out the registers from the cupboard in the vestry and almost dropped them onto a handy table. He pulled over a chair and sat down, flapping his handkerchief at his face as the fast jaunt on his bicycle finally caught up with him. He was still puffing and sweating when he heard the flower ladies come in to ready the week's floral arrangements.

Fourdrinier dabbed his forehead with the handkerchief and tucked it away in a pocket. Then he pulled forward the first register and opened its pages. He scanned to 1831, the year the Stewarts came to Syderstone. In fact, that could be his first question, Margaret Stewart should know when her father came to the parish, but to be on the safe side (and to avoid giving Nancy any loopholes she could dive through, such as Margaret being too young to remember) he wanted dates that would be particularly significant to the alleged spirit of Margaret.

He scanned the registers. There were no baptisms of Stewart children, so he could not ask about the birthdays of younger siblings. He flicked the pages. There were a few notes in the margin of the register, so small they strained his eyes to read them. He picked out one and slowly made out the words "...Ilking called by. Served with him in Spain..."

Fourdrinier sat up straight. Stewart had been in Spain? He glanced about the church, hoping desperately there was something about the room that might help him. He went to the wooden safe (it's key blithely hidden under a nearby cactus pot) and searched among the papers inside. He pulled out something that looked promising; it was a brief handwritten letter concerning the credentials of John Stewart. It must have been sent before he was appointed. He glanced through it, the writing straining his eyes almost as much as that in the register, but it told him what he needed to know – what Margaret Stewart should know. John Stewart had served for several years as an army chaplain in Spain. Syderstone had been his first appointment back in England. Margaret had to have lived in Spain in her early years.

It was perfect! It did not rely on dates a child might mistake and it would be something Margaret would be certain of. She would remember her childhood in the hot climes of Spain. She would know her father served out there!

He put everything away, locked it all up and headed for the Talbots' farm with a new sense of purpose. Aunt Ida would be furious with him, but that was not the point.

Nancy was perpetrating a fraud on them all and he intended to stop it at once.

Charlie was in his yard feeding the cart horse when Fourdrinier cycled towards him.

"Early aren't we, Fourdrinier?"

"Charlie, I think I can prove Nancy duped us all last night!" Fourdrinier thought Charlie would join him in his excitement, instead the younger man looked uncertain then turned away.

"You are positive of that?"

"Yes. I've been reading about spiritualism all night. These séances, they are a trick. They pick out information from peoples' responses to questions. It is very clever, but a trick nonetheless."

"What will your aunt say?"

Fourdrinier licked his lower lip nervously.

"I shall cross that bridge when I come to it. This must be done tactfully and gently. Are they awake?"

"Your aunt was up at dawn," Charlie yawned. "Nancy rose about an hour ago. She is a sullen thing."

"How so?"

"Oh, I don't know, maybe she isn't a morning person. But you can't speak to her. I said hello and she virtually glared at me."

"She'll be glaring at me in a minute," Fourdrinier predicted. "Go round them up."

Great aunt Ida was draped in a red and gold kimono with her grey hair nipped back in a bun when she presented herself to Fourdrinier in the dining room.

"Well, Norman?"

"I have devised a test for Nancy."

Ida gave him the glare he was expecting.

"Nancy does not need to be tested."

"Excuse me aunt, but I believe she does. She claims to be in touch with a dead girl and on her word alone you want me to begin investigating what became of this child and the riddle of a locked room."

Aunt Ida 'humphed' and sat in a chair.

"What sort of test do you propose?"

"Nothing drastic," Fourdrinier had read of the tests investigators had previously performed on mediums and the indecency of some of them had made him shudder. "I just have a few questions, questions that Margaret Stewart should be able to easily answer."

Ida narrowed her eyes at him suspiciously.

"You think me an old fool, a dupe. That I came upon Nancy one day, she threw me a story about being psychic, and I fell at her feet in awe."

Fourdrinier restrained his first response of "Well, didn't you?"

"I confess I don't know how you met Nancy."

Ida leaned back in her chair, her hands spread out on the arms.

"I was told of her by a friend. I have studied Eastern religion for a while, as you know, and I came across Theosophy. Have you heard of it?"

Fourdrinier shook his head.

"Dear Norman, you should keep up-to-date with your competition. Theosophy was founded by a Madame Blavatsky who, I'm afraid to say, proved to be the biggest fraud of the period, and I mean that both figuratively and literally. She was a woman of considerable girth. Blavatsky morphed Buddhism with Spiritualism, but denied that it was possible to speak with the dead. She considered such communication only a means to allow malicious spirits to sneak into this realm. She was popular enough in her own way, she taught of spiritual powers, such as the gift of healing. Sadly her powers largely involved the correct timing of opening and closing a hidden hatch in her rooms through which objects could be 'spiritually' removed or added.

"I studied Theosophy for a while, intrigued by its possibilities. That Madame Blavatsky was a fraud does not mean there was nothing in it, and then I stumbled upon a small circle of spiritualists via my Theosophy connections. A few of the spiritualists in fact dabbled in both religions, and one invited me to see the error of my Theosophy ways by attending a séance. I was unconvinced, as Blavatsky had taught communication with the dead was impossible. I believed her when she said a séance was a means of contacting demons or bad spirits and nothing more. You probably would have liked Blavatsky, Norman."

Fourdrinier shrugged. Somehow it did not surprise him that his aunt had drifted between two opposing religions.

"I spent some time with the spiritualists and I became intrigued, but I was not convinced. Their mediums were dubious to say the least, I am certain I saw one regurgitate cheese-cloth, though my companions were convinced it was this substance they refer to as ectoplasm. Anyway, I returned to Theosophy, there is a small society in London, and there I met this young girl called Nancy Hope Walker.

"Nancy was a very fearful little thing. Her mother had brought her to Theosophy as something of a cure. A cure for what I was not at first sure. She was nervy, but it appeared her mother was concerned with something more dramatic than that. Well, I befriended them, as I do everyone. I am a bored, rich lady and talking to the young improves my mood. I prefer not to leave the house if I can help it, my constitution being delicate, so I suggested the Theosophy group meet in my drawing room and spare themselves the expense of renting a hall once a week. That they did and before long I came to know Nancy and her mother a little better.

"I'm not sure how it cropped up, but I remarked to Nancy that I had also studied spiritualism. This seemed to strike a chord with the girl; it was like her whole being was suddenly struck by lightning. She sat bolt upright and looked me dead in the eye.

"'Do you think there is an afterlife where we go to after death?' she asked. I must point out Theosophy emphasises reincarnation as opposed to an immediate 'heaven'. I remarked that I was quite convinced there was an afterlife.

"'And do you think, if it was important, the dead might try to come back and speak with us? Ghosts I mean?' she continued. I had to think on that one, but eventually I said I thought that likely. Then her mother appeared and she changed the subject.

"I gave it little thought until the following week when Nancy caught me alone and desperately clung to my arm.

"'I have been beside myself all week, I must speak to you and confess all.'

"'Confess? What on earth could you have to confess?"

"'Ghosts! I have seen ghosts in our house and they have tried to speak to me. I told mother and she was appalled and insisted I come with her here. Theosophy teaches that only bad spirits would want to interfere with this earthly plane, but the ones I see in the house, they do not seem bad, they seem earnest. And they torment me, they will not leave me be, because they know I can see them. What must I do? I tell you all this because you have been to the spiritualist meetings and you seem so open-minded.'"

Ida gave a sigh.

"Nancy was frightened. She thought she was going mad. Her mother was not helping by trying to ignore the problem. I suppose I felt sorry for her, so one night I arranged for a few spiritualist friends to come around and Nancy made her excuses to pay me a visit. I introduced her and, upon my word, there was a woman among them who instantly saw Nancy's problem.

"'This child is being haunted by spirits in anguish!' she said. It was remarkable. Nancy lit up like a beacon. It took little persuasion to convince her to tell her story. The spiritualists were certain she had to act and free the trapped souls in her home. They wanted to hold a séance, but arrangements were difficult with having Nancy's mother about. Well, without boring you, we arranged the event to coincide with the mother being out of town. Nancy went into a deep trance and spoke with a gentleman called Henry who had died in the house during a fire. He didn't seem to understand he was dead and he was trying to find his daughter who he believed was still trapped in the house. The fire he mentioned occurred thirty years previously. The daughter had survived, married and was still living we learned later.

"Anyway, it took two hours but we convinced the poor man he was dead and his daughter safe and that he must move on. The last we knew he was speaking of a bright light and then he was gone. Nancy was exhausted afterwards, but we all felt we had achieved something remarkable.

"After that the spiritualists were convinced Nancy had a gift she must not ignore. Secretly she began helping them, communicating with spirits in trouble. Nancy found the task daunting, but wanted to help. I watched a few of her séances and couldn't believe the amount of detail she obtained. Slowly I came to believe in her too.

"Then her mother found out. Needless to say it caused a scandal within the family. The mother wanted Nancy to give up the séances and when her daughter refused she kicked her out. Nancy arrived on my doorstep looking every bit a waif and stray. I took her in and she has been with me these last five years."

Ida finished her story and waited for Fourdrinier's response.

"I suspect I would be on the mother's side," he said solemnly.

"The mother was wrong, Norman. If a person needs our help we must aid them."

"A living person, yes."

"A soul then. If a soul is distressed do you look away? Do we not pray for the dead?"

"It's more of a Catholic thing."

"But for centuries we did, didn't we? Tried to help them through Purgatory?" Ida frowned. "Norman, I really did not think you were the sort to refuse to help someone if you could."

"We don't know there is a 'someone'," Fourdrinier said calmly. "We don't know if that someone is Margaret Stewart."

"So you have your tests," Ida nodded. "And they will prove what?"

"If the questions I ask are answered correctly it will prove that Nancy is indeed in communication with the spirit of Margaret Stewart."

"And if not?"

"Then you can choose your interpretation. Either Nancy is a fraud or she is talking with a spirit, but it happens to be the wrong spirit or one impersonating Margaret."

Ida held his gaze for several moments.

"Nancy is not a fraud."

"Then she has nothing to fear."

At that moment the medium appeared in the doorway looking unhappy. Fourdrinier's first thought was how tired she looked despite a supposedly peaceful night and long lie-in. Nancy was in the same dull, old skirt and blouse, the jacket discarded in the warm house. She rested one hand on the doorframe and turned to Ida.

"What is this all about?"

"The usual, dear," Ida remarked blithely. "Norman wants to test you."

Nancy gave a soft sigh and her head fell forward.

"You think I am lying, Reverend Fourdrinier. Why?"

"I am sceptical, as any right thinking man would be in this day and age when fraud has been exposed over and over again within the spiritualist movement. I hardly need to over-state the case, you must be aware that virtually all mediums that have been in the public eye have been proved charlatans."

"And what of those not in the public eye?" Nancy cocked her head defiantly. "I do not deny that a number of fraudsters have portrayed themselves as mediums for the money and the fame it would bring. But they are the exception. Most honest mediums do not seek to use their talents for gain, only to help others. Name me one of those who has been exposed?"

Fourdrinier shook his head.

"I admit I can't."

"This is an idle test, and pointless. I do not need to prove myself to anyone."

"Yet you will?" Fourdrinier asked calmly.

The young woman glared at him, but she did not walk away.

"Yes, I will. But not because of you, but because Margaret needs your help and only by convincing you will she get it."

Fourdrinier was discomfited by her conviction. She spoke very plainly about the extraordinary. He took a small black notebook from his pocket and motioned it to his aunt.

"I came prepared."

"I shall summon everyone," Ida responded. "But just remember, Nancy has my full trust."

In a short space of time the room was prepared and the Talbots were present. The morning sun, fragile as it was, was banished from the dining room by the thick drapes and the candles were once more lit on the mantel. Fourdrinier kept a close watch on Nancy as the preparations were made.

"I don't do tricks, Reverend Fourdrinier," Nancy told him sharply. "If you expect to catch me throwing a vase or tilting a table you will be sorely disappointed."

Fourdrinier gave her a smile.

When everything was set they gathered round, Fourdrinier to one side again as the unbiased note-taker. Ida was still giving him reproachful looks, but on this occasion his aunt would not dislodge him from his course. He settled into a chair as the circle began chanting hymns.

As before it was a long time before anything appeared to happen. Fourdrinier sat by his candle and resisted the urge to tap his pencil on the side of the notebook. In the dimness he watched Nancy's outline, her fine nose and chin casting sharp angles in the darkness. She was breathing heavily and was distinctly swaying. That strange chill came over Fourdrinier again, the same one he had experienced in the old parsonage. He felt the desire to look over his shoulder, as though someone was there waiting for him just to turn around. He rolled his shoulders to shake the sensation.

Nancy parted her lips and wet them with her tongue. A long minute passed with her lips open and her breathing rasping from her mouth. Then the swallowing began. Fourdrinier watched her throat as the muscles contracted and relaxed almost violently. He understood Charlie's horror that something was taking hold of the girl's vocal chords, it was the exact impression the performance was designed to produce. He readied his pencil over the paper.

"Hello," the voice was not Nancy's. It came from her mouth, but it was much younger and childish. It had a sing-song quality Nancy lacked.

Fourdrinier had barely heard Nancy speak normally before that morning, so he had not noticed before how odd this second voice seemed. He started to make a note of investigating ventriloquism or voice-changing devices, when Nancy turned and faced him directly.

He felt her stare even though her eyes were shut. She had swivelled her entire upper body, but retained hold of the hands of the two ladies either side of her.

"You keep wasting time!" it was a surly complaint, tinged with a whine. "You are very mean."

"On the contrary," Fourdrinier was annoyed at being accosted like that, "I have every right to be sceptical. It is up to you to prove yourself to me, so that I might help you."

Nancy's lower lip bulged in a child-like sulk.

"Very well, if you shall be so mean I shall prove myself. I know what you want to ask, I know already."

"Do you," Fourdrinier remarked coolly, thinking Nancy was trying to bluff him, well she would not succeed. "What is my question then?"

"I'll give you the answer, not the question, then you will have to believe."

"Go on then."

"My father served in Spain with the cavalry. I was born in Cadiz, but I lived mostly in Madrid. I came to Syderstone when I was ten. It was my first time in England. I thought it very cold and dull."

Fourdrinier dropped his pencil. He stared at Nancy who stared blindly back. His mind tried to rationalise what had just happened – but she couldn't have known? She could not have known John Stewart's history or what Fourdrinier was going to ask. He had expected her to give some answer about the dates of her birth and death, something obvious Nancy could have picked from a gravestone to make herself look clever to the others. But not this, not his secret test.

"I watched you in the vestry this morning."

Fourdrinier said nothing.

"You were there alone until the flower ladies came in. Do you believe me now? Nancy was here all morning."

Fourdrinier bought himself time by stretching for his pencil.

"Norman, answer the child," Ida called softly from across the table.

Fourdrinier faced the blindly staring Nancy. He wished she would open her eyes instead of glaring at him like she was a mummy or a corpse.

"I did indeed go to the vestry this morning."

"And did I answer your question?" Nancy chimed excitedly.

Reluctantly Fourdrinier responded.

"Yes."

He felt Charlie's eyes stabbing into him, but he would not look back.

"Do you believe Nancy now? Do you believe this is really me, Margaret Stewart, talking?"

Fourdrinier wanted to give some plausible reason as to

how Nancy had done it, but he had none. Instead he slipped into silence.

"Please solve this, Mr Fourdrinier," Nancy begged. "The room binds me. I have never been free. There is this creature lurking within it. The story is old but it keeps going on. Solve the riddle of the sealed room, Fourdrinier."

"Look here..." Fourdrinier was startled into silence by a spark of light dancing across the room like a lightning bolt.

Maud screamed and jumped from her seat. There was a fine rent in her blouse sleeve and a long red mark.

"It burned me!" she cried, bursting into stunned tears.

Charlie grabbed her in his arms, his face deathly pale.

"It was the Devil," Maud sobbed. "I'm certain of it."

Fourdrinier was shaken, but his rational self was resurfacing.

"I would say it was a jolt of static electricity. The weather has been rather stormy. It probably built up and then happened to pop at this precise moment."

Maud was shaking violently in her husband's arms.

"Fetch some brandy," Charlie begged.

Fourdrinier bounced from his seat looking for the drinks cabinet. His gaze passed over his aunt who was quietly speaking to Nancy and drawing her out of the trance.

"Doesn't do tricks!" Fourdrinier snapped to himself as he marched to the cabinet. He poured out a good dose of brandy and gave it to Maud.

"There was no call for frightening her like that!" he snapped almost instantly, his fury directed at Nancy.

Nancy had a dreamy expression on her face. She clutched Ida's hands and swayed pathetically.

"She didn't do it," Aunt Ida said firmly.

Fourdrinier went to counter her but was halted by the look of unabashed horror in his aunt's eyes.

"That has never happened before, Norman, never, I swear to it."

Fourdrinier was taken aback by the serious tone of his

aunt's voice.

"There is evil here," Nancy's voice was weak but it cut through the tension in the room, she coughed lightly. "Not the Devil, but a piece of him. It hangs over Syderstone and snares the unwary. It has Margaret. When she comes through to us she only has so long before it follows. I knew it last night, I knew it before, but I could not think how to explain it."

Fourdrinier tried to grapple with this new logic. He found himself at a loss.

"Reverend Fourdrinier, Margaret has been waiting for just such a man as you. A man so rational and sceptical he will not be seduced by this darkness. You know what I am saying is true, you felt it when you went to the house."

"Nancy," Fourdrinier's tone had softened. "What just happened was some fluke of nature."

"Please do not be such a fool! There is evil about this village and it is very close to breaking loose and causing chaos."

"This is a parlour game," Fourdrinier stumbled back from the table and grabbed up his hat. He was out the door before his aunt could protest. Charlie chased him.

"Fourdrinier, don't do this!"

Fourdrinier stopped and faced his old curate.

"Do what?"

"Deny what you saw and leave us in this... this peril! I told you my thoughts last night and I am now even more confirmed in them. Something is wrong in Syderstone, you must sense it? Surely it is your duty as a man of God to root it out?"

"I don't sense anything, Charlie."

"That is a lie! I saw your face when Nancy answered your question. She was completely right and you know it! She could not have guessed that. It was your own test Fourdrinier! How could she have faked that?"

Fourdrinier could not answer.

"Let us put aside thoughts on mediums," Charlie said,

trying to sound reasonable. "As a spiritual man you believe in such a thing as evil?"

"Yes," Fourdrinier admitted. "The temptation to do wrong encouraged by the Devil."

"What about disembodied evil? The sensation within a room, a place, a community that something is out of kilter and that that something leads people to act in ways they otherwise would not do?"

"I suppose that is a type of temptation. Perhaps we might argue that is how the Devil works, an influence on susceptible people."

"And if that force, for some reason, became trapped in an area, could perhaps build up upon itself like rain water filling a bucket, what then?"

At that point Fourdrinier was out of his depth.

"You never saw the concentration camps in Germany," Charlie persisted. "Places of torment and pure, pure evil. I went there twice. Once to get people out and the second time when the camp was empty. I sensed it the first time, but I was too busy to consider it. When I returned it was stronger than ever; a feeling of deep evil embedded in the ground, seeped into the concrete. I'm not sure if the evil was there first and the Nazis fed on it, or if they brought it with them, but it had eaten into the soil and no matter if we pulled down the huts, stripped the wire fences and turfed the ground. It would still be there."

Charlie had to take a deep breath before continuing.

"My first thought was 'how could God let this happen?' Back then I had no answer, now I think I do. God did not let it happen. He tried to prevent it by opening the eyes of those he could reach. The clergymen of Germany, perhaps politicians, even ordinary citizens. He tried to show them and they would not listen. Just like how we are now. You are being shown Fourdrinier and you are too stubborn to listen. Is that how it was in Germany?"

"God does not talk through mediums," Fourdrinier replied.

"God uses whatever means he has. And besides, this started with your history project, not with any medium. You don't have to like Nancy or believe she has powers, but you do have to see something is wrong here."

Fourdrinier was tired of the debate. Charlie had dragged him into this misadventure and he was sorely loathed to be cowed into going further.

"You are going to turn away from me, Fourdrinier. I know you. But think on this, there is a sealed room and you have seen it and you go pale whenever it is mentioned. Is that Nancy's doing?"

"I need to get home," Fourdrinier turned away as Charlie had predicted, but he did not move, only stared at the gatepost near the wall that divided the farmhouse garden from the farmyard. "How long have you had a black cat, Charlie?"

Charlie stood by his shoulder and stared ahead.

"I don't. Old Marmalade is ginger."

The two men paused, watching the black, sleek creature sitting on the gatepost watching them back with vivid green eyes. Suddenly it jumped away and skittered across the farmyard.

"Are you not scared, Fourdrinier?" Charlie asked softly.

"The Devil doesn't scare me, my own foolishness does," Fourdrinier couldn't quite remove those piercing green eyes from his mind. "There is supposedly a pond with a witch buried beneath it in Syderstone."

"Really? Someone believed in evil then."

"I need to do my research, come up with some answers that will make this all seem like nonsense."

"You do that Fourdrinier. Perhaps you would be prepared to report your findings to me this Saturday in the pub?"

"Perhaps," Fourdrinier donned his hat and strode to his bicycle.

He was looking for a black cat the entire time he cycled from the yard and onto the road home.

14 - The Diary of Reverend William Mantle

Winter 1785

I have been gravely ill. There were fears for my life. My own imaginings were filled with horrors. I only recall a little of that night so many weeks ago that led me to this grave position.

It began when I confronted the squire's son. The lad is weak and vile. He sits in the inn enthroned among his cronies, preaching about his adventures in London or abroad. I have never seen a man so destitute in his body and morals. He leers at any woman who passes, quaffs his ale until it slugs down his chin and neck, and seems content to rest in his own filth. I am supposed to look at this youth with respectful eyes for he is allegedly my better. When he looks upon me he laughs, for I am deemed the bumbling parson who has neither sense nor courage.

But I had courage that night. I called him out. I told him I knew of his sins, of his debauchery and the wickedness of his ways. I told him I would see him chased from Syderstone and he laughed in my face, his breath damp and bitter from the beer, his teeth brown and rancid from tobacco.

"See here?" he pointed at the men who sit around him including Josiah Smith. "These are the men you would need to chase me out and they side with me. So what can you do?"

I was in a fury. I hardly knew what words I spat out. I told him that with those men or not I could see him from this village. I would seek out his father and place before him all his son's crimes. The man was indulgent, but not so indulgent. I would make it a matter of choice; he must send his son away or I should begin pursuing the magistrates and stirring up a good deal of trouble. No decent squire wants his name dragged through the mud and every squire's son knows his crimes will only continue while no one brings them to the awareness of his father.

He whored and debauched in the village out of his father's eyesight. But if I was to tell him, to reveal all... well, the man was bound to believe in the honest word of a man of the cloth!

I saw the boy pale. I knew I had him where I wanted. I pushed my claim. Told him if he were to leave at once I might see fit to forestall my complaint. His podgy eyes bulged, his filthy gut trembled. I saw that fear and I knew I had him, for where would he go? No village would be so amenable to him as the one where his father held sway. Perhaps he could disappear into London again, perhaps...

I wanted him out of my sight, either willingly or unwillingly. If he made me speak with his father then he would be forced away, if he spoke himself then he might be able to arrange some trip to the continent where he could continue his wickedness anew. I could not prevent that, but I could chase him from Syderstone.

I saw his fear and I gravely misread it. I was virtually upon him for I believed myself winning. I failed to remember that a scared animal reacts more violently and dangerously than a calm one. I am not certain who struck me first. Josiah was nearest and he was well in his cups, but there were others too. All I know is that on a word from the boy they leaped at me and had me on the ground in moments.

I am not such a sore fighter. I have scuffled before. But

five men against one is almost unbeatable. The inn erupted in chaos; I was dragged outside. I felt blows on my head and covered my face, only for someone to kick at my stomach. I doubled in pain and a boot came down on my arm. I heard the snap, but I felt little. I was scrambling in the midst of the onslaught, trying to deflect blows and escape from the gang.

My memory weakens. There were more blows, someone kicked my cock and tried to deprive me of my manhood. Another fellow was at my throat. I think they aimed to kill me in their drunken stupor. Parts of my body went numb, at some point I lost my senses. From a dark place I heard painful cracks and unpleasant cries but I was no longer aware if they were my bones breaking or my shrieks, my only notion was of an overwhelming sense of tiredness.

I am told Carter the blacksmith saved me. If this is true I must thank him when able. I awoke some days later in my bed, tied down for, as I later learned, I had been feverish from the pain and had thrashed about wildly, threatening to further damage my broken body.

Dear, sweet Octavia was there to attend to me, despite being swollen with child yet again. She was red-eyed and sad. I sensed her fear as she mopped my brow with a wet cloth. I was close to death, they thought more than once they had lost me.

I found myself assessing my body as I lay in that bed. I started at my head, where there was a throbbing sore patch at the back. Someone had stamped on me and the surgeon had been concerned there was water on my brain. I still find it fearful that I came within a hair's breadth of having my head opened by this good man to relieve the swelling. Fortunately the disfigurement went away.

My chest ached with each breath and I felt as though I could count each broken rib. My left arm had been snapped and several fingers broken. They were bound in bandages and I was admonished any time I moved them. Of my legs only the left ankle had sustained damage. The surgeon remarked it was how I had lain on the ground. He was confident once my fever broke I should be able to recover fully.

I had one nagging concern that could not be breached with my wife present, and in the end I had to conduct a secret self-examination to ensure I had not been prevented from enjoying the company of Octavia in the future.

I appear in one sorry piece. Stiff, sore and covered in bruises. My right hand remains able and I have been allowed the dignity of sitting up in bed and writing so as to occupy my time. I have read a little, but my mind wanders and I find greater solace in putting words to paper. For odd things have been happening to me since that incident.

But first I shall relate what I know of the outcome of my assault for the individuals involved. It was naturally too dramatic an event to forestall the intervention of the local magistrates. There had been numerous witnesses and it is no minor thing to badly beat a man of the cloth. The squire's boy had gone too far in his drunken state, he had not reckoned with the consequences which were greater than if he had merely heeded my words.

Josiah was arrested first and shortly after several other men were taken into custody, most of whom I only had a vague acquaintance with. I am sorry for Josiah's wife, for her husband is in serious jeopardy, being marked as the ring-leader by the others. If I had died it would have been murder and the noose would have been around his neck. As it is, I am told he will likely face a long custody charge or, worse, transportation. Apparently it need not matter that I am alive, it is his intentions that will have to be answered for.

I feel I have failed him yet again. His wife will be destitute if he is convicted, which he will surely be, and with so many mouths to feed I have no idea how she will survive. Their cottage is tied to the land Josiah works, so with him gone they will be rendered homeless. I have voiced the suggestion to Octavia that we offer them respite here. The parsonage is adequate to house us all and the good woman will not be left on the streets to starve. Octavia cocked her head at me when I made the suggestion and looked displeased. I think she feels the wife of a would-be murderer unpleasant company to have in the same house as the victim.

Suffer it I must, however, for I have led us down this path. And then there is the squire's lad, ah, how unchristian it is of me to wish the rope about his neck. He has not been arrested, but the talk in the village is that if he shows his face he shall be. So he has abandoned the county, and will no doubt shortly abandon England altogether. I hardly mourn his leaving, if only it had been sooner. But perhaps this was how things were meant to come to pass? God has his motives as much as man, and I must value His counsel and not question His ways.

So I find myself at the heart of this strange matter that has fallen into my lap, for my misadventure was only the start of something even more preposterous.

This bed has been my comfort and my cage for a month now, and during that time I have come to familiarise myself with every corner, every nook of this room. I know this place as if I was born here. I look out my window and I see the same tree and the same glimpse of garden. I look up and I mark the lumps in the plaster and the way they shift in the light. I sit in candlelight and I dream softly and the room swaddles itself around me... and then I see her.

Forgive me God, for I do not converse with the dead lightly, but on her first appearance I had no knowledge that dead she was. I lay here struggling with the fatigue of pain. There is opium on my nightstand, but the stuff gives me bad dreams and I take it only when necessary. So I lay as still as I could and tried to tease my mind away from bodily woes, and she just walked in and stood by the window staring out into the garden.

What visitor is this? I asked myself. The afternoon was growing dull, but she was vivid in an orangey-brown gown, her hair dressed upon her head and covered with a white veil. She clasped her hands and stared pitifully out into the garden.

"Who are you?" I asked innocently enough. I have had the odd visitor since my sickness, but never one dressed so finely – there were seed pearls dotted down the sleeves of her gown – or so completely unknown to me.

She turned her head and gazed at me. It was a very sad expression.

"I am the lady of this manor," she spoke fairly enough, but I noted her Norfolk accent nonetheless. I assumed her to be the squire's wife, or perhaps sister.

"I have been meaning to speak with you for some time, but I was never able. Now there is this," she vaguely motioned to my broken limbs. "At least now I can speak to you at length without disturbance."

"Forgive my poor manners. I cannot offer you a chair..."

She brushed aside the gesture with a flick of her hand.

"What need have I for chairs? I must talk with you William Mantle, for I hope you shall understand and listen to me," she came a little closer and I saw that her hair was blonde beneath her veil. "I have been dead these last two centuries."

A man can hardly prevent himself from starting at such a revelation. This elegant creature who breathed before me, who moved like a solid person, who appeared to fill the room with her presence, was asserting that she was dead? Long dead, if her words were truth. I must have looked at her stupidly for she laughed.

"You see how I must capture you when you are unable to run from me so I might tell my story? I am sorry I made you start. My name is Amy Dudley."

She held out a hand that I might take it in greeting and plant a kiss on the soft skin. I did reach out, but grasp her hand I could not. It was not there.

"I am spirit, that is all. I am sorry to disturb you thus, I would not if my soul rested easy but it does not."

"Amy Dudley?" my thoughts were spinning.

"Look in the history books and you shall see my family once owned the Syderstone estate. There was a country house but it fell into ruins long ago. I am all that is left, and the memory."

I stared at her like a man in a dream. She still looked solid and as alive as any person, but I noted the edge of her sleeve regularly passed through the end post of my bed.

"You are a demon?" my voice went harder, I was afraid.

"No, you insult me."

"Only demons loiter on this earth!"

"And what of lost souls?" she looked at me desperately. "Could I not be one of those? I am trapped William Mantle, in a snare that still lurks in waiting for the unwary. I was the first caught but I shall not be the last, unless you help me."

I did not want to hear her nonsense.

"A snare? A trap?"

"Of the Devil's invention. He found a path through the evil of man and he took me as his first victim, but there will be more. These last decades I have done all in my power to prevent others falling victim, but I am weary and weakening. I cannot hold the door closed. You must help me to chase the evil from this house, from Syderstone!"

Shame forces me to confess that I shook my head at her, despite the pure desperation in her voice. She looked at me almost with pity, but also anger.

"You will come to believe what I say."

Then I laughed at her. Her pretty face contorted into a scowl, but if I imagined the demon would drop its mask I was wrong. Her frown eased and she merely nodded.

"Mark my words. But I push you too hard. There is time enough yet," she gave a long sigh. "We must save their souls, William Mantle, or we will both be cursed."

She was gone. As though I blinked and removed a speck of dirt from my eye. Gone and only the long shadows of the room to remind me she had stood just there, with her sleeve fading in and out of the bedpost.

There was a nausea in the pit of my stomach that I could not place. I was not afraid, the encounter had been too absurd to scare me, but I was left feeling out-of-sorts. The room was colder than before. I sat very still and my mind raced. She had been there and yet not there. I was awake, of that I was certain, and I had not suffered such visions before. The opium I was resisting, so I could not blame that. Instead I found my thoughts turning to other possibilities. I have heard legends of ghosts and spirits sent to man, some come to try us, others to request help. Discerning if they are sent by God or by the Devil is the hardest part.

As I write this several days on I am still as baffled as before. I cannot decide if I believe myself sane or mad. I have spoken to no-one, what point would there be? But I have prayed and prayed for some glimmering of understanding, and the more I have prayed, the more fixed in my mind have become those strange words – we must save their souls. Whose souls? If I am somehow to conclude this matter I must answer that question, I know this now. Something is wrong in Syderstone and it goes deeper than a drunken squire's son and illicit gambling. Yet what madness am I entering upon? I must think on this still more. I must not rush into anything.

If I have witnessed a divine being bringing me a message, then I must prove it to myself. God must prove it – for otherwise I know not how to act!

15 – Norwich, Norfolk 1955

Fourdrinier put down the loose pages of Reverend William Mantle's diary and stared into the flickering flames of the fireplace in his study. He sagged back in his chair and steepled his fingers beneath his lower lip.

Mantle was in on the mystery too – or else some bizarre coincidence was befalling him. He shut his eyes and thought of Nancy in her corpse-like trance. Was he prepared to believe yet? Unless some enormous conspiracy had been unleashed against him, perpetrated by both his aunt and friend, then there was simply no way Nancy could have known of the contents of William Mantle's diary. Steward had said he had not known the contents himself and the leaves of the manuscript had come to him looking untouched and still iced with a century's worth of dust.

The problem was, this left Fourdrinier with more and more unpleasant conclusions. If Nancy was telling the truth, where did that leave him spiritually?

Fourdrinier stood and stretched his legs, noting that it was raining again outside his window. He moved to his bookshelf and picked out a directory of ecclesiastical figures in Norfolk, past and present. He consulted its thick pages that smelt faintly of dust and decay. Mantle was there, but his entry was barely a footnote. He arrived in Syderstone in 1783 and died there in 1797, nothing else remained about who he was or what he believed. The entry was so unremarkable it brought a pang of sadness into Fourdrinier's heart. That such an individual, obviously caring, obviously trying his best for his parish, could be so quickly forgotten. He flicked to the entry for John Stewart and it made him bitter to see the awkward, unforgiving and mildly sinister reverend had warranted a fuller entry. He was listed as having gone to Cambridge, served in Spain and written several titles of ecclesiastic poetry, none of which rung a bell with Fourdrinier. Unusually it gave no mention of his death, only that he left Syderstone in 1844.

Fourdrinier replaced the volume and sat at his desk, rubbing at his tired eyes. Logic had to prevail. If he approached the matter rationally he would find a reasonable solution. The main figures in this mystery were only mysterious because their lives had been so casually forgotten, but there had to be something else, something someone remembered.

Someone, who? Fourdrinier drew out a sheaf of white paper and placed one piece into his clunky, black typewriter. Gingerly, with the one-fingered imprecision of the failed touch-typist, Fourdrinier compiled a letter for The Church Times, one of the most widely circulated periodicals in the ecclesiastically world.

𝄞

"Dear Sir,

I wondered if one of your readers may be able to assist me with the history of the parishes in Norfolk. I am currently researching the little village of Syderstone and, in particular, two of its incumbents: William Mantle 1783 – 1797 and John Stewart 1831 – 1844. The latter was also remarked upon as a poet. If anyone could provide information on these elusive figures, I would be most grateful.

Yours
Reverend N. Fourdrinier
Norwich, Norfolk."

𝄞

He read the short note back to himself and nodded. It was better than nothing. Folding it into an envelope and addressing it, he slipped it into his pocket and headed out into the Norfolk rain.

His path was not entirely clear even to himself, but when the post box had kindly eaten his letter, he found himself stumbling on to the library in its grey old building. He pushed open the doors and took in the scent of so much paper bundled together in one place. There was only one girl at the front desk and he gave her a passing nod as he made his way to the records section, tucked at the back. He wasn't sure what he might find, but almost instantly he had success as he browsed the shelves and came upon a thin, old volume in green labelled simply 'Stewart'. He pulled it out and scanned a few pages of mediocre poetry. Somehow that restored a smile to his face.

"You were a pompous old prig, Mr Stewart."

He returned the book and made his way to the desk of the records clerk, his hands idly clasped behind his back.

"Would you mind telling me what records you have for the parish of Syderstone?"

The records clerk looked up from a slip of card she was diligently filling in and eyed him with a look of irritation.

"The card index is there, anything you want look it up and then bring me the number," she pointed in the rough direction of a wooden set of drawers.

Fourdrinier smiled warmly and nodded at her, hoping it might bring some grace to her manner, and ambled his way to the case. Syderstone, as he might have guessed, was rather devoid of records. One card did catch his eye though; it was entitled in blue ink 'Syderstone Ghost' and underneath 'correspondence re: the alleged haunting of Syderstone'. Fourdrinier gazed at those words as if they were the announcement of the Second Coming. Some strange mixture of excitement and terror sat in his belly. He jotted down the number dutifully and returned to the desk.

"Not much there," he remarked as he handed over the number.

The woman glanced up and, for the first time, appeared to notice his dog collar; either that or his smile had worked.

"We are entirely reliant on people from the relevant areas depositing records with us," she said as sternly as ever, and then relented. "Have you tried the papers? We have a complete collection of the Eastern Daily Press and if you know of any particular events or dates that are important you could look them up in the paper. We have an index for that too."

She motioned to several thick, red binders on a shelf.

"Have a look while I fetch this," she suggested as she left her desk and trotted off.

Fourdrinier obeyed. The thick binders looked enticing. But once inside them he felt a wave of despair at the sheer number of entries and the confusing numerical index the compiler had given them. He thumbed through pages for a while and then found there was a general index at the back. He scanned for the obvious word 'Syderstone' and found a short list of entries. The general cattle show winner and the summer flower festival were easy to mark as uninteresting entries. The controversy of a proposed new road through the town was too recent to be of any good, but there was one small note that caught his eyes. It read 'Syderstone – Obituaries'. Since it seemed unlikely many of the inhabitants of Syderstone would warrant mention in a big paper he decided to take a chance and hope that out of the five number references given, one would refer to someone he knew.

Almost immediately his hopes were dashed when he realised the paper had not begun publication until 1867, putting it well out of the scope of William Mantle and possibly also John Stewart. He came close to giving up there and then, but something caused him to hesitate and check the descriptions for the entries nonetheless. He was in for a surprise, the oldest entry in the obituaries for Syderstone was that of 'Eminent Church Poet and Former Norfolk Curate' John Stewart. The year was 1868 and John Stewart had died at the grand age of 82 in Lincolnshire.

Fourdrinier sat still, contemplating this strange turn up for the books. After a moment he remembered himself, took note of the date and number, and made his way to a stack of shelves full of tall red bound folios. Inside each he discovered six months' worth of the EDP, stretching right back to those earliest editions of 1867.

His palms were sweaty with a strange mix of excitement and trepidation as he drew out the relevant folio and took it back to the table. He opened it and stared aghast at the tiny, cramped newsprint that was presented to him. He had to waste several moments finding a magnifying glass near the archivist's desk before he could begin looking for the correct entry.

Syderstone had not featured heavily in the newspaper, why would it? It was a quiet parish which shared a curate. There was hardly anything remarkable or noteworthy happening in the district, it suffered little crime above petty theft and was home to no one of celebrity. In short it was the sort of quiet parish people these days longed to retire to and, as such, hardly worth remembering by the newspaper reporters. But the death of John Stewart had caught their eye, not least because his time at Syderstone had been marked by rather strange goings-on.

Fourdrinier read with interest the lengthy obituary of this 'eminent' man.

The late Reverend John Stewart, formerly of the parish of Syderstone, will be long remembered for his ecclesiastical moral poems. A man of stout beliefs and firm principles he is still fondly remembered by all in the parish where he was once just a humble curate.

Fourdrinier wondered if this included the children he had so kindly marked out for posterity as 'base-born'.

Stewart served in the army in Spain for a number of years before returning to England. He was remarked upon as a fine horseman and good shot, and left his regiment with full honours and the regrets of his men at his leaving. Stewart spent twelve years in Syderstone, where the most peculiar aspect of his long career occurred. The good reverend deemed his residence haunted and his delicate daughter the target of a malevolent entity. The circumstances of the matter were widely reported in the Norfolk Chronicle of the time. Several fellow clergymen were asked to inspect the house and render an opinion, which resulted in lengthy debate and inconclusive results. The matter was laid to rest upon the tragic death of Margaret Stewart in 1834, whereupon John Stewart threw himself into his works of ecclesiastical poems and reached the pinnacle of his literary reputation.

Subsequently Stewart moved to a living in Lincolnshire where he is lovingly remembered for his work with the poor and the immoral. His charity work extending to the education of working class infants to promote good manners and regular habits.

In his seventieth year Stewart produced a work on the legends of Lincolnshire which was warmly received by fellow folklorists and is remarked to have been unfairly neglected and forgotten. As an academic and enthusiastic antiquarian, Stewart never forgot his Irish roots and used these as a basis for his discussions on the origins of ancient English folklore and customs.

Stewart passed away on the first of this month, having suffered in his last years from apoplexy and rheumaticks. His funeral was carried out in grand style at Lincolnshire cathedral, his coffin carried in a hearse drawn by four black horses with purple plumes and silver studded harness. His mourners included the Lady Beatrice McCaver...

Fourdrinier lost interest as the piece descended into a long list of names. But he had read enough, and now he was deeply troubled. He had always known Margaret had died young, barely twelve, but for the paper to call it a tragedy... Was that poetic license or something more meaningful? What really bothered him was the reference to the haunting. A man of the cloth, especially a man like Stewart, would be unlikely to publically shame himself by talking about ghosts if he did not firmly believe in their likelihood.

Fourdrinier removed his spectacles and rubbed at his eyes. Stewart believed his house haunted, his daughter was at the centre of the case, and then she died, and so too did interest in the story. Should he take it at face value or try to read between the lines? Was Stewart masking some other controversy by blathering about spirits? Stewart seemed a man who would not risk his reputation lightly and certainly not for something he did not believe in. There could be another answer; Margaret Stewart could have faked a ghost and convinced her father, though for what purpose eluded Fourdrinier. Besides, he had to take into account what was happening now and that made him deeply uncomfortable. Unless he was prepared to say that his great aunt and Nancy had gone to the effort of investigating this case as he was now doing, how on earth could they know the things they did?

"Reverend?"

Fourdrinier glanced up and saw the archivist had returned to her desk with a bundle of papers. He approached her feeling suddenly elevated with a new hope.

"Could you tell me when last these records were looked at?" he asked as calmly as he could.

The archivist seemed unfazed. She glanced at a paper ticket on the cardboard folder that housed the bundle of papers.

"These were deposited in 1945. No one has looked at them since. You're the first."

"Thank you," Fourdrinier said with a smile, even if inside his last hope had been dashed. Nancy had not been here.

He took the package to the table, it smelled slightly musty and the cardboard had a chill to it that suggested a prelude to damp. He set it on the table and untangled the ribbon that kept the bundle together. The papers inside consisted of a series of letters and a few newspaper clippings. Fourdrinier glanced at one and realised it was the same obituary he had just read; it seemed someone in Syderstone had maintained an interest in John Stewart.

Another clipping was a short piece from 1944 dated 20th October. The brief article explained how an American serviceman visiting a girl in Syderstone while on leave, had been frightened by strange lights and ghastly sobs coming from a supposedly empty house. Thinking someone was in distress, he had tried to enter the property, only to find it locked and upon knocking for the lights to abruptly go out and the sobs to desist. He was so unsettled he finished his leave early and returned to his base. The journalist had made vague suggestions this episode was linked to other ghostly legends that circulated about the village, but failed to elaborate.

Fourdrinier put aside the interesting, but far from illuminating, article and concentrated on a collection of letters. Again he needed the magnifying glass to decipher the spidery handwriting which struck him as familiar. He scanned to the bottom of the letter to know who had written it and his heart jumped. John Stewart's name was inscribed in black ink at the base of the page.

⬜

16 – The Letters of John Stewart

To
No.11 Hercules Place, Belfast
March 30 1833
From
Syderstone Parsonage, nr Fakenham, Norfolk, England

My beloved sister,

Yesterday at this time I asked that the Lord who is our rock and strength will sustain us. Dark as are the clouds which surround us here, there is but everlasting sunshine hereafter. Nor, even now, will he desert his praying creatures. Has Jesus forsaken a soul that trusted him? Never! I feel, I know, I see with the eye of faith, that our days of trial shall not always last; and that when his infinite wisdom has disciplined the heart in the uses of adversity, we shall fain to confess with Holy David, "It is good for us to have been afflicted." Thanks to our Divine Hope, the wife and children are well, as well, nay better than under existing circumstances (and which I am now to relate) can be expected.

In this parsonage lived 36 years ago the then curate, the Revd. William Mantle. His wife, a remarkably fine woman, was Octavia Huntingdon, whose family of much respectability resided near Hull in Yorkshire. He likewise was a Yorkshire man. They came to Syderstone from the curacy of Docking, a large village or small town about 5 miles distance. When first they arrived they were normal in their characters. They had a numerous family. Gradually they formed an intimacy with a very dissipated circle of gentlemen farmers around the place, which insensibly led them into vice. There was one of these named Temple who from an improper admiration of Mrs Mantle, seduced the curate into the vilest debaucheries and latterly he was so much addicted to drunkenness as to go in that state to the Church to perform the Divine Service. Nay, when performing the Burial service the bystanders were obliged to hold him by the elbows of his surplice lest he should fall into the grave upon top of the corpse! Well, he died in a miserable state, and before his coffin was removed for interment, strange noises began to be heard in the parsonage. The Revd. Mr Evatt succeeded Mr Mantle and Mantle's shade has been seen, it is averred, twice distinctly, the latter time in his silk gown. Most violent noises have been heard repeatedly during the entire period since, but only at long intervals. The last curate, Mr Skrimshire, as well as his predecessor Mr Evatt knew this. All the parish almost had long known it, but not one could be found to make us uneasy by hinting that any such occurrence had ever been known. We had resided in the parsonage for eleven month before it seemed the will of God to make us know it.

Ever since the beginning of this month my clever little girl had been complaining when we met at breakfast that she had heard so many hours strike on the clock on such a night, and such a night. At length she firmly declared she knew not why, but she could not sleep. We tried to laugh her out of it. However, becoming more and more wakeful she at length heard plainly a loud knocking on the wall of the room within hers, (and where the two maid-servants slept) the door between my little girl's room and theirs being always kept open. She called to the servants repeatedly before she could so far awake them as to enable them to hear it. They became greatly alarmed. "Well," said the heroic child, "I'll secure the bolt at the foot of the back stairs (off the landing of which the two rooms run) I'll go and bolt it since you two great women are so frightened as not to be able to move from your bed." Saying this, and in the midst of all the most awful knockings, she went to the bottom of the stairs and shot the bolt.

Next night, the eighth, the knocking was renewed, and the maids were actually incapable of motion. They persuaded my little dear to ascend the passage to her brothers' room and awake William and John. We had desired to be called. I arose at 2 o'clock, heard it and proceeded down to the kitchen and passages and cellars underneath and examined most perseveringly every spot there was. There could have been no human agency. The knocking stopped the instant I set my foot on the stairs going down to examine. I stopped a minute on my return, all continued silent. I went to bed. Before I had time to sleep, we were called upon, the noises, louder and more continued. Mrs Stewart would go this time and refused to suffer me. This was 3 o'clock. She remained away until near 5. The loud, hollow, unearthly tones that were given by the struck wall I cannot describe. Speak to it and it will give you whatever number of strokes you name. This was on the Sabbath morning. All was quiet that night – until Monday. Monday night all these frightful noises returned. Next night, Tuesday, Mrs Stewart and I, having first removed the children and servants into the centre of the house from the North wing, resolved to sit up and watch. I must stop as I dare no more trust whole drafts or notes. Acknowledge by 'cut corners' (as usual) the receipt of this first half of draft. God Bless you All.

Yours most truly,
J. Stewart
~ ~ ~ * ~ ~ ~

To
No.11 Hercules Place, Belfast
March 31 1833
From
Syderstone Parsonage, nr Fakenham, Norfolk, England

My beloved sister,

God has witnessed our suffering and shall not forsake us. We suffer as he wills it and must not complain for only through suffering do we find our true strengths and merits. But again I say does he abandon a soul in distress? No! He watches us and guides us, he gives us the courage to continue and sustains us when despair looms. My sustenance shall be prayer and I shall not falter in my diligence.

As I mentioned in my last draft, on the Tuesday night, Mrs Stewart and I waited up in the room where these dreadful noises have been heard. This room is at the back of the house, one of the finest appointed in the building, with, as I mentioned, an internal room running off it where the maid-servants sleep. This room, when I arrived, was completely boarded up, permitting no entry. Though I sought high and low, I could find no one who could explain the purpose for sealing this room, nor who committed the deed. I came to some conclusions, based on my other knowledge, that it must have been upon a whim of that unfortunate curate William Mantle, whose shade seems to have trapped itself in the house.

I have come to wonder if some dark practice or terrible deed did not occur in this room causing it to be sealed, though when I first saw it I considered it a nonsense and had a carpenter come to rip away the boards. Margaret was given the room since it afforded her privacy, while allowing the servants to be nearby. Since these noises have begun I have found myself regretting that decision and asking myself if I have not caused this problem.

Tuesday night last, Mrs Stewart and I sat in the room and heard the hollow bangs issuing from the wall. For a time we just listened then I felt emboldened to ask a question of this spirit that is so determined to disturb our peace. I asked plainly who it was, but received only further bangs that came in no intelligible order. I asked again, this time inquiring its age. The entity rapped out 35 or 40 bangs, which seemed to be decisive in proving this misplaced soul as the late William Mantle. He was around that age when he died from dissolute living.

I asked how long had it been dead, but it rapped inconsistently. First only two and then 9 or 10 and then random rapid bursts. I concluded it had no knowledge of time passing and could not formulate an answer. I asked if it could answer yes or no, by rapping once for yes, twice for no. It seemed to rap once. So I asked if I was speaking to the Revd. Mantle and received a singular knock. Satisfied with this I asked if Mantle knew he was in Syderstone. One rap. I asked if he was aware of the time and that he had been greatly disturbing the family. Two raps. I asked if he was wishing to draw attention to himself. One rap. Did he need help? Two raps? I asked him if he intended to persist in this annoyance? One rap. I wished to ask why he felt such a need but there was a limit to our conversational topics, so I tried to speak to him logically. We are in this house now, I said, and he must depart. Two raps. Did he not know how he disturbs a small child? Two raps. I informed him he most certainly did and should desist. Two raps.

Finally my patience was exasperated and I demanded of him, did he not realise that he was dead? A furious burst of raps followed that lasted for several minutes, long enough at least for the clock which had only recently chimed the hour to mark the quarter hour. When he had done the house seemed to go completely quiet, as though he had worn himself out with his fury. I was determined to rid my family of this menace as soon as I could and intended to perform an exorcism the following morning.

Saying nothing of this decision to Mrs Stewart we retired, but in the morning I was ready with my prayer book and cross. Dear God protect me. If I am to be punished for a sin I have forgotten then at least it need not cause suffering to my family as well. Your Divine Will Lord is my guidance and my hope. I trust you will spare me from the worst of this world and that your mission to open my eyes to this torment is for a purpose I have yet to discern. Something inside me failed that day. I took my cross and I said my prayers, I asked God to bless the room and release the soul of William Mantle from its bondage to this place. I knelt on my knees and prayed with all my will, I forced my faith into a physical thing I could wield as a sword against the beast that lingers behind any form of haunting. I felt the strength of God fill me. I felt my sword forming from my very heart. Perhaps I was impatient, but I did not win my battle that day. I faltered at the last for the rappings began as I knelt on the floor. First on the wall and then slowly they came towards me. They rapped on the base of the wall, then on the wood of the floor, then each instant they rapped a little closer to me, like a singular footstep approaching. In my mind I had visions of the beast marching towards me, a cloven hoof causing that bang on the floor. I saw him so completely that I was overwhelmed, my sword shattered. I stared at the floor, anticipating each knock, willing myself to stay in position. Each time they came closer my body quivered with fear, but I resisted, I focused my faith and strength until they were just before me.

Then, at the last, at the moment the knock would reach my bent knee, my will snapped, my faith crumbled. To my shame I fled the room. I despise myself for it, for failing my Lord at this final trial. The knocks continue, I hardly imagined for a moment they would not, but now I see there is evil behind them and I must be rid of this thing in my house. If it cannot be done alone with prayer and cross, then I shall summon other clergymen and have them aid me to vanquish this creature.

God Bless you All.

Yours truly

J. Stewart

To
No.11 Hercules Place, Belfast

April 6 1833
From
Syderstone Parsonage, nr Fakenham, Norfolk, England

My beloved sister,

Your last letter shook my sensibilities. I am fond of your wisdom and guidance, indeed I have coveted it at times, a sin I freely admit, but your last words could not have come from your own lips, I cannot accept that. To hear you suggest my child might be a liar, a dreadful sin I might add, to suggest she is manifesting these noises and thus colluding with some dark and sinister force, is not only absurd but scandalous. I never imagined such thoughts would come from you. Have I not always been honest? Have I not always found fault before being persuaded of truth? Am I not hardest of all on those nearest me so I cannot be accused of being persuaded by love and kinship?

Perhaps you have failed to grasp the seriousness of the matter I have presented to you. Two letters I sent, concerned that they might be intercepted and expose myself to ridicule. Does a foolish man concern himself so? I do consider my reputation in all this. I consider it every day, do not feel you have to preach to me on that score. My little dear is no criminal in this matter. She suffers the worst of all. I see a paleness about her features, a slight drawn quality to her lips and cheeks. I see she is exhausted, but also troubled. The maids confirm what I have told you and will testify they have heard the bangs when my little one was tucked in her bed and could not possibly have made them. And what of the bangs I heard when I was in the room quite alone?

You suggest rats as another possibility. Rats that count? I have tried many attempts to speak with this spirit and on all of them it has been able to answer rudimentary questions. I need hardly say that it appears confused at the situation, as any soul would that finds itself neither in the land of the living nor that of the dead. Have you not told me of similar stories from our homeland? Stories of lost spirits and haunted houses?

I consider your comments on my rationality to be unnecessary and blunt. I am not biased or deluded by my daughter. Who I might add you hardly know. Does it seem fit to you to condemn a child you had never met before last year? Or one who you can hardly judge of her character and nature? God has seen fit to bring this frightening happening upon us, for His purpose and His design, I look upon it as a trial that will lead to better things. Perhaps I shall gain wisdom from this matter, or shall simply be made stronger. In any case, I see my thoughts on this matter will not impress you, so I shall desist from informing you of the developments. Needless to say the wife and children are well, despite circumstances.

I hope your complaint has cleared and you were able to attend the party you were so good to describe to me in your last letter. God Bless you All.

Yours Truly
J. Stewart

To
No.11 Hercules Place, Belfast
9 September 1834
From
Syderstone Parsonage, nr Fakenham, Norfolk, England

My beloved sister,
This will not be the long letter you must have been anticipating, for I have been inconsistent in my writing of late. God has granted me strength in this dark hour to take up my pen and at last write to you.

As you are aware, my dear child has been suffering from a complaint no doctor could specify, let alone cure. She has been withering away before my and Mrs Stewart's eyes. I have not wished to trouble you greatly with the matter, knowing of your sensitive nature to such things, so my notes on her health have been brief and optimistic to avoid concerning you. Your remedies were much appreciated, I might add, I had forgotten of grandmother's book with the various herbal medicines for such complaints. I avoided, of course, all the implied magic in the suggestions. Collecting nettles at midnight smacked too much of paganism. I write all this to let you know it was not from want of trying or from lack of medicine that I must describe to you my latest misery.

God preserve me, I feel cut to the bone. My hands tremble and I cannot eat. Mrs Stewart fears I am falling sick too, but it is not that, I am certain of it. God does not intend to take me yet, not while there is work still to do.

Yesterday my little one complained of restlessness and fever. She was bathed in cold water and seemed to settle. The doctor was due around midday and we hoped he might finally have something to eliminate these strange fluctuations of health Margaret has suffered. I returned to my work as always, distracted only once by the loud bangs that we have come to accept within this household.

At midday the doctor came and we looked in on Margaret, but she was not there. Her bed was empty, the blankets thrown back carelessly. I hardly knew what to think, but I hardly feared the worst. I anticipated she had gone downstairs for water; she has these moments of sudden recovery when she appears a normal child once more. I went downstairs but there was no sign of my dear one. Mrs Stewart was as perturbed as I, and rapidly searched the house. When it was clear she was nowhere inside we went outside.

By now I was fearing she had been seized by a walking fever, the sort I have seen in Spain, where a man stumbles from his bed unaware of where he is and wanders away. We searched the garden and I sent maids into the churchyard next door. I headed down to the foot of the garden where there is a lane just beyond the hedge.

There I stumbled upon her. I was not prepared for the

sight of her small body floating in the reeds of the pond. It hardly seemed real. May God have mercy on her soul! She must have fallen in while walking in the garden. She was still only dressed in her nightgown. I need not distress you further with this account. My dear one is gone, that is all that matters. God has seen fit to take her into his fold. If I have one regret it is that I still believe the entity that calls itself Mantle and lingers in my daughter's room was responsible in some manner for this tragedy. How can I know that? The answer is I do not, but I have senses beyond my logical mind and I feel the spirit's presence in the house. You have heard enough of this, I know, and you tire now of this missive. I apologise. I hope my next letter might be full of better news. God Bless you All.

Yours Truly

J. Stewart

☐

17 – Penshurst, Kent 1554

John Dudley the younger is dying. He lies in a soft bed at his friend Henry Sidney's house and contemplates the cruel hand fate has dealt him. He has been out of the Tower for three days, but he has been sick some time. His body aches and he craves water for a thirst he cannot quench. Sweat constantly wets his brow and his breaths come in rasps. It has been this way since the ordeal of the Tower. Imprisoned and forced to stand by while his father and brother were executed, John has suffered hardest of them all. Confinement sickened him, even though he insisted on occasionally walking out on the leads, being crazed for want of air. Queen Mary might not have ordered his execution, but it seems his time detained has weakened him gravely and the false monarch will claim another Dudley life yet.

Still, being sick has earned his family some grace. His mother, Jane, Duchess of Northumberland has worked tirelessly to have John and his brothers released. John is now the Second Earl of Warwick, inheriting his father's title, but he has only been allowed three days of life to enjoy this title in freedom. At least Robert, Ambrose and Henry are free too. Mary granted them mercy on account of their elder brother's sickness.

With sticky eyes, crusted with feverish sleep, John looks over at his forlorn younger brother Robert. Robert perches on a stool, looking drawn himself. Has ever a family suffered so? John wants to reach out to him, but he has no strength left, instead he just looks. He thanks God that at least this slow death has saved the lives of two of his siblings.

Ambrose is by the window. John cannot see him, but he

hears his feet shuffling. He wonders where his mother went, but then thinks it does not matter. She should not see another son die. He thinks of Anne, his wife, of that fine day four years ago when they were wed with much pomp and ceremony, supposedly to unite the Dudleys and the Seymours. But Anne's father is dead, his execution manoeuvred by John Dudley's father, and now he is dead too. Both their fathers have been casualties to the game of royal politics.

For a moment he drifts into a strange sleep and thinks of Anne; pretty and delicate she has been a reasonable wife, though never has their marriage been loving or simple. She has strange whims and moods; can suddenly be whipped into a frenzy over nothing and, despite his efforts, she has not borne him a child. Oddly that turns his mind to Robert, who too has failed to sire an heir with the fair Amy Robsart. Perhaps, he thinks, there is more to this sickness in the Dudley line than meets the eye?

A shivering sensation racks his body and he opens his eyes to see the concerned face of Robert. His body stills, he rests back on the pillows propping him up.

"Tell me, what is the day?" he has asked this three times, he wants to know every time he wakes in case he has slept yet more precious hours of his life away.

"The twenty-first day of October," Robert tells him gently. "Rest, brother."

"Talk to me. How is Elizabeth?"

Robert glances at Ambrose. His brother refers to the forgotten princess, the woman whose name had been carried as a banner by the Wyatt rebels.

"You know all we do. She is safe, free from the Tower."

John's eyes close again.

"Good. I think she shall be queen one day."

Now Robert laughs.

"Truly? She has more chance of being king! Mary might be old and as plain as a palfrey, but she is determined to produce an heir and from what I hear her Spanish husband is game enough for the opportunity to try."

"Though I suspect he would prefer fairer, fitter game," Ambrose smirks.

"Do you think Anne is well?" John asks randomly, his thoughts wandering. "She has been odd lately. Sometimes I fear for her..."

A breath rattles in his throat.

"Stay close brother," Robert pleads in his ear, but John is gazing beyond him.

Life has run its course in his body.

He is yet another sacrifice on the Altar of Queen Mary, a flesh and blood payment for the safety of his kin. So be it.

John Dudley's body relaxes.

John Dudley dies.

18 – London 1555

It is a strange feeling to be pardoned by the woman he has come to loathe and hate. In his court finery Robert stands near a wall and breathes in the subtle scents of spring. Distantly a child screams in play and his mind is lost for a moment. Amy finds him. Presses her hands onto his chest.

"I am sorry," she rests her head on his doublet and he places a hand on her hair, what little is not covered by her headdress.

Today his life began again, while far away his mother died. Jane has been granted her dying wish, to see her sons pardoned, but he can't help but feel deeply bereft by the losses that have marked his life. In less than a year both his parents and two brothers, not to mention the strangely appealing Jane Grey, have been snatched from his family. What does he have to show for their parting? He has danced at court, even taken part with Ambrose at a tournament, but he knows he is distrusted.

"Will it always be like this?" Amy asks, muffled by his clothing.

"Perhaps," Robert answers carelessly and feels her stiffen. "No, my love, things must change. Mary shall not be queen forever."

Amy looks up. Her heart-shaped face, rustic to some at court, still sparks a beat of excitement within him when he sees it. She touches his chin where a beard has replaced the smooth skin of his youth.

"I wish it was over. I wish Mary would see you had nothing to do with Wyatt."

"She sees that," Robert sighs. "What concerns her is

how much I am my father's son. How much do I despise her Spanish husband? She asks herself, and she is right to do so."

"But she could ask that of most nobles at court!"

"Yes, but none of them tried to prise the crown from her grasp and put a slip of a girl in her place."

"Poor Jane," Amy looks away. The two girls were not so far off in age.

Robert stares up into the blue sky where grey clouds are looming.

"Mary wants me out of the court during her confinement."

Amy pulls a face. It has become noticeable that Mary is with child, she crows about it indiscreetly.

"That is months away," Amy shrugs.

He senses her fear. Though he is pardoned, he is not in favour, and the old palace he used to play caretaker to has been handed over to someone else. Now with his mother dead, and an Attainder still hanging over his and Ambrose's head, the queen can confiscate the property his mother willed to him and his brothers. Robert is feeling the pinch of destitution.

"There is a rumour that Mary will allow Ambrose to inherit after all."

Amy looks sceptical.

"Yes, it is a rare generosity on her part, even exceptional. But my sources are certain that is how she now feels and Ambrose was always good at appealing to people. He has a fine charm."

"He can be coarse," Amy interrupts. "Not like you, you know how to speak with a lady."

Robert grins.

"Maybe I do. But Ambrose knows how to speak with the queen's male advisors," he laughs. "Besides, he never was so embroiled in my father's plots."

In an instant despair engulfs Robert and the amusement is gone.

"Something will come," Amy says, though her commitment to the statement is hollow. "I am sure if I spoke with mother..."

"Your father bequeathed his estate to your mother on his death, we could not ask her to relinquish that right," Robert pulls away from her, Amy grabs his arm.

"But if I ask..."

"No!" Robert snaps. "I have my pride!"

He glares at her, but she is not afraid of him. After a moment she lets his arm drop and glares back.

"Are we to be homeless then?"

"I shall find some way..." Robert turns aside. "Phillip is keen to have me accompany his entourage to the Continent. I think he is beginning to trust me."

"When?" Amy has a new urgency in her voice. "I have only just got you back."

"Later this year," Robert turns back to her, anger makes way for appeasement. "It will do us both good to have his favour. I shall ensure you are safe while I am gone."

Amy shakes her head. Knows this is how it is, how it always will be with a husband at court.

"I shall see Ambrose. We shall arrange something," he takes her hand and kisses it delicately. "Do what you can Amy, befriend everyone, but never trust them. Earn yourself a place."

Amy's eyes take on a startled expression. He knows how she hates court life.

"Try at least. For me. For us," he reaches in and kisses her lips. "I must go. If Phillip is genuine about including me in his entourage I need to show I am willing."

Reluctantly he lets slip her hand and studies her pretty face.

"Soon Amy. Soon everything will be well again."

Then he is gone, and so is the spring sunshine.

⬡

19 – The Diary of Reverend William Mantle June 1786

My first son is born. William Mantle is a red-faced creature who screams and screams. He has his father's nose and his mother's dark eyes. I was fit enough to baptise him myself. He yelled at me for dousing him in water. He is a fighter, as one must be in this world. I am delighted that my brood grows despite my own misfortunes of late.

My bones heal, but nothing seems to staunch the pain in my limbs, especially my arm and ankle. Just raising William in my arms was agony, and standing for more than a moment leaves me trembling. I come back to my bed and I rest myself on the edge and feel almost faint from it. My opium is my only solace; it dulls the tremors and brings me, for a time at least, to a place of contentment and happiness. I am managing my services with this small aid, but it seems each passing day I need it more often to ease my body.

No matter. The doctor tells me it shall cause no ill and that I might take it as often as I wish. I am up to three grains a day, which is truly a fortune for a humble curate, but I have sacrificed my wine and, God willing, this shall only be temporary.

Besides, the opium has had an effect I could not foresee. I do not care to understand what has been happening these last months within my household. All I know is that since my misfortune I have been visited on more than one occasion by a creature I can only describe as an angel. I was locked in a fever for days after the assault and from them on I would get regular periods of debilitation, when my body seemed to burn and shiver. Those were the times – when I lay in my bed too sick to weep even in despair – that she appeared to me, rested a hand on my brow and cooled my tortured body.

Dreams, you cry! Delusions! I told myself the same. But my physician would come and remark I was much improved since he last saw me, almost remarkably so. He believed me at death's door more than once when I made a spontaneous recovery. Only I knew the one thing that had occurred between his visits was the cool touch of an angel's hand on my brow.

I turned to my Bible and read through the stories of angels being sent from God as messengers. Surely this is what she is? I turned next to other books I had about, old ecclesiastical texts and philosophical books I acquired during my days of study at Cambridge. All confirm my interpretation. There is no scientific evidence for recurring delusions which can heal a man! But much evidence for the kindly intervention of angels and spirits in the workings of man. I have read of a case in Russia where a woman saw an angel several nights in a row which told her there would soon be a great disaster and she must prepare for it. She was uncertain, as I was, but after some time was convinced enough to do what the angel said. He told her to make blankets and save what food and water she could. He had her stockpile wood and all manner of other things. Her neighbours thought her feeble-minded. She would have been cast into an asylum except she proved no harm to anyone. Then one night there was a dreadful accident in the mountains nearby, an avalanche that buried many alive, including children. Men with shovels and dogs dug for them, and the victims were hauled from the freezing snow close to death. The only house near to the disaster was the old woman's cottage, so they bore them there. Even so, they were bound to die for they needed warmth and sustenance and a lowly cottager could not provide that – except the woman could! She had been stockpiling as the angel had said and now she used all her wood and blankets and food and water to save the lives of dozens of people. The angel never came to her again, and the villagers recognised her as a true miracle worker.

Can any of us blame them for their scepticism of the woman? Would I not have sighed and said "What a dear lady, such a shame about her delusions"? I start to see a path forming before me. My angel is here and has approached me with great care and delicacy so as to win me over slowly. She has yet to ask anything of me, but I know she shall, I know she has a plan for me. God has given me this opportunity as I prayed for and now I can either turn away from him or listen with an open heart.

My angel calls herself Amy. She comes the clearest when I take a grain of opium and lie back on the bed to let it work into my system. Then a calm descends upon me and she emerges from the shadows. I have concluded the drug makes me most receptive to her presence; it enables my mind to relax and sense her. She uses these moments wisely and does not rush our conversations. Indeed, it has taken many weeks for me to piece together what little I know of her. Sometimes she speaks in riddles, or her words are not ones I understand. She is very patient and forgiving of her slow pupil.

She will not talk of death, but she loves to speak of life – of the life she had before her death. She mentions a garden full of trees that she remembers from her childhood and a large dog called Hodge which was always at her side until its death one winter. Her father was a farmer, (that much I discern) but wealthy, and she talks quite knowledgeably of sheep and cattle. She thought she would marry another gentleman farmer, but she did not.

Amy talks of a manor house not so far from here. Syderstone manor. It should have been her home but it fell into ruin. She saw it only once and can barely remember it. When she died she had a strange urge, not yet realising she was actually dead, to go and see it. She describes the moment feeling as if she had just got up and decided to leave the house to go for a walk. Only she got up from her body, not her bed.

She left the house she had been in and strode out across the meadows. Within her she just knew the direction she had to go to find this particular house. So she walked, not noting the time and never aware of what occurred when they found her poor cold body.

She came across the manor and this was where things grew confusing. She knew the house in her earthly life was ruins, but in her spectral form she saw a standing house, grand as anything, nestled in the grass and with a pillar of smoke coming from the chimney. She approached and, to her surprise, the door opened and she stepped in feeling welcomed by something or someone invisible. She says no more on this subject. I tried to press her but she merely smiled. I am not sure what caused her to leave that beautiful manor, though I can only think it was by force, for I doubt she left willingly. The little I have discerned alludes to her wandering for many years as a lost soul before stumbling onto my humble home. Here she felt safe and welcome again, she also felt needed.

I asked her why she had not flown up to Heaven as the Bible tells us we all will? Amy was uncertain, she considered a long time, so long I thought she would vanish without answering – for she regularly vanishes mid-sentence. Then she turned to me with a strange smile.

"I still have much to do here," she said. "Once it is done, then I shall go."

I want to ask her so much, but she is elusive. I cannot get her to talk of family, of whether she had a husband or children, or of what her life consisted of before her death. I believe she is very sad and that some repentance, or task, is due before she can concede her soul to Heaven. She will not discuss that further.

Lately she has persisted in standing by the window and staring down the garden. Her brow is furrowed and I think she is distressed. She is, she says, but she will not explain why. Her eyes watch that old pond at the bottom of the garden as though she expects a monster to rise from it.

"How well do you feel?" she asks every time she comes.

I always say better or stronger, because I aim to please her. Whether she knows I am lying, whether she sees my trembling limbs and my gasps of pain, I cannot say, for who knows what a spirit may do?

"I will tell you soon," she says.

"Tell me what?" I ask.

Her smile is the only reply, but I understand. She intends to tell me soon what she has planned for me, what my great task is. Like the woman in Russia I shall be set a challenge, one that may cause me ridicule or distrust from my parishioners. I shall do it nonetheless. I trust in God's will for me. Perhaps my name will be remembered for these efforts, but I must not seek fame. It is enough to serve Him and serve well. Thank you God for bringing me through my crisis and offering me another chance to do your will. I shall take my time and think carefully of every action. Tomorrow is another Sunday, and perhaps tomorrow she will finally tell me what my mission is.

20 – Syderstone, Norfolk 1955

Fourdrinier knew how impolite he was being descending unannounced on an old man in the late evening. But his mind was whirring from what he had found in the archives and he needed to discuss it with someone and, in a strange way, it only seemed appropriate that that person should be the old antiquarian who had opened his eyes; Donald Steward.

He arrived at the old rectory out of breath, propping his bike against the garden wall with such haste that it clattered to the ground as soon as he left it. He had scrawled down everything in John Stewart's letters with a speed that had made the archivist look up unpleasantly at him. The words had startled him, how could they not? John Stewart, in every other regard a rational man of the cloth, believed a ghost was haunting his property, a ghost that was fixated around one room. Fourdrinier could still not quite bring himself to believe in the reality of such a thing. It defied every rational bone in his body, but he couldn't deny it either. John Stewart had summoned other clergymen to help him. He said so in his letters. He had insisted to his sister that the matter was true and clearly the sister had felt strongly enough on the subject to rebuke him.

Fourdrinier was strangely excited. He could not explain it. Perhaps it was the discovery of something no sensible clergyman would admit to believing in. Perhaps it was just the unravelling of the mystery including the odd death of Margaret Stewart. There had been no mention on her headstone or in the parish records that she had drowned. Certainly it seemed to have been kept hushed from the village, for that piece of gossip would have lasted, along with the legend of the ghost.

Fourdrinier paused at the back door to catch his breath. He could see a light burning in the kitchen, the curtains were not drawn and deep in the house he thought he heard the lulling hum of a radio programme playing. He rapped on the door, hoping he wouldn't give Donald a heart attack by appearing like this.

The radio droned on. The evening darkened so the light from the kitchen window illuminated an old hydrangea with an orange glow, but no one came to the door. He knocked again, letting the old brass knocker, shaped like a deformed horse's head, clatter on the wood. He was impatient, he realised, almost bouncing with the need to talk to someone. He had to explain and, just perhaps, he had to gasp out how he was coming to believe in the things Nancy and his aunt were saying. He still did not have an explanation for the shot of electricity that had hurt Maud Talbot, though his memory of the moment was vivid. He could have sworn it came from the direction of the window, where there was no socket or lamp that could have fused and emitted it. Not that he was pinning it to the supernatural, not yet anyway. But there was too much else going on to completely ignore his instincts, or the way his hackles lifted whenever he thought of Syderstone rectory.

Still there was no answer. He rapped again and for longer. Perhaps the old boy had fallen asleep. Inside the radio programme concluded and there was silence. Fourdrinier stood on the doorstep and listened to the wind moving the grass and a robin singing a final song before retreating to its roost.

And something else.

He stood very still and concentrated on the sounds around him. The world whispered; sighing as it drifted into sleep. He shut out the sounds of the garden, listened beyond the rustle of leaves and heard the sound again, ever so faintly.

It sounded distinctly like a moan.

Fourdrinier briefly recalled the story in the newspaper about the ghost. The report that someone passing had heard moans coming from the rectory as though someone was ill and dying. A superstitious man, Fourdrinier thought to himself, would leave now. He was not superstitious and if he heard a moan, especially a faint moan, he was more inclined to think a living person was in distress than a spirit one. He leaned his ear against the door and listened hard, but there was nothing but silence.

Fourdrinier wasn't sure what to make of the matter. Donald Steward's home showed all the signs of someone being there, but no one answered his knocks and there had distinctly been a moan. Hadn't there? He walked to the kitchen window and peered in. The room showed all the usual indications of evening domesticity. A frying pan was waiting in the sink to be washed and several wet tea towels were hanging from the warm range and steaming. Most conclusive of all, on the table was a portion of fried bread, spam and eggs, barely eaten, as though someone had started them and then hastily put down their knife and fork. In fact, there was a chunk of fried bread still caught on the fork prongs and dripping yellow egg yolk. Fourdrinier was worried. Something had disturbed Donald during his dinner only moments before the reverend's arrival and now he was failing to answer the door.

Fourdrinier hurried back to the doorstep and tried the latch, trusting to his luck that Donald followed the country custom of never locking his doors. That was indeed the case. The door swung inwards into the pitch dark hall.

"Donald?" Fourdrinier called out. He hesitated slightly in the dark, trying to recall the layout of the house. "Donald, are you about?"

The moan this time was marginally louder. Fourdrinier headed through the far doorway into the main hall which was only lit by the light coming from the living room and kitchen on the right. He turned that way first, took a pace forward and then checked himself. He turned around to face the left side of the hall, almost completely dark, and saw Donald instantly.

Donald Steward was lying sprawled face down at the foot of the stairs, his legs still resting on the steps, while his torso and head were spread out on the hall carpet.

"Donald!" Fourdrinier ran forward and went to his knees beside the old man.

He heard him groan helplessly into the carpet. Though the dark hid a lot, it was just possible to see a puddle of blood seeping from underneath Donald Steward's forehead.

"What happened?" Fourdrinier asked, desperate to know if the man was actually conscious. "Do you have a telephone?"

Donald groaned again, it seemed the only sound he was capable of making. Fourdrinier glanced about the hallway looking for a phone. When he saw none he headed to the living room and searched there. Among the clutter of antiques and ornaments he saw a pile of notes laid out on the sofa that distracted him for an instant, before he jumped back to his task. He went into the kitchen but there was no sign of a telephone, finally his search took him into a back hallway, oddly at an angle to a pantry, and there was a large, brown Bakelite phone sitting on a battered side table. He asked the operator to put him through to the hospital as speedily as she could. A vision was coming back into his mind of a similar incident many years ago when he and his wife had called upon an elderly parishioner and found her collapsed in her living room. In the time it had taken to realise she needed an ambulance and to summon one, the poor old woman had died. Even for a religious man it had been stunning and upsetting. Fourdrinier prayed that this time would be different.

"Hello, Norfolk and Norwich General Hospital."

"Hello, I have an elderly man who appears to have fallen down a staircase. He has a head injury and I need an ambulance. Yes, at once. I am at the old Syderstone Rectory, right next to Syderstone church. Thank you."

Fourdrinier replaced the receiver and hurried back to Donald Steward. He was relieved to see Donald trying to push himself up from the floor.

"I think you should stay put," Fourdrinier said hastily. He lowered himself to the ground, grimacing at the griping of his knees. "You've had a bad fall, Donald, and there is an ambulance on the way."

Donald had been trying to negotiate his arms and hands into a position where he could thrust himself off the floor, but the manoeuvre was proving too complicated for his bruised brain.

"Stay still," Fourdrinier commanded and the hands went still.

"Who... iss... that?" Donald's voice was frail.

"Reverend Fourdrinier, I called before if you recollect. I had come tonight to speak with you again."

There was silence as this insight was absorbed.

"...bout the ghost?" Donald's voice faded in and out like a badly tuned radio programme.

"Yes, that's right. At least I was asking about the legend. You let me borrow William Mantle's diary from you."

"...ny good?"

Fourdrinier took a moment to decipher the question.

"I've only read a portion, but it is interesting, no doubt about that. Mantle was a curious chap, tried his hardest to do his best, or so it seems."

"Shorry...."

"For what?"

"...can't make 'ou a 'up of tea."

Fourdrinier chuckled at the joke. He was feeling more confident by the moment that Donald would be all right.

"What happened? Did you slip?"

"Pussshed."

Fourdrinier registered the single word with a strange sensation of nausea.

"I wondered if there had been an intruder. Long gone now I imagine, at least I've seen no-one while I've been about, nor heard anything."

"Shtill here..." Donald seemed to try to laugh. "Always here."

The sensation of nausea settled in the pit of Fourdrinier's stomach and threatened to force up his supper. He looked up the staircase, suddenly nervous.

"Burglars these days are getting so bold," His voice sounded like it was coming from someone else, someone who was trying to comfort the uneasy priest.

"Don't be shtupid... Fourdrinier!" Donald coughed suddenly and his body twitched unpleasantly. "No burglar!"

Fourdrinier was relieved to hear the distant sirens of an ambulance; it must have been somewhere nearby to arrive so quickly. It saved him from probing the meaning of Donald's words, even if he did have a nasty idea what he was trying to imply.

"I think that is your ride. I shall go flag them down."

Fourdrinier hurried to the top of the garden where the gate led onto the road and stood on the path waving at a large cream van rumbling down the road with blue lights flashing. It pulled up to the curb and the driver jumped out.

"You call an ambulance?"

"Yes."

Another man jumped out the passenger side and started to open the back of the ambulance. He manhandled a stretcher out.

"Head injury?"

"Yes, there may be other injuries too. He has tumbled down the stairs."

The ambulance men followed him up the garden to the back door.

"You out doing parish relief work, vicar?" the driver said, having noted the white dog collar around Fourdrinier's neck.

"Just visiting, actually."

"This ain't your rectory then?"

"Oh no, this cottage has not been church property for many years."

"Good job you came by then," the driver seemed quite chipper as he went into the house and found Donald.

"Any chance of more light?"

Fourdrinier cursed himself for not thinking of it sooner. With the race for the telephone and the confusion of the moment, his eyes had adjusted to the dark and he had forgotten about switching on more lights. He hurried now to find a light switch and illuminate the hall. He instantly wished he hadn't. What had looked a very minor puddle of blood in the dark, seemed to suddenly double into an unpleasant pool of scarlet in the bright light. He gave a sharp gasp.

"Can you tell me your name?" the ambulance driver was asking Donald.

"Donald Shteward."

"Now, Donald, we are going to move you onto the stretcher."

Fourdrinier grimaced as Donald was untangled from the stairs and deposited on the old brown stretcher. Though the men were clearly being as careful as they could, there was no getting around the fact they had to pull and twist the poor man to negotiate him out of the tight hall. Donald moaned with each movement.

There was a brief debate between the ambulance-men whether to keep him facing down on the stretcher or to turn him over. They eventually agreed on the latter and Donald was once more shifted and pulled before the straps of the stretcher were wrapped over him.

"Can I come?" Fourdrinier asked as they were awkwardly moving out of the house.

"Sure vicar, hop in the back," the driver grinned at him. "Lucky for you and him we had a false call to the village just over. Woman thought her waters had broke, but the silly cow had fallen asleep with a glass of water in her hand.

Quite shame-faced she was."

Fourdrinier failed to enjoy the humour, though he appreciated it was probably necessary to enable the men to carry out what could be quite a grim job, especially at night. He clambered into the back of the ambulance and placed a comforting hand on Donald's.

"Everything's going to be fine," he promised.

Donald blinked slowly and seemed confused. Fourdrinier sighed and wondered why he could not have had the fortune of arriving at the rectory a few minutes earlier.

The next few hours Fourdrinier spent sat in an uncomfortable chair in the hospital waiting room. He nipped out briefly to telephone his wife and explain where he was. He described what had happened and promised to ring back when he had any news, only then realising he was out of change. By the time the hands on the clock in the waiting room were crawling to nine o'clock he knew it was going to be a long night. He sat watching the empty corridors, the odd sister wandering back and forth, thinking about what had just occurred.

Terrible accidents happened, especially to old people in old houses which were cluttered to the hilt. Really it was surprising Donald had not taken a fall before. It was just the way Donald had said so firmly 'pushed' that disturbed Fourdrinier. He was cold and tired, his stomach growled at him, hunger replacing his earlier nausea. He closed his eyes and tried to pretend he was at home in his own chair beside a warm fire. Instead his imagination conjured up the hallway in Syderstone rectory, Donald's body gone but the big red stain vivid on the carpet. He opened his eyes sharply.

"Reverend Fourdrinier?"

He looked up and saw a nurse standing in the doorway. She had the usual look so many nurses bore of sympathetic concern.

"Yes?" Fourdrinier stood.

"The doctor would like a word and then you can pay a visit on Mr Steward."

"Thank you," Fourdrinier followed her out the room, only then realising it was rather odd for him to be allowed to visit outside usual hours, even in an emergency like this. Unless things were more serious than he had first thought.

He was shown into a side room where a doctor in a long white coat was making notes on a clipboard.

"Reverend Fourdrinier?" the doctor held out his hand to shake. "I'm Dr Huxton."

"Nice to meet you," Fourdrinier said, feeling the rigours of politeness wholly unsuited to the occasion.

"I wanted to see you before I went on my rounds. I have a few questions, if you don't mind."

Fourdrinier relaxed a little.

"No, I don't mind."

"Good. Does Mr Steward have any family locally?"

Fourdrinier racked his brain.

"Not locally."

"Next of kin?"

"He has a daughter, but I don't know her name or address."

"May I ask," the doctor looked serious, "how exactly you come to know him, outside of your ecclesiastical duties."

That was easier to answer.

"I am researching the history of the clergy in Norfolk for a book, a pet project of mine. Mr Steward is an antiquarian and a keen local historian. Also he happens to live in the old Syderstone rectory. Our conversations are strictly about history. He has been good enough to lend me some original documents."

"So you don't happen to know if he has any close friends in the area?"

Fourdrinier's suspicions were rising again.

"No, I'm afraid I don't, though I was under the impression Mr Steward was something of a recluse who very rarely left his house. Why all these questions, surely you can ask him when he is feeling better?"

"That is just it, Reverend Fourdrinier," the doctor let out a professional sigh. "Mr Steward suffered a heavy contusion to the skull. At first glance it did not seem dangerous, but x-rays have shown the skull is smashed in more than one place and a fragment of bone has lodged itself in the brain. Quite frankly it is remarkable he is breathing, let alone talking to us."

Fourdrinier felt a little dizzy. He reached out for the back of a nearby chair.

"There is nothing you can do?"

"There is heavy bleeding, we have given drugs to counteract that, but the damage is done and we cannot remove the bone fragment. Not the way it is lying. We have no idea how it will continue to affect Mr Steward's brain but I am of the opinion that he has hours only."

Fourdrinier somehow managed to nod.

"I wondered why the nurse said I might visit him," Fourdrinier tried to steady himself. "If I had only been a few minutes sooner maybe I could have prevented the accident."

"Don't be too hard on yourself, if you had been a few minutes later he might never have been saved at all. At least he has a chance to say his goodbyes."

"I just stood at the door knocking," Fourdrinier was barely listening. "If I hadn't of heard him moan..."

"Perhaps you would like to see Mr Steward now? I shall have a nurse see if she can track down any details of relatives, you never know, he may have been in the hospital before and there will be something on record," the doctor moved Fourdrinier out of the room rather too eagerly, not a man who wanted to have to play at being a comforter. "He is in room 219."

Before Fourdrinier could ask anymore the doctor had bustled off and was accosting a nurse with a stack of clipboards.

Fourdrinier shook some of the shocked stupor from his body and made his way down the corridor looking for 219. He expected it to be a ward, but it was another side-room. Fourdrinier slipped in and looked at Donald lying beneath the crisp white sheets and the stiff red hospital blanket. Donald opened his eyes and looked at him.

"S'not gooood," he hissed.

"No," Fourdrinier settled in a chair beside the bed. "What a mess, Donald. This was not how I expected the evening to go. I was coming to talk to you about some letters I had found in the archives at Norwich. They were written by John Stewart."

Donald smiled.

"My letters."

"Sorry?" Fourdrinier feared his friend was confused.

"I 'ut 'em in there," Donald articulated with his hands the action of giving, his tongue and vocal cords frustrating him. "I 'ave them."

"You have them?"

"I 'ave them. G... g 'ave them."

Fourdrinier realised what he was explaining.

"Oh, I see, they were in your keeping like the diary and you donated them."

Donald smiled again.

"Have you read them?"

" 'es."

"They tell an interesting story, I wanted to discuss them with you tonight."

"No time," Donald's face fell. "No time, Foooourdrin'er."

Donald seemed to be mustering some great effort to say something. His features curled in concentration and when he spoke again he strained himself to say the words as clearly as possible.

"I was pussshed, down stairs, by the ghost."

Fourdrinier opened his mouth to speak but Donald glared at him with his eyes, instructing him not to interrupt.

"Something 'as changed. Never left 'oom before, now it can. I always look after 'ouse. Like father before me. Make sure no one gets in 'oom."

"You've been guarding the house?"

"Since 'urch sold it. Once no... re-li-gi-os man in it, real danger. Like Mar-gat Ste-art."

Fourdrinier thought back to the letters.

"Margaret Stewart slept in that room and she heard bangs. Thumps like someone hitting the wall. Her father tried to have the phenomena removed but it would not stop and then Margaret mysteriously died."

"No 'un, must enter that 'oom. So my father, grun-father swear. Evil is trapped in it," Donald looked exhausted by his efforts, he rested back on the pillows and groaned slightly.

"I shall ask a few more questions Donald, but you only need answer yes and no, do you understand."

"...es."

"You say you were pushed down the stairs?"

"...es."

"By the ghost that inhabits the room upstairs?"

"...es."

"But that 'being' has never left the room before?"

"No."

"No, as in the creature never left, or no that that statement is wrong?"

Donald flickered his eyes.

"Since Ste-art."

"It hasn't left the room since the time of the Stewarts?"

"...es"

"When the room was prevented from being used."

"...es."

"But it was there before the Stewarts?"

"...es."

Fourdrinier nodded, there was a sort of pattern emerging.

"Why did you go upstairs tonight? No, wait I shall ask

that better. Did you hear a noise upstairs?"

"...es," Donald summoned his flagging strength again. "...oom was open."

"But it shouldn't have been, because it was locked."

"...es."

"Has anything happened like this before, other than when Margaret Stewart was in the room?"

"No."

Fourdrinier had expected that, his mind was creeping back to the séance where Maud Talbot had apparently been scorched. He should have been stronger in his convictions that such dabblings could give strength to the wrong spirits, was that not why the Church had such strong views on spiritualism? Worse, had he not caused this tragedy to happen to Donald by allowing the séance which strengthened whatever was in the room?

He listened to his own thoughts and nearly baulked at the tone of them. It seemed suddenly he was a believer in ghosts, but seeing a man bleeding to death and insisting he was pushed with no human agency in sight had a tendency to make the irrational seem almost rational.

"You locked the room again?"

"...es."

"Then you went to go downstairs and were pushed?"

"...es."

It still could have been a burglar, Fourdrinier told himself. That was the logical assumption. The burglar found a locked room and investigated it, made a noise by accident and alerted Donald. He hid when the old man came upstairs to look and then pushed him down the stairs. That still didn't quite explain how Fourdrinier, arriving mere moments after the fall, could have failed to either see or hear a burglar.

"...ou don't believe me."

"I'm struggling," Fourdrinier admitted. "It is hard to take this all in. You say your family has been watching over the house, to make sure no one uses the room again?"

"...es."

"Does someone being in the room strengthen the entity somehow?"

Donald frowned.

"...on't know. Just what father said," Donald faintly smiled. "Didn't believe either."

"Why on earth is this happening in Syderstone of all places?" Fourdrinier was feeling more baffled than ever.

"...on't know."

"Look, I'm not sure how long they will let me be in here, so let's talk practical matters. Do you have any family."

"...es."

"Local?"

"No."

"A daughter?"

"...es."

"Can I find an address for her at your house?"

"...es. Ruby Brandon."

Fourdrinier carefully impressed that on his memory.

"Now, the house, what shall I do about..."

Donald suddenly started to thrash violently in the bed, he began foaming at the mouth and his eyes seemed to pop from his skull. Fourdrinier ran to the door and shouted for help. Urgent footsteps came crashing down the hallway. A sister appeared, her headdress flying out like the wings of an angel. Within moments there was another nurse and a third; the last was sent scurrying for a doctor.

Fourdrinier slumped against the doorframe and watched the women plunge into action. Donald was thrashing violently, caught in some type of seizure. It did not take a lot of imagination to assume this was the prelude to the end.

A doctor arrived – not Dr Huxton – but he was too late. Donald was still in the bed, a nurse checking his pulse and shaking her head. The doctor swung a stethoscope from his neck and listened for a heartbeat. It seemed so pointless to Fourdrinier. He turned away and looked across the corridor out of a window into a tiny, concrete courtyard. The rain was falling again and he felt momentarily concerned about his bike left scruffily on the ground outside Donald's garden. He hoped it would still be there when he returned.

The doctor distracted him.

"I'm sorry, are you a relative?"

Fourdrinier tugged his dog collar.

"A friend, but also spiritual support," that seemed a highly appropriate thing to say considering the circumstances.

"You are probably aware... well... Mr Steward has suffered a cardiac arrest, that means..."

"You don't need to spell it out, he's dead. God rest his soul."

The doctor was thrown by this bluntness.

"His next of kin should be contacted," he finally managed.

"He has a daughter. I will head back to his house in the morning and get her address for you."

"Thank you, is there anyone else?"

"Not as far as I am aware," Fourdrinier sighed. "I was just popping in to visit him."

"It is well you were. Would have been awful for him to be left lying at home. At least he was not suffering at the end."

Fourdrinier nodded, but he doubted that. Maybe physically Donald had been numbed to pain, but mentally he was fully aware of the implications his death would have and the calamity he was leaving behind. Fourdrinier had seen it in his eyes; he had been caught out by whatever thing he was trying to keep from harming the world, and all he had left to rely on was a strange, old vicar who thought he was crazy. What a way to die – troubled by the thought of what might happen in the future and blaming oneself.

"If that's everything?" Fourdrinier wanted to get out into the fresh air. The smell of the hospital corridor was suffocating him.

"Yes, I expect you want to get home. Miserable night. Good of you really to wait here all this time."

Fourdrinier gave another nod, too exhausted to ask what else any decent person could have done but wait? He wandered away, negotiating the warren of corridors towards the reception. What had happened in those last few hours? Well, for a start Fourdrinier had been shaken from his cynicism into something close to belief. He wasn't all the way there yet, far from it, but he was thinking hard and finding his logic insufficient to explain the situation he was in. He was a man of God, as such he understood the spirit world, he knew there were things that happened that one could not see, he had felt the hand of God in his life, knew it was there guiding him. So what of the opposite side? What of evil?

Fourdrinier found the reception and noted a sleepy looking fellow manning the admissions desk. He walked over.

"Do you have a phone I can use?"

The man pointed out a public telephone on the wall and Fourdrinier felt irritated beyond his usual patience.

"I came in with an ambulance. A friend was hurt in an accident. He has just died. I used my last change to call my wife earlier, and I want to make a phone call so I may somehow get home."

The sleepy man gave him an insolent shrug.

"Damn it!" Fourdrinier's normally mammoth patience was exhausted. He slammed his open hand on the counter and actually made the man jump. "I have no time for your rudeness! I am tired, I want to go home. You are a public servant and so you will help me and damn it if you want to argue about it costing you a few pence! Have you never heard about the Good Samaritan?"

"Alright!" the man blinked at him. "It's just I have my own rules to abide by."

"I want to make a phone call to get home, you can bill

me if you so wish."

"It's ok, no need to get sharp. As you are a man of the cloth and all, I'll trust you."

Fourdrinier felt like thumping the man as he attempted to give him an affable grin, as though he was performing a huge favour.

"Just don't tell the boss," the man handed over a black phone with a sheepish grin.

Grumbling under his breath, Fourdrinier picked up the receiver and took a moment to think who he was ringing. There was no point calling his wife – they had no car – he would ring Charlie. In any case, they needed to talk. The phone rang.

"Charlie? Hello, it's Fourdrinier. Look, could you come and pick me up? I'm at the Norfolk and Norwich. No, I'm fine. I'll explain when you get here. It's a bit of a story. Thank you."

He hung up the phone and looked at the fellow on the reception desk, who gave him an appeasing smile. Fourdrinier bit his tongue and moved away.

An hour later he and Charlie were slowly winding their way back to Charlie's farm. Charlie had offered to take Fourdrinier home, but the reverend wanted to go straight to Charlie's. There was a lot they needed to discuss.

"So Donald says that the spirit from the room attacked him?"

Fourdrinier was tired of questions, he wanted to shut his eyes and sleep, but there was more to come. He had yet to explain this all to his aunt and Nancy.

"That's a fine story. Scary, actually. Should we be worried do you think?"

"Dabbling, that's what they've been doing," Fourdrinier grumped. "Waking things up."

"You can't blame your aunt. This might just be a coincidence."

"Charlie, my aunt does not deal with coincidences. If something happens in her domain you can be damn sure she was firmly behind it."

"Not like you to swear, old man."

Fourdrinier sighed.

"It's been a long night."

The lights were all blazing at the farm despite it being past eleven. Maud appeared at the door when she heard the car pull in and was clearly worried. Fourdrinier got out as soon as it was possible and went to her.

"Are you well?" Maud fretted.

"I am perfectly alright. I was ministering to another poor soul."

"Well come in, quickly. Would you like some tea?"

Fourdrinier agreed he would, then excused himself to ring his wife and explain where he was. When he was done he found everyone in the front parlour waiting impatiently for him.

"I didn't like to say anything," Charlie announced as soon as Fourdrinier came through the door. "I thought it best to leave that to you."

Fourdrinier sat down heavily in an armchair and was instantly handed a cup of tea and a slice of bread and butter by Maud.

"Thank you. I do apologise for the late hour."

"Don't apologise, just explain," Ida was perched on the edge of her chair like a slightly dishevelled parrot in her Arabian style clothes. "What has been going on with you?"

"It has been quite a day," Fourdrinier was only just realising himself the strain that the events of the last few hours had had on him. "I went to visit Donald Steward who lives in the old Syderstone rectory. I found him semi-conscious on the floor having fallen down the stairs. Donald claims the entity that inhabits a room in the house pushed him down. I'm afraid he died about an hour ago."

Everyone was silent. Nancy was staring at the fire, her eyes wide as saucers. Ida was mouthing the word 'dead' as though trying to impress it on her mind. Maud just looked stunned and Charlie, already aware of the news, was clasping her hand.

"What room?" Ida finally broke the moment.

"The sealed room. Within the parsonage there is a room that is forever locked, it is the same room Margaret Stewart once slept in."

Ida went from fraught to excited.

"You solved the riddle?"

"Not exactly."

"What has this to do with Donald Steward?" Nancy interjected.

Fourdrinier prepared himself for the long explanation.

"From what I gather, the room had a strange reputation. My research today, at the Norwich archives, has shown that John Stewart, Margaret's, father was convinced the room was haunted. There was often banging in the room and something seemed to be trying to communicate. He came to the conclusion it was unfriendly, especially after trying exorcism. His daughter then began to wither away from a mystery illness. She finally appears to have drowned in the pond at the bottom of the garden while enfeebled with fever."

"Poor girl," Nancy mumbled, her wide eyes suggestive of tears.

"The room was apparently left unoccupied. Donald Steward was not in the best position to explain things to me, however, from what I understand it was felt that as long as a man of the cloth was resident at the rectory the evil that was trapped within would be prevented from causing harm, providing the haunted room went unused. But when the Church sold the property, and it risked becoming a private dwelling, Donald's grandfather was concerned and bought it. He took over the house and kept the room locked so the spirit could not escape and no one would be harmed. Finally he passed it to his son with the proviso that the room remain locked. Donald at first didn't take this seriously when told by his father, but apparently a night or two in the place changed his mind."

"From what you are saying this... evil should be permanently trapped in that room?" Maud asked.

"Yes."

"But tonight it attacked Donald?"

"It has not emerged from the room since Margaret Stewart was living there. Until tonight. Something gave it the strength to overcome the boundaries of its lair and attack Donald. Something I expect we did."

His gaze went to Nancy and she actually shrank from him.

"The séance was necessary, how else were we to contact Margaret?" Ida stepped in.

"Perhaps we should have left alone?"

"And let the soul of a child live in perpetual torment? Shame on you Norman!" Ida crossed her arms. "We weren't to know this would happen."

"Wait," Maud had gone icily pale, "that spark in the room that hit me, was that caused by... this thing?"

"It cannot really harm us," Ida assured her.

"But it harmed Donald!"

"Before a séance Nancy puts up protective barriers and we all pray for God's protection. Norman will tell you, the battle between Good and Evil is an unequal match with the balance of favour falling on the side of Good."

"We still need to be careful," Fourdrinier's voice had almost shrunk to a whisper, but everyone heard him.

"I am intrigued Norman. Do you believe now?"

Fourdrinier hesitated.

"Not precisely."

"Then, what must we be careful of?"

"I am prepared to accept something very odd has happened here, and on a spiritual level I am prepared to believe there may be more going on than rational thinking can explain."

"A lot of words to say nothing," Ida snorted. "You believe even if you won't admit it. Else you would not be here telling us. You would have chalked it up as a sad accident and gone home. But you don't need to say any more, your actions speak louder than your words."

"What do we do Fourdrinier?" Charlie suddenly spoke out and for a moment Fourdrinier felt as though the room had narrowed to just the two of them. He looked at his old friend, his confidant and his comrade in arms.

"No more nonsense, we have to be practical and behave as the men we are. If there is a..." Fourdrinier held the words uneasily on his tongue, " ...a demonic presence in Syderstone, then it is our duty to subdue and remove it."

"You forget, I'm not a curate anymore."

"But you once were. You will need to find a way to conquer your doubts and have faith in God. Else I think this thing will ensnare you. Do you understand?"

"I do, but it is not that simple."

"You must make it so."

Charlie nodded, but Fourdrinier could not tell if that meant he was agreeing or merely could not be bothered to argue further.

"Our priority is to investigate the house," Fourdrinier continued. "Beyond that we must continue research into who came before us and what they did, so as to avoid their mistakes. I must also explore the spiritual side of matters, look into the topic from a theological perspective."

"Evil does not just appear from nowhere," it was only the second time Nancy had spoken, her voice was firm though she was still clearly shaken. "It was drawn here for some reason. Some event brought it into existence."

"How do you know that?" Fourdrinier asked.

"Nancy has spent much time studying this topic," Ida elaborated. "We do not come at this as naively as you imagine."

She and her nephew exchanged looks.

"My point is, to truly root out this spirit, you must do more than merely exorcise it. That will only delay the problem for a future generation," Nancy was speaking slowly, determined for them to listen to every word. "You must find the source and that will give you the key to ridding us of this demon."

Fourdrinier realised how bizarre the conversation he was involved in was becoming.

"Of course, Donald might have been surprised by a burglar and we are exciting ourselves for nothing," he tried to smile, but no one was with him, nor were his own convictions. "Tomorrow I will go to the house and start putting things in order. Donald's daughter needs to be contacted."

"I will come with you," Charlie said instantly. Fourdrinier was rather glad he had, he had not relished going alone.

"Will you stay the night here?" Maud asked. "It is getting so late and at least then you can start early."

Fourdrinier sensed she wanted his presence in the house, perhaps it brought her comfort.

"If it is no bother..."

"No bother and I would rather that than have you and Charlie on the roads at this time of night. I'll pull out the old camp bed," Maud was up and bustling away. She looked more composed now she had a task to do.

Fourdrinier finished his cup of tea as the others dispersed, Nancy hugging herself as she went to find her bed, Charlie giving him a nod and masking a yawn.

"Got to be up in a few hours milking cows," he said as an apology.

Ida ended up sitting alone with her nephew. For an instant he had almost forgotten she was there, she was so quiet, completely unlike her usually vibrant and noisy self. He was close to dozing off when she spoke.

"You need to be careful, Norman. Promise me."

Fourdrinier put down his tea cup and reached out for her hand. It was very cold.

"Don't worry."

"I won't as long as I know you are taking this seriously. If you do not, I fear you will not realise the dangers you are facing."

"Don't I sound like I am taking this seriously?"

"Better than you were, but not enough," Ida clasped her other hand over his. "I still believe that this was meant to be. We were directed to this moment, brought together in this way because we were the only ones who could solve this problem."

Fourdrinier was uncomfortable with her earnestness.

"What does God say about demons, Norman?"

"He doesn't much like them."

"There used to be all that trouble about witches."

"That was centuries ago and sparked by King James I's own paranoia. A witch is merely an old woman without friends."

"No, more recently than that. There was that woman during the war. Predicted attacks on shipping, I think. They prosecuted her for it. Said maybe she was giving secrets to the Nazis, but even so they got her under the Witchcraft Act."

"Yes," Fourdrinier said noncommittally.

"I mean, if even the government can consider such a thing as witchcraft, then surely a man of God should?"

Fourdrinier rubbed her hand gently.

"I will try my best."

"I hope that is enough," Ida pulled away her hands and left him alone in the parlour.

⬚

21 – England 1556/1557

Robert Dudley is in good grace with the royal household. Though it might have caused consternation to his father, he has no qualms in befriending the Spanish associates of his new king and even finds himself liking them. Secretly, however, he maintains favour with the exiled princess Elizabeth. It is fortuitous that he is able to house his wife at Throcking with Elizabeth not far away, and he has even gifted the princess money and books.

Ambrose has spared him the indignity of being penniless. He was generous enough to give Robert the house their late mother had left him, in return for Robert paying off her debts. Even so Robert is rarely there, travelling as he must to Spain and France, and he sees his wife even less frequently. She spends her time at different residences, often with family friends to alleviate the loneliness. There is no time to be Robert Dudley's wife, not when he is so busy. They have been married half a decade, yet there are no children to show for their union. Sometimes Amy wonders if there ever shall be, her husband's visits are so infrequent she begins to forget him and moulds her life around herself. In her darkest moments she wonders if he is as lonely as her, or whether the gypsy has found female company to keep him warm at nights.

Amy's misery is deepened by the loss of her mother. Apoplexy snatched the old woman from life and cast Amy loosely into the world. Syderstone is now hers and Robert almost immediately started selling off portions and mortgaging the rest to pay off his ever increasing debts.

Even more worrying is Robert's talk of going on the king's planned campaign to St Quentin, France. He has re-mortgaged parts of his estate to raise a company of men, but only five have come to his muster. In the meantime he is appointed Master of the Ordnance to the Earl of Pembroke; it is an impressive role for one so young but it does not please Amy. She is simply scared.

Her one love, who she has so rarely seen these last years, whose life hung in the balance in the Tower, now goes to fight once again. She cannot complain for is this not how many wives must suffer? But still she aches inside.

Robert leaves with 6,000 men to fight the everlasting feud with the French. Amy does not see him off. She is sickening again, as she has before, and vainly she hopes this is a good sign; an assurance that her prayers have been answered and Robert has a reason to come home alive.

On the French battlefield the fighting is fierce and grim. St Quentin is laid to siege. Robert has memories of those days so long ago when his father laid siege to the enemy-held city of Norwich. That day he was charging down a rebel, since then he has been a rebel himself. Was it on such a faint, far away day he picked human flesh from his helmet and tried to erase the vision of a pretty Norfolk girl from his mind?

A cry goes up. There is a rush. Robert is ready for the fight; Ambrose is to one side of him, his younger brother Henry is on the other. Ambrose is alive with battle fever, ebullient, joyful. Henry hesitates.

"Damn horse's bridle is loose!"

Robert turns to tell him to hurry up, just as the cannon ball collides with Lord Henry and his horse. Man and beast explode. Parts of them scatter the ground. Henry is dead before he even knows it. Before his very eyes Robert has seen yet another brother die. He turns his horse and charges headlong into the fighting. It is 27 September 1557.

Robert does return home, but not to a pregnant wife. Amy is as maidenly as ever. She greets him, but he is stiff in her arms. He kisses her hair, but how can a man open his heart when he has witnessed such horrors?

Henry's sacrifice has earned the Dudley's one last piece of royal grace. Mary removes their Attainders, meaning they can now inherit the last of their family property. But times are changing again. Mary's pregnancy, for which Robert was banished from court, never came to anything and Phillip has turned to campaigning to part himself from his queen. Now Mary has suggested she is pregnant once more, but the court does not hold its breath. In fact Mary seems to grow weak and ill. Her half-sister, Elizabeth, the forgotten princess, has been restored to favour and quietly loiters at the court. It is known, according to her father's legacy, that she shall be next in line to the throne. The country holds its breath. The ill-fated reign of Mary, that saw a foreign prince commanding the country and a persecution of Protestants, might be finally coming to an end. Robert waits too. He has courted and flattered Elizabeth since she was a girl. He has given her money and acted as her friend and protector. Now, finally, his game of politics might be succeeding. But he is so very tired with being at the whim of others, so tired of the death threat the ruling elite hold over him. He wonders, even as he holds Amy, who the princess Elizabeth has thought to marry. If only... if only... Yet he is married and despite his ambition he loves Amy. It is just a thought. But Ambrose remains single and Amy has yet to bear him an heir. To compete with his own brother... To abandon his wife... Yet... To be King!

22 – Syderstone, Norfolk 1955

Fourdrinier held the door open for Charlie.

"He was lying just around the corner."

They entered the parsonage uneasily. Fourdrinier felt there was a strange heaviness in the air, like the moments before a thunder storm. Charlie edged into the hallway and looked a little green as he faced the patch of blood on the carpet.

"I've got to find the daughter's address," Fourdrinier moved passed Charlie, being very careful not to look at the spot where Donald had fallen.

Charlie was casting his eyes up the staircase.

"It's an awkward fall, you know, Fourdrinier. Down a dog-leg."

"Yes, well I wasn't really thinking along those lines."

Fourdrinier had entered the dining room which seemed to double as a sort of office. Charlie joined him briefly then wandered into the living room. Fourdrinier was still shaken from the night before. His head ached over his temples and his heart would inexplicably start pounding every once in a while. Sometimes a sensation of panic almost overwhelmed him as his mind flicked back to the previous evening. Even as he moved around the dining room, examining papers, opening cupboards and drawers, he was aware that he was also listening, trying to hear the slightest sound out of place, particularly from the floor above. He was frightened, he hardly dare admit it to himself, but it was true.

He picked up a book that looked well-worn and flicked through a few pages. It was a notebook and he scanned the entries, trying to pick apart Donald's spiderish handwriting.

Wednesday 10th Heard footsteps

Thursday 11th Ditto

Friday 12th Thought heard a moan, also footsteps about 10pm

The notebook recorded Donald's experiences within the house. Fourdrinier flicked back to the front and realised it had not been begun by Donald, but by his grandfather. The ink on the very first few pages was brown with age and was clearly written by a less literate hand. Fourdrinier noted the date. The book had been begun the same year John Stewart left the parish. He now flicked to the very end and found the last few entries. Donald had been thorough in his catalogue and at a glimpse the phenomena in the house had consisted of no more than footsteps and moans, with occasional bangs that may or may not have been paranormal, but over the last week it had changed.

Sunday 25th Heard door handle rattle upstairs, went to look, no sign of anyone. Removed key.

Monday 26th Visited by Reverend Fourdrinier. Showed him room. Afterwards terrible crashing sounds like furniture being moved upstairs in sealed room.

Tuesday 27th House feels wrong. Small electrical shocks are coming from anything metal, door handles, etc, such as before thunder and lightning. Footsteps, and door handle rattled again.

Wednesday 28th Found key in lock of room, though I know I left it in my bedside table drawer. Heard laughter.

Thursday 29th More laughter. Lots of bangs. Thought someone called my name. Found room unlocked but door not open.

There was no entry for Friday, but then poor Donald had been lying on the floor in the hall and hadn't had time to write it.

Fourdrinier pulled himself out a chair and sat down heavily. The notebook was revealing, but also frightening. Something had definitely changed and Fourdrinier knew what that was. His aunt and Nancy had a lot to answer for, not least Donald's life.

"Fourdrinier, have you seen these?"

Fourdrinier jumped at the sound of his name. Charlie was in the doorway holding a small bundle of loose papers. They seemed familiar.

"I saw those lying on the sofa in the living room last night. What are they?"

"Notes, mainly on the history of this property," Charlie joined him at the table and spread the papers before him. "Mr Steward was tracing the history of the house. He had gotten as far back as 1558 when it was being used as a farmhouse. Seems it only fell into the Church's hands in the eighteenth century. He also made notes on its former occupants. They are not very insightful, but he has written here that his great great aunt was Phoebe Steward, who lived in this house in the 1780s and 1790s and knew the Reverend William Mantle. He was Stewart's forerunner and apparently a number of people blamed him for being the ghost here."

Fourdrinier's ears had pricked up. He had recognised the name at once, he had read about Phoebe very briefly in Mantle's diary, but it had never occurred to him to connect her, centuries on, with Donald Steward. Phoebe did not appear to have children for a start, but of course, she was not a direct relation but a distant aunt. Elderly aunts had a tendency to crop up in their nephews' lives, he had noticed.

"There is a chart here. It seems Phoebe Steward stayed in the parsonage after the Reverend Stewart had gone and when the house was deemed unsuitable for the clergy's continued use and it was to be sold off her brother bought the property and passed it to his son. "

"Donald's grandfather," Fourdrinier stared at the notebook in his hand. "The Stewards have been caretakers here all these years. They kept a journal of occurrences, right through to Donald."

He showed the book to Charlie.

"And now?" asked Charlie. "Who is the next

caretaker?"

As he spoke a series of heavy footsteps rumbled across the ceiling above them. Both men fell silent and stiffened. The footsteps paced about, stopped briefly, then turned and walked back. At last they could hear the rattling of a door handle and silence.

"It has gotten loose," Fourdrinier said very quietly. "Whatever it is."

He indicated the last few entries in the notebook.

"We need to lay it then," said Charlie, eyes on the ceiling.

"I want rid of it," Fourdrinier's face grew stern, he was thinking of Donald lying on the floor, his last few moments spent trying to stop a demon unleashing itself on the world. "I have no time for softness. It shall be dealt with, sent back to the corner of Hell that spawned it, and shall never darken this world again."

"You mean it!" Charlie stared at him in surprise. "I just thought... you really mean it!"

"For some reason we crossed paths Charlie, I do not believe in coincidences, I believe in God guiding us to places we need to be. I needed to be here, I needed to deal with this. Last night I awoke to a horrible thought. What if my reticence to believe had cost Donald his life? If I had listened could I have saved him? I do not know, I suppose I never shall, but I owe it to him to prevent anyone else from being dragged in and destroyed by this..."

The footsteps interrupted him. They stomped back and forth.

"I wonder," Fourdrinier rose, his mind remembering something, "if Donald happened to have copies of the Norfolk Chronicle."

He went to a bookcase in the far corner of the room and spent several moments examining the titles, most were informative volumes on antiques or auction catalogues and price guides.

"There was a bookcase in the sitting room," Charlie left

him to explore.

Fourdrinier read through the titles slowly, unnerved by the rapid pulsing of his heart which had started with the footsteps. Seeking out the books had been a distraction, he had had to stand up and move away from the table in case his friend noticed his unease. The pounding was slowing again now, yet his nerves were as on-edge as ever.

"Is this it?" Charlie returned with several green volumes in his hands. "They are the bound copies of six months' worth of issues. You know how the Victorians liked doing that."

Fourdrinier took a book and read the date.

"Too early, look for 1832."

Charlie handed him another book, Fourdrinier ran through its contents quickly.

"No, nothing there."

Charlie handed over the Chronicle for 1833 and there, almost immediately, printed in black and white on the contents page was the plain title "The Syderstone Hauntings"

In Syderstone Parsonage lives the Rev. Mr. Stewart, curate, and rector of Thwaite. About six weeks since an unaccountable knocking was heard in it in the middle of the night. The family being alarmed, not being able to discover the cause. Since then it has gradually been becoming more violent, until it has now arrived at such a frightful pitch that one of the servants has left through absolute terror. The noises commence almost every morning about two, and continue until daylight. Sometimes it is a knocking, now in the ceiling overhead, now in the wall, and now directly under the feet; sometimes it is a low moaning, which the Rev. Gentleman says reminds him very much of the moans of a soldier on being whipped; and sometimes it is like the sound of brass, the rattling of iron, or the clashing of earthenware or glass; but nothing in the house is disturbed. It never speaks, but will beat to a lively tune and moan at a solemn one, especially at the morning and evening hymns. Every part of the house has been carefully examined, to see that no one could be secreted, and the doors and windows are always fastened with the greatest caution. Both the inside and the outside of the house have been carefully examined during the time of the noises, which always arouse the family from their slumbers, and oblige them to get up; but nothing has been discovered. It is heard by everyone present, and several ladies and gentlemen in the neighbourhood, who, to satisfy themselves, have remained all night with Mr. Stewart's family, have heard the same noise, and have been equally surprised and frightened. Mr Stewart has also offered any of the tradespeople in the village an opportunity of remaining in the house and convincing themselves. The shrieking last Wednesday week was terrific. It was formerly reported in the village that the house was haunted by a Rev. Gentleman, whose name was Mantal, who died there about twenty-seven years since, and this is now generally believed to be the case. His vault, in the inside of the church, has lately been repaired, and a new stone put down. The house is adjoining the Churchyard, which has added, in no inconsiderable degree, to the horror which pervades the villagers.

"We aren't blaming this on Mantle, are we?" Charlie asked as Fourdrinier paused.

"No, Mantle knew there was something here too, he was just a good scapegoat because of his problems and his early death."

Unconsciously they both fell silent and listened to the floor above them, but there was nothing moving.

On Wednesday night, Mr Stewart requested several most respectable gentlemen to sit up all night namely, the Rev. Mr Spurgeon of Docking, the Rev. Mr Goggs of Creake, the Rev. Mr Lloyd of Massingham, the Rev. Mr Titlow of Norwich, and Mr Banks, Surgeon of Holt and also Mrs Spurgeon. As if to give the visitors a grand treat, the noises were even louder and of longer continuance than usual. The first commencement was in the bedchamber of Miss Stewart, and seemed like the clawing of a voracious animal after its prey. Mrs Spurgeon was at that moment leaning against the bedpost and the effect on all present was like a shock of electricity. The bed was on all sides clear of the wall; but nothing was visible. Three powerful knocks were then given to the sideboard, whilst the hand of Mr Goggs was on it. The disturber was conjured to speak, but answered only by a low hollow moaning; but on being requested, to give three knocks, it gave three most tremendous blows apparently in the wall. The noises, some of which were as loud as those of a hammer on an anvil, lasted from between eleven and twelve o'clock until near two hours after sunrise. The following is the account given by one of the gentlemen: "we all heard distinct sounds of various kinds from various parts of the room and the air in the midst of us nay, we felt the vibrations of parts of the bed as struck; but we were quite unable to assign any possible natural cause as producing all or any part of this. We had a variety of thoughts and explanations passing in our minds before we were on the spot, but we left it all equally bewildered."

On another night the family collected in a room where the noise had never been heard; the maid-servants sat sewing round a table, under the especial notice of Mrs Stewart, and the man-servant, with his legs crossed and hands upon his knees, under the cognisance of his master. The noise was then for the first time heard there "above, around, beneath, confusion all" but nothing seen, nothing disturbed, nothing felt except a vibratory agitation of the air, or a tremulous movement of the tables or what was upon them. It would be in vain to attempt to particularise all the various noises, knockings, and melancholy groanings of this mysterious something.

The two men sat in silence as Fourdrinier reached the end of the text.

"What do we do?" Charlie finally asked.

Fourdrinier stared at the book in his hand; a whole party of clergymen had descended on the parsonage and failed to dislodge whatever creature was making the disturbances.

"I need to think about this. To understand better what we are dealing with," Fourdrinier felt his tired mind struggling to rationalise everything he had read. "Nancy believes we need to look to the source of the haunting to deal with this spirit."

"And how do we do that?"

Fourdrinier did not answer. He had noted there were soft footsteps above them again.

"Look, I didn't want to say...." Charlie hesitated. "Your aunt wants to come here and Nancy is adamant about a visit too."

"That would be foolish," Fourdrinier snapped the book shut. "Dangerous, even."

"I agree with you on this, after the last time..." again Charlie trailed off. "But I also know how determined they are and I suspect they will come on their own whether we agree or not. My thinking is we should come with them to try and mitigate any damage. Better that than let them run amok alone."

"They cannot come to this house!" Fourdrinier said even more sternly.

"And how do you propose we prevent them? I can hardly lock them in their rooms."

"I shall reason with my aunt."

Charlie's look summed up how effective he thought that would be.

"They don't seem to understand the gravity of the matter," Fourdrinier persisted. "You don't mess lightly with evil."

"From their perspective I believe they would say the same about you," Charlie glanced up at the ceiling. "This thing has caught us all off-guard. I never thought I would be involved in such a situation. Fourdrinier, by all means try and convince your aunt to let the matter rest in our hands, but if you cannot, at least consent to coming with her here."

"I've already crossed that line, any more dabbling will make things worse."

"Then we don't let her dabble, but we let her look, listen and feel what this place holds. Maud is still shaken from the last time, as am I. I thought it was a folly Fourdrinier, I never expected real spirits or phenomena. Now I realise why the Church is so aggressive in its attacks on spiritualism."

Fourdrinier stood slowly, his whole body aching with exhaustion. He thought of Donald living in this house alone year after year and wondered how the man had the courage. The hair was standing up on his body and he felt twitchy like a rabbit catching the faint scent of hounds.

"We must talk them out of this," he insisted.

"And I repeat, if we cannot?"

Fourdrinier failed to answer, when Charlie went to repeat his question the reverend held up a hand for silence. Both men listened. A whispery voice was singing above them;

"Ring-a-ring of roses, pocketful of posies, atischoo! Atischoo! We all fall down."

The nursery rhyme ended with laughter that drifted down the stairs and seemed to fill the empty rooms, then, as if to emphasise itself, the singer repeated softly;

"We all fall down!"

A terrible commotion echoed in the hall, it was as though a bed had been slung down the stairs and was thumping on each step, banging into the railings, clanging to the ground with a thud. Fourdrinier ran to the hallway expecting he knew not what, but at least expecting something. Charlie pursued him his heart beating fast. But the hallway was empty; nothing was out of place, no sign of anything thrown down the stairs. Only above them the sound of hissing laughter and footsteps rapidly running in circles. Fourdrinier stared at the empty hall.

"I think we just heard the moment Donald was pushed," he said stiffly, a cold sweat was drifting over his entire body. "We have been duly warned."

23 – London 1559

Bay Prince has a sore eye. Robert looks him over in the Royal stables and nods to a groom to dress it. His life now revolves as much around these horses as it does around the royal court. As Master of the Horse he is walking in his brother John's footsteps, maintaining the new queen's stables, improving the blood stock of her horses and planning for the queen's royal progress during the summer months, when he will ride at her side – her ever watchful guardian.

Robert smiles. The last years have been hard, but now he is a valued subject, a respected courtier with duties at court and, above all, the queen smiles upon him. When Mary died the country feared another civil war, yet Elizabeth came to the throne with surprising ease.

Robert thinks of that girl he knew so long ago, with vivid red hair and a spirit that shrieked to be released from the strains and restrictions of royal politics. He had never thought then that she would be queen, and even later he had only hoped. He likes Elizabeth, only daughter of the ill-fated Anne Boleyn. She is fiery and spontaneous. He heard she feigned a headache when her sister Mary tried to have her arrested, and postponed her detention for several days. He likes how cunning she is, yet she does not suffer from the excessive ruthlessness of her half-sister. Elizabeth does not spare those who threaten her, but she does not lash out so blindly or as randomly as Mary.

Rumours are still rife at the court that Anne Boleyn was a witch. That, some say, was how she ensnared Henry. People talk of her having a sixth finger and a third nipple from which the Devil might suck. Her daughter casts a similar aura about her. People are slightly afraid of their queen, and not just for the usual reasons which cause courtiers to tremble around their monarch. They say she can read your thoughts, or at least it seems that way, since she is always so well informed on what everyone is doing – particularly those who might be plotting treachery.

Robert has to smile at this. He knows exactly how Elizabeth is so well informed and it has nothing to do with sorcery or extra fingers. She inherited a spy network from her father when she came to the throne. It was flawed and demoralised, some of its member having been persecuted by the zealous Mary, but it still remained, and Elizabeth, forever one to see the advantage of information, ensured it was revived and restored. Like all monarchs Elizabeth is naturally paranoid, but while her half-sister let this fuel her mass slaughter of protestants in a blind attack on potential rebels, Elizabeth just sits back and listens to her many eyes and ears dotted about the court. Then she strikes precisely where she needs to, not rashly, not with swathes of fire, but with the pointed tip of an arrow straight to the heart of her would-be destroyer.

Robert knows all this for he is at the centre of the new order. He is Elizabeth's 'eyes', her most trusted informer and confidant. Beneath his doublet he has a folded letter that bears this nickname in the form of OO. This is the name Elizabeth always uses for him and he writes back in a similar manner. It is their secret, but he knows he is as much watched as he is the watcher.

There is talk. So far he has assured himself nothing has reached Amy, still safely tucked away in Norfolk, but around the halls, courtyards, parlours, bedchambers and latrines of the palace he knows his relationship with the queen is discussed. Elizabeth is fond of him, perhaps unduly fond, some will say. She bestows favours upon him and always tries to keep him by her side. When he must travel she pines for him. He has even heard it said there is no other prince she would rather marry than Robert Dudley; her words spoken in private often reach his ears and delight him.

In return he dotes on his queen, and it is not hard to do, for she is youthful and handsome, her copper hair crowning her pale face. She still looks like a girl, though her mind is already that of a mature woman. He likes the queen, he likes her company, he likes the prestige being with her gains him. He has coddled her affections – secretly aiding her when Mary was baying for blood – and he has been repaid a hundredfold. His father taught him well how to manage the royal head of England.

Still, he will not go so far as to call it love. Ambition maybe, lust even, but love? How can one love a queen? It is too hard, too fraught with danger. One must dance with royalty with a cool head, not be imperilled by an ardour that might make for rash or impulsive decisions. Robert does not think of love much these days. Love was something of his boyhood when he still had a large family about him and the world seemed to be welcoming him with open arms. Love was a plaything to be toyed with, like a wooden sword. Deep down he is hardened to such emotions. Deep down old wounds fester and boil. He doesn't dare speak in terms of affection for anyone about the court, for affection can be twisted and turned against you. He is not even sure these days if he still loves Amy. He thinks less and less of her, all his time devoted to his queen. Indeed he acts much more like a doting husband to her than he ever did to his wife.

Many are jealous. They think he would marry the queen if only he was a widower and no one is entirely certain they want a Dudley for a ruler. He is aware of plots to kill him, often no more than actions discussed over a pot of mead, (nothing serious to trouble him) but there are plenty who would welcome his death. In many ways having Amy is good insurance for his continued life. While she is alive he cannot marry the queen, and so he can dote and bend his knee and curry favour, without worrying his cohorts unduly that he might be thinking of marriage. No, Robert is very pleased he has a wife, it has probably saved his life more than once, truth be told. He is not a real threat with Amy alive. So he can carry on, enjoying the horses in the Royal Mews, spending time with his queen in relative safety. Amy is his shield and, if nothing else, he loves her for that.

24 – Syderstone, Norfolk 1955

"You understand I do this under protest?" Fourdrinier glared at his great aunt in the darkness.

She turned her nose up at him.

"Go home, Norman."

"And have you endanger your life? I would never forgive myself, even if it is foolishness to be doing this," Fourdrinier snorted as they crossed from the church to Donald's home.

"You said all those prayers in the church, surely that has satisfied you?"

"Hardly. They were prayers for protection, but I am not sure God protects those who are determined to stumble onwards into the lion's den."

"I am not the one stumbling."

"No? Then what is this dare I ask?" Fourdrinier gestured to his aunt and Nancy, each carrying a blanket filled with belongings. "This reeks of witchcraft."

"I told you Norman," Ida was getting increasingly infuriated with her nephew, "They are various experiments for detecting the presence of spirits. Not goat's blood or black candles, as you seem to imagine. I suspect you have been reading too much Dennis Wheatley!"

Fourdrinier almost fell down a rabbit hole as he spluttered out a response.

"Haven't you done enough harm already? Donald is dead because you stirred something with that séance."

"And you think it would not have stirred on its own?"

"Yes!"

Ida came to a complete halt just before the gate into the parsonage.

"Norman, I have dedicated the last few decades of my life into investigating the supernatural. I am aware you have mocked me and laughed at my attempts. I know you thought little of my time with the Egyptian spirit guides, who, I might add, proved very informative on matters such as this. But you hardly know a thimble-full of the things I have been doing. In London I am a member of the Society for Psychical Research and I have conducted experiments time and time again on hauntings and mediums. Now, whatever you may think of that you must admit I have more experience in this field than you do, seeing as only a few days ago you considered it poppycock!" Ida puffed out her chest, turned sharply on her heel and headed into the house.

It took a moment before Fourdrinier had enough courage to follow her after this outburst. She was still, after all, his aunt and he had always been taught to be respectful to his elders, even when they were clearly quite insane.

"And even you must admit this is a new experience," Fourdrinier countered as he arrived in the hallway, attempting to mollify his aunt.

"In 1951 I was part of an investigation conducted by the SPR concerning the apparent possession by demons of a well-to-do banker. He had come upon an old book on magic and had been experimenting with certain spells. He thought it harmless enough, but he went from being quite normal one day to being violent, murderous and savage the next. He tried to kill his wife and children, howled like a dog, threw about furniture and terrorised the servants. Eventually the butler and a neighbour managed to secure him in the cellar. Their report was that his eyes were bulging from his skull, that his nails had grown into claws and his features were no longer human," Ida paused for effect. "Medical men failed to produce a diagnosis. He ended up in a mental hospital of course, but no one could discern what was wrong. Finally the SPR was contacted by the family when they discovered all the magic paraphernalia the banker had collected. We went in and conducted a series of experiments. The SPR are naturally sceptical in all matters, but in this case we became convinced he was indeed possessed. We sent for a priest, as should have been done in the first place. The banker was exorcised and almost immediately returned to normal. He was released and to this day he is living quite contentedly with his wife and children, with never so much as a twitch of violence."

Ida stood before her nephew looking defiant and determined.

"There would have been a rational explanation..." Fourdrinier began, then checked himself. "I just don't want anything to happen to you or Nancy, or to anyone else. Look at Donald."

"We are aware of the dangers involved," Nancy spoke quietly from the dimness of the hall, not far from the spot Donald had fallen. "He is still around, you know, watching over us. I think he will try and help."

Fourdrinier raised an eyebrow in his aunt's direction.

"Be brave, Norman, and take this flour and sprinkle it about the upstairs hall."

Fourdrinier froze; the thought of mounting the stairs enough to cause him to hesitate.

"Why?"

"We may get footprints in it," Ida explained slowly. "You know, in the shape of a cloven hoof."

Her words were heavily laced with sarcasm.

"Upstairs?"

"Norman, there must be a rational explanation for Donald falling down the stairs, mustn't there? So no reason you shouldn't humour your old aunt and sprinkle some flour on the carpets."

Fourdrinier knew when he had been beaten. He headed to the stairs with ill-grace, just as his foot went onto the first step his aunt spoke again.

"Go with him Charlie."

Fourdrinier was certain he heard a trickle of fear in her

tone.

Upstairs was quiet, just as an empty hallway should be. Fourdrinier looked around at the head of the stairs, expecting... well, he could not say what he was expecting. A presence? An ominous shadow? A sense of foreboding? He reminded himself that up until a day ago Donald slept on this floor in a bedroom he could see just in front of him. Only now it did not seem such a comforting idea when evil had learned how to unlock doors.

Charlie joined him and flashed a torch down the hall.

"Shall I turn on the lights?" he fumbled on the wall and found a light switch. A bulb in a brown lampshade flickered into life and illuminated the hallway for them. Automatically they both looked towards the empty room.

"It looks locked."

Charlie headed carefully down the hall and tested the handle on the door.

"Yes, locked," the key was in the door. He removed it and slipped it into a pocket. "Have you thought what people would think of us acting like this?"

He laughed, though it was forced. Fourdrinier had not given much thought to outside interpretation – he was enveloped enough in his own doubts and confusion.

"Exactly how am I to sprinkle this flour?"

"Like you are dusting a table for making pastry or bread, have you never watched your wife cook?" Fourdrinier's expression told Charlie he had not. "Shake the canister lightly and leave a fine sprinkling over the carpet here."

Fourdrinier obeyed, working backwards from the locked door, when he reached the top of the stairs again he paused and looked across at Donald's room. He wondered, was that the room William Mantle had slept in? The room where he had seen his visions of a beautiful woman? He had yet to finish the diary Donald had loaned him but he was almost convinced Mantle's ghostly lady was nothing more than an opium-induced hallucination. Still, it thrilled the historian within him to realise that he was just feet away from the place this man had slept. That once Mantle had tread upon these stairs...

"Are you done?"

Fourdrinier was startled back to his thoughts by Charlie's voice. He used the last of the flour to dust the stair treads as he worked backwards and then joined the ladies in the kitchen.

"Good, you are finished," Ida had emptied her bag of tricks on a table. "Charlie, tie this cotton tightly across the bottom of the stairs, about ankle height. It will warn us of movement."

She rang a small bell that was fixed to the cotton; it reminded Fourdrinier of the sort people put in canary cages.

"Norman, set these thermometers in the dining room. Nancy says we shall work best in there. I want one near an outside wall, and one near an inside wall – not in the corners mind – and one on the table."

Fourdrinier went off with the big thermometers reluctantly. He nodded at Charlie working on his own task as he headed to the dining room. When he returned his aunt was carefully laying out a pack of blank cards.

"They are painted with phosphorescence and will give off a slight glow when turned over," she told Fourdrinier without looking up. "I also have a device kindly loaned from the SPR which is supposed to monitor any unusual electricity fluctuations."

She pointed to a wooden box that looked to contain a metronome.

"Lastly, I have this."

Fourdrinier almost laughed as she handed him a huge, old fashioned camera with an enormous flash bulb.

"The room will be dark. At the opportune moment I want you to take a picture with this."

"I could have brought my Box Brownie if you had said," Fourdrinier hefted the camera which weighed a ton.

"I have no faith in these new cameras. Old ones are the

best. The flash is powerful, so when you go to use it warn us, please," Ida looked in her bag to check it was empty. "Right, just to light the candles then and to sit quietly. You will be pleased to know Fourdrinier we are not attempting a séance."

Fourdrinier felt himself relax.

"Nancy will just read the room and the atmosphere. She is quite good at that actually. I don't think we will need to encourage anything tonight."

Fourdrinier glanced over at the girl in her plain woollen dress. She was sat by the cold oven, head slightly bowed, hands lightly draped in her lap, eyes closed as if asleep. Not for the first time he found himself thinking she seemed alien and strange.

They retired to the dining room. Charlie was smoking a cigarette to calm his nerves. Fourdrinier preferred to place a hand reassuringly over the miniature Bible in his coat pocket. Ida was practical but anxious, only Nancy exuded any sense of calm. She allowed herself to be escorted to a chair at the head of the table and sat down with the grace of a queen.

"He is here. Donald is here," she looked around the room, still illuminated by the electric light bulb. "He is pleased Fourdrinier has come back. He did not think he got across his message at the hospital."

Fourdrinier felt that familiar chill run down his spine, but told himself sternly the girl was a good actress and stating the obvious.

"He wants to talk about a lot of things. He is talking very fast," Nancy frowned. "He is too fast for me. I think he is trying to talk about the history of the house. He doesn't know all yet, but he has ideas about how this all came about... the room, he means. He thinks we need to look at the pond more closely."

"The one that used to be in the garden?" Charlie asked.

"I would call it more of a pool now," Fourdrinier nodded. "It stinks in summer."

"It is important though," continued Nancy. "As is the diary he gave you Fourdrinier. He wishes he had done more himself, but he never seemed to have the time. He thinks the clue lies with...."

Nancy paused with her mouth open. She didn't move her head, but her eyes flicked right and she seemed to be listening.

"Margaret is here," she said solemnly. "She is very upset and scared. She knows what happened to Donald, she says the same thing happened to her."

"Margaret Stewart drowned in the pond," Fourdrinier said carefully.

"Yes. But not by accident. She was pushed," Nancy listened again. "She feels very bad that by her talking to us she has somehow given the evil energy. She is very sorry. She was only trying to help. Margaret? No, don't go."

Nancy gave a shudder and sighed.

"She has vanished into the ether, she is afraid to help us anymore. But Donald is here, he is eager. He says he will watch over us all, and he says 'thank you', Fourdrinier, for being with him at the end. He says if you can contact his daughter, then he has some letters and papers wrapped in a parcel in his bedroom for her to have. He doesn't think she will come to the parsonage though. She always hated it here."

Nancy's hands suddenly groped out for the table as if she was steadying herself. Ida reached out and gently took one hand.

"Don't strain yourself."

"There is a woman, but she won't come forward."

Nancy gripped the edge of the table.

"You don't need to do this," Ida continued. "This is not our purpose tonight. We are merely here to discover the strength and nature of the thing we must deal with."

"I wish you could see her," Nancy gasped. "Her dress is so fine! I have never seen anything so beautiful. It is a pale brown in colour, but not a muddy shade, and it is decorated with embroidery. Flowers and leaves, all in the simplest of hues, yet they stand out like the real thing. She doesn't realise how fine her dress is. Oh, she is so sad! She thinks herself plain, so plain. She thinks herself unloved."

Nancy's hands came together and she toyed with her fingers, pulling at her knuckles in agitation.

"She still won't come forward and tell me her name. She is a very old spirit. The oldest here, in fact. She comes from the start, oh..." Nancy smiled to herself. "She was here when it began, when the room was sealed and the evil took hold, but she didn't cause it, not directly anyway. Ida, I don't think that quite right, I think she feeds into this place because of her sadness and misery. Oh, Ida she is a lost soul too like Margaret. This house traps and eats them. It lives on souls who die before their time. If we are not careful Donald will be trapped too."

"Don't fret Nancy, you have to be strong," gently Ida pulled Nancy's hands apart and laid them flat on the table. "Tell me more about this woman, she sounds important."

"She is. She has blonde hair and a pretty smile, but she frowns a lot because she is confused. This is not her real home, not really, but she found herself stuck here. She has been here a long time. I'm trying to work out how long," Nancy counted under her breath. "I think... at least four centuries. When would that make it? Yes, four centuries. I think she would like to help, but her spirit has been here so long it is weak. She has been drained of her energy all this time by the leech in the room and it has left her muddled. I don't think she really knows she is dead."

Fourdrinier was listening in silence, trying not to show the spark of recognition on his face at Nancy's words. He could imagine who this lady was, the same lady William Mantle had conversed with almost two centuries before them. Except then she had been able to speak lucidly and understood what was happening. He must finish that diary when he had the chance!

"Donald says he doesn't think anything will happen

before midnight," Nancy's trance seemed to lift. "They have all stepped back for the time being."

"Very interesting," Charlie spoke with complete sincerity. "If we have a lull, could we perhaps have a cup of tea?"

"Honestly!" Ida shook her head.

Going against her, Nancy looked up.

"I would like a cup of tea. Maybe then I will stop trembling," she lifted her hands and demonstrated them shaking.

For the time being the tension was lifted. Fourdrinier took it upon himself to head for the kitchen and boil some water. Charlie exited through the front door to get some fresh air and smoke another cigarette. The house seemed neutral for the moment. Fourdrinier felt nothing untoward, even when he glanced at the staircase. He lit the stove and knew it would be some time before it was hot enough to boil water.

Charlie emerged from outside.

"There is a storm brewing," he said, a look on his face indicating the slight anxiety this caused. He had cattle out in his fields and sheep close to lambing, but Fourdrinier suspected there was something else that made him nervous about the turn in the weather.

"I thought we should take a closer look at that pond," Charlie said. "Before it rains."

"I don't like leaving the ladies alone in the house," Fourdrinier replied.

"Nothing is happening for the moment. They could come."

Fourdrinier returned to the dining room and poked his head around the door. Nancy was sitting rigid at the table with her eyes closed. Aunt Ida was by the window staring towards the gateway to the churchyard.

"We are going to look at the pond," Fourdrinier said.

"Good," Ida answered without turning.

"Care to come?"

"Do not fret that we will come to any harm while you are out there," Ida said with more than a hint of exasperation in her tone.

Fourdrinier didn't like being caught out.

"I just thought..."

"Do go outside and get out of my hair for a moment, Norman. I need to think."

Fourdrinier still hesitated in the doorway.

"Norman, please! You are driving me to despair. Go away."

Stung, Fourdrinier retired from the room and went to Charlie at the back door.

"Are they coming?"

"Charlie, my advice to you for a long and peaceful life is to never possess a great aunt."

Charlie grinned in understanding. He shoved open the back door and they walked outside. The sky had turned an indigo colour and the air was growing heavy. Fourdrinier sensed the storm too, like a presence bearing down on him and cracking into his skull. He glanced about the horizon, trying to catch sight of where it was coming from – a sea storm perhaps swept in from the coast? But there was no sign of where the storm had come from, it just hung over Syderstone and drew a sweat onto his brow.

"Remember that strange bolt of lightning that got Maud at the last séance?" Charlie was making his way down the garden carefully, it was well-grown and, in the gathering dark, it would be easy to stumble into a bush.

"Are you losing your nerve?" Fourdrinier followed as best he could. "I would not blame you. I am not at ease myself."

"Fourdrinier, do you not understand what we are facing?" Charlie paused and turned to his old friend. "You are still uncertain about demons. You don't take them seriously enough."

Fourdrinier sighed heavily at the return to such an old and tiresome conversation.

"I refuse to let them scare me, Charlie. Evil is not equal to God's power, that is why it must act insidiously. Faith is the only weapon I possess, but it is a good one, and I will not tremble in the face of the unknown."

Charlie watched his face for any sign of reticence or deceit behind his words, then he gave a nod.

"I wish I had that too."

"You used to."

"Yes, I used to."

They moved past a neglected vegetable patch and towards the far wall. It was made of old brick and low enough to let a person look over easily.

"What do you make of the pond in all this?" Charlie negotiated an old holly bush and leaned on the wall to stare at a muddy pool just beyond.

"In English folklore the pond is the place to bury a witch's soul and trap it. Restless spirits can also be confined to a pond. It used to be part of old exorcism rites," Fourdrinier caught his leg on a bramble and felt the prick of a thorn. "This pond is manmade, got to be."

They both peered at the small patch of water. It was nearly a perfect circle and at one time had, no doubt, been considerably bigger and deeper, but it had become clogged with dirt and what looked like brick rubble, the rest had dried up over the course of long summers and dry winters. Its days as a pond where numbered unless it was dug out again.

"Purpose-built, are you suggesting? To lay a witch?" asked Charlie.

"A carefully prepared pond right next door to the church and the parsonage haunted by an evil spirit? Yes, I think that is what I am suggesting. However, if a witch was laid here I have seen no record to suggest who she, or even he, might have been in real life. There are no accounts of witchcraft in the parish records or the court transcripts."

"Ah, but what of a ghost? You said yourself restless spirits were also bound to ponds."

"For a finite period, the exorcism would run for, say, a few hundred years."

"And what if the pond was disturbed or started to dry up?"

The water before Fourdrinier could have been no more than a few inches deep, more a hollow in the ground than a pond.

"I suppose the witch or spirit might attempt an early release."

Charlie turned around to face the house, which was now silhouetted against purple-grey clouds.

"Margaret Stewart drowned in that pond after spending time in that sealed room. Tell me if I am wrong that in a lot of pagan rites and black magic a human sacrifice is necessary?"

Fourdrinier could not answer immediately.

"That is out of my scope of knowledge."

"Magic gains power from blood, doesn't it?"

"Charlie, I have never dabbled in such stuff."

"I have," Charlie's eyes suddenly blazed in the darkness and Fourdrinier felt a pang of fear as he looked at his friend. "In France, when I was in my darkest period. Fourdrinier, I fell in with these people..."

"Who were they?"

"Some were old, rich fools, who had been through the first war and couldn't face another. Others were just bored, so very bored. Then there were servicemen like me, trying to find a way through, a way to survive. When you think every day is going to be your last, sometimes you do stupid things."

"The war tested our faith, I know."

"You hardly know anything," Charlie was abruptly so angry it caused Fourdrinier a moment of doubt. "I didn't lose my faith, I gave it up!"

Charlie sank his head into his hands and gasped.

"Oh, Fourdrinier, at every turn I lie to you! I try to cheat you, make you say the things I want to hear because, in truth, I have been trying to lie to God for the last decade. I said I lost my faith and that is almost true. I lost my trust in God, not my conviction that he exists," Charlie trembled and drew his breath shakily. "I have been so scared, Fourdrinier, for so long. What you said just now, about evil being weaker than God, I so desperately want to believe that true."

"It is true," Fourdrinier said softly.

"I haven't dared tell anyone what I did one night in France."

"Tell me and be honest Charlie, I shan't condemn what you say."

"You will."

"Then you don't know me as well as you think. Tell me everything, because tonight we have some serious work to do and we don't need secrets among us that might weaken us."

Charlie rocked on the spot, a strange moan creeping from his lips.

"This crowd I fell in with, they practiced magic. All manner of stupid stuff. It was a game they did to take their minds off what was happening. The women would dance around the room naked, oh God Fourdrinier, if Maud knew!"

"She does not, unless you care to tell her. Go on."

"There was drink and drugs. I took the former not the latter, I still had some sense and I wanted to survive the war and you couldn't do that with a brain addled by drugs. A lot of it was just drink and drugs. Sometimes the girls would act as mediums, sometimes the men would too. It would invariably end in sex. I was scared. I knew I was wrong to follow them but I couldn't resist. I drank their strong spirits and I slept with the women. Sometimes, for a moment, it even made me happy, but always in the morning there was the war and fresh misery. I hated myself and yet I went back night after night, because the alternative was sleeping alone in my bunk and dreaming of death."

Charlie stopped to catch his breath. He had started his confession shaky but now he was speaking in a rush.

"I used to go with two friends. They were good friends, Fourdrinier, good men. They were killed unexpectedly. Something perished inside me when I heard. I couldn't believe it. I truly felt those two were the only thing keeping me sane and they had been snatched from me. I worked myself up into a fury with God. I was so angry he had stolen my friends from me. I went to the meeting that night so badly wanting to hurt God, to spite him for the wrong he had done to me. Can you understand that?"

"Yes. Very well."

"I was also terrified that I would be next. I had gotten into this habit of charms and superstitions to keep myself alive. I had a rabbit's foot and a four-leaf clover. I used to walk backwards out of my quarters so I never appeared to be leaving. I had all sorts of phrases and words I would say to keep myself safe. If someone dropped something I used to have to say 'no harm done' three times to prevent myself being jinxed. I cast spilt salt over my shoulder. I always tied my right shoe before my left. In short, I was a nervous wreck and despite all my obsessions I still feared I would die. So I went to the meeting that night and they saw the state I was in and they knew how terrified of death I was and they said they had been wanting to try something new and I would be the perfect subject."

Charlie reached out for the wall and steadied himself. It was more than he could bear to look at Fourdrinier.

"That night I wanted to spite God and so I did. When they suggested a way to guarantee my survival I jumped at the chance. I was vulnerable, but I was also a fool. When they talked about me selling my soul, I agreed without thinking."

If Charlie had expected Fourdrinier to be shocked, he was to be disappointed. His old friend reached out a hand and squeezed his shoulder.

"It is not so easily done, selling one's soul."

"They conducted a ceremony, they killed a cat!"

"God is not so easily fooled."

"But I survived the war, Fourdrinier, don't you see? It worked, and now I am condemned. I shall die and go to Hell..." Charlie broke into sobs. "I am so, so sorry."

"It was a foolish thing, yes, but no one is irretrievably damned. At least not by the God I know and love. Have you asked for forgiveness?"

"Every day since, I woke the morning after and could have slit my throat for the shame. God has never answered me."

"Have you taken the time to listen?"

Charlie shoved himself away from Fourdrinier.

"Yes, I have listened!" he snapped.

"Then, perhaps, you don't want to be forgiven?" Fourdrinier folded his arms and stared sternly at his companion. "Perhaps you like being a martyr."

"How can you say that? Don't you see I am torn apart? You don't know how I ache!"

"When was the last time you went to church?"

"Before the war."

"Why?"

"You know why!"

"God has forgiven that."

"How do you know?"

"Because you asked sincerely for forgiveness and God always forgives those who ask sincerely. You just don't believe that, because you want some huge display of proof, you want to feel different, to know for certain. But you won't know for certain until you give up this mantle of shame you are wearing."

"You think I am forcing this on myself?" Charlie was pacing the garden, his temper boiling over.

Fourdrinier picked his way forward carefully.

"Guilt is a very human thing, Charlie. I fear for the man who never feels guilt, but it is a burden too."

"If I knew for certain that I was forgiven I could stop

feeling guilty."

"That brings us back to your original problem."

"What?"

"You lost your trust in God. You don't trust him to have forgiven you."

Charlie stopped pacing.

"How do you trust someone?"

"A person? I think that is impossible. Humans are flawed. Complete trust in any one of us would be bound to be proven wrong sooner or later."

"Then God, how do you trust God?"

"Because God is not human. Because God does not break his promises and he has promised to forgive those who truly repent," Fourdrinier moved forward and to Charlie's surprise embraced him. "I wish you had come to me sooner. Your soul is quite safe Charlie, you are not condemned."

"I wish I could believe that!"

"How can I prove it to you?"

Charlie shook his head.

"Maybe if we defeat this thing, maybe then I will be able to believe that good can conquer evil. I am so tired, Fourdrinier. I am so tired of this doubt and anxiety."

Fourdrinier clapped him on the back.

"That's enough, this instant I want you to open yourself to God and trust him."

"Fourdrinier..."

"No, don't argue, just do it. You will need your faith tonight. This thing will come at us and we will need every ounce of God's protection to spare us its wrath. If you cannot believe it in your heart, at least speak it."

Charlie was silent a long time. He moved away from Fourdrinier and kicked loose pebbles into a bush. There was a distant rumble of thunder.

"Can it be that simple?"

"Why should it be complicated?" Fourdrinier decided it was time to move on and take Charlie's thoughts away from his inner turmoil. "Come back to the house, I imagine that kettle has boiled bone dry by now."

He strode purposefully back up the garden. Charlie watched him. He plucked at a loose thread at the cuff of his coat. He walked backwards and forwards a few more times. Finally he took a deep breath and strode towards the house. Under his breath he whispered the four words he hoped would save his life.

"I trust in God. I trust in God. I trust in God..."

25 - The Diary of Reverend William Mantle

July 1786

My doctor declares I take too much opium and must desist. He says it is responsible for the clogging of my bowels I have experienced lately and the sleeplessness, followed by deep, nightmarish slumber. I wish to stop, I have promised Octavia I shall, but I have a secret that makes me want to clutch to my last few grains.

It is the woman. Amy. My angel who visits when I am lulled into opium induced haziness. She only comes then. I tell myself it is because I am then most receptive. Perhaps, rather, it is because I am dreaming or delirious? I wish I knew for certain. She seems so real and she sounds so real.

Yesterday afternoon my leg was troubling me and I took a dose, then she appeared about an hour later. She was as stunning as before. Her gown seemed to ripple about her and she had the strangest aura of light hovering over her shoulders. I was lying on the bed. She held out a hand to me.

"Come William, I shall show you something."

"My leg pains me," I protested. Her ghostly hand was offered closer.

"Come William, I shall show you something."

I saw I had no choice but to obey. I summoned my strength and eased myself off the bed. The muscles in my leg tensed and vibrated as though about to snap, but I moved nonetheless. No one else was in the house. Octavia was visiting neighbours and had taken the children, the servants were at the market and cook, well cook was usually drinking a pot of cider at that hour of the day in the graveyard where she thinks I shall not see. So had I fallen no one could have come to my aid for many hours.

Why was I so determined to take this risk? Merely because my angel had asked and I will do all she requests. I fear I am in love with her. What she feels I dare not ask. She has an iciness to her sometimes, as though she is thinking of something that pains her deeply.

I followed her, anyhow, and we crossed the hall from my bedroom and stumbled towards the far wall. My angel paused.

"Do you see it William?"

I saw a plaster wall that could do with a lick of whitewash. Octavia has been on at me to try and do something, but opium dulls all sense of responsibility. I looked at that accusing wall again. Did my angel want me to notice the chips in the plaster? The smoke stains?

"I know you do not see," she placed her hand on mine, I felt nothing but a chill, yet though no solid thing gripped me, my hand moved. "Here is the handle."

My hand travelled towards the bare wall and fell onto what should have been nothing more than plaster. Yet, there it was! Beneath my fingers; an old metal latch handle. It was square and flat, with a spiral end like the doors in the attic. I stared at this strange thing which had suddenly emerged in my hallway and slowly, ever so slowly, my eyes came to make out the outline of a full door.

"I have masked it from you William, but I grow weary. I cannot persist."

I glanced at her, then back at my hand. I realised, rather laboriously, that there was a room in my house I had never considered before. I naturally pulled down on the latch.

"No!"

My angel spoke so sharply I stopped. Her face, normally

so radiant, was grey.

"I only warn you, this is all. You must never enter this room. It has been sealed for a reason. Look again."

I did look again and to my surprise I now saw planks of wood nailed across the door and set in place with thick, heavy metal nails. I reached out a hand and touched them.

"Who has done this?"

"It was done at the time the pond was built. The pond was not enough. I am so sorry William, they failed to understand and I could not make them know. They sealed one spirit in this room and the other in the pond. I was supposed to be the one in that room, but it went wrong. I went into the pond instead, but found it an imperfect prison."

At that point I laughed. Finally my insanity had taken a step too far. I had believed in my angel blindly, but sealed rooms and spirits in ponds? These were medieval tales not decent for a man of the Enlightenment to listen to. Nonsense, utter nonsense.

"You doubt me William?"

My angel showed her temper.

"Why would you be cast into a pond?" I said. "You, who are no harm to anyone?"

"Not because of my actions," admitted my angel. "But because of the creature that attached itself to me."

I laughed again.

"Please William, do not mock. I am serious. I have tried all these years to right the error made by the priests. I have seen to it this room was kept sealed by keeping people blind to it. Once the legends were forgotten I knew someone would try to use it. That would not have mattered if it was just my soul behind that door, but the thing within, it is pure evil."

I shook my head.

"I have been taking too much opium, the doctor is correct," I started to walk away.

"Please William!" my angel begged, but now I saw her

for what she was, a delusion influenced by my addiction. I was ashamed of myself, shamed by the man I had become. I thought of Octavia and my children, so long I had neglected them. And what of my parish? Again I had ignored it and swamped myself in my own daydreams. I have failed so often. I am unworthy of the responsibilities I have been given. I declared there and then to give up this drug. I took my last grains and cast them out the window. I did not regret seeing them scatter, even though I know I shall when my last dose wears off. I lay back on my bed and allowed myself to drift into sleep. I thought I heard Amy weeping in the passage outside my room. I ignored it. Whatever this drug has done to me I do not intend to be drawn back to it by false pity for a figment of my imagination.

I awoke several hours later. Octavia was back and I heard the voices of the children. I drew myself from my bed with care. I knew the pain would be sharp and indeed it sprang to life in my leg as I placed it to the floor. Whatever has become of me? The doctor swears this will one day end, but I do not ascribe to his optimism. In that horrid moment of awakening I reached out automatically to seek my opium, just a small dose, I told myself, just enough to take off the edge. Yet, of course, it was gone.

I hated myself. I slapped my face, bit my hand, punched my own ribs; so furious was I with my own actions. Gradually reality slipped back in. I recalled why I had finally thrown away the drug. Still some desperate part of me scoffed at my actions. How could I be sure Amy was a delusion? Could I not be wrong? Had I not sacrificed my only release from torment for a false assumption?

I forced myself up. My leg does not seem to have any strength these days. When I walk I often fear I will stumble and fall. I edged towards the door, in pain. I gritted my teeth. Usually it eases with movement, sometimes it will even fade to just a dull stiffness, but today it burned like fire all down my thigh. It is in moments like this that I come to rejoice in the deaths of my tormentors. Josiah got the noose after all.

Oh God, how I write! My brain is feverish with rage. I try to forgive but all I want to do is strike out at the men who brought me to this.

I stumbled on. I limped along the passage and I paused at the spot Amy had shown me the door. There was a blank wall facing me. I reached out and touched the plaster. Nothing. So I had been right. I managed a smile, I grinned at myself, backing the desperate addict within me into a corner. See, I told myself, I was right, it was just an illusion. I had chosen to be free and so I would be. In fact, I find myself tempted to burn what I have already written, all that stays my hand is that this might open the eyes of someone else, and then maybe they will too realise the perils of opium.

Though perhaps I shall still burn it. My ego may not survive the revelations I have written down. I shall burn it. As soon as it is safe. The next time Octavia is out and I will not be noticed. No more angels, no more waking dreams. Just this pain.

At least that I know is real.

26 - England 1564

"In her privy chamber there is a desk and in that desk are diverse papers each with a name upon it," William Melville laughs. "And if she did not ask me to look upon them. Showed them to me. And picked up the first one and drew it close to her breast. 'Tis my lord, she says of this one, and I say, your majesty, might I not see. Nay, nay, she says."

Melville glances at his audience of fellow ambassadors and courtiers to see if he has their full attention.

"Well, that is fine talk, ain't it?" continues the Scottish ambassador. "So I say, mistress, for she is but a wee slip of a thing, mistress, you have shown me these papers will you not show me this one too? Will you not show me who your lord is? And she smiles that strange smile, not a girl's smile, sometimes I think of it as a hag's smile, cunning and old."

"Mind your tongue, Melville," Roger D'Arcy says bluntly, he is a courtier dressed almost entirely in black, stretching back on a chair languidly.

"She cannae hear me."

"Can't she? Her eyes and ears are everywhere," D'Arcy picks at a nail. "You know who I mean, I saw him only this morning prowling about her chamber."

"I hear he prowls inside too," Blunden, a minor man at the court and a little too young to understand the full implications of the scandal, says.

"Which man wouldn't, given the chance?" D'Arcy sounds wistful. "She is queen after all. Look at us, degrading ourselves to act as the old mistresses of Henry did. Vying for room in her bed chamber, in her confidence, in her very heart."

"Ach, you ain't listening," Melville slams a hairy fist on the table. "Let me finish my story, you'll like what I saw."

"Go on then Melville, enlighten us," D'Arcy stretches back further, smirks.

"She held this little picture, a miniature close to her heart, and I see it is important to her. Let me look upon it, I say, what harm can it do?"

"You would tell us!" Blunden laughs.

"Ach, she is no fool to think I would do otherwise. Nothing is sacred in court and truly if she had not wanted to show me no persuasion could have won her over, but I see that really she wants me to see. She wants to brag about her lord. She is young after all, and she is a keen filly, she wants for a husband, but that shannae be for so long."

"Did she show you the miniature?" D'Arcy drawls, bored.

"That she did and I tell thee the face on it was none other than the man you have just been talking of. I had to bring a lighted candle near to see and I looked down into the eyes of Robert Dudley, no less. The queen's special lord, the one she keeps close to her heart."

"That is no news," Blunden slumps his head down onto one hand, so his cheek nestles in his palm, and looks disappointed. "I could have told you that."

"Melville, everyone knows Robert Dudley spends time in the queen's chambers. Everyone also knows it is far from respectable or dignified, but we say nothing because, at the end of the day, she is the queen, and not a bad one at that," D'Arcy has hardly risen from a slouch for his speech. "Did you see her other favourites in her desk? I would like to know if my face was there."

"Or mine," Grins Blunden. "I doubt it though."

"If you hadnae interrupted me I could have made the story better."

"Melville, it is old news," D'Arcy yawns. "She calls Dudley her little dog. He follows her everywhere and I have heard it said you can know when the queen is coming for

Dudley will appear moments before. If they are not lovers, they would sorely like to be."

"Excepting for Lady Dudley," Blunden says.

Silence.

"They say Lady Dudley has a malady of the breast and may be short for this world," D'Arcy sounds almost pained. "I wonder if Dudley was widowed he would marry the queen."

"He would be a fool not to."

Melville scratches at his beard.

"What if she doesn't die?" he says, almost to himself. No one answers immediately. "I mean, what if she is not so sick?"

"Melville, Robert Dudley and the queen are awaiting the death of the lady, mark my words. If she were not to die from this, then..." D'Arcy leaves the rest unspoken. All know that monarchs can be impatient when it comes to the demise of obstructive people.

Melville suddenly feels less merry about his story, about seeing how close to the queen Dudley has become.

"If Lady Dudley dies be prepared to say 'your highness' to Lord Dudley," Blunden says.

"It may not be as simple as that," D'Arcy interrupts. "A truly troublesome wife would ensure even in death she is a thorn in the plans of her husband."

"How do you mean?"

D'Arcy flicks his nail.

"I think it rather all depends on just exactly how the lady dies."

⬚

27 – Syderstone, Norfolk 1955

The night was unpleasantly quiet. Fourdrinier considered that an odd thing to think, but it was true. They had sat several hours in the house and nothing had occurred except for Charlie's heartfelt confession. Fourdrinier gazed over at his friend. How sad he felt for him, how he wished to comfort him. He had stumbled, but that was all, only a hypocrite would claim to have never stumbled at least once in his lifetime. Mistakes happened, that was surely the reason for forgiveness? Because God knew his people would falter and fall.

In truth, Fourdrinier was not worried for Charlie's soul. He was sure that was safe. Charlie was too torn up to risk it again and certainly had repented. No, it was for Charlie's mental state that he feared. A man tormented with guilt could lose himself, lose the sense of who he is. And they were all now in a position where bad things were liable to happen, when any doubts would be brought forward and it would take a strong heart to face all that was to come. Would Charlie be strong enough? Would he stand before whatever demon had risen in the house and declare himself safe in the clutches of God? Fourdrinier feared not, and yet he also suspected that that was what it would come to. This thing, this evil, would challenge them and it would be a dangerous thing for any of them to be found wanting.

The clock in the hall struck the first hour of a new day. Dawn was not so far off. At once Fourdrinier was relieved – perhaps they would survive this night unscathed? – yet at the same time he was nervous. The unsettling silence suggested to him something was waiting, building itself up for the right moment.

Nancy was still at the table, hovering in some sort of trance state. At least that was what Ida said. Nancy seemed asleep; that she didn't slump over was the only thing miraculous about her performance. Ida, in contrast, was struggling to keep awake. She had settled herself in an armchair and had consented to have a standard lamp switched on, so she might see the needlepoint work she had brought with her. Even so, she was close to sleep and every now and then her head fell forward as tiredness overcame all else. Charlie was smoking. He had smoked continuously since his chat with Fourdrinier. Each cigarette was lit, dragged on, finished and stubbed out in a matter of minutes. Fourdrinier had never seen his old friend so agitated and he wondered what had tipped him over the edge – a night in a haunted house or his confession?

"Perhaps I should take you home, aunt?" Fourdrinier said when Ida's head tumbled forward once more and she lost her needlepoint onto the floor.

"You have no patience," she declared, grabbing up the fabric and stabbing the needle into it viciously.

"I think Nancy's asleep."

"You can leave her alone too!"

Fourdrinier sighed and tried to make himself comfortable in the hard chair he had moved away from the dining table. At least he was in no danger of drifting off.

"I'm starting to feel rather foolish," he admitted to no one in particular. "When I was last here I could have sworn I heard footsteps and laughter, but now I am wondering at myself. Perhaps it was just the wind."

"Believe what you like, Norman, but we aren't done here yet."

Fourdrinier toyed with his cup and saucer, drained to the very dregs in an effort to pass the time.

"Shall I make more tea?" he suggested.

He received no answer, but got up anyway and collected the cups. He took them through to the kitchen and set the

219

kettle to boiling again, while he rinsed out the china. His fingers fumbled in the water. He almost dropped a cup off the draining board. He groaned to himself, craving his bed after two nights of sleeplessness.

"I know how you feel."

He didn't recognise the voice. He raised his head slowly and looked to his left, not turning his head fully, just glancing from the corner of his eye. A man leaned on the cupboard next to the sink. He looked haggard and thin, but his face had once been very handsome, before time and suffering had taken its toll. Fourdrinier blinked, but the man did not vanish.

"I am not in the custom of seeing ghosts," he said carefully.

"Nor was I," the man strained to smile at him. "Turns out they struggle to show themselves to fully awake people. Better when the mind is tired, otherwise the rational senses tend to block out what they deem irrational."

"Who are you?"

"Reverend William Mantle," Mantle stood and gave a deep bow. He was in breeches with knee height stockings, and a loose white shirt. A cravat hung limply around his neck. "I dressed for you. I am usually seen in my nightgown."

Fourdrinier carefully reached out for the back of a chair and gripped it. He felt the hard wood beneath his palm, the pain as he gripped tighter, and his fingernails curling around and digging into his skin.

"I've fallen asleep."

"Please do not say that," Mantle was suddenly weary. "I said that so often too. I saw you take home my diary, how far have you read?"

Fourdrinier licked his lips, wondering how sleep deprived a man needed to be before he began to hallucinate.

"You have just given up opium."

"Ah, yes. That does not go so well," Mantle sighed. "I

ruined a lot of things, Reverend Fourdrinier. I stumbled through life ignorant and foolish. I tried my hardest, but I always made some mistake, some error."

"You tried to help people," Fourdrinier assured him, finding it impossible to not respond.

"I turned away from Amy, please, do not do the same. Do not turn away from me."

Fourdrinier found himself lowering into a chair. He clutched his hands together.

"What do you mean?"

"You are not afraid, that is good, and you are listening, even better," Mantle moved across the room so he could face him. "This thing in here, it eats souls, and with each soul it eats it gets stronger. At first I thought it nonsense. I still find it hard to comprehend what has happened. I'm trapped here, I cannot leave. I have been trapped from my death. If a soul dies in this house then more than likely they will be sucked in by this presence and forced to stay. The sealed room is only some protection for the living, none for the dead."

"Are we talking about a demon?" Fourdrinier pressed, perhaps this was only his subconscious talking, but even so it might help him to order his thoughts. Perhaps rooted at the back of his mind was the knowledge he needed.

"I am not sure about demons," Mantle said. "I do understand evil though. That thing is evil, not just in its actions. It is a presence of evil. I suppose, if enough malice and badness occur in one place it could become a force of its own. That is all it is really, but over the years it has formed itself into a persona – a creature that communicates and has impulses and desires."

Fourdrinier took a wedge of skin from his arm and pinched it hard. It hurt considerably.

"You are not dreaming, Reverend Fourdrinier. I came to you for a reason, because you can finish this thing once and for all. I am certain this entity can only be destroyed by a priest. That is why God has allowed it into this house, but time and again the people He has put on this quest have failed. Some because they did not believe, others because they did not care," Mantle wrung his hands together, Fourdrinier noted the blue veins he could see in the knuckles; for a dream or spirit Mantle was extremely real. "I am sorry about Donald Steward. I knew Phoebe Steward. Donald is trapped here too, that grieves me."

"Reverend Mantle, why have you come to me? Why now? You did not come to Nancy."

"I do not hold with spiritualism. I see the forces at work behind the words she speaks. Some are true, the rest are spoken by a malicious spirit intent on harm. I could not be sure my own words would reach you."

"But, this..." Fourdrinier pointed at the shade before him, he was strangely calm in himself and he wondered if his exhaustion had numbed him to shock.

"I came to you because you have been reading about me. A lot of unpleasant things have been said about me. Could you imagine me appearing to Reverend Stewart? He might have had the house exorcised. I had to bide my time and wait for the right person. I think you are it."

"Are we in a great deal of danger?"

"Everyone is if that thing is allowed to break free."

"I mean, tonight?"

Mantle strode away a little. He was rubbing his hands together furiously.

"It wants to harm you. I really only sense it, not understand it. Amy is better at this than me, but she can come forward so rarely these days. You must destroy this thing, Reverend Fourdrinier."

"How?"

Mantle shook his head.

"Just not by exorcism, I know that at least," Mantle stopped and looked to the doorway. "Someone is coming. I just wanted to make my presence known to you. If I can help I shall, but I fear I will fail in this as I did in life."

Fourdrinier suddenly felt annoyed with the self-disparaging spirit which moped before him.

"You have to be stronger than this Mantle," he said firmly. "You have to stand up for yourself."

"Yes," Mantle nodded and appeared to be trying to appreciate what Fourdrinier was saying.

There were footsteps in the corridor.

"Take care and God speed," Mantle hissed.

He walked towards the wall and vanished. Fourdrinier stared at the spot the man had last been in and wondered what he had just witnessed. The footsteps grew louder.

Abruptly Fourdrinier was lifting his head and opening his eyes as a hand shook his shoulder.

"How could you fall asleep with this thing screaming at you?" Charlie moved to take the kettle off the hob.

Fourdrinier came to himself. So he had been asleep and he had dreamed of William Mantle. To his surprise he felt a pang of disappointment. He had actually liked the idea of meeting a man he had read so much about and come to know rather fondly. He looked at the wall where Mantle had vanished. How sad it had been a fantasy, for a moment it had given him hope.

"Do you want a cup of te..." Charlie was interrupted by a loud scream.

In an instant Fourdrinier was on his feet and running with Charlie to the dining room. Nancy was sobbing in her chair, aunt Ida was clutching at her; a dead bird lay on the table before them. The tableaux took a moment to sink in.

"What happened?" Fourdrinier stepped forward and looked at the body of the blackbird resting on its back before the women.

"Nancy sensed something. It scared her. Then that fell from the ceiling," Ida motioned to the bird.

"No doubt there are lots of dead birds in the attic, they huddle in such places over-winter and perish," no one was listening to Charlie's rational explanation, even Fourdrinier found it hard to see how a dead bird could fall from the attic through at least two floors.

"It's coming for us," Nancy whispered.

Fourdrinier heard the footsteps race over his head. He automatically looked up.

"I suggest a prayer," he glanced at the group. "Unless you have other suggestions?"

They heard the twisting of the door handle of the room above them.

"Charlie, you still have the key?"

Charlie reached into his pocket and placed the brass key onto the table. Fourdrinier relaxed a little.

"Let us pray. Our Father, who art in Heaven..."

The door handle rattled furiously as though someone was wrestling with it. Abruptly it stopped and footsteps scampered about the room, as if running in circles.

"Thy will be done..."

There was a grunting sound, then something like the snarl of a dog. The handle was turned furiously again. There was the quiet scrape of a latch lifting. Fourdrinier glanced at the table. The key had vanished. He faltered.

"Charlie, did you move the key?"

Charlie glanced at the bare spot on the table. In horror he turned to Fourdrinier and just shook his head.

"It's out," Fourdrinier said breathlessly before he carried on with the prayer. "Give us this day our daily bread..."

There were footsteps in the hallway; for a moment they were light like a child running, then they stomped and all the time they were heading in one direction; the staircase.

"Forgive us our trespasses..."

The first tread on the staircase had a creak, and it cried out beneath the weight of a foot.

"Lead us not into temptation..."

There was another step; steady, paced.

"But deliver us from Evil..."

Fourdrinier clutched his hands in prayer, begging God to preserve him, shaking from the terror of the unseen thing descending towards them. How less frightening it had seemed when it was apparently locked in a room!

"For thine is the Kingdom, the Power and the Glory. Amen."

The bell at the bottom of the stairs jingled furiously and then there was nothing.

They held their breath collectively. Charlie was closest to the door and couldn't take his eyes from it. He was as tense as when he was marching through France, ears tuned for the shots of battle.

Fourdrinier decided to take control.

"It cannot harm us, not if we hold fast to God..."

The doorway exploded with a bluish light. A noise like the fierce hurrying of a gale-force wind reached their ears before Charlie was picked up off his feet and flung across the room, smashing into a mirror over the fireplace and cracking the glass in a star-burst of shards. The wind died; Fourdrinier ran to his friend and reached him as Ida was bending to him.

"Charlie!"

Charlie shoved away the helping hands.

"I'm ok. It was like the after-blast of an explosion and, God knows, I've survived those before," Charlie pulled himself to his feet, staggering dizzily. "Remind me that this thing can't harm us."

The sound of a cackle filled the house. It started in the floor and they could almost feel it bodily as it worked its way upwards, trembling through them until it ringed in their ears.

"Ida!" Nancy cried out.

They all turned to her and Fourdrinier felt his heart almost stop as he saw the girl crouched under the table, her skin ashen and taut, her hair, her auburn flowing hair, now a shocking white. Ida scrambled over to her and pulled her from under the table.

"It's in my head," Nancy sobbed. "I can feel it inside."

Fourdrinier found he was shaking; all around him the room echoed with laughter. Outside the first crackle of a thunderstorm rippled.

"What does she mean?" Charlie asked, plucking glass from his jacket.

"I'm not sure," Ida took Nancy by the arms and tried to calm her. "Explain what you mean, Nancy."

"It's in my head. It's inside, laughing."

"No, that is outside. We can all hear it," Fourdrinier reassured her.

"No..." Nancy trembled into a sob. "It is in my head, I can feel it. Ida, I think it is trying to possess me."

"Don't be silly," Ida pulled the girl into her arms. "We talked about this, remember? You are in control of your powers and you can force out spirits who are not welcome. Close your mind to this thing, push it away."

"I can't," Nancy suddenly broke from Ida's grasp. "It wants to use me."

The laughter rose around them in a crescendo, taunting them, sneering at them. Fourdrinier had finally had enough; glaring out into the darkness he shouted;

"Be quiet!"

The laughter instantly stopped. For a moment they waited for it to restart, but it didn't. Ida nodded at her nephew.

"The voice of a true Churchman has a power over these things. For the first time I'm rather glad you are here."

"Thank you, aunt," Fourdrinier forced himself to say. He was furious, not so much with this demon, though that had incurred his wrath, but with his aunt and with himself for allowing this charade of a performance. They never should have been here, never should have allowed Nancy to dabble in such a dangerous place. He could never forgive himself for the terror on the girl's face right now.

"Nancy," Ida approached the girl, "be seated. It's gone, isn't it?"

Nancy took her hand. Slowly she looked around the room, blinked, swallowed.

"Yes. Gone."

"Good, sit down a moment," Ida pushed her into a

chair. "Charlie, I want you to look at that thread on the stairs, find out if it was broken. Norman, look at the thermometers and tell me their temperatures. We should have used the camera too."

Charlie exited the room apprehensively. He made a determined effort to keep his back to a wall as much as possible. Fourdrinier checked the temperature of the room while Ida sat with Nancy and cradled the girl in her arms.

"I would say the room is quite normal in temperature," Fourdrinier said as a lightning strike outside lit up the room.

Thunder rumbled steadily overhead.

"There is a measure next to the main glass tube. It will tell you how far the temperature dropped," Ida said softly, stroking Nancy's hair as the girl huddled into her.

"Oh, I see," Fourdrinier brought the gauge closer to a candle. "Yes, it has left a faint mark. I can't quite see it."

Ida blinked at another lightning strike.

"It will feed on this energy," she muttered to herself.

Charlie reappeared.

"The string was unbroken, but we all heard the bell."

"As I expected. Only a human agency would have broken it," Ida touched Nancy's skin and wondered at how cold it was. "Charlie, can you see that the camera isn't broken?"

Charlie fumbled with the old black box as Fourdrinier gave a huff of triumph.

"It dropped to -5 from 8 degrees Celsius," he noted. "I never even noticed how cold it had gone."

"I had," Ida stroked Nancy's face. "You're freezing child, Fourdrinier bring over that blanket."

Fourdrinier obeyed, pulling a heavy woollen blanket from an old chair, while still marvelling at the thermometer.

"I cannot explain it, such a sudden drop in temperature. This is almost a science!"

He still had the thermometer held out in his hand, gazing at the impossible when he brought the blanket to Ida... and saw the mercury in the glass tube suddenly drop,

drop, drop as he came close to Nancy. Ida saw it and caught her breath at the same moment as Charlie half-dropped the camera and set it off.

The room was vividly illuminated by white light. Fourdrinier and Ida were blinded, but Nancy howled like a banshee, leapt from the chair and snarled at them. Tearing at her white hair she drew blood from her scalp, but Ida did not run to stop her.

"She's gone," Ida's face suddenly sagged, she half fell into Fourdrinier. "It's possessed her."

Nancy was crying out, but her anguish was fading, being replaced by a look of utter fury and contempt. She looked at them all, her lip twitching into a sneer. Then she lunged at Charlie, grabbed the camera and beat him over the head with it before he could react. He used one arm to protect his face while he punched out with the other, catching Nancy on the arm and causing her to stumble.

She spun, grabbed a vase from a nearby sideboard and flung it at him. The porcelain smashed, but not before the heaviness and force of the throw took Charlie to his knees. Nancy flew at him again, landing on him and scratching at him with her nails. She howled and cackled as she clawed at him, laughing at the blood she drew. Then her head went down and she bit his ear.

As Charlie cried in pain Fourdrinier was crossing the room as fast as he could, a poker in his hand. Conscious that he was about to attack a woman, yet terrified for his friend, he struck a blow on Nancy's upper arm rather than aim for her head, where, no doubt, a good blow would have killed her. Nancy retreated from Fourdrinier, hissing and spitting. Charlie pulled himself into a ball clutching at his ear, as the clergyman stood over him with the metal poker.

"I might be old, but I'm still a bloody good batsman in the local cricket team," Fourdrinier growled, brandishing the poker like a sword.

"You won't hurt her!" Nancy spat back. "You won't harm her, so you won't harm me!"

Fourdrinier tried to pin the voice; the weird, twisted tone. It was not human. It seemed to slither from Nancy's lips and yet at the same time not come completely from her at all, but from the air. Yet this thing – demon, evil spirit, whatever – it had managed to perfectly mimic Nancy and fool them. That really scared him.

"I shall have you out of her!" he snapped, trying to summon his courage for another attack. But how? If he struck too hard he was in real danger of killing Nancy, but if he held back he would surely be at the mercy of the entity that possessed her? He hovered in indecision as Charlie regained his feet.

"We can't let her leave, Fourdrinier," he said, still clutching at his ripped ear. "If she does who knows what damage she might do."

Nancy laughed. Suddenly her eyes caught on Ida standing by the table, close to tears at the horror of what was happening to her friend.

"Did I scare you auntie?" the Nancy-creature teased. "Did I frighten your little soul? Are you trembling, auntie?"

Nancy took a step towards Ida.

"Don't you dare!" Fourdrinier closed on her and waggled the poker.

Nancy grinned.

"Stupid man!"

And she lunged. She had the poker in a moment. Her strength was enormous. Fourdrinier fought with her and felt as though he was wrestling a bear or some such animal, not a woman at all. Suddenly she yanked backwards and the poker slipped from his grasp. Charlie was hurrying to help as Nancy swung the poker with all her might.

Fourdrinier never knew how it missed. It should have taken his head off, it should have finished him. Yet in the split second it should have connected with his skull, the poker suddenly seemed to pull up short and not only miss, but with its momentum unchecked, fly from Nancy's hands and across the room.

Charlie grabbed her and tried to pin her arms. Nancy writhed violently, twisted up her hands and sank her nails into his flesh. Charlie gritted his teeth and hung on, badly wanting to repay her for the agony in his ear. Nancy shrieked again, wriggling her body like a snake. Abruptly she drew up one knee and kicked backwards, connecting with the soft flesh of Charlie's inner thigh with her heel. There was a strange, soft ripping sound and Charlie gasped, his eyes bulging as his flesh was ripped open. As blood gushed down his leg, the strength went from his arms. Nancy pulled an arm free and shoved her elbow into his face with a crunch, giggling as he crumpled to the floor.

She turned, triumphant, and stepped straight into the hands of Fourdrinier. He clutched her upper arms and she started to twist again.

"Stop it!" he snarled.

The Nancy-creature slowly went still. She turned her head towards him. Looked him straight in the eyes and smiled.

"Get... out... of... her... body," Fourdrinier said through clenched teeth, he was all too aware that his fingers were digging into Nancy's flesh and would bruise her.

"Bad priest," the Nancy-creature smirked. "Shouldn't you go help your friend?"

Fourdrinier didn't dare break his gaze from her, not for a moment.

"Get out of Nancy!"

Again the being in his clutches smirked. Up close he could see how wrong Nancy had suddenly become. Her muscles twitched painfully, her flesh was so cold and icy it seemed like that of a corpse, her eyes seemed to have a shadow behind them and she smelt... yes, just faintly... she smelt of sulphur. An awful thought crept into Fourdrinier's mind that Nancy might already be dead, that in the moments after the gale had stormed the room she had perished and this thing had taken up residence. The creature saw his doubts.

"Perhaps you'll have to kill her? Only way to be sure I am gone," the thing gave a snigger.

Fourdrinier was flustered and afraid. He knew he had to act, but to do what? He was holding her still; he seemed unable to do more. That he had clutch of her at all was a miracle, considering the beating she had given Charlie who was a young man and stronger than Fourdrinier. Yet he held her... A thought came to Fourdrinier's mind; he had commanded quiet and received it, he had told the creature to stop struggling and it had. In the spiral of chaos only he and Ida had escaped, and what they shared in common (though in Ida's case it was complicated) was a firm belief in spirituality and God. Fourdrinier felt a new strength fill him. He allowed himself to smile. The Nancy-creature glared at him.

"Our Father, who art in Heaven, Hallowed by thy Name..."

"Gah! Bad priest! Bad priest! You think they didn't try that before?"

"...On Earth as it is in Heaven, Give us this Day our Daily Bread..."

"Mantle prayed! Stewart prayed! They are all dead!" the creature began to writhe. "I'm not scared of silly poems!"

"...lead us not into Temptation, but deliver us from Evil..."

"Gahhhh!"

Nancy went limp in Fourdrinier's hands. He suspected a trick and refused to stop until he had finished the prayer.

"Amen!"

There was a pause. Nancy drooped like a doll in his arms. There was no sign of life. Gingerly Fourdrinier lowered her into a chair and felt for a pulse. Her skin was warmer. The pulse was faint but regular. He gently lifted her chin and looked at her face, wishing she would speak, before he decided he could spare her no more time and went to Charlie.

"How bad is it?"

Charlie was propped up on one hand, the other was pressed firmly on the slice into his leg.

"She gouged out a chunk of flesh but I think the bleeding is stopping," Charlie was pale, but he spoke firmly. "It's not done yet. Watch that girl like a hawk."

"I'm more concerned for you at the moment."

"I'll take care of him," Ida had appeared almost out of nowhere, she was clearly still shaken and she looked frail, but she moved to help Charlie with quick steps and no hesitation. "See if you can rouse Nancy, please."

Fourdrinier took a moment to decide. He loathed to leave Charlie, but the thing behind them could still present a danger. Slowly he rose and went to examine Nancy again.

He felt her forehead, checked the pulse in her wrist, then he spoke her name.

"Nancy?"

Perhaps she was comatose? He tapped her cheek with a finger, his memories of first aid in such situations proving hazy. He glanced back over his shoulder at Charlie, a desperate pull drawing him to help his friend first. He shouldn't be angry with Nancy, she could not help the attack, but it was still hard to separate the brutal assault on his friend from the innocent woman unable to stop it. He had never had a stronger desire to hit anyone in his life as he did now towards Nancy. He told himself off and patted the woman's hand gently.

"Nancy?"

He thought he saw her eyelids flicker; it was hard to tell in the dark. It was then he realised the thunder storm had passed and outside the sky was showing the first hints of dawn.

"Nancy?"

Her eyes opened and closed. She gave a long sigh and then trembled violently. A hand spasmodically came up to her face and she pressed at her temples. Painfully she focused on Fourdrinier.

"It's not gone," she said in a whisper.

Fourdrinier had feared as much, but this, he was certain, was Nancy talking. He could see the clearness of her eyes and the warmth of her spirit. For the moment the beast was tamed.

"Prayer is only temporary, and the longer it is with me the stronger it will become," Nancy was fraught, she clutched at Fourdrinier's hand. "Kill me!"

"Nancy, I shall do no such thing. We shall perform an exorcism. I am sure I can discover how."

"It's not enough. You know that as well as I do. The longer it remains the more risk you take. If you kill me it cannot use me."

"I know this is frightening, but I shall do no such thing," Fourdrinier squeezed her hand. "This thing has not beaten either of us. I told you this is not an equal battle and God's forces are far stronger."

"I'm so sorry I let this thing in," Nancy wiped at tears, her throat choked with them. "I was not quick enough. You said I should not come, I refused to listen."

"Never mind that. We all made mistakes tonight," Fourdrinier tried to smile at her, unfortunately he was distracted by the groans behind him.

A sharp cry made him turn around anxiously towards Charlie.

"What is it?"

"His leg is bleeding again, I think we need an ambulance," Ida looked up. "He won't listen to reason."

"How do you intend to explain this to an ambulance-man?" Charlie interjected. "Get me back to the farm, I have medicines there. You think I've never had to staunch the bleeding of an injured cow? Maud knows how to do stitches."

"We can hardly walk you there," Fourdrinier left Nancy to attend to his friend, he pulled away Ida's hand and was relieved that the bleeding was not as profuse as he had feared.

"Drive my car!" Charlie snapped, cross from the pain.

"I do not know how!" Fourdrinier replied.

"I do," said Ida. "We should get them both back..."

She was gazing over Fourdrinier's shoulder.

"Where is she?"

Fourdrinier turned with a groan. He would have thought it impossible until that moment for a girl to slip past all three of them with no one noticing. He got to his feet and hurried out of the room. There was no sign of her in the living room. His first instinct was to head upstairs to the creature's lair. Surely that was where it would limp back to, to lick its wounds? He was just heading for the stairs when he heard a clatter in the kitchen.

Knives! That was now the thought springing to Fourdrinier's mind. How many weapons must there be in that kitchen? He did not fancy his chances against an armed demon and he could not risk more harm to Charlie or Ida. He ran as fast as he could, praying to God for strength, imploring Him for help, wishing he had had the sense to leave this problem well alone.

He stumbled around the door. Nancy was leaning over the sink. Fourdrinier glanced at the knife rack on the Welsh dresser. Sure enough there was a space where a knife was missing. He caught his breath. His best chance was probably to try and sneak up on her and wrestle the knife away, what other option was there? He stepped forward, cringing at the soft creak of his shoes. He was no sneak-thief and each step seemed to give him away. Nancy didn't turn. He felt he was being drawn into a trap; she would swing around at the last moment and plunge a knife into him. Still he stepped forward.

Just as he was coming within a foot of her Nancy suddenly sagged and a bloody knife clattered from her hand to the floor. Fourdrinier stared at it stupidly. Its significance took several moments to register, then he dived forward and grabbed Nancy into his arms. He spun her around and gazed at her slit throat.

"It will come back," she said, blood dripping from her

lips. "Unless I'm dead."

"Nancy!"

"Tell Ida, I'm so sorry."

The girl was barely conscious. Fourdrinier lowered her to the ground and snatched a towel off the door handle of the range. With shaking hands he wrapped it around Nancy's throat, watching it soak with blood instantly.

"Aunt Ida!" he was panicking. Nancy could not possibly live long with this sort of blood loss.

Ida was in the doorway.

"Call an ambulance!" Fourdrinier shouted. "She has cut herself!"

Instead of running for the phone Ida came towards him and knelt down as best she could. She reached out a shaking hand and felt for Nancy's pulse through the blood.

"They'll never get here in time," she said.

"We still try!" Fourdrinier started to stand, his aunt took a firm hold on his arm.

"And tell them what? She was possessed and attacked one man before turning a knife on herself? Charlie is right. You have been here twice when someone was bleeding to death, try explaining that to anyone. Try explaining Charlie! They won't make it in time and we will only get caught up in a police investigation, this house will be sealed off and we will never be able to stop this thing..."

Ida broke down. Fourdrinier wrapped his arms around her, shaken to see the woman he thought so strong suddenly caving in on herself.

"We have to do something," he insisted.

"Yes!" Ida pulled her head away from his chest. "We have to stop this evil!"

"I meant about Nancy."

"I know you did, and my point is still the same."

Ida had composed herself, though it was a fragile state. She knelt stiffly beside Nancy and touched her hand.

"Oh Nancy," she let out a little sob.

Fourdrinier stared uselessly at the pair of them. He

heard a scuffling sound and turned to see Charlie painfully limping towards them.

"I wasn't inclined to stay on my own," he muttered as Fourdrinier went to his aid.

"Nancy cut her throat," Fourdrinier whispered.

Charlie looked past him, down at the floor tiles crimson with blood, the saturated towel pointlessly pressed to the girl's throat, Ida crying.

"This is worse than I ever imagined, Fourdrinier."

Fourdrinier hardly knew how to respond. Everything he believed, everything he knew to be certain had been shaken. He had seen the face of evil up close and he was more scared than he could muster into words. He had never even imagined such a thing existed as he had seen; there was no logic or reason to it. He trembled.

"We need to get you home," he said solemnly, trying to focus on an achievable task.

"Then you must go to work, Fourdrinier, find out how to deal with this thing."

Charlie's earnest face scared him even more.

"Perhaps a Catholic priest..."

"Don't you ever listen, Fourdrinier?" Charlie snapped, he was wincing from pain in his thigh. "I'm the one who is supposed to be having doubts with his faith and yet you are the one who can't seem to grasp that God caused us to meet and set you on this path for a reason."

Fourdrinier bit at his lip. He wanted Charlie to be wrong. He didn't want this role, this tumbling into an unseen adventure that made no sense and threatened to strip him of his reason. He was a rational churchman, adverse to stories of demons, possession and evil spirits. Everything about that night was wrong. The only thing he could do was change the subject.

"Aunt Ida, is Nancy..."

Fourdrinier glanced at his aunt who could only nod and sob.

"We underestimated this," Charlie said.

"I'll find a blanket to wrap Nancy in. Aunt Ida, if you could fetch the car? Are you able?"

Ida removed a handkerchief from a hidden pocket in her robes and wiped her eyes.

"I shan't let anyone else down," she said firmly.

They cleared out of the house faster than Fourdrinier would have thought possible with an injured man and a dead girl. He wrapped Nancy in a blanket and heaved her light frame into his arms. He tried not to think of the blood that splattered his shirt, or that dripped across the carpet. He was last out with the corpse and he could not help but pause at the door and listen. The house was silent. He thought of the hissing, spitting thing that had taken over Nancy – how could such a thing exist? Where had it come from? How was it created, if 'created' was the right word for it? There was too much to think over, too much to consider. The one thing it appeared there was not too much of was time itself.

🙞

28 – The Diary of William Mantle March 1789

The death of Joseph shook me. It was not a good period for dearest Octavia. She was sick and weak throughout her confinement. Sometimes I fear myself evil, for was it not I who put her in such a predicament with my carnal lusts? Can a man be forgiven for loving his wife too much?

Joseph took his first shaky breath on a cold morning in February, he died fourteen days later, with icy rain tumbling down the windows. We have been fortunate, in truth, of all our dear little ones this is the first to pass. Have not others suffered worse? Another of Josiah Smith's children has perished, I fear through hunger. His wife scuttles about the village without meeting anyone's eye. No one can say how she continues to exist. I keep trying to visit her but it is awkward and on the few occasions I have steadied my bravery and knocked on the door she has appeared to be absent.

My grief though, is hard to stomach. Telling myself I have been fortunate does not still the pounding in my temples, or soothe my wife. The bairn was beautiful – so small, but perfect. Phoebe Steward looked on him and declared he was a scrawny thing, for which unkindness I angrily told her to mind her tongue. Sarah, as ever, was peacemaker between us. She works at the house helping with the children, her daughter is the same age as Ann Elizabeth and the arrangement works admirably. I do not think Octavia could manage alone. Sarah came between myself and Phoebe and said there was an old legend that the smallest of bairns grow to be the strongest of men and that we only need look at the kings and military leaders of old to see that.

I wish her tenderness had been more fortuitous. Joseph did not live to become a strong man. He withered away. Life seemed to leach from him. When I buried him, Octavia was still too sick to come, but I promised I would have the bells of the church rung so she might hear them from her bed. She said they comforted her. She said they made her imagine little Joseph's soul flying up to Heaven. She is a brave woman. I am not so brave.

Sarah tells me I should seek out a man called Temple in the village. I ask her why and she looks at me knowingly. I have drunk more wine this last week than I dare say I have drunk in the last year. All I know is that it dulls the pain of Joseph's passing, not to mention the ever present soreness in my leg. I have never escaped the pain from that fateful evening with Josiah Smith and the squire's son. Phoebe believes the doctor failed to set my bone right, she makes hot poultices for it when it burns dreadfully, but I am never free of the torment. Even in sleep it disturbs me.

"Temple would give you what you need," Sarah says innocently enough.

I know what she means. Opium. Just the thought of those sweet grains enchants my brain and sends a shiver of excitement down my spine. But I will not falter, I promised Octavia. This agony will pass just as before, into a dull ache that I can live with. For now I merely smile at Sarah and tell her I shall consider it.

~ ~ ~ * ~ ~ ~

A strange thing occurred. I was down with Sarah's Ann and my Ann Elizabeth by the pond, looking at the big goldfish I bought last year to amuse them. All the fish have been christened by the girls and they delight, as the weather warms, to see them rise from their winter sleep and nibble at the surface of the water for breadcrumbs.

We sat by the 'Witch's Pool', as the girls call it since hearing Sarah's story, and watched shimmering red and orange shapes dip and dive beneath the water. Ann Elizabeth was fascinated by a big white one that none of us could recall from the year before. She wanted to name it.

"So name it," I said, laughing at the eagerness of the girls.

Ann Elizabeth took a moment to think of something suitable.

"I shall call her Amy."

"That is a name I hear rarely," I said. "Where did you come across it?"

"Oh, but it is the name of the Lady," Says Sarah's Ann.

I looked at them both curiously.

"Which lady?" I think of the women who might go by that term in the village, none I know are called Amy.

"We see her by the pool," Said Ann Elizabeth. "She is always crying."

"She is very sad," added Ann.

"One day we spoke to her, didn't we?" Ann Elizabeth looked at her cohort for back-up. "I asked her why she was sad and she said..."

Ann Elizabeth suddenly looked abashed.

"I wasn't supposed to tell you," she explained quietly.

I could not think who this woman was who has stood in my garden weeping and it troubled me.

"I am sure she would not mind you telling me, for I might be able to help."

Ann Elizabeth needs little cajoling, the innocent creature cannot keep a secret for more than a moment. It is too delightful to her to have news to deliver. She is the worst gossip I have ever known.

"She said she was crying because you would not listen to her and that I must not say anything, because it was up to you. But I asked her her name and she said it was Amy and I said 'should I fetch you' and she just went away."

"We see her sometimes, right there," Piped up Ann, as

keen as ever to aid her friend. She pointed helpfully to a patch of grass opposite where I sat.

I was perturbed by the conversation, because there is only one woman I can think of who goes by the name of Amy and I do know her, I know her all too well.

How many years since I thought of my angel? I do not know. Once the opium torpor wore off I never saw her and was convinced she was a figment of my imagination. Yet now my daughter and another girl have seen her? That means she is something else, does it not?

What if I made an error? What if, in my desire to rid myself of a vice, to purge myself so I might consider myself superior to this drug, I abandoned something important? What if I should have listened? I have been thinking of that last meeting with Amy, the strange appearance of that door that had never existed before, or had it? Could there be something in this house I never dreamed of? What did Amy call it? My mind betrays me, I cannot remember, but it was something that must not be released and she was growing weary of containing it.

Since the death of Joseph I have not been the same. I feel things, odd things. I think a person is behind me and yet they are not. I hear footsteps and I check on the children to find them sound asleep. Sometimes I think I hear crying... I blamed this all on grief until now. Have I been deluding myself?

I went and looked at the wall in the hallway again, I still can see no door, but it occurred to me there was another way to tell if a room was missing. I walked downstairs and made my way into the churchyard. My leg is bad today, it aches at every step, I limp badly and I crave a sip of wine to ease everything away. But I marched on and finally I leaned back against a tomb and looked up at my house.

I noted five windows on the front of my house. The problem is I can think of only three rooms with windows, which leaves two unaccounted for. Needless to say this concerned me, especially as I realised the extraneous windows happened to coincide with the area of hallway Amy had shown me as containing the hidden room.

Now I am confused. Have I deluded myself again? Am I counting the windows wrong, or is there something else here I am missing? I think of Amy often, how she was good to me when I was sick, how she comforted me. I cast her aside without concern. I called her a delusion, I refused to listen. Now her words are proven true. It is safe to say I am shamed and frightened. There is a room in my house containing I know not what. I fear for my children, for my darling Octavia. Worse, I think of Joseph and wonder if his death was due to more than ill health. Is there an evil lingering over us?

Tonight I will drink two bottles of wine before I go to sleep and I hope to induce Amy to appear. Then I must ask her questions and find out once and for all.

~ ~ ~ * ~ ~ ~

Amy did not appear last night. I am despondent. I write these words feeling troubled and scared. Must I feed my vice to find my angel? Must I ingest the dreaded opium? I may be able to take a few grains without suffering. Perhaps I shall not crave anymore after so long without?

I am afraid to try. I think I will falter and then what? It was horrible cleansing myself of addiction the first time, a second time I might not be able to manage it. I thought I would die sweating with fever, trembling with chills, tortured by pain I could not place or find, that was just there. But if I do not take it, how can I find Amy? I shall not concede defeat yet, there must be a way. Perhaps if I take myself into a higher state of prayer like a monk in olden days? Ah, Octavia, how I wish I could explain this to you? But I must be strong. Somehow I shall find my angel and I shall solve this riddle.

⧠

29 – Syderstone, Norfolk 1955

The police arrived at the Talbot farm in the early morning. Charlie absented himself to the sheep pens where he huddled on a stool, in pain mentally and physically. Ida stayed; her red-rimmed eyes and tearful demeanour could not be mistaken for anything but raw grief. Maud played the distraught hostess perfectly, though really it needed no pretence. Nancy's death had deeply upset her. She ushered the police in, past Fourdrinier who she introduced as the local reverend and Ida's nephew come to try and give spiritual comfort to his aunt, then whisked them upstairs.

Nancy had been put in the big enamel bathtub on the first floor. The ladies had concocted the scheme. Nancy's clothes were removed – they would have to be burned. Fresh clothes were laid haphazardly on a chair in the manner of someone getting undressed in haste, then Nancy was laid in the bath, one hand draped over the edge, her head leaning back to show the awful, gaping wound. Fourdrinier had had the foresight to bring the knife home that Nancy had used, now it lay discarded beneath the bathtub. Maud explained to the police how she had found the poor girl in the bath and drained the water which was red with blood. That explained why the body and the bath were so clean, there was no other way to mask that Nancy bled to death somewhere else. Out of dignity Maud had draped a towel over the girl and told the police over and over how horrid this whole thing was, how she would never be able to sleep again. The beauty of the statement was that every word was true.

The police interviewed aunt Ida delicately. The sight of

an elderly woman ensconced in a bright mauve, crimson and gold kaftan was enough to make any constable wonder about her sanity. Ida's hysterical tone only added to their impression that they were dealing with a mad woman. Fortunately, being a woman of means, Ida was deemed eccentric rather than crazy. Ida hardly needed any help from her outfit to give the police the impression she was maddened by grief. Her eyes were red raw from weeping and she had worked herself overnight into a tizzy of guilt and despair. Seeing Nancy in the bathtub again had tipped her over and, half-fainting, she had to be helped downstairs by the police constable and settled into a big armchair by the window.

"Take a breath of fresh air," the plump constable told her with a kindly tone. He opened the window a fraction then bent forward with his hands clamped on his knees. "Do you feel any better?"

"It is such an awful thing," Ida sobbed. "She was my friend, constable, and I blame myself for all this."

"Now, now, you hardly put the knife in her hand, did you?" the constable was unfalteringly calm in his handling of Ida. "My sergeant wants to ask a few questions, just routine for a thing like this. Are you up to answering?"

Ida managed a nod.

"Just you hold fast and I'll fetch him," the constable turned and exited the room, passing Fourdrinier as he went.

"Rum old do," he muttered to the reverend as he hastened upstairs.

Fourdrinier joined his aunt in the parlour. They did not acknowledge each other. On Fourdrinier's part this was because he could not bear to look at the woman he blamed for bringing Nancy into this mess, encouraging her 'talents', filling her head with ideas. This had all begun with aunt Ida's obsession with Margaret Stewart and it had ended with Nancy's death. Once he had thought her fads and crazes harmless, if embarrassing, now he found himself seeing the danger behind them all too late.

He was angry at himself too. He had gone blithely into this business. He had not had the courage to stand by his principals, instead he had allowed himself to be cowed and persuaded. He had trodden a path full of sin and deceit and the result could hardly be unexpected. He would never forgive himself for Nancy's death, nor would he ever forget that moment in the kitchen when he realised what she had done, when he had seen the awful wound in her throat and felt his stomach churn in revolt. When he closed his eyes it was a vivid image before him. He wondered if this was how Charlie had felt when he stepped into the Concentration camps?

The constable reappeared with his sergeant.

"Just a few questions now," the sergeant was tapping a pencil on a pad of paper held together by an elastic band. "I know this is hard."

"No, you do not sergeant," Ida said, gnawing at the edge of one finger. "You are just saying that. You cannot know how it feels to see a friend, a girl one thought of as a daughter, take her life in such a way. You cannot know how much I wish I had acted differently and prevented this tragedy."

"People always think they could prevent these things, but in my experience if a person is determined, they will do it as soon as they get the chance. Do you know why she harmed herself? Was she unhappy?"

Ida pulled the hand away from her mouth and looked at the tip of her finger which she had caused to bleed. Fourdrinier was pleased she did not look at him. A glance his way might have seemed suspicious. Instead Ida composed herself and faced the sergeant.

"Nancy did not talk about herself. I am from a generation who rarely discussed their emotions, it was frowned upon in my home growing up, so I was not one to elicit the feelings of others from them. Perhaps that made Nancy reticent with me, I cannot say. But she did not talk to anyone else as far as I am aware, I don't think she was the sort," Ida took a trembling breath. "You could describe her as lonely, I suppose. She fell out with her mother and I was her only friend. She did not socialise, she was very quiet. But she never seemed bothered by this. I don't think she was a person who needed company."

"So she wasn't unhappy?" the sergeant pressed.

Fourdrinier clenched his fists. If they could not give a good explanation for Nancy's desperation then the police might start to look harder at them. He knew Maud and Ida had talked long into the night about what they would do, surely they had covered this?

"Sergeant, Nancy came to me because we shared an interest in spiritualism, do you know what that is?"

"Yes, ma'm, my own grandmother, rest her soul, was one."

"Then you understand that spiritualists believe we can contact the dead?"

"Yes ma'm," the sergeant gave an apologetic smile. "I can't say as I believe that."

"Well, what you believe is irrelevant," Ida brushed aside the remark. "Nancy believed, in fact, she had the abilities of a medium. She could hear the voices of the dead. Sadly her mother considered this devilry and terrified the girl, leaving her torn between the powers that came to her unbidden and the wrath of her mother. It was our friendship that changed everything. She came to reside with me, in a household where she would not be constantly berated for her gifts."

Ida stopped herself. There were tears in her eyes and she started searching frantically in one voluminous sleeve for a handkerchief. The sergeant kindly offered her his.

"Thank you. I'm sorry about this sergeant. It is just that I now feel I was wrong encouraging Nancy. I believed her mother oppressive, now I fear I see why she was so concerned for her daughter. She will never forgive me for what has happened. I shall never forgive myself."

"Are you implying Miss Nancy's death was to do with

this spiritualism lark?"

Ida stiffened at the awkward comment, but she refrained from arguing. Now was not the time.

"Nancy was a very sensitive girl and she did have very strong views, perhaps almost fears, of sinfulness and negative spirits. I was aware of this, but I did not appreciate the depth of her feelings. Nancy became convinced she had been possessed by an evil spirit," Ida suddenly turned to Fourdrinier. "My nephew can explain better, we were here to see him."

Fourdrinier was thrust into battle a little stunned.

"You were visiting today in your professional capacity?" the sergeant was looking at him, tapping his pencil.

"Yes and no. Sergeant, I do not hold with possession. It is a Catholic idea and the Church of England has no time for it," Fourdrinier felt he was blustering, but his outburst seemed to please the sergeant who nodded and wrote on his paper. Fourdrinier decided to continue. "Stories of demon possession in the past are now known to have been the result of a misunderstanding of certain diseases and conditions, epileptic fits for instance. That being said, if rationally we cannot believe in possession, it is feasible for a person of sensitive nature to become irrational on the subject. In short, a person can believe themselves possessed even if medical evidence and Church opinion says they are not."

"And this was the case with Nancy?"

Fourdrinier's mind went back to the night before; Nancy's hair turning white, her wicked laughter, her attack on Charlie and her ultimate death.

"Yes. Nancy believed herself possessed. I was trying to be of assistance. In cases like this arguing that possession does not occur is pointless because the affected person simply does not believe you. Instead you must play along and try to convince them that they have the power to drive out the evil."

"Bit like psychology," the sergeant mused. "We have

one of them psychologist fellows come in the station sometimes to talk to suspects that are unhinged."

"Nancy was not unhinged," Fourdrinier said firmly, noticing the scowl on his aunt's face. "She was merely tormented by an anxiety to be a good person. She believed that the demon possessing her would cause harm to others. I tried to explain we would remove the demon and that she was in control of her actions, but I am sorry to say I was not convincing enough. She had expressed the view that she must die to rid herself of the demon and, by her reasoning, keep her loved ones safe. I failed to realise that she was in danger of taking her own life."

"You did your best vicar. We'll be sending an ambulance over for the body. In the meantime, I suggest you try and eat something and put this thing out of your minds. Surprising how often stuff like this occurs, sorry to say. It's been worse since the war," the sergeant put on his helmet. "There'll be an inquest, but I think it will be quite straightforward. Don't fret too much on the matter. Good morning all."

He turned and gave Ida's hand a sympathetic pat, then left with his constable trailing behind. From the sofa Fourdrinier could watch them leave the yard and head for a pair of bicycles propped by the wall.

"You are a good liar for a man of the cloth," Ida said spitefully.

"Would you rather I had said the truth?"

"Between you and that police sergeant you made me feel like a silly old woman with a head full of air!" Ida flung the handkerchief the sergeant had gifted her to the floor and cupped one hand over her eyes, rocking back and forth in the chair.

"Aunt, I have seen things over the last few days I would not care to try and explain to myself let alone a policeman. You are not a silly old woman. Well, not most of the time, anyway."

"I caused this to happen, Norman. I was so arrogant on

the matter!"

"Perhaps, but if this is a war – albeit a small, spiritual one – then we have to expect casualties. Now, we have to ask ourselves do we surrender? Or do we fight on and avenge Nancy?"

"Norman, what will you do?"

Fourdrinier gave a sigh and watched a sparrow perch briefly on the windowsill before fluttering off.

"I have every intention of fighting on."

Ida gave a shuddering sob that cut off suddenly.

"Don't get yourself hurt, Norman, promise me?"

"I told you before, evil is no match for good," Fourdrinier went to his aunt and squeezed her shoulder. "I wish Nancy had listened to me. But I must get on because I greatly fear time is running out. Nancy might have denied the demon her body, but her soul will have gone to feed it and made it stronger. I'm not sure how much longer it will be confined to the house."

"Hurry then," Ida nodded.

Fourdrinier kissed her gently on the temple, then went to find Charlie.

"Could you run me to the library?"

Charlie was by the cattle shed at the far end of the yard when Fourdrinier came across him. He was leaning on a door, staring into the darkness of the barn.

"I'm hoping to do more research," Fourdrinier explained as he drew level with him. "What are you looking at?"

Charlie pointed into the shadows. It took Fourdrinier's eyes several moments to adjust to the dim light and see what he saw. A big black cat was sitting on a beam at the far end of the shed, glaring at them with large, angry golden eyes.

"It's been about all day. I would like to think it was just another feral that has stopped by, but the cattle are petrified of it. Since it has been in there they have refused to go near their feed. At one point they seemed ready to dash themselves through a hedge to get away from the sight of it,"

Charlie rested his chin on his folded arms. "It's a very strange thing."

Fourdrinier peered at the cat, which greeted him with a low hiss. He saw what Charlie meant. The beast felt a little too calculating and intelligent for his liking, it seemed to be studying them.

"Should I get my shotgun?" Charlie asked.

"I would rather have this thing in plain sight," Fourdrinier replied. "If it wants to follow us as a cat, so be it, at least we know where it is."

"I wish I had your confidence," Charlie pushed himself away from the wall and hobbled painfully to one side. He had brought a stick from the house and he leaned on it heavily. "The police have gone then?"

"Yes, about that lift, if you are not fit I have my bicycle..."

"I'll drive you Fourdrinier. It will be quicker and we need some answers soon."

"Steward seemed to imply that we must unravel the mystery of the former house owners first to know how to defeat the entity. I assume this is because they are all interconnected. The being feeds on them, but how? I have to find the root of this problem and then I shall know."

"I've been mulling over that too. It seems to have a rudimentary intelligence, but I wouldn't call it clever. It took over Nancy and it could have escaped the house altogether if it had not been so determined to attack us."

"It has limited ability to plan or think through consequences?"

"Precisely, it acts spontaneously and impulsively. That is a weakness. I don't think it can predict our own moves, it just reacts."

"Its reactions can still be deadly," Fourdrinier half smiled to himself. "But I appreciate the insight."

"Well, I had to do something, because any way you look at this it is going to fall to me and you to resolve the matter."

Fourdrinier turned to his friend and suddenly embraced

him in a hug.

"Fourdrinier..."

"I am very glad you are alive and at my side," Fourdrinier said quickly before he could protest. "There now, I have said my piece and I expect to never have to say it again."

Fourdrinier pulled away and both men shifted awkwardly apart.

"If you would mind not doing that in future..." Charlie said uneasily.

"Do not anticipate it happening again," Fourdrinier assured him. "But sometimes these things have to be said, or rather, expressed."

Charlie rubbed the back of his neck.

"I appreciate your friendship too."

"Good, now that is settled perhaps you would care to escort me to the library?"

"Yes, of course. It won't be a smooth ride, mind."

"Charlie, this whole fiasco is shaping up to be a disaster, so let's not worry about your driving."

⧫

30 - The Diary of Reverend William Mantle

August 1789

I have come to a decision. For many nights I have prayed for an answer and finally I feel I have one. This morning I woke and heard my daughters laughing together, they were singing ring-a-ring-of-roses and their feet were stomping on the floor as they danced with the words. But they had altered the last line and I shall never forget what I heard.

Ring-a-ring-of-roses
A pocketful of posies,
Atishoo, atishoo!
Amy falls down!

Amy falls down! I heard those words so plainly I could not be mistaken. I am certain now that I must seek her out, this strange angel of my dreams. Some meaning is hidden here and only she can explain. I must apologise for my last words to her. Perhaps I shall face her fury and be cast aside, but God bids me to try and so at least I must.

I have fetched the dreaded elixir from the man Temple. He is an evil looking soul, so thin I swear a gust of wind would carry him away. He has a bad leg and rotten teeth, but he is not short of a penny or two, I saw as much when he opened his pouch to accept my coin for the drug. No, he is a miser, but a wily one. He keeps a scarred, old mastiff at his side and a knife in his pocket. He appeared in Syderstone about a year ago and since then I have heard no good of him, except that he is a fine medicine man who can provide any cure a person might need. I know many in the village now seek him out before they try the surgeon. Perhaps he is a villain, but he is a helpful one. Anyway, from his ragged coat he drew a key and with the key he opened a chest and from that he dispensed the white powder I clutch in my palm. It is wrapped in a twist of paper and I am half sick with the thought of taking it. A part of me craves the ease it will bring, while another part dreads it and recalls the suffering I went through to cleanse my body of the substance the first time. I have only bought one, singular dose, so I shall not be tempted to consume more. If I can thus monitor myself then perhaps I shall keep this illness at bay.

There is wine at my hand, once I mix my drink I shall lie back and put this paper to one side until it is over. I am afraid, I confess. Who do I write this for? Perhaps for my children or for their children? Whoever reads this, do not judge me harshly for I have every mind to be strong, if only I could. I must see my angel again. I believe this is God's will and if only by poison can I do it then so shall it be. The twist of paper has split open in my hand. I have no choice now.

~ ~ ~ * ~ ~ ~

God's will is a blessing, I am wont to forget. My troubles leached from me as I supped my opium and lay back on my bed. The ache in my leg eased for the first time in years and my body stretched out in utter contentment. I was at peace, yet my thoughts were still lively and fresh. A sudden clearness of vision pervaded my senses. I saw perfectly how things must be, how they must become. There is a darkness in my parish, in my very home. I have avoided it, chased it behind the rational logic of my upbringing, but it is there nonetheless, and so too is my angel.

I wish I might have asked her how I had changed since

we had last spoken. I am certain I have aged, my injuries weaken me and I have grown thin and lost my grace. Where my arms were taut and muscular, they now look scrawny, their suppleness now flaccid, their tone diminished. I see myself as I am, and cannot lie. These years have been hard. But here was Amy! And her beauty was as radiant and perfect as ever I had remembered.

She stared at me a long time. It was not an angry or accusing look, nor even sorrowful. I sensed she was amused.

"I am pleased to see you again," I said, somewhat pathetically. It was a poor thing to say considering how I had stormed off and declared her a fantasy of my mind.

"I have seen you every day," Amy said simply. "Just, you could not see me."

"My daughter has though."

A puzzled frown flitted over Amy's face.

"The girl at the pond?"

"Yes."

"She saw me weeping."

"Yes, Amy. And because of that I have made this effort to find you and renew our friendship," I started to wonder how long this dose of opium would last for me, how long did I have? I wished to hasten her. "I was wrong, I now see, about the room. I have come to rethink all that I said."

She cocked her head on one side.

"I know."

"Then you understand why I have sought you out?"

"You wish to understand the secret of the room and I dearly wish to share it, for I think only you can disperse this evil that lingers about us."

"What is this evil, Amy? How does it come to be here?"

Amy studied me for a moment and then she removed the embroidered headdress that kept back her golden locks. I had longed for such a moment, to see her hair flowing freely down her shoulders. But when she turned about, so I might see the full extent of her glory, I cringed at the nasty, bloody gashes at the back of her skull.

"I died William. It was an evil death because of its execution, and because of that an evil was born," Amy replaced her headdress and moved closer. "Emotion is a truly powerful thing, do you not agree?"

"I do," I said, still sickened by the wounds I had witnessed.

"When I died I was deeply sad and desperate. I was already ailing in both spirit and body. I prayed to God that he would relieve me of this burden, but I did not pray for death. I expected a visitor on the day I perished. I do not know if it was he..." Amy shook her head. "I died suddenly and cruelly, in my last moments I was angry and hateful. I screamed hate with all my soul at my husband who had forsaken me for the queen. I let out this venom in a curse I hardly knew I spoke. It is said, when a person dies through violence or misadventure their soul lingers, and sometimes the strength of their despair at that moment is strong enough to impress itself on the very fabric of the place they died."

I understood some of what Amy said, but the rest was riddles to me. She saw I was confused and smiled.

"William, this evil came from my death. It sprang into existence as a vague idea with my death throes. It was no more than a thought or feeling that lingered in the air and made people imagine they felt a chill at the spot where I died. And so it would have remained until it faded away, except I could not leave and take my place in God's realm. I was bitter and jealous. I was angry. I would not leave, would not heed the angels calling me. I chose to remain and to let fester the darkest emotions I was capable of, and so this strangeness I had first summoned now fed on my rage and hate, and it grew into something else."

Amy touched the edge of her headdress as if adjusting it. I feared she might remove it again and braced myself, but instead she pushed back a strand of hair and started to talk.

"My ghost was a burden on the people of the house

where I died. They had a priest cast out my spirit and it was necessary for me to wander the countryside, a lost soul seeking... I do not know what I sought. Perhaps, a home? It took some time to realise the evil had come with me. It seemed attached to my spirit somehow, so wherever I wandered it followed. It was like an imp at my side. I hardly sensed the harm within it, not then at least.

"I found my way to my mother's home at Syderstone. At first I was welcomed. I saw the fine building as it had once been and it was the most handsome of places. I was safe there. I could have stayed as long as I desired, until I was ready to heed the call of the angels. But still I could not relinquish my bitterness! It grew and grew, and so at my side grew the imp it had spawned. And as it festered, so the beautiful dream I had been welcomed into started to fade. Reality slipped in. I started to see the house as it was, rather than as it had been. Oh, but it was a ruin. It had fallen down in my lifetime, yet somehow I had seen it restored. It made me so morose to see it like that. It seemed to mock the life I had led, ruined as it was too, falling apart. Again I was hateful and again the evil fed on my anger and grew. I stumbled away. I came slowly to the church next door. I thought to pray. I could not. Then I saw this house. I came inside because it seemed to welcome me," Amy glanced at me. "The curate was handsome. I decided I should stay. He reminded me of Robert. I did not realise how great the evil had grown or that others might sense it, but he did – the clergyman. He saw me too, once or twice. The evil did not wish to be grounded in one place and it set to cause mischief with noises about the house. I do not know when it became cunning. Perhaps it acted out of some animal intellect. It tried to drive me away and I would not go and then the curate decided to perform an exorcism.

"Can I blame him? His house was tormented by one forlorn ghost and this evil spirit that broke his sleep and disturbed his thoughts. He seemed to understand there were two of us and he attempted to seal my spirit in the room I showed you, confine me there so I might not disturb him. He chose to cast the evil spirit into the pond in the garden. I do not know what went wrong, but my spirit went into the pond and the evil was trapped in the room. As soon as it realised what had happened it set to work tormenting the curate. His maid slept in that room and was chased out by footsteps, rappings and manic laughter. When the curate tried to sleep there he was also overcome. In desperation he nailed shut the room and told no one to ever use it. I think he hoped the evil within would fade away with time."

I was fascinated by Amy's story; how it reminded me of the witch's legend Sarah had told me of. She seemed so penitent and sweet stood before me. That she had created this darkness seemed almost impossible, yet I believed her. Really what other choice was there?

"Over the centuries the exorcism has faded," Amy continued. "At least, where it concerns the pond. I am free to wander within the limits of this house and grounds. I cannot reach the church, though I have tried. The seals around the room are kept strong because of the men of God who inhabit this place and cast their prayers into the ether, and so the evil remains trapped, but it does not weaken, instead it too strengthens. It feeds on souls, especially hate-filled ones. But it can only do limited harm. If someone was to spend time in the room with it, be exposed to its full menace, that would be different. Which is why I found a way to hide the room from people's eyes. Except, now I am so tired and my strength for such things is almost gone. You must do something William, or else this thing will keep growing. I'm not sure what it will become, but it cannot be good and it dreams only of harming those it can reach."

"Are you sure of this?" I asked.

Her pale face turned to me and she dabbed at her eyes.

"As sure as I am that it was my folly that brought it to life."

"Amy..."

"I should have accepted my fate and left this world to the living, then no harm would have followed. I just could not go William. I missed Robert so and I had hoped he would come to me again, one day."

"Your husband?" I racked my brains for the full name of the man Amy had been married to, I was certain I had once known, and then her surname pounced into my memory. "Dudley, you married Robert Dudley."

"Yes, and I loved him too," Amy sounded miserable. "He was my handsome lover, when we danced at our wedding I could not remember being happier, but our happiness grew stale and cold. He dedicated himself to our queen, turned his love from me to her, and I could not bear him a son. That ruined us."

"I am sorry Amy," I said, and I meant it.

"I have had many years to realise that such unhappiness occurs and a woman can do nothing about it. I just wish I could be certain he was not the one who wanted me dead."

I was stunned.

"Wanted you dead?"

"I believe I was murdered William. I am not certain because I saw no one, but in my last few days I was aware of tension about me and danger."

"No, surely, this is not what a loving husband does?"

"Ah, but as I said he was no longer my loving husband. He loved the queen, or at least her power. Who was I to rival her? The country girl who could not even give her husband an heir in eleven years of marriage? Once dead, I was an obstacle no more. Do not pity me William, I have done that enough. I should have realised a marriage born of carnal desires, would result in disappointment."

Amy was such a sad creature to me then. I wanted to say how wrong she was, how my love for Octavia had begun with carnal thoughts. I admit as much, I lusted for her and this became love, and we were certainly not disappointed. Then I checked myself, because Amy had said her husband had cast his affections elsewhere and was that not exactly what I had done when I fell in love with Amy? I was upset with myself, but I could not show it, we needed to keep talking.

"You want me to chase out this evil?"

"Yes, you must."

"I do not know how. I do not know how even to begin."

"Then you must learn."

Amy suddenly stood.

"Your opium is wearing off."

I suddenly realised the dull ache was beginning in my leg again. The dose had been small, yet even so I had expected it to last longer. I started to doubt Temple's honesty and the purity of his products.

"You must not seek me out again William, do you understand? You must forsake the opium and concentrate on the task at hand."

"Yes," I said, but I lied. I had every intention of finding Amy again, of continuing to talk to my beautiful angel. I would not let her go again, besides, I had been reminded of the pleasure of the drug coursing through my system, the way it removed all anguish and anxiety.

"William, I shall not come again."

She was insistent and I nodded at her, agreeing even though I really did not care. I was falling under the spell of the poppy and found it impossible to contemplate her sternness.

I slept. When I awoke my leg seemed to burn as though I had only just broken it. I cried out in pain. The house was quiet, apparently empty. For some reason this angered me. Should they not be here when I was suffering? I buried my head in a pillow and groaned, my fingers bunching the fabric. I suffer God, I weep, and you do nothing to spare me? Why do I fall so low in your regard? Why have you abandoned me?

I am confused. Amy is gone and all I can think of is how soon I can risk seeing Temple again. I apologise, dearest

Octavia, for this weakness that fills me, but if I do nothing I fear I shall go insane. Who would begrudge me another dose?

I shall cease writing now, for my thoughts are plain enough. I must ease my agonies and then I shall contemplate the problem of the room and what lies behind. If I had not the proof of my daughter's eyes I would think myself as insane as before. At least I have Amy back, this consoles me. I must end. I must think. There is much to be done.

31 – Norwich, Norfolk 1955

The librarian could not find a book on Amy Robsart alone – she had not constituted a biography to herself – but she was able to find two volumes on Robert Dudley which might prove useful. Fourdrinier took himself to a quiet corner, drew out some sheets of paper and a pencil, and started reading.

Amy Robsart did not attract a great deal of attention from the authors of the books. Her early marriage to Dudley was uneventful in comparison to the political life he was leading. Embroiled in the plot to put Lady Jane Grey on the throne, cast into the Tower and in real danger of losing his head, Robert's story had little time for the humble wife left behind in various neighbours' country homes. Amy was as silent as a church mouse in the records. She might as easily have not existed. Robert courted the new queen, Elizabeth I, and was soon her favourite and rumoured lover. It seemed obvious in his younger years that, given the chance, Robert would marry the queen without hesitation. Elizabeth's views were less clear, but she did seem to favour Dudley over all others. The one thing standing in their way was Amy.

Robert's early love for his wife seemed to dwindle to resentfulness. He was disappointed that she bore him no heir and that she prevented him from aspiring to wed a monarch. By the 1550s, the royal court was awash with rumours that Robert wanted his wife dead and had plans to poison her. By all accounts it seemed Elizabeth was equally anxious to see the lady out of the picture. Yet at the same time there was news that Amy was grievously ill with a malady of the breast. Fourdrinier understood this to mean she was suffering a form of breast cancer and was probably not long for the world anyway. Robert's biographers were divided on how he accepted this situation; one argued he was still fond of his wife and grieved for her, the other considered he was just biding his time, pleased nature had acted in his favour. Fourdrinier chose, magnanimously, to side with the former.

If Amy was initially a fleeting presence in the story the biographers wove, that all changed in 1560 when she, briefly, became the star of both volumes. It was 8 September and Amy was staying at Cumnor Place, Oxfordshire with family friends. Robert had not been to see his wife in a year and it was obvious to those closest to Amy that she missed him and wished he would come soon. If Amy was sick there were no particular signs, though she was prone to sudden angry outbursts and, on the day of her death, she insisted that her whole household go to the local fair. Fourdrinier mused, as the biographers did, that this was a strange thing to do. Did she just desire to be alone? Or were other thoughts on her mind? It wasn't helpful to speculate, but it was interesting to ponder that if some of her household had stayed behind, Amy might have lived out 1560.

The fair kept the household out all day. When they returned it was to be greeted by the body of Amy Robsart lying at the foot of the stone, dog-leg staircase. Her neck was broken. At first glance it seemed she had fallen down the steps. Robert's immediate response seemed to be grief-stricken shock. He insisted the full truth of the accident must come out at an inquest and asked Amy's brother, John Appleyard, to be present. The verdict was perhaps foregone. The tragedy was ruled an accident, though there was some small talk that Amy had been depressed and wished to free herself from the constraints of her unhappy life. The coroner suspected no foul play and Amy was buried in grand style with dignified mourners dressed in black following her coffin. Robert frugally removed her diamond ring and sold it, but then he was again deep in debt.

The funeral was not an end to the controversy. Robert's enemies suggested he had killed Amy – not personally because he had been away, but by hiring someone to do the deed. Had Amy been pushed? No one could quite dismiss the thought, even if it did come from those who wished Robert ill and also wanted to end any risk of marriage between him and the queen. It certainly had this effect on Elizabeth who delayed and delayed before finally declaring she could never marry her favourite. Robert's hopes were dashed. His brother-in-law, John Appleyard, who had at first supported the verdict of accidental death now sided with Robert's enemies and threatened to bring more disgrace on the former favourite's reputation. Robert found himself fighting fires on all sides, with no prospect of marriage to the queen to make his burden worthwhile. If he had killed his wife, it had been all for nought.

Fourdrinier closed the books and sat back in his chair. His paper was a heap of notes and question marks. Was Amy ill? Did Robert still love her? Did she trip? Did she jump? Was she pushed? How did all this speculation help him? Amy Robsart was the key to the mystery; that was clear from William Mantle's diary and the words Donald Steward had whispered. Amy's death had been unexpected and unfortunate. She had died barely 28, an unhappy soul, who felt she had failed in all aspects of womanhood. Her husband had left her and she could not bear his child. She wandered from house to house, not even with a home to call her own, and always tormented by the rumours that filtered from the royal court of her husband's activities with the queen. Such misery and despair has an effect on people.

Fourdrinier recalled a story he had heard in the trenches during WWI. In 1915 there had been heavy fighting around a Belgium village called Hooge. The place had been in and out of British hands on several occasions. Earlier in the year the Royal Engineers had laced the area with tunnels filled with explosives and sent several tons of earth (and more than one German) soaring into the air when they detonated them. The Hooge crater still remained as a monument to the exercise. Fourdrinier had arrived in Ypres in 1916, fresh to the trenches and scared out of his wits. The older men told him tall stories to pass the time; tales of ghostly Germans or lost friends returning to say goodbye. Despite his nerves, Fourdrinier was smart enough to avoid being spooked by their legends. There was one story, however, that had everyone upset, one that even the officers bought into. Near Hooge there were a series of trenches that had been heavily fought over, at some points the British were spitting distance from the German trenches. They had been overrun and retaken dozens of times and the ground heaved with the blood of the dead spilt upon it. Men called it an 'evil' place. Considering there were many such miserable trenches about, equally blood-stained, it seemed odd that this trench had earned a distinction. Fourdrinier only went to it once and once was more than enough. He understood what his comrades had meant the instant he exited the communication trench and stepped into the narrow world where hundreds had died. The place had an atmosphere. It was the smell, or the appearance, in all other regards it was a plain trench. It was not littered with bodies at that moment in time, nor were the signs of death and destruction more obvious there than in other trenches. But he sensed it alright, that feeling of evil. As if something unpleasant and malicious was watching over the trench and seeking to delight itself with more death and sacrifice.

Fourdrinier had not thought of that place in years. Amy's words, spoken to William Mantle over a century before the Great War, had brought it all back. She was right. Strong emotion, particularly negative emotion, imprinted itself on the landscape and could give a place a presence, an atmosphere that others could sense. Perhaps, under the right circumstances, that presence could be transformed into something more – into the entity Amy spoke of. Fourdrinier thought of the Concentration camps Charlie had alluded to. Those sites had been left untouched; people thought of them as cursed. No one would build on the land or try to farm it for fear of what had occurred there, for fear of the evil that had once flourished. Fourdrinier shuddered. Yes, a demon could be raised from such a place. Surely it was just a translation of the demons that dwelled within a person? If a person could project love and have it felt by others, then an equally strong, yet negative, emotion such as hate should produce the same effect? And once it was projected, why should it not stay if it were strong enough? Could you not feel the love in a letter written to a sweetheart a century ago? Could you not feel anger or bitterness in the same way? Was it just the words, or something more intangible, something that had been trapped in the paper at the time of writing?

Fourdrinier's mind was whirring. There had been surprisingly few deaths in the parsonage, since the curates living in it often moved out before their earthly years had ended, so how many souls had perished there for certain? William Mantle, dead before his years, as yet what had caused it was not clear to Fourdrinier; Margaret Stewart, drowned in a pond as a child, again dead before her time; then Donald Steward and Nancy, murdered.

Murdered? Fourdrinier felt a fool. Had they not all been murdered? Each death had somehow been engineered, he could not say for certain how in the case of William Mantle, but now he was certain of it. It had all begun with the murder of Amy Robsart, the girl had not tripped, no, she had been pushed and that was why she had struggled to move on, why such hatred, anguish and fear had escaped her in her last moments! There had been so many rumours concerning the manner of her death and how convenient it had been for her husband and the queen. What began with a murder had to end with...

Fourdrinier had no solution, not yet, but a new fire was burning within him. Demons had to be slain, be they personal or infernal. The only question was how, and even that was becoming clearer to him. He was thinking of William Mantle, the shade that had stepped before him and spoken. William Mantle had tried to destroy the demon, but had failed, why? Was it because like John Stewart he had lost his courage? Fourdrinier thought not. Mantle was flawed, but he was a good man with perhaps more courage than sense. He had marched into a gang of thugs and paid for it. There was something else. Stewart had been scared off and left, why not Mantle also? Because he had gotten too close? Because he had almost succeeded? It might be in the diary, but Fourdrinier was troubled that there were only two pages remaining in the manuscript he had been given, and they were sparsely written, the last in a hand that seemed to shake and dance about the page.

He pulled the papers out now and turned to the last but one entry.

32 – The Diary of William Mantle
Christmas 1789

I have been visited by my angel no more. God forgive me, but I dosed myself with opium to reach her and before long I was hopelessly under its thrall again. Octavia saved me. She found the drug and cast it away, saw to it I had no coin to spend alone, and spent days with me, nursing the fever and pains that came with my release.

I am free now, but only of the opium. In a daze of agony and obsession, when the world spun and strange insects seemed to leap at me from the walls, I reached up to my Lord and swore that should he deliver me I should remain forever his faithful servant and do as he willed. I was delivered and I know what he wills. The demon resides in the room down the hall. Each day I pass, I notice the door a little more and I know Amy is withdrawing, that she cannot hold on any longer. I must help her. I have read what little I could find on exorcisms, but I fear my knowledge is incomplete, I also fear what others will think should they know of what I am about. Therefore I have determined to do this in secret and to write not another word on the matter. Already I had a fright when the maid turned up these papers, had she read them I doubt they would have allowed me back into the pulpit on Sunday.

I am not mad! If I was could I think so rationally and logically? Octavia says I have a new light in my eyes, as though finally I have come out of my slump and reached a resolution. If only she knew that resolution was to destroy a demon! I shall begin with prayer and see how my actions affect the thing. I have not sensed it yet, Amy's barrier prevents such. Soon, however, I shall know exactly what I face. I hardly dare think what I am about. When I say it to myself I am shocked at my own thoughts. No rational man would ever believe what I intend to do, what I believe I must face!

But I digress. My hand shakes because I am so excited, yes, excited at the prospect of triumphing over evil! I am a soldier going into battle! No one shall know of this skirmish except my wonderful Lord. He is sufficient. I must close now.

Signed William Mantle 24 December 1789
꒰

33 – Norwich, Norfolk 1955

On the final page of William Mantle's diary, Fourdrinier squinted at the rough writing that scrawled across the paper. He picked up a pencil and a new piece of paper and tried to slowly translate the letters. With patience he found words forming, though there were still holes in the text;

1797 ¬– God forgive me! Only ... solution to face on own ground. Death ... to defeat this thing. My death. To keep them all safe.

The writing tailed off into what appeared to be Mantle's signature. Fourdrinier gave a sigh and leaned back in his chair. He was sorry for Mantle, a man who tried so hard and in the end gave his life – was that what he meant? – to destroy the demon and yet still failed. He also had a pang of anxiety, was this the way his fate was destined to go? Would he too be slain?

Removing his glasses he looked over at the wall clock and was shocked to see it was nearly five o'clock. It was rapidly growing dark outside and Fourdrinier had no desire to be outdoors when night truly fell. He had an ominous suspicion that darkness would draw out the evil he was hunting, and spring it from its lurking spot. It knew now he was after it, and it had also fed on a fresh soul. How strong would it be? What would it be capable of? Fourdrinier thought it best to reach Charlie, Maud and his aunt before they discovered without him. He found a phone and called the farm.

Within an hour they were at the dining room table

awaiting a meal of pork and cabbage Maud had prepared. Aunt Ida was hollow-eyed and quiet. Charlie was rubbing the spot on his leg where Nancy had stabbed him with her heel. The stitches had taken well, but they itched. Fourdrinier was looking out the window and noting how dark the sky seemed.

"Isn't it heavy weather?" Charlie remarked, his ears pricked to the sound of his cows lowing unhappily in their stalls. "Thunder storm brewing. Always sets them off."

Fourdrinier felt as though a lead weight were pressing down on his skull.

"Storms help spirits," Ida said softly. "The electrical energy gives them strength."

"Thank you, I needed that comfort," Charlie groaned.

"I don't think the storm is a coincidence," Fourdrinier muttered to himself.

Maud hurried in with a bowl of potatoes.

"I'm all in a fluster, it's so hot in the kitchen," she flapped her apron in her face. "What sort of weather is this for spring?"

She bustled off. Fourdrinier simply shook his head. It struck him no one was really paying attention. A storm last night and a storm tonight with the weather so cool? Coincidence? He thought not. He anticipated the arrival of 'something' very soon.

"These are the last of the crop I pulled in the winter," Charlie said, serving potatoes onto Ida's plate. "They have almost a buttery taste, I always keep some back."

He dropped a fluffy potato onto the plate and then they heard the shriek.

Fourdrinier jumped back from the window at the same instant a lightning bolt skirted the farm and harmlessly extinguished itself on the weathervane. He turned and chased after Charlie and Ida, already heading fast for the kitchen where Maud was.

In the sweltering room Maud was clutching one arm to her bosom, blood dripping through her fingers, while a black cat sat on the draining board and hissed at her. One clawed paw was raised and the thing was about to pounce when the others swept into the room. It turned its head and gave them a wide-mouthed hiss, exposing its sharp fangs.

"It came in the window!" Maud was trapped between the cat and the range stove.

Fourdrinier was slow to catch up with the situation. The black cat had leapt into the house and attacked Maud. The black cat! The one they had wondered about. He was about to step forward and do something when Ida sprang forward in her flowing robes like an avenging angel. With her draping sleeves about her arms she scruffed the cat, ignoring its hissing protests and the claws that flailed everywhere. Swinging back her arm she heaved the cat through the open window. It flew through the air and landed with supernatural grace on the vegetable bed. The second its feet were on solid ground it turned and came racing back towards the window. It jumped at the opening as Ida wrenched it close. There was a horrible moment as the spitting, growling cat jammed itself in the gap of the window and tried to scramble back in. Ida, still holding the window latch with one hand, grabbed up a wooden spoon and lunged out at the monstrous cat, poking and jabbing it, until finally it lost its grip and disappeared from sight. She pulled the window shut fast and pushed down the latch. A moment later the cat appeared on the windowsill outside and hissed at them through the glass.

"Is everything else closed and locked?" Fourdrinier asked, going to his aunt as he spoke and taking her hands to see if she was injured.

"I only opened the window in here because it was so stuffy," Maud assured them.

Charlie slipped his arm around his wife.

"Don't worry, old thing. Not your fault."

"Here, I'll bandage up that arm, while you boys finish serving dinner and make some strong tea," Ida yanked herself from her nephew's grip and took hold of Maud.

"I've got a feeling we will be needing all our strength tonight."

As Maud left the room, looking more dazed than distressed, she suddenly turned back.

"There's an apple tart in the oven, take it out so it doesn't burn!"

Charlie half laughed as he found a tea towel and used it to remove the blisteringly hot pie from the oven.

"That's Maud for you, tough girl. No fretting. She's handy in the calving season, I tell you."

Charlie put the tart on the kitchen table and looked at his friend. Fourdrinier was staring outside. The cat had vanished, replaced by heavy drops of rain.

"What are you thinking?"

"That we have scared it and it is coming for us," Fourdrinier said solemnly.

"Can it harm us? I mean, just on its own? If we don't let it in surely it can do nothing?"

"We shall see," Fourdrinier answered unhelpfully.

Back round the dining room table they ate in silence. The rain noisily pelted at the windows. Maud had gone to close the curtains but Ida had insisted they stay open. She wanted to keep an eye on the outside world. Fourdrinier ate pork and potatoes that tasted like ash in his mouth. The cabbage was sickening as he tried to chew it. There was nothing wrong with Maud's cooking, only something wrong with him. He was afraid.

By the time the tart came through to be served with cream, Fourdrinier was so anxious and bottled up the mere thought made him almost gag. The anticipation of danger was worse than anything else. It felt as though something was just waiting to happen. He ran through in his mind possibilities; but the house was sealed up tight, both chimneys were covered with grills to prevent birds nesting inside. He just had to survive the night he told himself and then tomorrow... What about tomorrow? Would he be any closer to understanding Mantle's cryptic last words or what to do?

"It's a nasty thing, but it has no real power," Ida reflected, spooning up pie as another streak of lightning lit up the clouds.

Fourdrinier cringed as though the bolt had seared every nerve in his body. The next moment they all heard the screaming pandemonium coming from the cattle sheds. Charlie jumped to his feet and grabbed his coat.

"It's luring you out!" Fourdrinier cried.

"Well it's working! I am not letting my cows be slaughtered while I sit indoors!" hauling on his rubber boots and picking up his shotgun Charlie was almost out the door when he sensed Fourdrinier beside him. The vicar was putting on a mackintosh and rain hat.

"Lead on McDuff!" he said with as much courage as he could muster.

Charlie gave him a faint smile as he yanked open the door and stepped into the storm. The weather was worse than Fourdrinier had imagined. The wind whipped at their clothes and pummelled them backwards, the rain hammered down like icy stones and the thunder rolled ominously and continuously. The noise was so loud and constant, Fourdrinier could not hear a word Charlie said, but merely followed him as, rain dripping down their faces and wind lashing their clothes, they hurried for the barns.

It was as dark as a deep pit in the sheds, but the frantic bellowing of the animals led them onwards. Charlie grabbed a torch from a shelf and flashed it about. The beam caught rolling, wide eyes, pale whites exposed in terror. The shed was warm and fuggy, with a sensation of static in the air, but there was a tangy taste that hit the back of their throats as they breathed in. Blood. Charlie moved onwards, light shining from side to side, gun slung over one arm. He was panting hard, anxious and nervous, like the days in the army during a raid.

His torch beam caught a huddled lump on the straw and he dashed forward. Fourdrinier almost lost him as darkness fell about him. The torch vanished with Charlie, and he only kept up because of the sheer terror of being left alone in the dark. Charlie had found what had startled his herd. He was swearing and cursing, rubbing at the massive head of a bull calf lying dead on the floor. Throat slashed open, blood drained out. He was angry and fat tears rolled down his cheeks at the senseless slaughter, at the miserable cruelty. Fourdrinier patted him lightly on the shoulder, thinking he had always been slightly too sensitive for the farming life.

A rustle behind them made them spin around. The cat was perched on the cow shed wall licking at its filthy paws. It was extremely cocky sitting there and, Fourdrinier realised in the split second before the shot, it had clearly not taken into account Charlie's gun. The boom of the shotgun barrel sent the cows into a frenzy again. Fourdrinier felt a heavy body barge into him and almost fell. That could be fatal if the animals stampeded in the confines of the shed. Fortunately Charlie grabbed his arm and kept him on his feet as he raced them to the doorway and back out into the rain.

"Did you get it?"

Rain tumbled into Charlie's eyes. He wiped at them.

"I think so. Better look."

They patrolled the side of the building, Charlie guiding the torch in short sweeps back and forth ahead of them. They both stopped at the same time. There was a black cat lying dead on the path. Fourdrinier gave it a nudge with his foot.

"You got it."

Charlie looked up at the storm clouds overhead.

"So why hasn't the storm abated?"

"It's far from over yet," Fourdrinier answered.

They walked into the centre of the farmyard, Charlie scanning around for any other signs of disturbance.

"What else can it throw at us?" he shone the torch up into the clouds. "I've been through a war! I shouldn't be frightened by this!"

"I don't think the two can be compared. Have you other weapons in the house?"

"An old pistol, somewhere."

"And bullets? We may need it," as Fourdrinier spoke they heard the howl.

At the gate of the farmyard the pouring rain dripped off the sleek black bodies of two of the biggest dogs Fourdrinier had ever seen. Had it been any other night he might have assumed they had strayed from a farm, but he would never have made such a silly assumption under that grizzling storm cloud with the worst the world could offer, in terms of spiritual evil, headed his way.

"Eyes as big as saucers," Charlie gaped at the dogs. "And red, Fourdrinier, red!"

"I had noticed, shall we go inside?" Fourdrinier was edging back towards the door to the house. Charlie followed.

"That's black shuck as sure as I am stood here, Fourdrinier! The demon dog."

"I know the legend," Fourdrinier lay his hand on the door handle and in the same moment the dogs screamed forward.

The speed they crossed the farmyard was astounding, each pace seemed to take them further than was physically possible. Three galloping strides had them almost on Charlie. He shot blindly into the face of one and it wheeled back, while the other plunged at him. Fourdrinier had the farmhouse door open. He threw himself at Charlie and took him to the ground as the frenzied dog went for his throat. It missed and ended up soaring straight over him. The dog landed and spun for the next attack as, somehow, Fourdrinier grappled Charlie in through the open door. The dog was springing at them as the door slammed shut and Fourdrinier shot home the bolts.

Outside the dogs began to pound on the door and it shook terribly in its frame. Both men edged away.

"Will it hold?" Fourdrinier asked?

"I don't know!" Charlie broke open his gun and loaded two more cartridges. "But I'm ready if it breaks. Ask Maud for the pistol."

Fourdrinier's heart was racing painfully; he had visions of himself collapsing with a heart attack through all the strain as he headed back to the dining room. The women were stood up waiting for him, remarkably calm.

"What are they?" Maud asked.

"Demon dogs. Maud, I would not normally ask, but do you happen to have any of those superstitious devices used to ward off witches?"

"Like corn dollies and witch balls?"

"Yes."

Maud glanced about the room as if trying to locate something, then nodded and went to the fireplace.

"There is a box in the chimney with a child's shoe in it, said to ward away evil," she reached in and pulled out an old cardboard box, handing it to Fourdrinier.

"We need more than that. Something we can place at every possible entry to this house."

"I don't think there is anything else in the chimney," Maud reached in her arm again. "We found the shoe when we gave it a clean."

Suddenly she jumped back and gave a scream, flinging her arm about and yelling in terror. Her arm was covered in crawling, biting black spiders, racing down her skin from the wrist to her neck heading for her face.

"Get them off! Get them off!"

Ida grabbed a hand brush from the fireplace and swung at the spiders. Maud was shrieking as they grew closer and closer to her face. She turned her head, trying to separate herself as far as she could from her arm. Fourdrinier came to her other side and plucked off the stray insects that Ida missed with her brushed. He snatched one from Maud's cheek and squashed it with a satisfying squelch, then he nipped another from her ear. Ida was stomping on the ones she had brushed onto the floor, hopping on them as they ran this way and that. Fourdrinier pulled the last spider from Maud's hair and she slumped backwards against the table, trembling and pale.

"I hate spiders," she said in a voice that was barely a whisper.

"What's that noise?" Ida asked, glancing up from the floor.

"It's coming from the fireplace."

As they looked on in horror, a thick mass of spiders leaked out of the chimney and poured onto the hearth rug. They were like a hideous river, a torrent of black bodies and legs. As they leaked out of the chimney so they spread out, widening into a flowing swarm upon the rug. Maud gave a horrific yell and leapt completely into the table, clutching her arms around her knees.

"What's happening Fourdrinier?" Charlie yelled from the hallway.

"Just concentrate on those dogs!" Fourdrinier called back.

There were spiders running over his shoes, heading towards his trouser legs, creeping over his socks. The skin on his calves began to tingle as small feet touched him and then vicious fangs bit him. Ida was attacking the floor with the brush sweeping, this way and that, sending heaps of black bodies dancing into the air. She was like a madwoman, smiling and cursing, stomping her feet about and shaking out her robes when one wing of the spider army tried an assault.

Maud, upon the table, was starting to shriek again as the spiders swarmed up the legs of the table and headed towards her from all corners. Curling herself into as tight a ball as she could she cowered and sobbed, watching her worst nightmare approach her.

Fourdrinier slapped at his legs, jumped from one foot to the next, shook his trousers and hoped to God these strange things weren't poisonous. And still they were coming! There was no halt to the stream of them seeping out of the chimney. Soon the room would be awash with them and for as many as they killed a hundred more would replace them.

"Stopper the leak!" Ida shouted at him, now half covered in spiders despite her fury.

"What?"

"The box! The child's shoe! It was protecting the chimney! As soon as Maud removed it we gave this witchcraft an open doorway!"

Maud gave a whimper as spiders crawled up the bottom of her skirt. She struck at them in panic, lashed out only for dozens to latch onto her hand and arms, and start the journey up to her face again. She wailed like a woman deranged.

"Put back the box, Norman!" Ida snapped. "It was you who said we should place warding objects at every entry!"

That he had. Fourdrinier clutched the box tighter in his hand. There were spiders throughout his clothes, some were sidling up his neck, they bit him at every step and he dreaded what would happen when they reached his mouth and eyes. Behind him Maud was gurgling in stupefied horror and Ida was exhausted at trying to hold back the tide. He went for the chimney, but here the deluge was at its worst and as he stepped forward he felt soft bodies breaking under his shoes and then others flooding over his legs. It wasn't the odd bite now; he was encased by the creatures. He moved another step and it was like wading through heavy water. The spiders were falling from the chimney so fast he could not make out their individual bodies and he had to stick his arm in there? He panicked at the thought, the idea of putting his arm into that dark cavity while these menaces fell down on him. He was not afraid of spiders, but even he could feel a pang of nauseating terror at braving the chimney-breast.

Yet there was no choice. If he did not do something he would be overwhelmed anyway. He could not even see his legs anymore, they were one heaving mass of spiders, there were so many upon him that the bottom layer was doomed to be crushed by the many above. He braced his hand on the mantel over the fire, clung to it as a source of hard reality, then leaned forward as far as he could. His hand touched the falling spiders and the feel of the pellet-sized thoraxes hitting him made him withdraw with revulsion. He sucked in his breath and pushed forward again. Maud was crying and retching in terror, Ida was trying to keep the spiders off her face. Around them the bodies were building and building, mounting into arachnid walls, flooding the room.

Fourdrinier closed his eyes and shoved his hand forward as fast as he could. He tried not to let any thought enter his mind as he fumbled for the ledge the shoe had come from. If for even an instant he allowed himself to imagine what was going on around him, what the stuff was that was running over his arm, he would never be able to finish this. He ignored the surge of arachnids that had landed on his shoulders and were heading up into his hair. His fingers nudged writhing bodies and were pinched by fangs. He felt the scurry of the unpleasant creatures on his skin as he located the ledge in the brickwork. He nestled the box on the edge, it almost fell from his grasp as he adjusted his hold. For a moment it hung in the balance whether he would drop it or not. Then a spider nipped his arm and the pain sent a surge of action into his numb body. He gave the box a shove onto the ledge and stumbled back, the skin across his body rippling with disgust, his flesh itchy and taut. He shuddered several times, the violence of the last convulsion throwing him back into the table.

He opened his eyes when he heard Maud being sick. At first he could not believe what he saw and then he yanked up his shirt sleeves and trouser legs. The spiders had entirely vanished. Maud was still rocking on the table.

"I've... always... hated.... Them," she said in a staccato fashion.

"I dare say we will all feel that way from now on," Ida said with some sympathy.

Fourdrinier touched the skin around his neck. There was no sign of a bite. He even examined the bottom of his shoes, but there was no sign of an arachnid infestation. He was beginning to relax when he heard the crash of the front door and the boom of a shotgun.

"Aunt Ida, fetch a bowl of water or a mirror, anything that will cast a reflection and bring it to the front door fast!"

Fourdrinier raced to the front door and saw Charlie pressed against the wall opposite it, loading more cartridges into his shotgun. He glanced at the door and saw the glass pane in the upper portion had been smashed. It was probably not big enough for the dogs to haul themselves through, but from the marks of shot in the woodwork around it, it seemed they had tried.

"What was going on in there?" Charlie said as he slammed the gun barrel back into place.

"Spiders."

"Huh?"

"Really, don't ask. Did you get one?" as if in answer a demon dog's head appeared at the broken window and lunged through. It had longer jaws than Fourdrinier had reckoned on and he came close to being snatched into them. Charlie aimed his gun and shot off two barrels. The dog's head retreated with a whining sound.

"They're tougher than the cat. The shot doesn't seem to do more than stun them," the hammering began again, but the dogs were being careful not to risk exposing their heads in the window.

"I have Ida and Maud working on wards for the doors and windows."

"How does a rational vicar like you know about wards?" Charlie managed a grin as he fed more cartridges into his gun.

"I read a lot," Fourdrinier replied with a huff. "I never thought I would be using any such superstitious stuff though. I don't suppose you have any crosses?"

Charlie shook his head.

"Pity. Those at least would be firmly within Christian tradition."

Ida appeared with a large mirror awkwardly held in her arms.

"Good, stand it where Charlie is," Fourdrinier motioned.

"Exactly how will rearranging the furniture in my house help?" Charlie asked as the mirror shoved him from his place.

"My dear boy, do you know nothing of the old ways?" Ida tutted at him almost cheerfully. "Evil cannot stand its own reflection, because reflections reveal the truth. Demons and evil entities won't look in a mirror. Same principle with witches."

Fourdrinier nodded to the front door.

"Notice anything?"

Outside there was no hammering or whining, silence instead reigned.

"Maud is filling bowls of water and putting them beneath every window, she said there might be some glass baubles in the attic for the Christmas tree if you would care to fetch them?" Ida's comment was directed at Charlie.

He gave them both an odd look and then headed for the staircase.

"Well Norman, this has been a fine evening so far!"

Fourdrinier had to hand it to his aunt for being so stoical under the circumstances.

"Those spiders, all of this, it's really a figment of our imaginations, isn't it?" he replied.

Ida considered.

"I suppose we could perceive it that way, but was the terror those delusions caused any less because they were not real?"

"No, that is for certain. Is Maud alright?"

"Embarrassed, but no real harm done. This thing, it is

determined to drive us insane or find some way of killing us off."

"You don't think it has the power to kill on its own then? I mean, it has to manipulate us into doing it ourselves. Nancy pulled a knife on herself. Steward, well maybe he thought he felt a push which caused him to stumble when in fact there was no one behind him."

"No, Norman, this thing can kill. Think of Maud's arm."

Fourdrinier did and then his mind flicked to the bull calf in the cow shed.

"I was just hoping..."

"You were trying to be rational again, trying to think of a logic for this situation. As I told you before, reasoning will only get you into deeper trouble, there is nothing rational about this, nothing logical. The sooner you realise that the safer you will be."

Fourdrinier gave a nod, then awkwardly wrapped his arms around his diminutive great aunt and gave her a hug.

"You were like a whirling dervish out there."

Ida gave a grunt of laughter.

"I have been a fool!"

"No, just maybe a little too rational, like me."

Fourdrinier squeezed her slight body, her shoulder blades digging into his arms. He had hardly had time to think over the last few days, but just in that instant he realised how awful it would be to lose his aunt to this evil. How he could never let that happen. For all her quirks and oddities, he loved the old woman wrapped in his arms and he would protect her with all his might.

Perhaps he had always known this battle would come down to him and him alone. Now he was certain. Whatever had made its home in Syderstone it was his duty to eliminate it. As a spiritual warrior – was that too pompous? – as a man of the cloth, this was his domain and he had to destroy the demon of Syderstone no matter what. But he would not risk others, he would do this alone.

Slowly he pulled away from his aunt.

"We best make this house secure."

Over the next hour the house became ornamented with shimmering bowls of water on the carpet, glass baubles hanging in windows and mirrors propped at angles to the doors. When everything was in place it seemed like some strange game was being organised and Fourdrinier wondered what he would have made of such a sight had he just happened upon it in one of his parishioner's' homes. The creatures outside had gone silent. They were either a spent force for the night or the superstitious trinkets were working.

Fourdrinier went to find Charlie who was just checking on the last fireplace in the main bedroom upstairs.

"This is a queer turn of events," Charlie said, his head half in the fireplace.

"Charlie, I'm nipping out."

Charlie extracted himself from the chimney at speed and stared at his friend.

"Were you not present for the last two hours?"

"I have a vague idea how to stop this thing, but I need to be sure and I won't put either you, Maud or my aunt in any more danger."

"Where are you going?"

"The parsonage."

"Not alone you aren't," Charlie folded his arms obstinately.

Fourdrinier had expected as much.

"Charlie, we both know out of the lot of us I am the least likely to be attacked. It can't get its spectral head around me, not yet at least. I shall say a prayer the whole way to the parsonage. If it dares pursue me it can risk the wrath of God. I know for certain that is not a risk I would want to take."

"But why the parsonage?"

"Donald had some papers there, I need to look through them. Papers that belonged to William Mantle and should contain some answers," it was a lie, but Fourdrinier was not about to admit his real reason.

"This is crazy."

"As an old soldier you know as well as I do that sometimes direct action is the only course available and that, pragmatically, the fewest number of men should be exposed to danger. The fewest number this time is me alone."

Charlie turned his head away. He didn't reply at once.

"My faith isn't strong enough, is it?"

"Not your faith, your trust. When you believe you can be forgiven and when you realise you can trust God then it will be a different matter. Look, I need you to be here and prevent the ladies from knowing where I have gone. Particularly Ida, I don't want her following me."

"What will you tell them?"

"That I am retiring for the night to meditate on the situation and to try to come up with a solution."

"Fourdrinier if you get yourself killed I..." Charlie gritted his teeth, the words refusing to come. "We'll all be stuffed, that's what it is."

Fourdrinier gave his old friend a smile.

"You see, that's what I mean about trust. Trust that the Lord has no intention of seeing evil triumph over him."

"Are you sure about this?"

"Absolutely."

They wandered downstairs and found the women in the kitchen. Fourdrinier gave his excuses for his absence, ending with the hope his research and meditation would finally provide an answer. He thought his aunt was not entirely convinced, but she made no comment. Then he retreated with Charlie to the front door.

Gingerly the younger man opened it. There was no sight of demon dogs, cats or spiders.

"I want to check on my cows," Charlie said.

Fourdrinier nodded. Calling over his shoulder to Maud that that was what he was doing, Charlie eased himself out the door. Fourdrinier strode out beside him.

"Good luck, old man," Charlie shook Fourdrinier's hand and looked close to saying something else.

Fourdrinier waited for a moment, but when no words came he placed his other hand over Charlie's and gripped it tight.

"I'll be fine," then he put on his hat and headed off into the night.

⬚

34 - Cumnor Place, Oxfordshire 1560

Amy sits on her bed and strokes a brush through her hair. She is alone. All alone. She has sent away her servants, her companions, even the women who are just resident in the house. She wishes to be all alone, to be away from their voices for just a while. Sometimes her ears pound with their chatter and she wants to bellow them into silence. The fair was a good excuse to see them depart, maybe now she can put her mind in order.

Robert has abandoned her. Of that she is now certain. A year ago she would have laughed and denied it, remembering his love-filled eyes at their wedding, the way he danced with her, the way he kissed her and took her to his bed. But that was a year ago and in twelve months she has not seen him, has not heard a single word. He lives for the queen now. Maybe he loves her majesty.

She knows there are rumours. As much as her household try to shield her she hears the gossip. A man was been arrested for saying the queen is swollen with child by none other than her favourite Dudley. He will probably have his ears cut off for spreading slander, but what if it were true? Robert spends more time in the queen's chamber than any other man, enough time surely to...

Amy remembers his hands stroking her white flesh, his teeth nibbling at her neck and ears, his confidence around her. She was a virgin, but for sure he was not, and the queen is still a young woman too, could she be blind to what Amy saw? What Amy still sees?

Amy stands and walks the room. A hand goes to her breast where the pain lingers. The doctors have been no aid, she is not sure if she will die. The malady swells on her bosom and she feels ill so much of the time. Perhaps this is why she has never had a child? Is that too the reason Robert has tired of her? Oh Robert! Why did she ever marry such a man? He was handsome and strong, and she loved him, loved him so her heart would burst. And who was it who stood beside him in the Tower during those dreadful years? She slams her hand angrily on a table. Not princess Elizabeth, that is for sure. Amy Dudley stood by her husband, comforted him on the deaths of his father and brothers, did what she could to ease his confinement. Has he forgotten?

Amy paces. Perhaps she should not have stayed alone. The thoughts she had hoped to reconcile in her mind have instead turned into a burning hate. She had aimed to bring some logical conclusion to her suffering, to restore her mental self. Now, rather, she wants to find Robert and scratch his face and spit in his eyes. She has never been so furious! When her mother and father died did they not think they had left their daughter in safe, kind hands? Did they not die knowing she would be cared for? And where is your care Robert Dudley, she cries to herself, where is your anguish for me as I feel anguish for you?

She goes into the hall. She is restless, though movement sends new pains up her body. If Robert had been around more often than maybe she would have fallen with child. She is so angry she could scream. Then the pain takes its toll and she slumps down on her knees and clutches her face in her hands.

She heard the newest rumour this morning. In the kitchens they talk so much that it is easy to hear what others try to hide. She was only walking past because of the pain in her breast which refused to leave her and which only the walking seemed to soothe a little. Sometimes it makes it worse, sometimes it heals, it is as though even her sickness cannot decide what it shall be. At the kitchen she heard them talking, the serving girls and the lad who lifts and carries because he is too dense for anything else. They spoke of Amy and she listened, of course she listened! They talked about how sorry they felt for the poor lady, with her disease and all, but hark, have you not heard what they say? Someone heard it from a fish merchant, who heard it from a boatman in London, who heard it from a woman who knows a woman who is a lowly servant in the royal court but hears all the news. Oh and isn't it dreadful! They say Lord Dudley and the queen are wishing for Amy's death! Some say they are even planning it and that Lord Dudley has sent poison! Is that why Amy ails so? Why a woman in her prime is stricken with agony in her most feminine parts?

The gossip was grotesque. It didn't just hurt Amy's feelings but destroyed them. She was too sick to her stomach to eat breakfast, and was it not this new information that had caused her so intensely to want to be alone? To think over this idea that Robert, her darling Robert, could wish her dead?

Amy is too weary to weep anymore. Too tired of all the thoughts that buzz in her mind. She realises that somewhere along the way anguish turned into bitterness. Sorrow into hate. Dismay into white fury. If she saw Robert now she might be just as likely to kill him if she had the strength.

She drags herself back to her feet. She should return to bed, but she wants to get outside and smell the fresh air. It won't be many weeks before it is too cold for her to venture outdoors. How she dreads winter! Once she longed for it as a time when Robert would return from the queen's summer progress. If only God had blessed her with children she might find some alternative to this misery, but God has not been kind. Amy reserves a certain portion of her anger just for him.

She reaches the top of the stairs, old and worn, treaded by a thousand feet, and now hers. She grips the bannister and for one moment it crosses her mind to jump. To tumble herself down the stairs and end all the misery inflicted upon her. She will not though. As angry as she is with God she still has faith in him and knows the penalty he imposes for a suicide. She suppresses the mean thoughts that tell her to fall and concentrates on lifting up her heavy skirts and finding the first step.

What's that? A movement? A shadow? Did she hear anything or was it imagination? As she looks right the blow comes from her left. Oh the pain! She clutches her hands to her head as the next blow descends and then in a daze she feels the hand push her, feels her feet leave the step. In that strange moment of suspense she thinks of Robert. He has done this. He has betrayed her. She falls, the stone has no mercy. Her neck breaks and then Amy Robsart is no longer a living mortal. Amy Robsart is a ghost with a heart full of hatred and sorrow.

⬜

35 – Syderstone, Norfolk 1955

Fourdrinier cycled along the road in almost complete darkness. His lamp on the handlebars was faltering, its battery old and drained. He pedalled on, trying to keep himself optimistic and positive, and above all else he resisted the desire to constantly look back over his shoulder.

There was an old legend in the county of the fearsome demon dog black shuck, that he followed his victims waiting for the moment they turned their heads and saw him. And then they would be cursed. Within a year and a day they or a loved one would be dead. Fourdrinier thought such stories nonsense; at least he had until recent events had disturbed his sense of reality. With each rotation of his wheels he was listening for the soft padding of a dog and instructing himself over and over not to look around. In-between he was reciting the Lord's Prayer and every psalm or hymn he could remember. He had just started on the last verse of Rock of Ages when Syderstone Church loomed before him.

He gently squeezed his brakes and came to a quiet halt outside the graveyard wall. How ironic; here he was pedalling as fast as he could to escape the terrors behind him, only to walk straight into their lair! But he wasn't afraid. He did not believe the entity was as powerful as it made out. Instead he believed it had over-played itself that night and had retreated to rest. The spiders, the cat, the dogs – it must all have taken a toll. He itched at a spot on his neck, the sensation of hairy feet crawling over him still strong.

Dismounting, he pushed the bicycle into the graveyard and headed for the gate that connected it with the parsonage. An owl flew low over his head and he ducked. The white shadow skimmed the gravestones and disappeared into the night. It had been nothing, just an ordinary bird, but still...

He left his bicycle propped up against the cottage wall and opened the door. The smell of blood hit him at once; it was a tang in the air. No one had been in to clean up the mess Nancy's suicide had caused and the scent was so strong he could taste it. He licked his lips and tried to calm himself. He had a mission to fulfil and he could not falter on the doorstep. He had come to seek out the shade of William Mantle. It was a long-shot, but it would be even longer if he left it until the morning. He doubted William would appear in daylight.

Bracing himself he strode into the house. He had come in through the front door and in the dark it took him a moment to orientate himself. The small hall leading to the dining and sitting rooms was on his right, to his left a door stood ajar leading to a cluttered study. He nudged the door open further to give himself some more light. The papers beyond the door smelt musty.

Directly ahead the hall stretched away to the kitchen. Fourdrinier would have preferred not to head in that direction, but since William had previously visited him in the kitchen he felt it the most likely place to find him again. He walked forward, his ears pricked for any sound. Distantly he thought he heard a cackle, but it might have been his imagination. The wind was picking up outside and the windows rattled. The house felt humid and there was a threat on the breeze of another storm. Fourdrinier hoped he was wrong about that, if a storm was approaching it seemed likely so was the evil of Syderstone.

Another step took him parallel with the hall to the front rooms. There was the unnerving sensation of something lurking to his left in the darkness and, (partly terrified, partly curious) he risked turning his head to look. Darkness loomed empty. With a slight sigh Fourdrinier went to turn back and gave a gasp.

Before him on the carpet the corpse of Donald Steward lay, with its eyes open and looking at Fourdrinier accusingly. As he looked on at the impossible vision, the corpse's stiff lips began to move, a croaky sound coming from the body's throat.

"You couldn't save me... Fourdrinier."

Fourdrinier cringed. He knew this could not be real, but he could smell the stench of putrefaction, see the blood pooling on the floor. He gulped and tried to look away, but his eyes seemed to keep coming back to Donald. Defiance took hold of Fourdrinier then. He would not be scared away by mind games, he would not be made to feel guilt! He stepped forward, focusing his gaze on the kitchen and ignoring the corpse.

"You could not save me!" the corpse on the ground wailed, then, from its thin lips, a set of black legs emerged, followed by six more. The spider plopped to the ground as another languorously stretched its legs out of the corpse's decaying lips. Suddenly there were spiders emerging from the dead man's clothes and hair, from his ears and nose, and pouring onto the ground. A bubbling sea of black bodies writhed on the carpet, boiling up over each other before, as one, they surged at Fourdrinier.

Fourdrinier stumbled backwards as the arachnid army came at him. Memories of just a few hours ago returned to him; Maud sickened with fear cowering on the table, the hideous sight of his aunt slowly being engulfed by spiders. Backwards and backwards. He was alone here with no witch charm to protect him. He skin was crawling just at the sight of the beasts, he could already feel them crawling over his body, biting his flesh. Backwards another pace, his foot catching on a ruck in the carpet and then he fell and the army was almost upon him. Scrabbling backwards now, kicking uselessly with his feet, waving with a hand, trying to think of any means to elude the wall of black facing him. Could they kill him? Just the thought of their bodies touching his was enough to make his heart race erratically, his body to clench, his mind to reel. The blood was pounding in his ears, whooshing like the crashing waves of the sea, panic was forcing him to breathe hard through a thumping in his chest and a new dread overcame him. Were he to faint now there would be no hope!

The spiders were clambering onto his shoes, he shook his feet wildly, twisted his body and stamped his feet on the creatures, feeling bodies pop under his heel. But it was not enough, not with thousands advancing. Just as he felt certain he was doomed, that even an attempt to get back to his feet would be too late, a thought struck him. Perhaps call it divine inspiration or instinct, or just pure luck, but Fourdrinier had the sudden urge to make the sign of the cross. Touching hand to forehead and breast, then to either shoulder, he made the sign with a strange lack of haste, at the same time he whispered Amen and closed his eyes.

For a long time nothing occurred, though he sat on the floor waiting for the attack. After several minutes it became unbearable and Fourdrinier opened his eyes. His body was spider-free, so was the hallway floor, and at the foot of the stairs there was no sign of a corpse, only a slightly darker patch in the carpet where Donald's blood had spilled. Fourdrinier trembled as he stood, but otherwise he was unscathed. He cast a wary eye about the hall. There seemed no indication of the spidery horror that had threatened him.

Fourdrinier's chest hurt in a bad way. It was tight, like an iron band enclosed it. Rubbing at his breastbone he tried to take a deep breath and winced as his chest muscles protested. He hoped this was not the start of a heart attack, not now when he was so close. He took another breath and the pain was less. He relaxed a little.

Cautiously he headed for the kitchen, expecting spiders or rabid dogs at any moment. At the doorway his nerve failed again. Seeing Donald was one thing, but if the demon now chose to show him Nancy he was not sure how he would react. Her death was still far too fresh in his mind. He hardly needed a mirage to conjure the scene of that awful night and the girl dying on the floor. Methodically he began to repeat the Lord's Prayer, using it as a mental shield. When he felt ready, about three lines in, he braced himself and, his voice rising, stepped into the room.

He was still chanting as he realised there was nothing there except the ominous stain left by Nancy's blood. The iron tang of it filled the air and several small flies were buzzing on the counters, disturbed by Fourdrinier's appearance. He stepped in and felt the instant urge to get the range working and make a cup of tea. That was foolish, there was no time, it just seemed needed. As though a lighted range would restore some cosiness, even some friendliness to the kitchen. Fourdrinier very carefully pulled out a chair from the side of the table nearest the range and furthest from the blood stain. The angle of the table masked almost all of it, but nothing would remove the smell.

The house was silent. Fourdrinier listened for a while to the emptiness, wanting to be alert to any new attack. Nothing seemed to come; perhaps the spiders had been its last attempt, at least for the moment. Taking a shaky breath Fourdrinier pressed his fingertips together and called out into the darkness.

"Are you there Reverend William Mantle?"

He felt like some hocus-pocus fairground medium, calling out for the sake of gullible patrons.

"I am not conducting a séance," he told himself firmly, appalled at the very thought. "William Mantle, I have finished your diary and I have a number of unanswered questions. If you are the man I think you are, you will talk to me about how we are to rid ourselves of this problem."

The room remained obstinately empty.

"I understand that you tried. You tried for, what, seven years? But you failed. I wish to know why you failed and how I, in your place, can succeed."

"You can't. Not alone."

Fourdrinier jumped out of his chair and a new surge of panic painfully constricted his heart. The shade of William Mantle stood just behind and to the left of his chair.

"Good evening," Fourdrinier said, trying his hardest to regain some sense of composure. "I half-thought I dreamed you."

"I'm sorry I startled you," William apologised solemnly. "Why have you come back here tonight?"

"This thing," Fourdrinier motioned to the room upstairs, "is after myself and my friends. It has grown a great deal stronger with the weakening of the old exorcism rites and the new... souls it has fed on."

"Yes, another woman joined us. I am sorry."

"How many of you are there?" Fourdrinier felt calm enough to resume his chair.

"Myself, Amy Robsart, though she is much faded and I hardly see her. The little girl and now the man Donald and the woman Nancy. She does not talk."

"How do you mean Amy is much faded?"

"It has drained away most of her soul. There is not much left. I'm not sure enough to save," William Mantle lowered his head and seemed overcome for a moment.

"Explain this to me William, I understand some. This Thing was created by the great evil done to Amy?"

"Yes."

"And because it is a projection of her emotions from the instant of her death, so it is tied to her?"

"Yes."

"Then it became, for want of a better word, alive? How does that work?"

William Mantle gave a shrug.

"If I was to hazard a guess I would suggest it was purely an accident, a fluke of chance. Perhaps Amy died in such a frame of mind, in such a place, in such a state as to cause such as this to happen. Perhaps it has never happened before because the circumstances are so rare."

Fourdrinier nodded along, it was as good as any explanation he had to offer.

"And it feeds off her?"

"Yes, or at least it did, until it began acquiring new souls. If that had not happened it would not have become as powerful as it is now. It desires souls that have died a violent death in this house. A natural death holds no appeal for it."

"A connoisseur of death, then?" Fourdrinier said morbidly. "I must ask, how did you die William?"

William took a few paces across the kitchen. He was vaguely transparent from the waist down and it caused Fourdrinier some consternation to see the countertops through him.

"I drank myself to death," he said softly. "I lost myself in my desperate need to purge this house. I drank when I was awake to still my nerves, and before bed to help me sleep. What started casually enough, began to over-take my life. In my last days I interspersed attempts to drive out the demon with heavy drinking, until I was taken dangerously ill. Octavia tried to save me by removing all the wine and spirits in the house. Instead she killed me. Such sudden withdrawal is fatal to an acute alcoholic. I convulsed in agony in my last hours, I recall that clearly. I was feverish and at times violent. I saw things that even now I can't be sure were illusions of my mind or tricks of the demon that dwells here. In some moments I was drifting along a river, in others I was being stabbed by a thousand lances while my children laughed. I wanted to die eventually. My body was so tortured, my mind so unravelled and all of me exhausted. I never imagined when I perished I would be sent from one hell to another."

"You tried your hardest, William."

William shook his head. He was staring at the spot Nancy had fallen.

"Whatever I did, I know now, could not be enough."

"Why? This is what I must understand," Fourdrinier

insisted.

"It does not like prayer," William said. "Or anything religious, that, I realised, was a weakness, but it was only half of the puzzle. You can confine it here, exorcise it even, but you cannot completely banish it."

"Why? What am I missing?"

William gave him a sad smile.

"You are not dead. I realised it too late. You are not fighting something of this realm alone. You are fighting a creature with one foot in the world of the living and one in the world of the dead. You must destroy it in both!"

It was so simple an answer, yet Fourdrinier saw that Mantle was intrinsically right. The demon merely projected a part of itself into this world, while its core being was safely housed in the world beyond, in some spiritual limbo where it lived in complete security.

"Then, if it must be destroyed in both realms, you must help me!"

William Mantle shook his head again.

"I am too weak."

"Have you given up?"

"It has been draining my soul for the last 150 years! I hardly consider that giving up, merely understanding my limitations," even so William looked hurt.

"You and I both know we are probably each other's last chance. If we do not work together, what then? The evil is loose, it is pursuing my friends, it almost killed us tonight. More will die William, that is a certainty."

"You do not know what you ask."

"Raise yourself a shield of faith Reverend William Mantle, forge yourself a sword of hope. Let God give you strength."

William's face contorted into a pained grimace. He wanted to sit, but there was no mortal chair that would take him. He wrung his hands together.

"Why me?"

"Because you have a strong faith, or at least you did.

Donald did not and I cannot speak for Nancy, Margaret is but a girl. If you will not do this for yourself you could at least try for them."

William paced and paced.

"A shield of faith, a sword of hope?"

"You know your Bible, William, you know how God cloaks his champions. Don't you want to finally leave this purgatory and go to Heaven? To meet Octavia once again?"

"A shield of faith, a sword of hope," William recited as he moved back and forth. "It has been so long since I thought of fighting."

"You were always a brave man, William. I saw that in your diary. You would not leave a wrong unpunished. You have risked your mortal life in ways others would never dare to."

"I was a poor preacher," William's shoulders hunched.

"Really? I found you quite remarkable. You tried William, that is more important than failure or success. Others never even get that far. You are too harsh a critic of yourself."

"Please, Reverend Fourdrinier, your kindness is appreciated, but it is misplaced."

"William Mantle, I see you through the eyes of a historian as well as a man of the cloth, and I know what I look upon. I see the potential for greatness, if only you could have more confidence in yourself. And please, call me Norman."

William stared at him for a while, then a smile twitched his lips and he laughed.

"You are silver-tongued."

"But honest. Now will you help?"

William had to turn away to consider. He was afraid, that much was obvious. He had fallen into this strange life of semi-existence, not happy but not miserable and at least in some way existing. He wasn't sure of the outcomes that might follow an attack on the evil upstairs. It would pain him to relinquish this existence for nothingness, even if it was a hollow way to dwell. Still, he was a man of God and he did not say that lightly. He had pledged to walk into the fire for his Lord, if he must. Perhaps this then, was the fire.

"Is there such a thing as death of the soul, Norman?"

"I would hope not, though perhaps what you are already experiencing is just that."

William rubbed his hands.

"I was never a coward."

"I know."

"I said a long time ago I would protect others from this evil. In that I failed. Yet now I have an opportunity to make things right."

"Good, then we have a plan."

William glanced at him in surprise.

"We do?"

"I fight this side, you fight the other, your battle will be harder but I shall be doing my best to distract the thing from here. I shall go to the room and pray continuously. If it chooses to strike at me all the better for it will give you a chance. Do you see?"

William nodded.

"A shield of faith, a sword of hope."

"You must visualise it."

"Yes, I understand the concept."

"Then we will begin at dawn, it seems weakest in the daylight."

William did not leave immediately, though it was obvious discussions were over.

"I want to be able to keep in touch with you, but I cannot do this," William indicated himself. "Do you know of automatic writing?"

Fourdrinier had a vague idea of what it was.

"Have someone sit by you with pencil and paper. I will send messages through that person, using their hand. It is easier for me and I may need to contact you urgently."

Fourdrinier went to disagree, the last thing he wanted was to bring another person into the house and risk their life. But William held up a hand as he began to protest.

"This is my only condition for helping you. If I cannot communicate I can only half aid you and may not be able to warn you of an emergency."

Fourdrinier relinquished.

"If that is the case..."

"It is."

"Then I agree to it. Reluctantly."

William smiled.

"I will leave you now."

"Agreed."

"Until dawn, Fourdrinier."

Fourdrinier expected William Mantle's shade to slowly fade away, instead it vanished almost with a pop. One moment he was there, the next he was gone, so Fourdrinier found it hard to determine if he had really just talked to a ghost or had deluded himself. Ominously he wondered how clever the evil working against him was. Could this meeting have been a trick? Could it be a means of luring a person in for possession? He hoped not and yet he could not exclude the possibility. If alone, he would still have taken the risk, but now he had to endanger someone else? And who? He slumped forward on the table with his head in his hands. His mind was a mess and he had no way of knowing whether the next few hours would bring triumph or sacrifice.

Fourdrinier now had the unenviable task of spending the last few hours of darkness alone in the parsonage. Nervously he looked out of the corner of his eye towards the kitchen doorway. There seemed to be no one about. He tapped his fingers on the table, an annoying habit he had once scolded Sunday school children for doing. He had to distract his mind and with no inclination to wander about in the dark outside, (where he still had the uncomfortable notion of demon dogs lurking) he decided to deal with a chore that had been assigned to him some days ago.

Tentatively he made his way down the hallway, carefully switching on every light he could find. It was no real defence, but it made him feel better. He had noted Donald's study on entering the house, now he pushed wide open the door and stepped in. Fourdrinier paused and for a moment anxiety was replaced with mild despair. Donald's study was no better organised than any other part of his house. Two bookcases stood guard against opposite walls and an old desk nestled in the small window bay. Every surface, including the floor, was stacked with books, loose papers, cardboard box files, folders and notebooks. There was no obvious coordination to the heap, though looks could be deceiving, and Fourdrinier suspected there had been some system to Donald's chaotic hoarding. For the time-being, however, he had to aim for a best guess at the location of the address for Donald's daughter. He took a rummage through the desk, turning up notes on scraps of paper and old documents, a receipt fell out for a pair of boots bought in Norwich 100 years ago and Fourdrinier had to smile as he noted the name read, 'Rev. J. Stewart'. There was more in the desk; household accounts from 1890 tumbled out with an old menu from a Christmas Ball hosted by the local cricket club in 1920. As Fourdrinier dug he realised the whole history of the house was tied up in the desk and probably the papers and books surrounding it. He could have spent hours among the papers, happily reading and cataloguing. Every moment or so he found something that caught his eye and stopped his searching. He was so absorbed the demon could have pounced on him and he would not have noticed.

Fourdrinier fumbled in a drawer and turned up old pocket diaries, flipping them open he found they were Donald's and the most recent – 1953 – had a short list of addresses in the back. He found one for a Ruby Brandon, including a phone number. Satisfied that he had finally completed part of his last task for Donald he pocketed the diary and was just going back to searching through the papers for more tantalising nuggets of information when he heard the front door slam.

Fourdrinier held his breath. His whole body went rigid. He listened intently, wondering if it would be better or worse to shut the study door and trap himself inside? Footsteps echoed into the hallway, they were slow and heavy. What was it trying now? Mind games? Or had it restored its strength enough to tackle him head on? Fourdrinier let his eyes move left and right, scanning for a weapon. Even if he saw one he was not sure what he would do with it, it seemed the only weapon that was in any way effective was his own faith. He told himself that sternly and cursed his fears. He had sent William Mantle away with words about shields of faith and swords of hope, well where were his? Hypocrite, he told himself, bloody hypocrite.

Stiffly he loosened his tense stance and took a pace back from the desk. The footsteps were moving through the lobby beyond the front door and into the hall. Fourdrinier cautiously turned and waited for the approaching phantom. He braced himself, whatever new horror was coming he would not let it daunt him. Was this to be a shambling version of Donald dripping blood? Or Nancy with her gutted throat? Whichever he would not falter. Though his heart was fluttering and his knees shaking he pulled himself into an attitude of firm command, determined to defy all that came his way. And then...

"Fourdrinier!" Charlie emerged in the hallway.

Fourdrinier didn't move at first.

"Stop there!" he called out.

Charlie obeyed, perplexed.

"Stand perfectly still! I shall have to make sure you are not some illusion."

"Fourdrinier!"

"It is a perfectly reasonable request after what we have both just experienced. We don't know how devious this entity is. Recite the Lord's Prayer."

Charlie cocked an eyebrow at him, almost flabbergasted.

"I can do better than that," he slipped a hand into his jacket and removed it curled into a fist. He presented it to Fourdrinier and slowly unfolded his fingers. A silver cross lay in his palm. "It's my Confirmation cross."

Fourdrinier took a step forward and peered down his nose. The artificial light glinted off the metal and the cross sparkled.

"Thank goodness," Fourdrinier released his iron grip on himself and almost instantly his legs seemed to turn to jelly. "It has been a nightmare here."

"What happened?" Charlie came forward rapidly, slipping a discreet arm under Fourdrinier's to prevent the old man collapsing.

"It created an illusion of Donald Steward lying on the floor as on the evening I found him, then it changed into those spider-things again," Fourdrinier gave a shudder. "I am going to have trouble clearing out the church cupboards from now on, you know. Spiders everywhere. They never fussed me before."

"But were you able to do what you came here for?"

"Yes, and more bizarre an episode I could not imagine. I would hate to think what the bishop would say."

"And you now know how to destroy this entity?"

Fourdrinier gave a long sigh.

"We can't just kill it in this world, it has to be undone in the spirit world as well."

Charlie's face captured the hopelessness Fourdrinier had felt when Mantle had told him.

"How?"

"Do not be alarmed Charlie, but I have been communing with the shade of William Mantle."

Charlie stared at him for a long moment.

"Last week that might have troubled me, this week... No, I still find myself struggling. Really Fourdrinier?"

"I can't explain it. If I am honest I am still uncertain myself, but I believe using the assistance of William Mantle is the only hope we have of defeating this demon. Mantle will fight the creature on his side and I must fight it on ours. He will summon all his spiritual strength, plumb the depths of his faith and conjure up a weapon that will strike the creature. I imagine a sword of light, but it could be virtually anything. I just trust Mantle will know what to do when the time comes."

"And if he doesn't?"

Fourdrinier had no answer. Instead he changed the topic.

"What are you doing here?"

"Helping," Charlie smiled. "Maud and Ida went to bed. I stayed up to do the cows, but came here instead. You can't do this alone, old boy, we both know that."

Fourdrinier shrugged off Charlie's arm and staggered his way to the kitchen. There he slumped into a chair.

"I didn't want to put you in danger."

"That was never your choice," Charlie took a gander in the cupboards to see if there was anything to eat. He came up with some digestive biscuits and offered them to Fourdrinier. "You need something inside you, what with the shock and all."

"Charlie, this thing could kill us."

"And?" Charlie sat down and faced his former superior. "I've come to help, so what can I do? Join you in prayer?"

Fourdrinier slipped a biscuit from the packet and nibbled its edge forlornly.

"Actually, there is one thing. I was rather loath to agree to it, but William Mantle insisted. He wants someone to act as a communication line for him. Have you heard of automatic writing?"

"It's one of Maud's fancies. You sit with a pencil and paper, close your eyes and allow the spirits to guide your hand. Maud has come up with some right nonsense using it."

"Well, now you are going to use it. If Mantle wants to communicate with us it will be done via pen and paper,"

Fourdrinier brushed crumbs from his sleeve. "Every time I talk about this out-loud it sounds more and more like nonsense."

"Oh right, shall we go home now then?" Charlie verbally poked him.

Fourdrinier gave a scowl.

"How many hours before dawn?" he said.

"Not many."

"Then you just better be prepared."

Fourdrinier deposited the barely touched biscuit on the table. He stared at it for a while, as if his greatest worries centred around crumbs and attracting mice. Then he shook himself from his despondency.

"Come on, I'll show you what I found. It will pass the time."

36 – Syderstone, Norfolk 1955

The Bible lay very neatly before Fourdrinier. There was a cushion under his knees; age had robbed him of the ability to rest pain-free on a bare floor. To his right Charlie also kneeled with several sheets of paper in front of him and a pencil in his hand. Occasionally he glanced at Fourdrinier uneasily. The vicar had been praying quietly for around half-an-hour.

They were in the sealed room and nothing untoward had so far occurred. Charlie wasn't sure what he was expecting, but it wasn't silence. He closed his eyes and rested his hand on the paper. He tried to clear every thought from his mind and focus on nothingness. Instead a stream of ideas poured into his skull; random thoughts on improving his cattle herd, what he would do about the leak in the attic, whether he could tell Maud her apple tart was too heavy for him. Every mundane thought that had ever occurred to him before, now swamped his mind. He bit at his lip and tried to refocus, instructing his rebellious brain to control itself. It was only then that he realised his hand had been moving for some time.

He opened his eyes and stared at the paper.

READY.

"Well I never. I think Mantle is communicating," Charlie whispered to Fourdrinier.

"You didn't think he would?"

"I was becoming convinced you had been with Ida too long. I guess I have to correct myself."

"Good," the reverend muttered back. "Brace yourself."

Fourdrinier began speaking his prayers louder but

always at a steady, solemn pace, as though dictating them. Charlie closed his eyes and wrestled again with his rampaging mind. The first indication he had that anything was wrong was the smell of smouldering fabric. He opened one eye, thinking he was imagining things, and almost went giddy as he saw both his and Fourdrinier's cushions were slowly catching fire.

"Fourdrinier!" he reached out a hand and swatted the cushion Fourdrinier knelt on. He couldn't fathom how they were catching alight.

"What is it?" Fourdrinier hissed.

"You're on fire!"

"Oh, I know that!" Fourdrinier went back to his prayers calmly ignoring the rising smoke.

Charlie started to panic; there were definite signs of flame on the edge of his cushion. He smothered one with his sleeve and another burst out further to the corner. Finally, in sheer desperation he jumped up and hurled the cushion into the hallway. He watched it smoulder slowly and then the hall carpet gingerly caught fire.

"That was really not a good idea, Charlie," he told himself, running out and snatching up the cushion again, stamping on the flames springing out of the carpet and at least extinguishing those.

The cushion was now burning hot and odd flames were leaping out of the fabric. The fire didn't look entirely real but when Charlie accidentally came too close to the flames they burnt the skin on his knuckles sure enough. He hurried the cushion downstairs to the kitchen, each step seeming to ignite it further until he could only hold it by one corner for the rest was a burning ball of flames. He dashed it into the huge stone kitchen sink and turned on the cold water tap. The cushion hissed with a whoosh as the flames were extinguished and smoke filled the room. Charlie coughed and spluttered, wafting smoke away with a hand.

When he was sure the cushion was utterly drenched he

grabbed a bucket and filled it with water. Then he ran back upstairs ready to douse Fourdrinier. He was only mildly surprised to see that Fourdrinier was unscathed. His cushion had stopped smouldering and he was calmly praying. Charlie knelt on the bare floor and wondered what was next in store for them, or more rightly, him.

An hour passed with no interference. Charlie kept the pencil in his hand and finally mastered letting his mind drift into a state of semi-consciousness. Somewhere between sleep and conscious thought, he found a nook he could slip into and disengage his mind for as long as needs be. Deep in this trough of the mind he was only faintly aware of his surroundings; the soft words Fourdrinier spoke, the ache in his knees and back, the chill of the room and his hand moving.

He dragged his mind back from its hideaway and looked at the paper.

ATTACKING

Charlie read the word twice and then repeated it to Fourdrinier.

"He has forged his weapon then," Fourdrinier did not budge from his position. "We shall be his distraction, Charlie."

Charlie closed his mind to everything, but this time his hidden place eluded him. Instead he was thinking of William Mantle; he had forged a weapon. What would it be? A sword? A mace? Maybe no more than a cross like the one Charlie had in his own hand. Charlie found his mind turning to how he would attack. It would be with a pistol, forged from his soul and firing Heavenly bullets. Six in total. He would not need more. He pictured the pistol perfectly in his mind. It looked like an old army revolver. He visualised himself inscribing his initials on each bullet, so the demon would know who they had come from. It was an oddly satisfying task and it gave him some comfort, which he sorely needed as his ears became attuned to a new sound – the skittering of tiny feet.

Spiders do not make sounds unless there are many of them and they are seeping out of the skirting boards. Then, apparently, they make a tremendous racket. Charlie opened his eyes and saw them billowing towards him. He quickly shut his eyes and tried to ignore them. That only worked until the first one bit his hand and their furry bodies started up his thighs. He had a dreadful thought about how close he was to the floor and how much faster they could crawl up him then if he was standing. He flailed out with a hand, scattered a cluster, but more swarmed onwards, a black mass that made his stomach knot.

Charlie risked a glance at Fourdrinier and saw the reverend was completely absorbed in his prayers and oblivious to the spiders. More significantly, the spiders were ignoring him, or at least they were unable to go beyond the very edge of his cushion. Not a single spider had crawled onto Fourdrinier's clothes. It appeared he had created a perfect spiritual bubble for himself.

Charlie swatted out with his hand again. It was useless; the spiders latched pincer teeth into his flesh and hook-like legs wrapped about his fingers. Panic threatened to overwhelm him again, but he could not face abandoning Fourdrinier to this calamity. He had to do something, but not flee – what if running away distracted Fourdrinier and left him open to attack? Charlie grabbed up the paper and started sweeping away spiders, but the room was starting to flood with them and his efforts were barely touching the flow. Trembling all over, skin itching and prickling painfully and spiders creeping up his body faster and faster, Charlie had to think of something, anything.

He folded his hands in prayer like Fourdrinier, but the words would not come. He pushed for anything, even the Lord's Prayer suddenly eluded his memory and he realised his fright had robbed him of his one weapon – and now there were spiders in his shirt and up his arms and on his neck. He was succumbing to them and he almost ran despite himself, almost fled from the room screaming. All his options were gone, his only weapon lost! Except...

Charlie shut down every part of his mind apart from the small corner he had found sanctuary in. There he went to work constructing his pistol. He imagined it as fast as he could, the smooth lines of the barrel, the rough surface of the grip. Then he mentally loaded it, placing each bullet into the cylinder and clicking it in place. He pulled back the safety and then he reached the hardest part. Still visualising the pistol he imagined the hoard of spiders around him. There was one at his mouth nipping his lip and he was terrified of the moment it would reach his eyes. He saw all the spiders in his mind's eye and it was almost enough to induce the panic again, but he clutched to his thoughts as his only safety.

"Oh God, save me!" he whispered as in his imagination he fired the pistol.

Black bodies leapt up from the floor. He fire again, at another part of the room, and more spiders erupted, their legs bunching about their abdomens as they curled up in death. He fired at another patch and another. To his amazement those that were not damaged turned about and fled away from him. Now he turned his mind to his clothes. He imagined hands, dozens of them, hundreds, plucking away the writhing bodies and squashing them into oblivion. They went over him like a flock of busy birds and took each spider until there was not any left but the odd confused one on the floor.

Charlie was breathing calmly again. The many bites no longer hurt and, though he still tingled, he could not sense the actual bodies of the spiders. Very cautiously, expecting to see a sea of spiders leaping at him, he opened his eyes. The room was empty. It took a moment to sink in. Fourdrinier was still kneeling and praying but the spider menace was gone. Cautiously Charlie looked all around him, but they were gone, all gone! Charlie was dazed. It had worked! His pistol of faith! He almost laughed out loud, had he really vanquished demonic arachnids by the power of his own faith? Then the laugh turned to a strange sob wrenched from his heart. So he hadn't forgotten, not really, and God... God had helped him. That was enough to drag a gasp from him, but he stifled it and returned to his pencil and paper. In the confusion there was no knowing if Mantle had tried to speak to them. Charlie grabbed up the pencil and felt an almost immediate spark in his hand. He closed his eyes and the words sped across the paper with ease.

I CAN'T DO IT.

"Fourdrinier, he says he can't do it."

Fourdrinier glanced over.

"William, you have to," he said loudly.

Nothing happened at first, then Charlie felt his hand being tugged and wrote on the paper.

I HAVE NOT THE STRENGTH

"William, you have to do this, there is no one else," Fourdrinier had read the words as they were written. "If you do not do this then there is no hope."

They waited for a response. Charlie's hand rested on the paper.

"Maybe he does not have the strength?" he said. "This thing is powerful enough to us, let alone in its true realm."

"I know," Fourdrinier admitted. "But there is no one else."

"Fighting a thing that leeches your very soul away," Charlie gave a shudder. "That uses your own strength against you."

"Remember, with faith as small as a mustard seed we can move mountains," Fourdrinier refolded his hands into a position of prayer. "Did you hear that William? I will keep praying to aid you."

The seconds ticked by. Charlie wanted to move and stretch out his legs, to ease their ache. Then his hand twitched.

I'LL TRY

"Thank you William, that is all I can ask," Fourdrinier exchanged a look with Charlie and it was far from hopeful.

"I have sent him into a dreadful battle alone."

"What other option is there?"

"I don't know," Fourdrinier sunk his head and began to pray.

Charlie stared at the paper for a while, the scrawled words filled with such despair. He knew nothing of William Mantle, but he recognised a desperate man from those short sentences. He had heard similar things from men in the war, men who were somehow chivvied to carry on, to pull themselves together and drag themselves into the fray. All too often they had never come back. Charlie shut his eyes. He had spoken to them just as Fourdrinier had spoken to William, beseeching them to carry on, when knowing all the time they were at the end of their resolve, of their strength. That really all he was asking was for another man to distract the enemy, to buy time, to eat up incoming bullets so there would be fewer for the next wave. He clenched his teeth painfully. At least he was able then to console himself with thoughts of a better next life, but what was there for William Mantle? What came after your very soul had been destroyed?

"Fourdrinier, we must do something for him!"

"Exactly what? The only weapon I have against this thing is prayer and faith. I am trying my hardest to send that to William."

"Beyond that," Charlie insisted. "He needs someone to fight with him!"

"How Charlie? He is dead! In the next world!" Fourdrinier knew his voice was rising and could not help it. He was worried, even beginning to contemplate the failure of this, his only chance. Then what?

"There has to be a way!"

"I have done everything I can. I have read the books and the papers! William himself told me there was nothing more I could do!"

"We can't just sit here and pray!" Charlie got to his feet, he was full of anguish, unable to stand still. "There has to be something!"

"Charlie, this is it!" Fourdrinier looked at him miserably. "I have no other answers!"

"Then I shall find one!" Charlie stormed off, wild thoughts racing through his mind. He was not so much angry with Fourdrinier, as frustrated. There had to be something he could do, some way of reaching William and offering help. He knew Fourdrinier was trying, but he was trapped within his own limited parameters, he needed someone prepared to take a risk.

It was then Charlie had an idea.

37 - Syderstone, Norfolk 1955

Knelt in prayer Fourdrinier rocked slightly. He had come to the battle confident, now he was shaken and unsettled. It had been several minutes since his last communication with William. He wondered what had happened. And where was Charlie? He stopped praying and looked around the room. He was waiting for something to happen, something to strike to tell him it was not yet over. The room had grown chilly, but that was about it. A streak of sunlight was peering through the window. He felt it gently warm his left hand.

John Stewart had knelt here. William Mantle had knelt here. Margaret Stewart had lain in her bed and heard a demon whispering to her here. Learned men had crowded in this room and heard the rappings from beyond and either declared them a ghost or the work of rats. This room had more history within it than any other in the village, and all of it dark and dismal.

Fourdrinier pressed a hand to the wall, not really knowing why. Oddly it felt a touch warm. He moved his hand to the right and the wall felt distinctly heated. He made a small circle with his hand, feeling where the warmth was strongest and then following it. Upwards it went, so far up Fourdrinier had to rise from his knees and stand. He followed the heat, recognising an outline forming on the wall, but unable to discern it. Then he found it – the hottest point. It was in direct line with his face, same height as him, maybe a touch taller. His hand rested on the spot and he found himself asking what it could be, what it might mean?

The wall beneath his hand flexed inward. Fourdrinier

snapped his hand back, startled. Before him the white plaster was bubbling as though it had water behind it, small flecks began to peel off and crumble to the floor. Fourdrinier started praying again, recognising his wish for a sign was coming true, only, unfortunately, it meant William Mantle was still failing.

The plaster bubble bulged unpleasantly, like a boil, and then the very centre split open and oozing red blood dripped from it in a thick stream. Fourdrinier concentrated on not retching in disgust as more blisters appeared in the plaster, following the area he had traced with his hand. Now it was becoming plain to see the shape it formed; a head, two arms, two legs. The entity was finally taking form.

Unconsciously Fourdrinier stepped back until he collided with the far wall. He quelled his panic as best he could, but an irrational fear was grasping hold of him. He was exhausted and weary and somehow his brain no longer seemed to perform as logically as it should. Was this mental block yet another trick of the creature? Fourdrinier licked his lips as another thought caught his attention, did this mean Mantle had been destroyed? He almost wept at the thought, shocking himself. He was not normally an emotional man but now it seemed everything induced him to misery or despair. He was certain now the entity was toying with his mind.

The blood was forming a shape, a figure. It had circled and forged itself into the outline of arms, torso and legs. The bloody form emerged from the wall, red and glistening, a shimmering creature that smelt of iron and death. A head appeared last. It had no features except for a nose and mouth. Blood constantly pumped over it in a sheen of red, so it seemed the creature's 'flesh' was constantly renewing, yet not a drip fell from the skull and touched the floor. The creature prised itself from the wall and took a step towards Fourdrinier. The mouth split open into a leer, then it widened into a wicked grin and Fourdrinier could see into the hollowness beyond. There was nothing inside, nothing.

He tried to pray again, the words fell off his tongue awkwardly and he realised he was making no sense. What was this? His mind had gone blank of good thoughts. Instead it was suddenly full of the worst moments in Fourdrinier's life; the death of Nancy and Donald, the funerals of friends gone to the war, his own experiences in the trenches. He had touched dozens of lives, maybe hundreds, in his time, but now it was the deaths he regretted the most that haunted him. He saw men he had almost forgotten howl in agony as shrapnel or bullets took them. He cried at himself, trying so hard to comfort the dying, so useless to them in their last moments. He saw the mother dying of flu who begged him to take care of her children, and all he had done was standby and watch them go to the orphanage. He saw the homeless man he had tried to help and then grown angry with for his drunkenness. He had failed him and he had died one winter in a ditch. It all flashed before him and broke his heart, each as fresh as if it had happened yesterday.

"You are doing this!" he growled at the beast approaching him, its body giving off a strange, trickling noise. It just smiled.

He tried to pull himself together, to banish the images, but they sprang back at him. It was like a nasty wound you could not help but look at. Every time he pulled away the images bombarded him from a different angle. At last the creature had learned his weakness; his love for others was proving his downfall. In awful realisation it dawned on Fourdrinier that his enemy had suddenly become more sophisticated and was attacking him not with random fears, but aiming at his very heart. That could only mean it had consumed William Mantle and taken on the last dregs of his consciousness. Fourdrinier snarled and forced the words of the Lord's Prayer to his lips.

"Our father..." he almost gagged as an image of his own father flashed before his eyes, half-rotted from his grave. He had died at sea and for years Fourdrinier had had a recurring nightmare of him rising from the seabed, dripping with seaweed, cadaverous and decomposing, heading for Fourdrinier's house. Now the same spectre rose up in his mind's eye and reached out a hand to him. The flesh was dripping off the fingers, odd muscles and sinews were still attached and moved the bones into a pointing gesture.

"No," Fourdrinier clutched at his head and sunk to his knees. The ghoul that was his father lurched forward in his mind and seemed to draw so close Fourdrinier shuddered violently and his skin rose in goose-pimples.

He opened his eyes to try and elude the image, but instead saw the bloody monster slipping towards him. He stared upwards into its grinning maw, smelt the overwhelming tang of its body and had new images of Nancy's death spinning into his mind. He wanted to shriek for it to stop. He wanted to run away from his own thoughts, his own mind. Somehow he must be able to shake them!

Before him the demon sank an arm into its slimy torso, the limb vanished into its depths. Then it drew back its arm and held a sabre formed of glistening blood in its hand. Fourdrinier's gaze was drawn inescapably to the blade, which rippled with the same shimmer of the creature's body. He took a deep breath and tried to pull himself up once more, but there was no strength left in his legs. They refused him. Was this what William had meant when he wrote of having no strength? Fourdrinier had been so short with him, commanding him to try no matter what. So quick was he to sacrifice another.

The sword hung in the air and then the creature raised its arm. So it was intent on finishing him. Yes, of course it was. It wanted no more disturbances. Had not aunt Ida warned him it could kill in its own right if it chose? Fourdrinier stared up at the ceiling. If only he could move! Was he now doomed to be trapped in this house too? To have his soul feasted upon forever? He tried to grab at the bare wall, but there was nothing to hold onto, nothing to drag himself away with. His legs were useless to him, they were numb and uncooperative. He found his throat letting out a shriek as the blade swung down and in a split second he envisioned the pain, the tearing of flesh, the agony of death.

It never came. A moment before the blade struck him and rendered his head from his shoulders there was a whooshing sound like the air escaping a tyre. Fourdrinier felt a sucking sensation tugging lightly at his clothes and hair, but the creature.... The creature felt it all. It was being drawn backwards, sucked backwards! It stretched out its arms, flailing at the air. The sabre was forgotten, Fourdrinier was, for the moment, reprieved. The beast grimaced and howled, opening its hollow head to shriek. It wailed and tried to steady itself, but whatever pulled at it pulled too hard to resist. Suddenly there was a popping sound and a bubble of blood burst on the beast's side, then another on its chest, then on its head, its arms, its shoulders. Each pop came with a small spatter of blood and left a hole in the beast. Slowly but surely it was being torn apart. Another pop exploded a hand, another a foot, now its entire face was gone and all Fourdrinier could see was the ghastly concave surface of the inside of its head. It popped again and its right leg disintegrated into globules of red on the floor. Then one arm fell. The creature lashed out blindly, a breeze was whipping about the room, pushing it backwards, backwards to the wall. The other arm dissolved, now the remains of the head crumbled. At last there was just a writhing torso and a single leg, the wind buffeted at them until they lost balance and fell backwards. The torso vanished into the wall with a final POP! Then the leg fell to pieces. The breeze flew around the room like a mini tornado, gathering every droplet of blood and herding it back to where it came from.

It had felt like hours, but the incident could have taken no more than minutes. Fourdrinier fell forward flat on his face, as though all the air had been knocked out of him. His hand flopped on the paper and pencil and he lay with his head turned towards the window, feeling the soft sunlight bringing warmth back to his body.

His mind was settling, but the images were still there. He shut them out as best he could, ushering them to the deepest corners of his mind and hoping they would not resurface. He shut his eyes; the desire to slip into sleep was dominating his thoughts. He had never felt so drained in body and spirit. The temptation to drift off was hard to resist, until he felt the twitch of the pencil under his hand.

Without turning his head he lifted the pencil in his fingers and felt it skate over the paper. When it stopped he pushed himself up from the floor and read the words written in such haste.

FIND CHARLIE!

Where was Charlie? Fourdrinier found that his rebellious legs were working again, if stiff and aching, and he was able to stand and glance about. Where had Charlie gone? Had the creature attacked him too? What if it had managed to get to him first?

Fourdrinier hurried out of the bedroom, glancing up and down the corridor. Where did he even begin? There were a dozen rooms to check and each one would cost him time.

"Here!"

He turned and there was William Mantle, almost transparent and in obvious pain, though how that could be Fourdrinier could not say.

"Here!" William said again and pointed at the staircase.

Fourdrinier hurried forward.

"Charlie!" he yelled. "Charlie!"

He stumbled onto the staircase, hurried around the dog-leg and almost crumpled to his knees again. Charlie was hanging from the bannisters, a noose around his neck, his feet swinging over the lower set of stairs.

"Oh no!" Fourdrinier was weeping as he ran to his friend and fumbled with the knot attaching the noose to the stairs. "Please God no!"

Charlie's body slumped into his arms and he dragged him down onto the floor, to the spot Donald had fallen, though he refused to recognise the coincidence. He removed the rope and felt for a pulse. Charlie's body was lifeless, but he was not deterred. He pulled open his shirt and then breathed into the man's mouth, inflating his lungs as they taught in first aid classes. He put his hands one on top of another and began to press rhythmically down on Charlie's chest.

"Charlie!" he called. "Do not die on me Charlie!"

He breathed into Charlie's lungs again and again, pushed down repeatedly on his chest. His mind was whirring. What had happened? What had the creature done? Disturbed Charlie's mind so much he had taken his life? He was sobbing now. He could not lose another person to this demon. It was too much to bear.

"Why didn't you let it take me?" he cast up to God, "I'm so bloody old, he has got so much life to live!"

He forced another breath into Charlie's lungs and pumped his chest, counting the movements. How long before he had to face the truth? He pushed that aside. He refused to have another bad memory to add to the store in his mind.

He clasped his mouth around Charlie's, breathed a little harder, pumped.

"Please save him, please save him," he begged softly.

He suddenly stopped and convulsed into violent tears. Charlie's body refused to respond to him and he had failed, oh how he had failed. All along he had been arrogant and foolish, unprepared to listen and open his mind, to see the danger God had sent him to resolve and now this had happened. He sobbed so hard he thought he would be sick, it seemed impossible to stop. Something had broken inside Fourdrinier. It seemed the demon had won after all.

The light touch of a hand on his arm did not register for several moments. Then Fourdrinier reached out a hand

and rested it on top of the first. It felt solid and warm. He turned his head and looked at Charlie.

"Wasn't expecting this, old man."

Charlie grinned at him wanly.

"What did you do?" Fourdrinier wrenched the hand off his shoulder. "Why? Why..."

Fourdrinier had to take a deep breath. He felt giddy and light-headed. He moved back from Charlie and perched on the last step of the staircase. Charlie rubbed cautiously at his neck.

"I wasn't intending to die, as such."

"You could have fooled me!"

Charlie took several, long intakes of air and then carefully hoisted himself into a sitting position.

"William couldn't do it alone, Fourdrinier, he needed help and the only help had to come from someone on the other side. So, I suppose, I volunteered."

"You killed yourself to help Mantle?"

"Don't make it sound so stupid," Charlie frowned with anger. "William needed help, else where would we be? He might lose everything, you might... it was horrible to think of. I was trying to think of something to do when this idea came to my mind. What if, just for a minute, I was dead and could help William Mantle? It was a frightening thought, I admit, but I decided to trust you would find me in time. Perhaps, more logically, I decided to trust that God would alert you to me within time. I took my leap of faith Fourdrinier, and I soared."

Fourdrinier wiped at his eyes, a sour laugh coming from him.

"I'm not so sure my faith hasn't been winded."

"Nonsense!" Charlie reached out as far as he could and grasped Fourdrinier's arm. "I saw you up there. You had your shield of faith around you, stronger than anything that demon could throw at you."

"Except at the last."

Charlie gently nodded. It hurt to move his neck much.

"You were exhausted. No man is an island, yes? But that is where I came in."

"I am so furious with you Charlie," Fourdrinier couldn't look at his friend. "When I saw you hanging there..."

"Can you forgive me? I only did it because it seemed the only way, and I saved your life."

Fourdrinier registered the words slowly.

"How do you mean?"

"I slipped into the afterlife and there was William Mantle. Oh Lord, Fourdrinier, he was a mess. I can't say bloodied, that doesn't make sense, but he seemed to be dripping, dissolving. There was this white streak of light between him and this, well, this black mass. It was eating his soul and he was writhing in agony. It was the most appalling thing. Alongside him was a broken sword. The black mass had strange slits in it, like a bag sliced open, so I presume he had had some impact. There was not much of him left though. He could not have done more.

"Then I realised the black mass was projecting itself against what I can only describe as a transparent wall. There was this shadow upon it and beyond I could make out you. The mass was pouring through and taking a human form, I imagine using William's soul for fuel. As I watched it came to you and you backed away. I saw it draw a blade from its own body, for a moment my dull mind couldn't grasp what was happening and then it dawned on me. In my mind I had forged a weapon before. It was not a sword but a pistol. It took me several precious moments, fortunately you and the creature seemed to be moving at a snail's pace. I crafted this pistol out of the air, and if you ask me how, I cannot tell you. It just seemed obvious at the time. And then I aimed at the black mass and I fired. Not only did the black mass react to the shots, but so did the creature attacking you. They began to fall apart."

Fourdrinier was reminded of the pops he had heard as the bloody figure had broken up before his eyes.

"Then what?"

"When the creature started to fall apart, then it released its hold on William Mantle. He stood with difficulty. He was speaking, at first I thought to me, but then I realised it was a prayer in Latin. He walked straight towards the black form that had shrunk considerably and he held out his hands and the prayer seemed to reach out from him and dive into the black mass. Suddenly there was nothing but light all around and this sensation of rushing, hot air. I had to close my eyes at the force of it.

"When I could open them again William Mantle was before me and he was smiling. Nearby there was a little girl and just beyond her a woman in old-fashioned clothes, who was crying joyfully. Behind them I thought I made out Donald and Nancy, they seemed to be heading somewhere and then... then I was here with you."

Fourdrinier let the words sink into his mind and mulled them over for a while.

"Did we release their souls?" he said, mostly to himself.

"Maybe, they seemed happy, at least."

Fourdrinier gave a heavy nod.

"Does that mean they are gone?" he looked around the hall as though it might hold some clue.

"I think that part has to be left in the hands of William Mantle."

Fourdrinier suddenly had a thought. He glanced back up the staircase, but there was no one, so he called out into the air;

"Thank you William Mantle. God bless!" he waited, only half-expecting a response and, when there was none, felt a flood of relief. They were gone, safe in the place they were supposed to be.

Charlie hauled himself onto the step next to Fourdrinier.

"I certainly hope this is the last demon I ever encounter."

"I assure you they are rare," Fourdrinier said assertively.

Charlie slapped him on the back.

"Last week they didn't exist, now you concede they do

but are rare? Why Fourdrinier you have actually admitted to being wrong!"

"I can positively say that shall not happen again!"

Charlie laughed hoarsely, he started to cough.

"I best get you home," Fourdrinier helped him to his feet. "You've been gone a long time sorting out the cows."

"It was worth it though," Charlie leaned heavily on Fourdrinier. "For a lot of reasons. Do you regret meeting me in that graveyard Fourdrinier?"

The old reverend snorted.

"I regret meeting anyone in a graveyard, but I have learned that life's twists and turns are often fortuitous. Besides, I do have some excellent material for my history of the clergy in Norfolk."

"I don't suppose it will include any demons?"

"Not if I want my bishop to approve it!"

They hobbled to the front door, Fourdrinier already noticing a change in the atmosphere of the house. It was lighter, and more peaceful. He could never forget the people who had died in there, who had perished on his watch, but at least he could know it was over. As he helped Charlie to his car he allowed himself a small moment of satisfaction.

38 – Syderstone, Norfolk 1955

Great aunt Ida held her suitcase in her right hand and stood at the door.

"It won't be the same going back without her," she said softly.

Fourdrinier gave her a hug with one arm about her shoulders.

"I know."

Over the last month Fourdrinier had worked hard to tie up loose ends. Maud had cleaned the blood from Donald Steward's kitchen, admitting mournfully there was no way to get it out from under the heavy cupboards that were mounted in place. They just had to hope Donald's daughter had no plans for remodelling the house. Ruby Brandon arrived in time for her father's funeral and bumbled into the parsonage shortly afterwards. She was a short, stocky girl, with bobbed hair and an affinity for tweed and brown walking boots. She took one look and declared she was selling the place. Fourdrinier did not have the nerve to ask her what she made of her father's stories of ghosts in the house.

He had no real desire to return to the parsonage, but he did, with Ruby's permission, to remove any papers concerning the history of the property and Syderstone. He found a wealth of material which he intended to use for his book before donating to the Norwich Record Office. A couple of days later there was a 'for sale' board sitting outside the garden wall. Fourdrinier suspected it would have no local takers.

Aunt Ida stayed with the Talbots throughout the

process. Maud said she could stay the whole summer, but Ida could not face it. She had refused to use the bathroom since it had been the stage for Nancy's fake death scene, and had taken to using the old outside toilet, and washing in a bowl of fresh water brought up by Maud in the mornings. Fourdriner thought she had aged in that time, as if a dozen or more years had been added to her. She suddenly seemed frail. He hoped heartily her usual vigour would be restored by a return to London.

"I started all this," Ida said miserably. This had been a common refrain of the last few days.

"Yes, you did," Fourdrinier said plainly. "But it worked for the good of us all."

"Except Nancy."

"We've talked about this. You cannot continue to blame yourself."

"Can't I?"

Fourdrinier felt his aunt's usual defiance surging to the surface, it gave him some hope.

"Get back to London, see some friends and take your mind off things."

"Don't patronise me, Norman! I remember when you were a bare-bummed babe!" Ida humped her suitcase out the door as Charlie drew up in the car.

"She'll be alright," Maud whispered in Fourdrinier's ear. "She's a tough old bird."

"And you?" Fourdrinier asked as he watched his aunt give Charlie an earful for trying to help with her luggage.

"Me?" Maud was surprised. "I'm fine, maybe the odd extra grey hair but nothing I will weep over. And Charlie is brighter than I have seen him in ages. He seems to have a new confidence about him. He doesn't sit of an evening moping about the world. Surely you have noticed?"

Yes, Fourdrinier had noticed, and it was one of the few things that pleased him about this whole sorry affair. Neither of them had ever told Maud of Charlie's near suicide, it was unspoken between them that it should remain a secret. But Charlie did seem happier and more content. That was something at least.

Fourdrinier gave Maud's hand a squeeze.

"I best see my aunt to the train."

"I've already told her, but remind her, she is welcome back at any time. I know she won't come, but I do mean it."

Fourdrinier gave her a kiss on the cheek and promised he would. He walked across the yard enjoying the sunshine, it had been a long winter and they were due a good summer. Just as he was about to open the car door a cat leapt on top of the car roof. Fourdrinier stumbled backwards, his heart pounding out of his ears, every nerve on edge. But the big white and ginger tom just looked at him mildly and started to lick a paw. Charlie came around and removed him.

"Off you go, lad," he glanced at Fourdrinier. "It will take time."

Fourdrinier knew what he meant, but he doubted he would ever be able to look at a black cat again without a pang of anxiety.

"We'll be late!" Ida scolded from inside the car. Life seemed to be returning to normal.

Fourdrinier got in and waved to Maud. They left the yard and Ida started muttering about arrangements at home; would her maid have remembered to air the bedclothes and open the windows? Did cook understand what she meant about a fish supper awaiting her on arrival? Fourdrinier found it strangely lulling to have this regalia of domestic concerns issued at him, none, of course, needed an answer. Ida's house would be perfect for her when she arrived, it always was.

Fourdrinier leaned back and found his mind turning to his sermon on Sunday. He had an idea of what it should be about, but getting the words just right was the problem. He wanted to discuss forgiveness and the need to trust in God, no matter how dire the situation was. He paused. Had he? Fourdrinier smiled to himself, perhaps he had or perhaps he hadn't, but that was not the point. What really mattered was that God had trust in him to complete the task. Fourdrinier had dealt with the Syderstone ghost, the sealed room and the legend that had gone with it. It might have been a messy adventure, with lots of mistakes along the way, but he supposed the result was really what mattered. He hoped William Mantle, Amy Robsart, Margaret Stewart, Nancy and Donald had found their way to a better place. One day he hoped to meet them all again.

One day.

Not today.